AUGUST MAGIC

AUGUST MAGIC

VERONICA ANNE STARBUCK

Windigo
P.O. Box 183176
Shelby Township, MI 48318-3176

This book is a work of fiction.
Names, characters, places and incidents are
either the product of the author's imagination
or are used fictitiously, and any resemblance to
actual persons, living or dead, events or locales,
is entirely coincidental.

AUGUST MAGIC

Publishing History
First Windigo Paperback Edition: September 1998

Inquiries should be addressed to:
Windigo
P.O. Box 183176
Shelby Township, MI 48318-3176

E-mail inquiries may be sent to:
info@windigo.net

The Windigo World Wide Web site address is:
http://www.windigo.net

ISBN 0-9658488-2-5
LCCN 98-90577

Jeep® is a registered trademark of the Chrysler Corporation.

Printed and bound in the United States of America.

A U G U S T   M A G I C

is dedicated to the memory of a Basenji
who brought some real magic into the world

Magic
12/93 - 6/98

A rescued dog is blessed when he finds a home where he's loved simply for himself; knowing he will be welcome for as long as he shall live. One of the most beautiful things you'll ever see is a rescue blossoming in a new home with a new family, learning every day to love and trust again.

This was so with Magic.

Abandoned by those who didn't understand him, rejected by those who should have taken responsibility for him, Magic was lucky enough to find friends and a family who loved him unconditionally.

Sadly, Magic's time was all too brief. He lives forever in the Happiness, and in the hearts and memories of those fortunate enough to have known and treasured him.

Veronica Anne Starbuck

August 1998

FOREWORD

THE DECEMBER TWILIGHT WAS CRISP

and cold, cloaked in a soft hush of pre-Christmas

snow. The frozen world glowed with the fresh

snowfall, sharply contrasting with the darkness

and warmth inside the animal shelter where an

old Basenji lay curled in a corner of his pen,

afraid to fall asleep.

Tears glinted in his dark brown eyes,

revealing for the first time in several days the

intense misery he kept hidden inside. He had

seen many springs and summers, and played

through countless years of brightly colored autumn leaves. Never could he have guessed that the last winter of his life would find him abandoned and forgotten in the county animal shelter.

The Basenji sighed, ignoring the harsh whisper from the dog in the next pen — a shepherd-something mix — who had angrily told him several times to shut up and go to sleep. Not knowing what else to do, the Basenji squeezed his eyes tightly, making the darkness even darker, forcing away his tears and willing himself to sleep.

Maybe, he thought sadly, *if I try hard enough, I won't have to wake up and face tomorrow.* He buried his wrinkled face deep between his snow-white paws, breathed warmly into the space, and after a time drifted to sleep.

He dreamed of walking along the ocean's edge, feeling the sand warm and dry between his toes. He had walked that beach countless times in his younger years, and now in the autumn of his life, he walked it only in his dreams.

The intoxicating scent of salt-spray mist hung soft in the air, and breathing it made him feel light-headed. It was summertime, and the summer day was all around him, pulsing and moving in sync with the greatness of the ocean and the vastness of the sky, so much alive that he soon forgot he was in a dream. Seagulls cried from dizzying heights, and tall grasses on the dunes whispered in the wind, calling him by all the old names he'd once had. Beyond him, to the north, an abandoned lighthouse towered into the brilliant summer-blue sky.

"There you are."

His mother appeared before him, a welcome sight, slim and young as he always remembered her, reflecting vibrant sunshine in her deep red coat. She danced happily along the shore, chasing frothy waves as they pulled away from the beach. When the waves returned, she'd spin and caper off toward the dryer sand, leaving deep impressions where her dainty, almost kitten-like paws had been. Glad to see her son, she bent low into a play-bow and wagged her curled tail merrily, yodeling a welcome.

"Come play with me," she invited. "I hope you're here to stay."

"No," the old Basenji replied, dropping his tired body to the sand. He hung his head shamefully, not wanting to meet her questioning eyes. "I can't stay with you. I'm in a terrible lot of trouble and I don't know what to do."

His mother moved close, pressing her warm body against his. After sniffing him carefully from head to tail, she began to clean his face as she had when he was a puppy. The velvety strokes of her tongue calmed him, her touch making him feel younger and stronger than he had felt in years. Overwhelmed by the love he felt pouring from her as she worked, he nuzzled her neck gently, smelling her sweetness.

"Tell me what's troubling you," she implored. "Tell me why you can't stay. Today is such a beautiful day."

"I've been abandoned," he replied. "I'm all alone in the world, with no one to love. How can I remain here with you when there's no one for me to watch over? What if no one comes for me?"

His mother stopped cleaning and gazed intently at her son, and gently placed a paw on his shoulder. "Not everyone has someone to watch over," she said. "But you do have someone, don't forget. Someone very special."

"It's not the same," he replied. "I've been apart from him for so long, he's forgotten me too. Besides, I failed him once; I don't deserve to watch over him when it's time."

His mother moved away and he felt coolness in the space where her body had been. She walked around him slowly, tracing out a large circle of pawprints in the sand.

"Love is a circle with no beginning or end," she whispered. "The lighthouse is built of a circle, and it will protect you." She continued to walk around him, each time moving closer until she'd left a spiral of pawprints in the sand. "If you want something badly enough, if you believe in the magic, the magic will take care of you."

"But where can I find the magic?" he asked, puzzled. "Where do I begin?"

"You know the answers," his mother explained. "They've always been inside of you. Everyone knows what to do, and how to do it. You have the magic in you, my son."

"I'm too old!" he exclaimed, feeling the years returning to his body. "I don't know where to start!"

"Follow your heart," came the reply. "Look deep inside, remember your past, and focus on what you treasure the most. Find love again, believe in friendship and trust, and find your way back home. Do these things and you will find what you seek."

"Is it possible?" he asked. "Do you think I can?"

His mother nodded and turned to leave. "I believe in you," she said. "And I will watch over you, my beloved." She walked a short distance, then stopped to look back. "Everyone else has come to stay," she added. "Your brothers and sisters, Violet, and your father have all been able to stay. I'm so happy with them here. We're waiting for you; certainly you won't keep us wondering too much longer, will you?"

"When I've done what I need to do," the old Basenji resolved. "Then, someday, I can stay."

"I've got to leave now." His mother turned and headed toward the lighthouse. He watched until she was nothing more than a tiny, dark speck on the horizon, her words echoing in his mind and heart.

Find love again, believe in friendship and trust, and find your way back home.

He awoke the next morning feeling as if he'd slept an eternity, unable to clearly remember the dream. The warm glow of sleep disappeared when he realized the dog that scolded him the night before was no longer there. Stale cigarette smoke lingered in the warm air, and it was no mystery where the missing dog had gone. Moments later, the Basenji's sensitive ears heard the dog's mournful howl cut short by a yelp of pain as a needle entered its body.

Several more minutes passed before the Basenji saw the dog's spirit appear before him, translucent only for the briefest second before dissolving into thin air. He felt its warmth brush past him, and heard it apologize for being so sharp with him the night before. Before the Basenji could reply, it was gone.

I can't let that happen to me! he thought sadly, returning to his corner. Why the strange dog's spirit had stopped for him, he didn't know.

Why had it touched him?

PART ONE

DISCOVERY

Blessed is the person who has
earned the love of an old dog.
— Sidney Jeanne Seward

ONE

CAROLYN WASN'T IN THE CHRISTMAS
spirit, and as she waited for the car ahead of her
to turn left, she wondered if she ever would be.
Funny how time came and went, she mused,
pulling one glove then the other off with her
teeth as she steered her way through the slushy
streets of downtown Romeo, Michigan.

Snow fell gently, silently swirling between
old red-bricked buildings that lined the main
street, making ghosts dance and twirl in the icy
air, as if a child had shaken a snowglobe quickly

then set it down to watch. Even though her vehicle was warm, Carolyn shivered in her wool coat, staring out at snowflakes that landed and melted on the windshield — silent, beautiful, fleeting. A finger of wintertime sun broke through the steel-gray clouds for the briefest moment, dazzling her eyes and making the snowflakes turn to glittering diamonds.

Not so very long ago it had been summer, humid and hot, when the now-barren branches were alive with green leaves drooping and wilting in that same sun. How could it be Christmastime when she remembered the crisp coolness and musky-leaf smell of Halloween as if it were only a week ago?

More puzzling, though, was why she had let her cousin Andie talk her into dropping five 40-pound bags of dog food off at the local shelter. She could still see Andie's blue eyes pleading with her to help the hungry dogs at Christmas.

"I'd do it myself, only I've got to take the kids to get their Christmas pictures taken," Andie had said. "I'd ask you to trade places but I don't think that you'd really want to do the Santa-and-crying-kids routine. Come on, where's your Christmas spirit, anyway?" She'd made it difficult for Carolyn to refuse. Good old cousin Andie, the giving one, the sprite that put the fireworks into Independence Day, the shine into Christmas, and the one who fed homeless and hungry dogs during the holidays.

"Andie," Carolyn muttered, shaking her head as she counted the bags stacked in Andie's garage. "How will I ever get this dog food into the shelter? You didn't think of that!"

"Oh, it's not that bad, Kay O'Lyn," Andie replied, slipping into the silly name she always used when they were children and she wanted to persuade Carolyn into doing something she really didn't want to do. "I'll help you load them in. For heaven's sake, you certainly have enough room in this oversized truck of yours. Just get one of the shelter workers to help you unload when you get there. It'll be no trouble at all, really."

Carolyn was never good at resisting Andie when she got her mind set on something. Even when things didn't turn out as easily as her cousin had promised, Carolyn couldn't help but allow her cousin's bubbly, outgoing personality to sweep her away on whatever wave she happened to be riding at the time.

"Andie, Andie!" Carolyn smiled. "What would the canine world do without you?"

As quickly as it had started, the snow let up, dissolving the large wet flakes into smaller ones, but sticking to the windshield all the same. Carolyn flicked on the wipers, fumbling with a neatly folded paper, hoping it was the one that had the directions to the shelter on it. A smile danced across her face as she squinted at the familiar scribbles of Andie's less-than-intelligible handwriting. The schoolteacher in her automatically noted the loopy letters, misspellings, and arrows on the paper that smelled faintly of peanut butter and baby powder.

She decided right then and there that Andie was just a little bit crazy. After all, who went out of their way to make sure homeless dogs that probably didn't care what they ate had a good Christmas dinner?

Guess that makes me a bit crazy too, she reflected.

Her life hadn't been the same since she'd lost her Golden Retriever Max late that summer. Convinced no dog could ever begin to touch that special place in her heart as he had, she consciously made the effort to avoid the places that would bring back memories of him. Andie had told her she was being silly, insisting that the old familiar places – the park, the feed store in downtown Romeo, the bike path through orchard row – would help her remember him as he had been – young, beautiful, and healthy. Wasn't that the way Carolyn wanted to remember him?

Sometimes she'd glimpse a bit of the past, catching a memory of him running through an apple orchard when it was in full bloom, or sleeping soundly at the foot of her bed – snapshots that would appear in her mind briefly then were gone in a flash. She knew in her heart Andie was right, and desperately wanted those images of good times to comfort her. But it was difficult to forget the devastation his cancer had brought down upon them; and as the days grew shorter and colder, Carolyn had felt the unwelcome chill of loneliness settle around her, encircling her in a cocoon of semi-depression she simply couldn't shake. Tearing up at the thought of Max, she almost missed her turn.

Feeding dogs at Christmas! she thought. *If I don't pay attention to where I'm going, they won't have a Christmas dinner at all.*

What kind of Christmas a dog would have in the shelter, she didn't know. Even though she'd lived in Romeo her whole life, she'd avoided the shelter like the plague after her mother (not an animal lover by any stretch of the imagination) had sent a stray dog to its death there years ago. Unbeknownst to her mother, Carolyn had secretly befriended the dog – a black cocker spaniel mix – and spent a great deal of time and effort cleaning it up and making it look as presentable as possible, hoping against hope that maybe she'd be allowed to keep it. She'd even gone so far as to name it Pepper after the Boston terrier her mother had grown up with. It was not to be, though, for unbeknownst to Carolyn, her mother had spotted the dog rooting around in a flowerbed while Carolyn was at school, and that was the end of the dog.

The coldness of her mother's act left an indelible impression on her nine year-old daughter, who spent many nights crying herself to sleep, unable to forget Pepper's awful fate, and hating her mother for it. In her mind's eye she had pictured rows of dark cages full of hungry dogs staring out through rusted bars. She could almost reach out and feel their emaciated furry bodies and see the hopelessness in their dark, liquid eyes. Even as an adult, Carolyn sometimes awoke from that nightmare in tears.

At least I'll know those shelter dogs will have a good meal, she consoled herself. *I've got enough dog food here to feed them for a month!*

The thought occurred to her that many of those dogs who would celebrate Christmas in the shelter might not make it to see the new year, and it dampened her spirits, saddening her even more.

Great, she thought. *As if I don't feel bad enough already. Merry Christmas, indeed.*

A trickle of something that could have been a tear started down her cheek, and she was suddenly overwhelmed with a familiar feeling of loneliness. The void Max's death brought into her life hadn't grown any less painful through time. All the cheerfulness and flurry of activity that surrounded the holidays only served to remind her of how empty her life was now that he was gone. She hadn't the heart to decorate or put up her tiny Christmas tree because she couldn't bear to watch the colored lights blink cheerfully when she was so sad. Time couldn't pass quickly enough to get her through the season and into the new year.

The tiny gravel-and-asphalt parking lot in front of the shelter was well salted and full of standing puddles. Seeing only one other car in the lot made Carolyn wonder if she was too late. A faded sign on the door said it was open until two-thirty; her watch showed only two-ten.

She stood in the decorated lobby for a few minutes, staring wistfully at the cheerful strands of garland and fake holly branches, peering curiously at the obviously fake Christmas tree. Photographs of homeless dogs and cats hung from its plastic branches on bright red ribbons, and she occupied herself by reading the descriptions on the backs of a few. A red and green sign above the tree read "HOLIDAY HOPEFULS."

That's me too, she thought cynically. *I'm just hopeful to get through the holidays too.*

Hearing the bells on the Christmas tree jingle, an animal control officer appeared, putting out his cigarette on the floor and blowing a large cloud of smoke from the side of his mouth. It hung in the warm air, curling and swirling around his head like a foul fog.

"Can I help you?" he asked, running his fingers through his thinning hair. "You looking for a dog, maybe?" he coughed. "There's plenty of pictures on that tree, if that's what you want. Just pick one and it's yours."

"Uh, no." Carolyn stepped back, her nose wrinkling at the cigarette smell. "I've brought some dog food," she said. "To donate for the dogs. The bags are kind of heavy, and I was wondering if someone could help me carry them in."

She saw the man's eyes widen, then narrow just a bit. He coughed again, making her take another involuntary step backward. "Guess that'd be me, then," he shrugged. "We're a little short of help this time of year. Short of folks to adopt, too. We get lots of dogs in, but few go out." He smiled hopefully at Carolyn. "You sure you're not interested in adopting?"

"I'm sure," she replied.

"Well, you never know," the man pressed. "If you don't mind me saying, you look like a dog person. Say, I've got a real nice collie back there. Nothing wrong with it at all; the owner gave her up because they're expecting their new baby any day now. Think you might be interested?"

"No, thank you."

"Terrier then? There's a cute little guy back there – kind of active, but with a little work he'd be a great companion."

"No, really. Thanks."

The animal control officer sighed. "Well, you can't blame a guy for trying. It's just that I hate having to put them down, you know? It breaks my heart, especially this time of year. If my wife would let me, I'd take them all home."

He followed Carolyn back into the cold to unload the heavy bags of dog food, making small talk and complimenting her on the color of her new sport-utility vehicle.

Carolyn toyed with the idea of asking him what other things the shelter could use, but lost the thought as she watched him heft the last bag onto his shoulder and slip on a chunk of slush that had fallen from her vehicle.

"Oh! Look out!" She reached out to steady him.

"That's okay. I've got it."

"Thanks for taking those bags in for me," she said. "Those were pretty heavy."

Peering at her from around the bag of dog food perched on his shoulder, the animal control officer grinned broadly. "I don't know how you managed to get them into your car," he grunted.

"Sport-utility vehicle," Carolyn corrected him under her breath. "It's not a car."

"Whoa!" The man slipped again, losing his balance and nearly dropping the last bag. The generosity of people at Christmastime never failed to surprise him. The dog food she'd donated wasn't the cheap kind that many people left during the holidays, and it gave him a good feeling about her.

"Are you sure you're okay?" she asked quickly.

"Sure," he replied. "No harm done. Say," he added, "If you don't mind me asking, what kind of dog do you have?"

"I don't have a dog," Carolyn managed. "At least, not anymore. He was a Golden Retriever. He died in August."

"Sorry to hear that," the animal control officer said softly. "If you want to go look around in back, go right ahead. You never know. Maybe there's a dog back there that will strike your fancy."

"Oh, I don't think so."

"Well then, I've got to put these in the back," he smiled. "If you're sure you don't want to look around, you can wait by the front desk for your receipt. I shouldn't be more than a minute or so."

Fifteen minutes later he hadn't returned, and Carolyn was beginning to wonder where he'd gone. Her watch said it was two-thirty, but the clock on the wall showed only two-fifteen. She sighed, regretting the deep breath she took instantly. The smell of dogs and disinfectant was overpowering, and a stale cigarette smell lingered in the warm air.

As she glanced at her watch and tapped her fingers impatiently on the counter, her gaze was drawn to the HOLIDAY HOPEFULS sign again. Humming to herself, she wandered over to the tree and stared at the pictures that hung there, not seeing any one of them clearly, but taking them all in.

What the heck, she thought, noticing that another car had arrived. Why not take a peek at the lucky dogs that were going to benefit from her driving ten miles out of her way just so they'd have a Christmas feast?

A haunting image of caged dogs was stuck in her mind, and she figured the only way to make it go away was to see them for herself.

At least I'll know, she thought. *Really, how bad can it be?*

She almost changed her mind when an older man and his teenage son walked in. Surely the animal control officer would return now.

The man cleared his throat and stared at her. "You work here?" he asked, pulling off his knit cap, running his hand over his face. His winter coat was dirty, and stuffing stuck out from a tear in his sleeve. The boy had long hair that fell across his eyes like a sheepdog, and he wasn't dressed much better.

"Me? No." Carolyn replied, taking a step backward. "No, I don't work here."

The man glanced around. "Does anybody work here?"

Carolyn nodded. "There's someone here," she said. "But I think he's still busy in the back."

The man snorted and turned to his son. "There's nobody here," he shrugged, signing the words. "We'll come back tomorrow, okay?"

The boy, who Carolyn immediately realized was deaf, signed something back to the man. She found it hard to meet the boy's crystal-blue eyes as they stared into hers, almost as if he didn't believe she didn't work there. She smiled at him and shrugged, but he turned away.

She shuddered involuntarily once they were gone. Something about them had made her feel dirty, and it bothered her that she didn't understand what the boy had signed. She'd taken some classes in sign language years ago, but hadn't recognized any of the signs he'd used.

Well, better take a look inside, she thought, her eyes falling on the HOLIDAY HOPEFULS tree again. *The minute I walk away from this spot, that animal control officer will be back here wondering where I went.*

Dog ears of nearly every shape and size turned toward the sound of her footsteps on the concrete floor. At least sixteen pairs of canine eyes turned her way, looking hard for a moment at the brown-haired young woman in a hunter green wool coat, half expecting to see someone they knew or remembered, hoping that whoever it was had come to take them home, and realizing in that same instant it was no one they knew.

Dark, wet noses pushed their way through chain link and worked the air, catching her scent and wondering if their eyes had made a mistake. Canine minds, simple yet painfully desperate were working feverishly, searching for the match to some familiar scent that wasn't there.

Do I know her? each dog asked itself. *Does she belong to me?*

Not recognizing Carolyn's scent, nor her slightly rounded feminine features, each dog made a brief mental note and looked longingly at the young woman who had mysteriously appeared from behind the metal door. They detected the faint aroma of fabric softener mixed with the fresh winter smell of outdoors as she passed, and they found the scents intoxicating. A hint of ham sandwich and pickles lingered on her, and there was the tempting, delicious aroma of her leather handbag. Maybe she'd take one of them home, give a good warm bath and a decent meal. Perhaps she'd even be willing to share her soft bed and warm blanket.

But Carolyn saw only what a human could possibly see. The thoughts that raced through the minds of these unfortunate dogs were as foreign to her as she was to them. She couldn't possibly know they saw right into the deep sadness she carried with her. Her body language gave her thoughts away, and it saddened them to see the unhappiness in her. Always eager to please as dogs are, she was a challenge that, if given a chance, any one of them would gladly have taken on.

In one large cage a hairy beast of a dog peered at her with liquid-brown eyes, one ear flopped over, and begged to be taken home. His shaggy tail wagged slowly from side to side as if someone had wound it up. Another cage held three black lab-mix puppies that tumbled over each other and crowded against the fence. Yet another held a matted and filthy blue merle collie with mismatched eyes. It tried to bark as she approached, but its voice was only a husky whisper from having been debarked. It stuck its elegant, slender muzzle through an opening in the chain link and whined softly.

Carolyn kept her arms close to her body, careful not to touch any of the dogs, unaware of how desperately they wanted to be near her. It wasn't that she found them repulsive; in fact, her heart cried out for each and every one of them. After what she'd gone through with Max, she was afraid of commitment, of growing close to something again only to have it snatched away.

Sensing her apprehension, the dogs moved away as she approached, afraid if they came on too strong they'd frighten her off.

At least there aren't any Goldens, she thought. *I don't think I could handle seeing one trapped in here*.

She turned a corner, her eyes dazzled for a moment when the clouds opened up, sending a brilliant ray of sunlight through a high window. Adjusting quickly to the unexpected brightness, she gasped when her eyes fell upon a small dog. Bathed in an aura of golden sunlight that made him seem almost otherworldly, she knew in that instant he didn't belong there.

TWO

THE SMALL DOG SAT QUIETLY BY himself in a cage at the end of a row. He was obviously a purebred, for his features and manner were regal and poised. His finely sculpted face held a multitude of wrinkles at his brow, giving him an intelligent but worried look.

Reddish brown in color, his coat was short and neat, with snowy-white markings on his face, neck and chest, and on each of his feet. He had velvety, hooded prick-ears that stood straight up at attention. Transparent whiskers moved forward with great precision as he carefully sniffed the air. His eyes were dark, exotic-Egyptian, rimmed with smoky black, as if someone had used eyeliner on him.

He straightened as Carolyn approached, making himself appear even more regal. Intense brown eyes locked into her green ones and didn't waver their stare.

She was taken aback by the dog's boldness, feeling even more unsettled from his silent gaze than she had been from the barking dogs all around her. She glanced away from him a couple of times only to find herself drawn back to him, staring right back into his dark eyes.

The dog's nose worked the air feverishly as she drew closer. One elegant paw was raised, held just off the ground, as if he were asking a question — almost as if he needed to tell her something. All she had to do was lean down to his level and she was certain that the red dog would begin to speak . . .

"Hello."

The voice was small but masculine, with a faint and unusual accent. It echoed clearly in her head, as if it had come from inside her, shutting out all the other shelter sounds momentarily.

Confused as to where the greeting had come from, Carolyn turned to see if the animal control officer had returned to find her among the dogs. Her brow furrowed in puzzlement, for she realized no one else was in the room with her — except for the dogs.

"Hello?"

The word was a question now, and Carolyn glanced back at the red dog, then back to the doorway from where she'd come. Surely someone was playing a trick on her.

It's a game, she thought miserably. *That guy probably does it all the time!*

Embarrassed and suddenly feeling unwelcome, she turned her back on the dog and started back toward the lobby. Her purse caught on a broken piece of fence that jutted sharply from one of the runs. Stopping in mid-stride she struggled, trying to free her purse without inflicting too much damage on the brushed leather surface.

"Don't go!"

The voice was gentle, not overly deep, but now clearly panicked. Carolyn studied the red dog carefully, seeing him with more detail. For the first time she noticed patches of gray showing around his finely shaped muzzle. A pink scar stood out prominently on his white neck, just to one side of his throat where the hairs swirled and grew in a different direction. Dark pigment spots were visible through the white markings on his legs and chest, and she couldn't help but smile when she noticed one shaped like a heart.

"You can hear me, can't you?"

"You?" To Carolyn, her voice sounded loud and shrill compared to the beautiful one she'd just heard. Several dogs resumed barking at the sound of her voice, and the puppies she had seen earlier squeaked loudly, pawing at the fence and making it rattle.

Nope, she thought. *Nope, nope, nope! I am not hearing a dog talk to me!* She said this last part out loud, without even realizing it, as if she could convince herself it wasn't true at all.

"What's wrong with a dog talking to you? We don't just talk to *anybody*, you know." A resigned sigh escaped from the red dog. "Ah, what's the use?"

He stood and shook himself, and paced back and forth in his cage, his dark eyes fixed on her, erasing any doubt about whose voice she'd heard. His nails tapped sharply on the cement floor. "You can hear me! I can see it in your face!"

He put two paws on the fence, hooking them through the chain link. Carolyn noticed scars on the inside of each, where dewclaws had once been.

"Tell me you hear me," the red dog pleaded, wagging his curly tail and trying to look as friendly as possible. "Whatever you do, don't go!"

"Why me?" Carolyn whispered, suddenly very afraid. *I am not crazy*, she thought to herself. *I am not crazy.*

"Why not?" came the reply, accompanied by a relieved chuckle. The red dog seated himself as close to her as the fence would allow, little tufts of his fine coat pushing through the openings. "Say, were you thinking of taking me home?"

"N-no," she stammered. "I was just here dropping off some dog food and . . ." her voice trailed off. What was she doing, explaining herself to a dog? "I don't know why I can hear you but I can, can't I?" Fascination replaced fear as she crouched to the dog's level and stared directly into his eyes. "Do I really hear you?" she asked, her green eyes wide with wonder.

"You do hear me!" the dog exclaimed. He sneezed, blowing air out of his nose with a *whoosh*. "You've got to help me! If you don't take me with you today, tomorrow morning, before they open the doors and let people in again, I'm dead. That's what happens here if nobody wants you," he whispered.

"I bet everyone in here is thinking the same thing," Carolyn said, reaching through the fence, letting the dog sniff her fingers. His breath came in gentle *wuffs* that tickled her, making her smile.

"Some of them don't have a clue what happens here," the red dog said. "Like those puppies, for example. They just got here this morning." He sniffed her hand, and gave it a tentative lick with his tongue.

Basenji. The word popped into her head suddenly, right then, so clearly she could almost see the letters hovering in the air. That's the kind of dog he was. A Basenji.

She'd read about the breed before, and knew it was an ancient, African breed. She knew Basenjis didn't bark, but none of the books she'd ever read had indicated that they — or any other breed, for that matter — were actually able to talk.

She studied the Basenji carefully, noticing that what she had thought was a white muzzle really once had been red, for a few red hairs were still visible through the gray. Clearly, he was much older than she'd assumed at first glance. She fingered his coat, thinking he was similar in color to Max, only she was having a hard time remembering exactly what that color was.

For a moment she wondered if it was possible for people to be reincarnated. Maybe the Basenji was someone who'd been brought back as a dog. It occurred to her that perhaps even Max could have been reincarnated, sent back to be with her again. Certainly, he must have missed her as much as she'd missed him.

You've been watching too many movies, she chastised herself, feeling foolish. *Reincarnated indeed. Get real.*

She brushed off the idea as just plain preposterous. The creature sitting in front of her was a dog, clearly enough. Four legs, wet nose, tail. A dog. Yet, he was talking to her, and she could hear him.

"Come on, then, there isn't much time!" The Basenji touched her hand with a paw. The pad was rough from the cement floor, and rubbed against her bare skin like sandpaper. "Please, you just can't leave me here!"

A strange feeling ran through as he kept his paw on her, and she felt as if she'd always known him. She didn't want to stop hearing his beautiful voice, and right then she knew she couldn't leave him there to die.

Boldly she flipped open the latch that held the cage door closed. It swung open with a groan so loud she was sure the animal control officer must have heard it. Fleeting second thoughts entered her mind, but she pushed them away and concentrated on the Basenji.

Gratefully, he pushed his way into her arms, sniffing her eagerly. "Thank you!" he breathed. "Thank you so much!"

Carolyn's hands were drawn to the dirty leather collar encircling his neck. As she scratched beneath it, her fingers found shorter, broken hairs, and she knew he must have worn it for a very long time. There were no tags or identifying marks on it.

Impulsively she held him close, smelling his sweetness that wasn't dog-like at all, reminding her of warm grass on a hot summer day. His heart beat rapidly in his chest, and she easily found his ribs jutting sharply from beneath his short coat. When she put her face close to his, a quick, pink tongue rewarded her.

Reluctantly she pushed the Basenji back behind the fence. "Wait here," she whispered. "I'll be right back." She turned to go, feeling strangely elated at the prospect of taking him home.

Suddenly afraid she wouldn't come back, the Basenji let out a whine that turned into a long, mournful yodel, silencing the other dogs. He pawed frantically at the fence, not caring how the metal hurt his paws. Somewhere another dog started to howl.

"Oh!" Carolyn hurried back, unlatched the cage door, and scooped the surprised Basenji into her arms. "Let's get you out of here," she said. "There's too much sadness here."

"It's more than just sadness," he replied, relaxing in her arms. "What you see here are a lot of hopes that won't ever be realized."

The thought troubled the Basenji, dampening his enthusiasm as the reality of his situation sunk in. Tomorrow morning some of the dogs left behind would die. His tail unfurled at the magnitude of the revelation.

How terrible it is to die without being loved by someone, he thought, feeling tears well up in his eyes. *How can this be allowed to happen? Who will they watch over when they get to the Happiness? They should all be this lucky*, he thought, troubled by the haunted looks he saw. Panic shone brightly in some of those eyes and his sensitive ears heard the low thumping of heartbeats quickening. He heard the soft, resonant sighs that came from dogs he couldn't even see.

This is no place to live, he thought. *A dog needs a family, someone to love.*

Sixteen pairs of hopeful eyes had watched Carolyn enter the room; now fifteen pairs, their hopes dashed, watched her carry the Basenji past their cages to the exit.

The barking and whining stilled as the remaining dogs realized they were being left behind. A resentful murmur started amongst them, whispering dog voices undetected by Carolyn but heard quite clearly by the Basenji.

"Purebred!" He heard one of them spit out the word as if it were poison. "What's so special about a purebred?"

"See if she keeps you!" Another called out from across the room. "I bet she won't for long!"

They're barking and whining, Carolyn thought as the heavy metal door closed behind her, shutting out the angry words only the Basenji could hear. *Why don't they have voices too?*

"Hey, you found one, after all!" The animal control officer appeared from the back room and stood at the counter, grinning widely. "I thought you might!"

His happiness was contagious, and Carolyn returned the smile enthusiastically. "I guess I did." She paused, and saw that the Basenji had his ears pricked forward, listening to her every word. *Am I the only one who can hear him?* she wondered, feeling him shift in her arms. *I have to know.* "This little guy just up and asked to be taken home," she continued, studying the animal control officer's face for a reaction – any reaction that would give away the fact that he knew there was something different about the Basenji. "He was pretty insistent. How could I refuse?"

The man reached over and let the Basenji sniff his fingers. "I know what you mean," he said, patting the dog's head gently. Carolyn's heart raced, pounding in her chest loud enough that she was sure he could hear it. Had he heard the Basenji talk, too?

"You do?" The Basenji and Carolyn said this together, almost as if it were on cue. They turned to face each other, surprised. Surely the animal control officer had heard both their voices in the room.

"You can hear me too?" the Basenji pressed, his eyes wide.

"Sure," the man smiled. "If anyone knows how irresistible some of these dogs can be when they want to, it's me. Every time I go back there, they're staring at me with that sad little 'take me home, please' look on their faces. Day in and day out, it's the same thing, only the dogs change."

Carolyn hadn't even noticed that she'd been holding her breath, and suddenly she let it out, feeling slightly disappointed but quite relieved. *So he doesn't hear him,* she thought excitedly. *If he can't, and he's standing right there, then I must be the only one!*

"Oh, I almost forgot. Before you go, you'll need this." The man reached behind the counter and handed her a brand new nylon leash and collar. "Let's see how he looks in hunter green." He snapped the new collar around the Basenji's neck, and stood back to admire it. "Looks good to me. Well, there you go, then. All set."

Carolyn set the Basenji on the floor and fished for her wallet. "How much do I owe you?"

"Well, seeing that it's Christmas, let's just say no charge. And, don't worry about the leash and collar, either. Last week someone donated a whole bunch of these so that all the adopted dogs get to go home with something new." He leaned over the counter and looked at the Basenji. "I'm glad you're taking him home. His time was up tomorrow."

"Thank you!" Carolyn said breathlessly. Her mind was moving quickly, almost as if she were in a dream. Only a little while ago she had despaired over Max, missing him so terribly that it hurt, and now here she was with a new dog at the end of a new leash. For some strange reason she didn't feel as if she were being unfaithful to Max by adopting the Basenji; in fact, she had the feeling that if Max could see her, he would have approved.

Maybe it's because I couldn't save Max, she thought. *But maybe in some way by saving this dog, I can make up for it.*

"Thanks again," the animal control officer said, walking her to the door. "I've got to feed the rest of these guys, and then lock up. Have a great Christmas!"

"I think I will," Carolyn replied. For the first time that season, she added, "And, Merry Christmas to you, too!"

THREE

"As for introductions," the
Basenji said, making himself comfortable on the
sofa. "Now that I know your name, I know what
to call you. But you don't know mine." He
turned around several times before settling
down, leaning heavily against a pile of pillows.
"Officially, I'm Champion Windswept of
Hatteras. My mother was called Savannah, and
my father was a champion, although I never
actually knew him." He stood and nosed the
pillows, circling again before settling down.

"Ah," he sighed. "This is nice."

"What should I call you?" Carolyn asked, watching him with amusement. "I mean, what's your name?" Surely he didn't expect her to address him as "Champion Windswept of Hatteras" every time she needed to call him — or, did he?

"Oh," the Basenji lowered his head to his paws, a multitude of creases wrinkling his brow. "You can call me whatever you'd like, I suppose." The answer was noncommittal, almost as if he didn't care to have a name at all.

Carolyn didn't know what to make of his reply. "You must have a name," she said. "Or, at least you must have a preference. Something somebody's called you before, maybe?"

"Oh *no!*" The Basenji's eyes narrowed into dark slits, and he pulled his ears close to his head, clearly offended. "I am *here* and now is *now*, and what *you* choose to call me is who I will be," he said, staring hard at the young woman before him. "It's simple."

When he got no response other than a puzzled look, he tried again.

"You can't call me by an old name, because that's not who I am anymore. I'm here, with you. Give me a name to remind me of being here with you."

Carolyn smiled. She glanced over at a small, framed photo that had been carefully placed on the coffee table. It was evident to the Basenji that, while the coffee table itself hadn't been dusted, the picture had been, perhaps as recently as that very morning. Clearly, the picture was something his new companion treasured.

Cousin Andie had taken that photo of Carolyn and Max the autumn before he died. Whenever Carolyn looked at the photo, she could almost smell the musky scent of burning leaves that had drifted on the gentle autumn breeze. Forgetting the Basenji, she closed her eyes, letting the memory flow over her like a warm comforter on a cold night.

Andie had captured the perfection of that day so well. Golden sunlight illuminated the backdrop of brilliant fall leaves; Max, his tongue hanging out of his smiling mouth, wagged his tail happily.

Carolyn had been shocked at the warmth the sun had given Max's silky gold coat, and she could almost feel him breathing beneath her hand, his sides rising and falling rhythmically, in sync with her heartbeat.

Andie insisted on taking the photo with Carolyn standing in the sun behind Max, instructing her to lean over and give him a great big bear hug. Carolyn remembered kissing the top of his broad head, smelling his earthy, doggy smell mixed with the freshness of the outdoors. Not long after, when the days became damp and cold, had he fallen ill.

I know what I was thinking when Andie took that picture, she thought sadly. *I was thinking how happy I was, how I was lucky to share my life with Max. I was counting my blessings, and he was the most important one.*

Her memory of that beautiful day was captured forever in one snapshot, and she recalled how often she'd wanted desperately to return to that single moment in time. She hadn't even realized how precious those last warm days of that autumn really were.

She shook her head to clear it of the painfully familiar sadness that overtook her whenever she thought of Max. She had many memories of happy times with him, but they seemed distant and far away. It was almost as if they weren't her memories at all, but instead borrowed from someone else.

She understood then what the Basenji had meant about memories, amazed how one photograph stirred a multitude of emotions within her. The photograph was in her hand, its intricate brass frame held tightly against her chest, her mind a million miles away. A sad smile appeared on her face, turning the corners of her mouth up slightly.

A sound, very much like a gentleman clearing his throat

politely, brought her back to reality.

"I think I know what you're thinking," the Basenji said at length, pausing long enough to let Carolyn collect her thoughts. "When you choose a name for me, please don't name me after your old dog. That's his name, for his time with you. Give me a name of my own."

As quickly as her smile appeared, it vanished. "You knew I was thinking of Max?" she asked, startled to hear herself say his name aloud, surprised to have even said it.

"You were in the picture," the Basenji explained. "You were remembering the day in the picture. I saw you looking at it."

The photograph was back on the coffee table in a flash.

Looking uncomfortable, and feeling for the moment somewhat unwelcome, the Basenji tried to explain. "He's still with you," he ventured. "Max. He wants you to be happy, and he wouldn't like it if I took his name. Not that I would, at any rate. It was a gift from you, and it belongs to him."

The golden rule of dogdom — one that all dogs, regardless of their breeding or stage in life strictly adhered to. Don't ever, ever share a name. Names were precious gifts, and the Basenji couldn't imagine taking someone else's name; it was unthinkable.

Carolyn was stunned. The thought of Max actually being in the same room with her made sadness and happiness all at once rise inside of her. All this time she'd thought she was alone, yet he'd always been with her. How could it be?

She'd entertained similar thoughts in the days and weeks after he'd died. Her denial had been so great that she actually believed he was physically with her, sleeping on the sofa or curled up on the bed, always out of sight, in another room, but always there. Her ears, so in tune with the familiar sounds of his comings and goings, actually believed he was lapping water in the kitchen, breathing softly as he dreamed, or tapping his toenails on the kitchen floor. She'd even gotten the nail clippers out so he'd walk more quietly. Sometimes at night she'd feel him in the bed next to her, his golden body warming her back. He'd always curled up against her back.

"You can hear him?" she whispered, wiping away a tear. "You mean, he's here? He talks to you?" She glanced around the room, clearly upset. "Is he a ghost or something? Can you see him?"

Frightened by the look in her eyes, the Basenji realized she didn't understand the nature of what Max was. He found the strangeness of the situation overwhelming.

"Well, he is here," the Basenji pawed at his face, thinking hard. "When dogs die, they become dog-spirits." Seeing a puzzled look cross her face his mind raced, trying to find a way to explain the essence of a dog's life.

He cleared his throat, and tried again.

"When we're born," he explained, "our mothers teach us that all good dogs are expected to do their master's bidding. That means we are to be companions, protectors, and workers — anything our people want us to be. We're not allowed to have true freedom in this life, because that's not what being a good dog is all about. But when we die, our bodies are left behind so we can become totally free. A dog-spirit is its own master, free to move between this life and the next." The Basenji thought for a moment. "In life, when we find someone we truly love, we become a part of them. We never, ever leave those we love all alone in this world. A dog-spirit never forgets the people who love him."

"Every dog remembers a place and time when they were most loved, and it's in that place and time where our spirit rests. From there, we watch over our beloved. Often, we leave the Happiness in order to be close to that person again."

The Basenji cocked his head to the side and looked at her through narrowed eyes. "Some dogs live a lifetime and can't get to the Happiness because their people loved them too much. The love binds a dog-spirit to this earth, and he can't be free unless his person allows him to be." The Basenji paused, and took a deep breath. "I'm sure you loved Max very much, and losing him was difficult — so difficult that you haven't been able to let him go. But keeping him from going to the Happiness is selfish and wrong." He pawed at the air, making his point. "Your sadness won't let his spirit leave here and be free."

Carolyn slowly sank to the floor and stared into the dusty oak top of her coffee table. Max's reflection seemed to appear in its smooth surface, floating ghostlike next to her own. When she moved her hand to see better, to brush away the dust, it was gone.

Can this all be a dream? she asked herself. *Can this really be happening to me?*

The Basenji had called her selfish, and she knew he was right. Max had been the center of her life, almost as if he'd been her child. He was on her mind constantly, so much a part of her that she still mourned his death as if it were only yesterday. Wasn't that all a part of loving someone?

"You don't want to talk about it anymore, do you?"

The Basenji was beside her, his voice gentle with understanding. She turned to him, her face pained, her eyes wet with tears. "Forgive me for not being able to explain it so you can understand," he said, placing a paw on her knee. "It's what life is to me, and how can I explain it when you don't see the world through my eyes? We learn about dog-spirits when we're very young. Maybe some other time, when you can tell me about the life Max shared with you, then I'll be more help."

He lowered his head, resting it tentatively on her leg. "This is as new to me as it is to you. I've never talked to a person like this before," he sighed. "There's so much about my world that you couldn't possibly know, and I never imagined how complex your world would be. I'd always thought we were essentially the same, just different-looking. It's not that simple at all, is it?"

"Maybe," he ventured, "maybe we can get this whole thing sorted out together. If we try, maybe we can understand what it all means, and why this has happened to us."

Carolyn nodded, afraid to trust her voice. A tear managed to escape from her eye, leaving a salty trail down her cheek. It threatened to dangle from her chin, and before she could reach up and brush it away, the Basenji's lightning fast tongue made it disappear.

"Everything will work out," he said simply. "I'm here with you now."

FOUR

"YOU DID WHAT?" ANDIE STARED AT her cousin in disbelief. She knew that sending Carolyn to the shelter might help interest her in considering a new dog, but she never imagined her soft-spoken, sometimes-timid cousin would do something so impulsive; it simply wasn't in her nature.

"Tell me again," she said, taking a huge bite from a sugar cookie that left crumbs tumbling down her chin and sweater. "Kay O'Lyn, this is so great!   Whatever made you walk into the

30

shelter and walk out with a dog?"

Carolyn regarded the plate of sugar cookies before her and selected one dusted with red and green sugar granules. She bit into it carefully, not wanting crumbs. "I don't know. Christmas spirit or something?" She wasn't about to tell Andie the dog had spoken to her. No, she couldn't tell *anyone* that. "And anyway," she added, "the only reason I even went there in the first place was for you, you know!"

Andie smiled. "Well, it was nice of you to take the dog food into the shelter for me, and I'm glad you decided to get another dog. It's about time." She reached for the coffeepot and filled Carolyn's cup, then her own.

Carolyn winced at Andie's words, but her cousin didn't notice. Andie always spoke her mind, even if it wasn't always tactfully done. Carolyn's admiration for her cousin ran deep, as did their mutual love for dogs; it had drawn them together when they were just kids.

Andie was secretly glad that her cousin had opened her heart again. They'd been too distant, drifting apart lately, especially in the months since Max died and Andie's second son was born.

"So what's he like, this new dog of yours?" Andie reached for another cookie. "Big, small, hairy, hairless?" she giggled. "Let me guess. Great Dane? Chinese Crested? Mutt?"

Andie can eat and eat and never gain an ounce, Carolyn mused. She was something else, alright. To look at her, you'd hardly know that she was the mother of a two year-old and a four month-old.

Carolyn had always envied Andie's deep blue eyes and long auburn curls. She still looked like a teenager, slim and pretty, while Carolyn's cat-green eyes glowed beneath her own dark hair and hid themselves inside her more rounded frame. Andie had been a cheerleader in high school, and just like in romance novels, she'd married her high-school sweetheart, who was a football player and the team captain. Her life was a fairy tale that Carolyn sometimes wondered if she'd ever find for herself.

"The new dog's a he." Carolyn smiled. "A Basenji. He's an older dog, a little gray around the muzzle, but overall he's really pretty. I can't imagine why anyone would have dumped him at the shelter, or left him out on the streets." She blew on her coffee to cool it, watching as the steam rose and curled from the cup.

"Purebred, eh?" Andie smiled. "Wow. Classy stuff."

She handed her two-year old son a cookie, and watched as he toddled off. "I wonder what his story is?" she asked. "I bet there are a million reasons why he could have ended up there. Who knows? You've got a real man of mystery there, cuz."

"Well, I don't know about that," Carolyn replied. "I'm sure he was locked up for the same reason the others were. Maybe no one wanted him anymore."

"Hmmm. I'm no expert, but Basenjis aren't the most common dogs around. I've got to believe he was worth something to someone, somewhere along the line," Andie speculated. "Maybe he was a big-time show dog who was kidnapped and held somewhere far away for years and years, and maybe only just now he escaped from his captors and was trying to find his way back home when he ran into the dog catcher."

Carolyn laughed. "I doubt it," she said, shaking her head. "He's way too old to be a show dog, that much I can tell you."

Andie narrowed her eyes and pointed a cookie in her cousin's direction. "But Kay O'Lyn, you really don't know, do you? It's not like you can just sit him down and ask him where he came from! No, I'm convinced," she said, biting into her cookie. "He's a man of mystery. His past is a secret only he knows. You, my dear cousin, will never, ever know. But," she relented, "it sure is fun to think about!"

"You're getting just a little carried away, don't you think?" Carolyn smiled. "He's a dog, and he was in the shelter. Now, he's living with me in my apartment. That's his story."

"How about this, then. Do you think he was running away from something terrible that he did, and just was unlucky enough to get caught?" Andie countered, her blue eyes wide. "Maybe he's a criminal!"

"Not likely."

"You never know, nowadays." Andie pressed. "The way some people treat their dogs is pretty awful. Maybe," she lowered her voice to a whisper, "just maybe he got fed up with his last owner — so fed up that he finished him off one dark and stormy night!"

"Come on, already!" Carolyn set her cup on the table with a bang, rattling the silverware and making her cousin jump. Coffee sloshed over the rim of her cup, staining the festive Christmas tablecloth.

"All I'm trying to say, Kay O'Lyn, is that you don't know much about this new dog of yours. And here, you've gone and left him alone in your apartment. Loose. You must be pretty confident that he'll be okay by himself."

Carolyn hadn't even considered the possibility that her new companion had been in some sort of trouble, or even a runaway. It made her wonder if, at that very moment, he was looking for a way to escape from her apartment. What had she been thinking, leaving a strange dog alone and loose in her home? She hadn't closed any doors to contain him, and he hadn't had a bath yet. What if he had fleas?

Impulsive! she thought nervously, angry at herself for not thinking things through. *That sort of thing can really get you into trouble if you're not careful.*

"Hello?" Andie's voice broke into her thoughts. "So what do you call this mystery man you've rescued for Christmas? What's his name?"

It was on the tip of Carolyn's tongue to tell her cousin the dog didn't have a name yet. After all, she hadn't even known him for a full day! She smiled ruefully, remembering the earlier discussion she'd had with the dog about names. What would Andie think of that?

She'd tell me it's all in my head, Carolyn thought, sipping at her coffee. *Just like when we were kids. She'd tell me to stop believing in things that only happen in fairy tales and children's stories. Like believing in magic, Andie would say. Believing in talking dogs is just like believing in magic.*

She could hear her own little-girl voice defending her position. *If you're so smart, Andie, then tell me why would people go and make up stories about magic if it really doesn't exist? Just because you don't understand it or see it doesn't mean it's not there! You believe in love, don't you? Isn't love magic?*

"Magic," Carolyn said after a pause. "His name is Magic."

"Magic," Andie repeated. "That's really neat. If anyone deserved a little magic in her life, I'd say it was you!" She smiled. "A little Christmas magic for my cousin Kay O'Lyn."

FIVE

THE BASENJI HAD SPENT THE HOURS after Carolyn's departure examining every inch of her spacious apartment. He sniffed under furniture, regretting his curiosity when he found dust that made him sneeze. He stuck his head into cabinets, sniffing with great relish the place where the garbage had been kept, disappointed that it had already been taken out. On a whim, he even made a half-hearted but unsuccessful attempt at opening the refrigerator door.

Not having had a dog around for awhile,

Carolyn hadn't thought to leave her new companion a bowl of water, much less something to eat. He had been thirsty for several hours, and now he was getting hungry, too. The rumbling in his stomach was getting harder to ignore, and he hoped she would return soon.

He squeaked happily when he discovered his first treasure — a box of tissues in the bathroom. After a quick drink from the cool water in the toilet bowl he spent several delightful minutes shredding the contents of the entire box, tossing the soft paper into the air joyfully, watching as it drifted lazily back down.

When the last tissue was shredded, he resumed his explorations, doing ferocious battle with a stuffed toy cat he'd found perched on Carolyn's bed. Tiring of the toy, he tried every piece of furniture in the apartment until he found one that was suitable for a nap. Exhausted, he settled into the sofa with a loud sigh, turning around several times before he was comfortable. He tucked his nose into the space between his front paws, warmed it with his breath, and drifted into a dreamless sleep.

He was snoring softly when his ears caught the distinctive click of a key turning in a lock. The sound startled him, and he watched the door carefully, cocking his head as he heard someone fumble with keys and shopping bags. He relaxed when he heard Carolyn's exasperated voice say "Darn!" as her keys jingled and hit the floor. After an eternity the doorknob turned and Carolyn walked in, her arms full of grocery bags.

"Hey," she said, smiling and coming over to the sofa where the Basenji was stretched out. Her green eyes rapidly scanned the apartment, looking for evidence of damage or attempted escape, seeing nothing immediate that was out of the ordinary. "Didn't get into any trouble, I see," she said sheepishly, feeling silly for having doubted the dog's house manners. "Did you have a good sleep?"

The little dog regarded her with smug amusement. "I was

wondering the same thing about you!" he said with a grin. "It's late and I'm hungry!"

He stood and gave himself a good hard shake, right down to the tip of his tail, ridding his body of sleep. This done, he hopped off the sofa and paced back and forth on the kitchen floor, his toenails clicking merrily on the linoleum.

He made sure he got a good look inside all of the grocery bags Carolyn had left on the floor, conveniently at his level. Beyond the smells of paper and plastic he found residual scents of the many hands the contents of the bags had passed through. And, of course, there were the tantalizing aromas given off by the groceries themselves.

Carolyn laughed and rummaged through the bags. Intrigued by all the rustling and the fact that something in one of those brown paper bags smelled really good, the Basenji stuck his nose into each bag again, wondering if he had missed something.

"Aha!" he exclaimed, pulling out a bundle of carrots with the green leafy tops still attached. He shook them side to side playfully, then let go. The carrots landed on the floor with a satisfying *thud*. "These are good," he said, holding them down with his paws and pulling off the tops. He munched on some of the greens, smacking his lips happily as he reached for more.

Suddenly, Carolyn swooped down on him as he was in mid pull, and he knew the carrots weren't going to be his for very long.

"Hey!" The delicacy was removed, deposited high on the countertop, out of reach. "Not everything in here is for you, you know!" She fumbled with another bag, keeping one eye on the little Basenji who stood on his hind legs in front of the counter. She watched with amusement as he stretched each front paw in turn as far forward as he could, trying to reach the carrots.

"But some things in here are for you. Did you see them?" she asked, pushing him away from the counter and back down on all fours.

His pride wounded from having the delicious carrots taken away, the Basenji sat amongst the bags and put on a sorrowful look. When Carolyn ignored him, he whined and cocked his head to one side, wrinkling his brow with the most pleading, "poor me" look he could muster. Although she tried, Carolyn couldn't help laughing at the faces he made. He pleaded some more, sitting with his paw held up in the air, his whole body begging for the carrots.

Some carrot greens stuck out the corner of his mouth, and hung down on one side. Realizing what had happened, and suddenly understanding why he wasn't getting any sympathy, the Basenji pawed at his face, trying vainly to dislodge the greens. They finally came free when he rubbed his head along the braided rug in the kitchen.

"Really," he said, smacking his lips loudly. "It's not *that* funny!" He held his head high and proud, curled his tail tightly across his rear, and stormed out of the kitchen, his toenails tapping on the floor, his backside swaying defiantly. He was embarrassed, certainly, but he also had his Basenji pride and dignity, and he gracefully retreated with what little of it he had left intact, relocating to the comfort and sanctuary of the living room. Carolyn heard him muttering to himself under his breath, just quietly enough so she couldn't make out the words.

"Hmmm." She watched him leave, and felt guilty that she'd offended her guest. After all, he'd just had a rough day. It occurred to her that being in the shelter must have been a trying experience for the old Basenji. Having narrowly escaped death would certainly put her on edge and make even simple things like a bunch of carrots a luxury.

She pulled two bright stainless steel bowls out of a bag and filled one with water. The other she filled with dry dog food. The clattering of kibble in the bowl brought the Basenji back to the kitchen doorway, ears pricked forward, his stomach grumbling at the sound.

She called to him several times before he came to her. Gently, she took him into her arms, stroked his wrinkled forehead, and whispered her apologies to him. It shocked her to see how much gray hair was in his coat, especially around his face and muzzle. As she stroked his body, she felt the tenseness leave his muscles. He leaned into her, resting his head heavily on her arm.

"I've got some dinner ready for you," she said, pointing at the shiny bowl heaped with fresh kibble. "Why don't you try some? If you don't like it, I can always get another kind."

The Basenji moved toward the bowl and sniffed hungrily. The wonderful, fragrant aroma of food filled his nostrils, and made saliva wet his eager mouth in anticipation.

Carolyn said nothing as she watched him eat, smiling to herself when she saw his tail curl tight with pleasure. She felt guilty that she hadn't thought to buy some food for him earlier that day when she'd taken him home.

She thought of her visit with Andie, and realized she hadn't told him his name. Suddenly, she was shy about it. What if he didn't like it? What would he think?

She remained on the floor beside him, watching happily as he devoured his dinner. *His name*, she thought. *I must tell him his name.*

"I've been thinking," she ventured. "If it's alright with you, I'd like to call you Magic."

The Basenji stopped eating, and turned his wrinkled face her way. "That's a good name," he said, feeling a happy warmth wash over him as she repeated it at his request. "In fact, it's just the sort of name I'd hoped for."

S I X

MUCH TO MAGIC'S SURPRISE,
Carolyn discovered and cleaned up the tissues
he'd shredded without so much as a grumble.
He'd waited silently to see how she'd react, for
his love of tissues had gotten him into plenty of
trouble in the past. He felt relieved, although a
bit confused, when he realized no
admonishments were forthcoming. He was
pleasantly discovering that, in a wonderful sort
of way, Carolyn was different from people he'd
known throughout his life.

"I have an idea," she told him, surveying his dusty coat with a critical eye. "How about a bath? You'll feel nice and clean after one."

"Bath?" Magic's ears perked forward, but then were laid flat against his skull. "No bath!" he squeaked, bending low into a play-bow. A hint of a smile glinted in his eyes. "No bath for the dog!"

She chased him through the apartment for several harrowing minutes before cornering him in the bathroom. He felt her strong hands close around his body and lift it high, his toenails scrabbling on the tile floor in a valiant attempt to escape her.

"Gotcha!" she exclaimed, planting a kiss on his nose. He pawed at the place, and sneezed playfully.

As much as he hated the thought of a bath, Magic found Carolyn's hands soothing on his dusty coat as she rubbed and lathered fancy-smelling shampoo into bubbles, careful not to get any in his eyes.

"Hold still!" she said, almost falling into the tub as he tried to slip from her soapy grasp. "I still need to rinse you off!"

"What I'd like to know," Magic grumbled, "is when you get your turn!"

The water was murky when Carolyn finally let him out of the tub to shake off. As she dried him with a thick towel, he closed his eyes, enjoying the feel of it against his coat. The comforting strokes brought to mind memories of his mother, and how she'd cleaned him when he was a pup. Other memories, dusky visions of a better time when he was a young and proud show dog, drifted into his mind.

"I've never liked baths," he murmured. "But long ago, when I was young, I didn't mind them so much."

"What was different then?" Carolyn asked.

"Lots of things," he replied, shaking himself again. "I was younger, and beautiful, and people thought I was something special. Hey, you left the door open!"

Clean and well-fed, mischief overtook the old Basenji and he bolted out of the bathroom with a trumpeting yodel. After a sudden burst of energy and a good roll on the soft chair that Carolyn shooed him off of almost immediately, he asked her about herself and about the apartment.

"I'm a teacher," she told him. "Lower grades, mostly. This year I'm teaching third grade. I've got a great group of kids."

"You're alone?" Magic was blunt with his question. He'd been over every inch of the apartment, and had smelled a great many people smells, and a faded, distant dog smell that could only have belonged to Max. One place he'd smelled nothing but Carolyn and the faint traces of Max, however, was in the bedroom.

Carolyn nodded. "I just haven't found Mr. Right, that's all," she said. *And I probably won't at the rate I'm going*, she thought.

She didn't pursue the topic any further, and Magic was perceptive enough to know better than to push it. Clearly she needed somebody as much as he needed her, and he wondered if he might be able to help.

After all, he thought. *Basenjis do make good conversation starters*. He decided to keep his eyes open for any opportunity that came along. In the short time they'd been together, she had been good to him, and had done so without asking for anything in return. Resolutely, he vowed to someday return the favor.

Fighting sleep but not wanting the day to end, they curled up to watch television, each lost in thought. Carolyn settled into her favorite place, an oversized plaid armchair with a matching ottoman that was equally huge. Magic found a spot on the sofa directly across from her, and studied his now-familiar surroundings. They said little, both overwhelmed and worn out by the day's events.

"Well," Carolyn finally broke the silence and turned off the television. She stretched and yawned loudly. "I don't know about you, but I'm ready for bed."

Magic hopped off the sofa and padded into the kitchen for a drink before bedtime. Listening to the sound of his tongue lapping the water, Carolyn closed her eyes, pretending that Max was in the kitchen. When Magic returned to the living room she opened her eyes, shamefully disappointed that it wasn't Max after all.

Don't be silly, she chastised herself. *What did you expect, anyway? Max isn't ever coming back.*

"Where do you want me to sleep?" Magic asked, feeling uncomfortable and not knowing why. He glanced around the room, feeling Max's presence strong around them. "If you don't mind, I'll just stay right in here." He leapt onto the sofa, circled until he felt just right, and tucked his nose under a pile of pillows. Carolyn heard him sigh softly.

"There's fine," she said. "If you're comfortable there." Secretly she'd hoped he would hop into bed with her and spend the night just as Max would have. Seeing that he was content to stay where he was, she bid him goodnight and went to bed.

By the time she was done brushing her teeth she could hear Magic's steady breathing from the other room, interrupted at intervals by loud snoring.

He must feel safe here, she thought, and it gave her a warm feeling inside. *Sleep well, little rescue.*

It was nearly one-thirty by the time she drifted off into sleep, a comforting vision of Max running through a field of tall grass in her mind. He was smiling at her, his long pink tongue hanging happily from the side of his panting mouth. His eyes were bright, and he seemed to be telling her that everything was okay, that he didn't mind the stranger in the house. The best dreams she'd had lately were the ones that brought Max back to life, if only for a little while.

Magic easily drifted off to sleep, but found it hard to keep the demons of his nightmares at bay. He tossed and turned on the sofa, falling off once and hitting his head on a corner of the coffee table. He could feel a small lump forming on his temple, and it throbbed painfully. Gingerly, he rubbed the sore spot on the carpet until the pain subsided.

When he finally fell asleep again, he dreamed he was floating on an irregularly shaped board, adrift somewhere in the ocean. He had to dig his toenails into the soft wood to keep from tumbling into the water.

From where he sat he could see land, and before he could decide whether or not to jump off and swim to shore, a large wave broke over his head, knocking him from the board into the water.

The roaring ocean was like a wild, angry animal that surrounded and swallowed him, pulling him under. He tasted the ocean's saltiness on his tongue, and felt it rushing into his mouth and nose, stinging his eyes and making it impossible to breathe. Struggling valiantly, he twisted and turned, finally breaking through the surface. Gasping for air, he swam with all his might but couldn't make any headway against the powerful current that spun him around mercilessly. The distant land grew smaller and smaller as he fought to keep from drifting further out, and he knew giving up meant he'd never see it again.

Terrified, he cried for help, but no one heard him except for a lone seagull who perched like a vulture on a rusted buoy, staring at him with sun-yellow, unblinking eyes. Before Magic could cry out again, he felt a heavy chain around his neck, weighing him down and making him disappear beneath the waves.

He awoke with a start, gasping for air, jumping as the clock on the bookcase whirred and struck the hour with loud, resonant bongs. After a few confusing minutes, he remembered he wasn't in the shelter anymore, but in Carolyn's home.

I don't like that dream, he thought, panicked. *I don't like it at all.*

He trembled uncontrollably, feeling chilled as if he'd really gotten wet. He had a hard time seeing in the darkness, afraid that the past day had been merely a dream.

What am I doing here? he whispered into the darkness. *How did I end up like this?*

Fighting back another wave of panic, he forced his mind to wander back into happier memories, recalling the sights and smells of better times, willing the warmth of comforting thoughts to calm his racing heart. Breathing deeply and feeling his body relax, Magic reflected on how good Carolyn had been to him, even though they'd only just met.

He'd seen a sadness in her, and understood that only time could bring her happiness and heal her deep sorrow. Max's presence was strong all around him, and he was grateful that the dog's spirit had welcomed him into his home. Max knew his mistress needed someone, and Magic wondered if the dog had helped bring them together.

Bits and pieces of a dream he'd had once before drifted through his mind, and he heard his mother's voice reaching out to him from somewhere far away, whispering.

Find love again, believe in trust and friendship, and find your way back home.

Where is my home? he wondered, thinking back to the many places he'd lived. *What is really my place? Where should I call home? Will I ever find it again?*

He tried to fix a picture of his first home clearly in his mind, but it had been so long since he'd seen the place that the image was fuzzy and unidentifiable. Magic closed his eyes and tried to remember something simple, like the way his mother had smelled after being out in the sun and ocean air all day, the way the aroma of grass and summer had lingered in her soft coat. Finding the memory was like opening a window in his mind and looking out, and before long he was remembering tall grass bending in the wind, brushing softly against yaupons weathered dark from salt spray and sand.

Where is it? I've got to remember!

Magic shook himself and turned around several times, feeling sleepy again. As fragmented as it was, the picture of home that began to form in his mind comforted him, helping ease his fears of being old and forgetting. Feeling safe in Carolyn's apartment, he knew she would take good care of him and, he hoped, grow to love him in time. He could hear her steady breathing in the other room as she slept, and wave after wave of warm contentment washed over him.

"Home," he murmured, curling his body into a tight ball. "If I try, if I really, really try, I can remember where it is and what it was like."

Images of a calm ocean caressing a sandy shore entered his mind, and he watched the waves move back and forth against the beach, feeling his eyes grow heavy with sleep. Lost in remembering, he gently drifted into contented darkness where the tiredness left his old body, and he didn't dream at all.

SEVEN

MAGIC AWOKE TO THE INTOXICATING aroma of bacon frying and coffee brewing. Slightly dazed from sleep, it took him a moment to remember where he was. He stood, stretched right down to his toes, and shook the night from his body.

Brilliant winter sunlight streamed through the apartment windows, leaving tempting splashes of warmth on the sofa and carpet. The blinds had been left partially open, and through the spaces in the slats Magic could see strips of deep blue sky dusted with feathery white clouds. He stuck his nose up to the window and sniffed the place where it didn't quite seal, and was rewarded by the pleasant aroma of a fresh snowfall.

Sniffing the air, he yawned and sat back down to scratch his ear, momentarily getting his foot caught in it. Embarrassed, he quickly worked it free, sniffed it, and licked it clean. Tantalizing cooking odors hung heavy and delicious in the air, making him salivate, encouraging the familiar rumble of hunger to begin in his stomach. Uncertain of what to do, he lay down again and closed his eyes, mulling over the events of the past several days.

His nightmare from the previous night still lingered in his mind, leaving him with an uncomfortable, fuzzy feeling, a foreboding that he knew had no logical basis. Safe and warm in Carolyn's apartment, he felt more relaxed than he had in many days, and was grateful when the strange feelings finally began to subside. Nightmares had haunted him for many nights, and he attributed them to having been in the shelter, unable to accept his fear of abandonment. Reflecting on his past, Magic felt sadness and a yearning for his younger years, and indulged the thoughts for a moment before pushing them aside.

Don't worry about the past, he chided himself sternly. *You can't ever go back and change it, and you certainly can't live it again. Look how lucky you are to awake to this beautiful day, and you have a fresh chance with Carolyn! It's a gift — an opportunity to live a different life. Be happy for what you are now.*

He could hear the cheerful sound of the bacon she was cooking sizzling and crackling in the frying pan, and he chuckled to himself as he heard her scrambling eggs and muttering over burnt toasts. He could tell she was doing her best to keep the noise to a minimum, but she wasn't being terribly successful in doing so.

It was the bacon smell that brought back the not-so-long-ago memory of his previous owner, an elderly woman he'd shared life with for several months. She'd pitied him with his dirty coat full of fleas, chained to an ancient maple tree in her neighbor's backyard. Lonely for a friend, she would sneak him treats and feed him table scraps when his owner was away at work.

Time plays tricks on an old dog, he mused. *It seems as if I could close my eyes and open them again, and find myself back in a different time and place. How can it be that the wonderful smell of bacon can take me there and make it seem like only a moment has passed; yet at the same time it's as if those experiences belonged to someone else, and happened long, long ago?*

Scenting was very important to Magic, and often he'd been amazed at the memories he was able to recall when coming across familiar odors. The heavy scent of an oncoming storm, coupled with the strangeness of ozone in the air never failed to make him apprehensive and watchful. Automobiles, with their oily, gasoline-vapor aroma excited him and made him long for the opportunity to travel as he had in his youth. Sunsets, cedars, clean laundry — the host of memories surrounding them all were scents labeled and stored in his mind. And, of course, there was the smell of breakfast cooking that stirred some of the most powerful emotions deep inside the old dog. Breakfast meant a sort of permanence, a reassurance that one was in the right place and all was well with the world. Breakfast was not only a comfort but an indication of stability, and where one found breakfast, one always found home.

I've called many places "home," the old dog thought, perking his ears at the sound of Carolyn's footsteps. He smelled the recently-showered cleanness of her, the halo of brewing coffee and other cooking odors that followed her into the room, and was comforted by them. *Yes, many places have been home. And today, I awake to another.*

"Good morning, Magic." Carolyn's voice broke into his thoughts. He felt her on the sofa next to him, her hand cool on his head, stroking in line with the way his coat grew. "I had the most remarkable dream," she said. "At least, it seemed like one. You talked to me, and I brought you here." She giggled and shifted next to him. "Just a silly wish for a lonely person, you know?"

"I wondered if it might be a dream," Magic whispered. "But here we are." He opened his eyes and gazed at her. "We didn't dream any of this. I was so afraid I'd wake up this morning and find out it had all gone away."

He heard her gasp, and she pulled her hand away.

"Don't," he said. "Please, touch me some more. It feels nice."

She obliged him, resuming her gentle strokes. "Can you tell me why you were in the shelter?" she asked. "I laid awake for some time wondering about it." She studied Magic carefully. "I mean, if it's any of my business."

"Oh," he replied, rolling onto his back so she could reach his stomach. "I don't mind sharing that with you, if you're really interested."

Carolyn regarded the old dog with wide, green eyes. "I really am," she assured him. "I can't imagine anyone just up and leaving you there."

"Well," Magic said, righting himself again. "I was left behind, but no one left me at the shelter." He paused and rubbed his face with a paw. "Being left behind means you're no longer wanted or useful. It's the end of a journey, where everything just stops and there's nothing left but memories and dreams you won't ever attain. It's like when darkness falls after a gray autumn day, and the gloominess settles on your back and shoulders like a damp fog."

He rubbed his face again, and leaned forward as Carolyn found an itchy spot on his neck. "But you took me out of the shelter. Being taken is entirely different than being left behind. It means you're wanted, and there's hope and a future waiting for you. It's the beginning of a journey; something to look forward to.

I like to think of it as an adventure waiting to unfold."

Carolyn let his words sink in, feeling the power of emotion he put into his explanation. She watched as he hopped off the sofa and began pacing around the room, sniffing the floor restlessly.

"Magic," she ventured, suddenly aware of what he wanted. "Do you need to, umm . . . do you want to . . . go outside?"

"Oh, yes!" the old dog breathed a sigh of relief. "Yes, I do!" Although he'd had the urge earlier, he'd refrained from urinating in the apartment. A proper Basenji was always careful about such things, and he was certain she wouldn't have appreciated a puddle on her carpet. In a flash of insight it occurred to him that he needn't have waited at all — he could have simply asked Carolyn to let him out when he first felt the urge!

This is incredible! he thought excitedly, watching as she slipped into her coat and replaced her slippers with tennis shoes. *We can communicate! There's no limit to the things we can talk about, is there?*

Together they stepped out into the bright December morning, dazzled by the prisms of light that danced on the fresh snow. The air was crisp and clear, and Magic could hear the scraping of shovels as people cleaned off their sidewalks and driveways. A strange sound made him stop and turn, his fine hooded ears moving to catch the sound and locate its source.

An older gentleman appeared, dragging a small Christmas tree behind him on the unshoveled sidewalk, leaving a smooth trail in the snow. The branches of the tree brushed softly against the snow, and Magic quickly realized it was the sound of the branches on the snow that had made the strange sound.

"Merry Christmas, Carolyn!" the man called, waving a mittened hand cheerfully. His cheeks were red from the cold, and his brown eyes sparkled happily. "Hey! You got a new dog! Wonderful!"

"Merry Christmas, Mr. Feldman!" Carolyn replied with a

smile and a wave. "You'll have to drop by with Mrs. Feldman and meet Magic when you're not so busy!"

"I'd like that," came the reply. "Have a great holiday, young lady!"

"Magic," Carolyn leaned down and gave the old Basenji a gentle pat. "I forgot to tell you! Do you realize that tonight is Christmas eve?"

"I wondered if it might be," he replied, lifting his leg on a nearby bush. "Ahhhh. That's better."

"Really?" Carolyn was surprised. "You know about Christmas and all that?"

The old Basenji squinted, for the morning sun was bright on the snow. "Sure," he answered. "You don't live as long as me and not learn about holidays. Besides," he added, "I was part of a family, once or twice before."

They walked in the snow, pausing at the end of the sidewalk. "Next time," Magic said, "You don't need the leash. Really." He sat and scratched his shoulder with one white foot. "I won't run away, I promise. That's how I ended up in the shelter, and I don't want to go back there again."

"Would you tell me about that?" Carolyn asked. Even though the shelter had been clean and well lit, memories of Magic being locked inside had haunted her all night. She hadn't been able to sleep well thinking about the lonely nights he must have spent there. "I'd really like to know where you came from."

Magic hesitated, making her wonder if he'd rather not talk about it. She watched him busily sniff the ground, avoiding her gaze. He cleared his throat, watching how his breath hung steamy and ghostlike in the cold air.

"I was a runaway," he said suddenly, not liking the word, embarrassed to use it to describe himself. "But I wasn't always a runaway," he added. "I've been many things, and have lived in many places, but something happened not too long ago that changed everything."

Eight

"One Christmas," Magic began, shaking some snow from his coat, "about three years ago, a man came to the house where I lived. He'd gotten a Christmas bonus and finally had enough money to buy a champion dog." He sniffed at the stair rail and lifted his leg on it.

"I'd seen this man a couple times before, but then, a lot of people came to the house, sometimes to see puppies and sometimes to see older dogs. Not once did I even suspect it was me he came to look at." Magic paused as a jogger ran by, startling the old dog and making the bristles on his back standing straight up. "I should have been paying more attention when he kept coming around," he continued. "But being sold never even occurred to me."

"Maybe we should go inside where it's warm," Carolyn offered. "I'd love to hear the rest of your story, but I'm freezing out here!"

Once inside, Magic stretched out over a heat register that warmed his belly wonderfully, and he continued his story.

"The man had saved up money for quite some time, and the bonus at Christmas was enough to give him what he needed to purchase me. He couldn't afford a younger dog, but I was a champion and that's all he really wanted."

"Compared to the kennels I had come from, his house wasn't much. It was just a small bungalow near a busy road. All day, and even at night, you could hear the cars passing by. Big trucks would make the dishes in the cupboards rattle and the pictures on the walls move. That road scared me, because everything on it always moved fast. In the summer, if the wind was blowing from the west, I could smell rubber tires on the hot pavement. In the winter the road noise was even louder, because then there weren't any leaves on the trees."

Magic's face wrinkled, and he rested his head on his paws. His face took on a faraway look, remembering. "When I got there I learned another Basenji was already living with the man. She was a black-and-white female called Violet."

He closed his eyes for a moment, seeing Violet's face reflected in the darkness. "She was indifferent to me at first, then refused to even acknowledge my presence. She didn't like having me in her house, sitting on her furniture, and eating out of the same food bowl as she did."

"The man figured we'd hit it off right away, but he didn't figure on Violet. I'd always had my own things before, and I was really confused when the man didn't bother to buy me my own food bowl or toys. Violet and I even had to share a crate when he left for work! Let me tell you, those were some long days that I spent locked up with her, because for the longest time she wouldn't even talk to me."

A smile lit up his grizzled face. "Violet was something else, alright. She'd snap at me if I accidentally brushed against her, but she wasn't a nasty or spiteful dog. She simply was happy to be left alone, and she didn't want another dog in her life. Oh, I tried to be friendly, under the circumstances." Magic chuckled. "But most of the time she pretended I didn't exist."

"Her attitude changed when late summer arrived and she came into season. She started talking to me then, flirting with me, and apologizing for the rotten way she'd treated me in the beginning."

"Like I said, Violet was black and white, and very pretty for the most part, although two of her teeth were slightly crooked in front, right on top, and her ears were just a little too large for her petite head. She had the most exotic eyes I'd ever seen in my life, and her tail had a kink in it, right where the black part ended and the white part began."

"She hadn't been many places, and she'd never seen the inside of a show ring. As I got to know her I learned she had lived with the man ever since she was a puppy. She didn't remember her mother or her other home, partly I think because she was taken from it at such a young age. In fact, most of her life had been spent in the house and was limited to the confines of its small yard."

Magic yawned and hopped onto the sofa. "She was fascinated when I began to tell her about the world I had lived in. Many nights she'd keep me up late, asking me questions and begging me to tell her stories about the places I'd been."

"I told her about the place where I was born, and about my

mother. I described in great detail the fireplace I used to sleep in front of, and she loved to hear about my days on the road traveling to dog shows. To me, my life was nothing remarkable, for I'd known plenty of dogs who'd been where I'd been and done what I'd done. But for Violet, even the most mundane things were exciting and wonderful to her."

"Poor girl, she'd never been all the way around the block where she lived, much less seen the world except for a once-a-year trip to the veterinarian for shots. She was a sweet creature, but if there was one person she truly hated, it was the vet. She loathed him like nobody's business. They had to use a muzzle on her to give her shots," Magic added, shaking his head.

"At any rate, Violet came into season, and two months later she had five beautiful puppies. Three boys and two girls," he added proudly. "All but one were red and white like me. The smallest girl was black and white, like Violet. Our little ones seemed so helpless and fragile that I would sometimes watch them and wonder how it was that these blind, deaf little creatures could become Basenjis. From the moment I saw them, I loved them."

"After the puppies were born Violet decided I shouldn't come near them. I don't know what she was afraid of — I assumed it was her maternal instinct and respected her wishes. I loved those puppies, and I wouldn't have hurt them. I used to spend hours watching them, and when the first one opened its eyes and wandered over to see me, I was ecstatic! Our joy was short lived, though, because when the puppies were close to being weaned, they began to disappear."

"Violet panicked when this happened, and then she became depressed. After all, her babies were everything to her. She searched everywhere for them, afraid the man had played a trick on her. Having lived in a kennel, I'd seen other females go through the same thing, so I did my best to reassure her and explain that the puppies had been sold and were gone for good. But, she wouldn't accept it; she simply couldn't understand she'd never see them again."

"Those puppies were the one thing she didn't think she should have to share with anyone, and it never crossed her mind that they could be taken from her. Before we knew it, they were all gone. I never saw them again, and never knew what happened to them, or what kind of homes they ended up in. I'd like to think they all found good homes, and I hoped they were loved more than Violet and I were loved."

"Violet's second pregnancy went smoothly, much the same as the first. Right from the start she tried to hide her pups, and begged me to help her find places where the man wouldn't think to look. There were only four in that litter," Magic added. "Two boys and two girls; half looked like me and half were like Violet."

He sat up and scratched his ear. "It broke my heart, watching her pick them up one at a time and hide them throughout the house whenever people would come to see them. She hid them under beds, in closets, and once she even hid one in the man's tall rubber boot. She would tell them to whisper, to keep their voices quiet, but they didn't like being away from her and cried. No matter what Violet did, the pups always gave themselves away. Violet threatened to run away and take them with her, but even with my help it would have been impossible, and we both knew it. And so, once again, our puppies were sold."

"Violet's next pregnancy was difficult for her. She became violently ill, and was rushed to the vet late one rainy night. The man came home many hours later without her, and I thought for certain she had died." Magic paused.

"The man acted as if I wasn't even there. I was worried sick over Violet, and he didn't bother to tell me what happened to her. A little while later I overheard him tell someone that the puppies had died inside of Violet. The only way to save her life was to

spay her, which meant she couldn't have anymore puppies."
Magic sighed and rested his head on his paws again. "At least she
wasn't dead, as I had feared."

"Losing the puppies made the man angry. He'd always
bragged to his friends how he made lots of money when he sold
them. That night he drank a lot, and talked to himself, growing
angrier and more upset. He said it was my fault the puppies had
died. I didn't know what to think or do then. Violet wasn't home
and the puppies were never coming home, and he blamed
everything on me. I couldn't understand why."

"The next morning, the man dragged me off the couch where I
had been sleeping and chained me to a big tree in the backyard.
He said Violet would be coming home, but that I couldn't see her
because she needed time to recover."

"When Violet came home she wasn't herself at all. She was in
constant pain from her operation, and there was an ugly red scar
on her belly where they'd cut and sewn her back up. I wanted to
be near her and watch over her until she was well again. Over and
over I rehearsed the things I would say to her, thought of new
stories I hadn't told before, and swore I would give her all my
dinners if it would help. I loved her, and I simply wanted to be
there for her. Unfortunately, the man had other ideas."

"True to his word, he kept me outside, as far away from her as
he could. He didn't bring me inside when it rained; he just made
sure my chain was long enough so I could hide under the
woodpile he kept against the fence. I had become invisible to him,
almost as if I had died. He never came to see me anymore, except
to feed me — when he remembered to."

Magic closed his eyes tightly, shutting out the bright
December sunlight that poured in through the window. "I would
never have done anything to hurt Violet. My heart cried out for
her, she was in my dreams and on my mind always. I only saw her
when she went out in the yard to do her business. The man kept

her on a leash so that she couldn't come near me."

"For many weeks she'd stare at me from across the lawn. Sometimes I'd see her looking out a window at me, always with the saddest look I'd ever seen. Her eyes were empty, sad eyes that made me feel like she could see right through me. I could tell she knew she'd never have puppies again."

"One summer morning Violet came out into the yard, and she wasn't on a leash anymore! She came over to me, and shyly asked if I would tell her stories about the world beyond the backyard. A million questions raced through my mind, but she didn't want to hear any of them. Thrilled to have her near me again, I began to tell her stories as she'd asked. After hearing several, she lamented how narrow and small her own world was. Those were strange words to hear coming from her; it was as if her body had healed, but her mind never recovered. She had always been content with her life, but something had changed in her. I don't know why, but she made me feel afraid."

"She began to spend lots of time with me, asking me all sorts of strange questions; things like what did one need to know when crossing a road, and about stray dogs and how to avoid them. I taught her to read the stars, and to find her way wherever she might be, although I didn't know why she needed to know."

"It all made sense a few weeks later — and it seems to me that autumn had just begun, for it soon would've been puppy time for Violet. One beautiful morning she came out into the yard and apologized for the way she'd treated me in the past. She thanked me for the puppies I'd given her, and said she missed them terribly. Then she surprised me by saying she was going to run away, right then."

"I wanted to go with her, because I didn't think she could make it on her own. I warned her it wasn't safe to go alone, and told her she needed me to guide and protect her. She reminded me that I was chained to the tree and said that if I could get free, then

I could go with her. Violet stayed with me for several hours as I tried to get free, and as time went on she realized how futile my struggles were. No amount of pulling or chewing was going to set me free.

Magic ran his tongue along his teeth, feeling the sharper places near the back where he had broken them trying to get free. He sat quietly for a moment, remembering.

"I'll never forget how Violet leaned her dark body into mine, pressing hard for a moment." Magic's voice trembled with emotion. "I remember smelling grass and sunshine in her coat, feeling her sweet breath warm on my face. I felt life and excitement vibrating through her body. She sniffed me carefully as if she was afraid she'd forget me; her whiskers tickled my face and neck. Then, quietly, she said good-bye."

"Violet climbed the chain-link fence paw over paw, just like a person would, I imagine. In a flash she was on the other side, pressing her nose through the links, telling me she loved me and someday she'd return so we could be together. I watched as she disappeared down the street, and I had a terrible, lonely feeling that I would never see her again. I envied her freedom, and more than anything I wanted to be with her. I cried and threw my body as hard as I could against the collar and chain, but it was no use."

"When the man discovered Violet was gone, he became very upset. He searched the entire house, and when he didn't find her there, he came back out into the yard. He shouted her name several times, turning in all directions. I could hear fear in his voice. While he didn't care about me, he was genuinely concerned about Violet. I heard him leave in his car, only to return a short while later. I saw him go out again, this time with some signs he'd made."

"It finally dawned on him that someone might have seen what happened to Violet, and I heard him mention her disappearance to the elderly lady next door. She said Violet had jumped the fence and run away."

"The man spent the rest of the day looking for Violet, putting up signs wherever he could. When he returned late that night, she wasn't with him." Magic sighed. "I was so afraid something had happened to her. I wanted to go out looking for her myself, but I couldn't, because I couldn't get loose. It was terrible, wanting to go but not being able to. I was completely helpless."

"Violet was in my dreams that night. I saw her cross the big road, nearly hit by several cars as she turned and dodged to avoid them. She stopped in the grassy median, breathing heavily from fear and exertion. Crossing the other side wasn't much easier, and I watched in horror as she hesitated just long enough that I was sure she'd be hit. In my dream I called out to her 'Run, run as fast as you can!'"

"She glanced back as if she'd heard me, and in the last possible instant she bolted. A truck rushed by, missing her by a tailtip. She stood unsteadily on the shoulder of the road, stunned, but safe. Before I could call out to her again, she disappeared into a grassy ravine. I knew at least for that day, she was safe." Magic paused and closed his eyes. In his mind he saw Violet, dark and beautiful, her curly tail wagging slowly from side to side.

"Very early the next morning, the man came out into the yard and paced back and forth for quite some time, smoking several cigarettes. He sat on the cement steps of his house, staring hard at me for the longest time. Suddenly, his face lit up, and for the first time in months he came over to where I was and placed his hand tentatively on my head. He asked me if I could help him find Violet." Magic snorted. "All that time it took him to figure out that I might be able to help him could have been spent trying to find her!"

"Well, hearing that he wanted me to help, I got very excited. At last I would get my chance to find her, to be with her. And maybe, if I brought her back, the man would forget he hated me and not keep me chained up anymore."

"He got a leash from the house — it had been Violet's leash — and attached it to my collar, freeing me from the tree. Immediately, I ran to the fence and found her scent was still strong there. In a flash I was over it."

"The man couldn't climb the fence as easily, and I had to wait as he tied me to it and went around through the gate. Impatiently I started to chew on the old leather leash, knowing that if I could get free, I could leave the man behind and find Violet on my own." Magic sighed. "Unfortunately, he was right there before I could really get my teeth working into it. What could I do but follow Violet's trail and pull him behind me?"

"Following her scent was easy, for she'd only been gone a short time. Her scent ended at the big road. Remembering my dream, I knew if I wanted to find her I would have to cross the road."

"The man swore when I pulled hard on the leash. Obviously he didn't like the thought of Violet crossing the road, either. I could tell he was afraid of what he might find on the other side. I knew better, of course, and pulled on the lead until he told me in a harsh voice to wait, that we would cross when the traffic cleared."

"When I finally found her trail again, I was so excited I yodeled, which encouraged the man. I guess we were both relieved that she wasn't lying along side the road, or in the ravine."

Magic yawned and stretched, giving himself a good shake. He jumped off the sofa and found the bowl of fresh water Carolyn had left for him in the kitchen. Noisily, he drank his fill, careful not to get water on his coat. When he returned, he rubbed his face along the carpet to dry it. Refreshed, he stretched out on the floor with his rear legs out behind him in what Carolyn called "frog-dog" style.

"What happened next?" Carolyn asked eagerly. She sat on the

floor next to him, gently stroking his back.

Magic cleared his throat before continuing. "Violet's trail led us to train tracks, then into a trainyard. A man who was working around one of the boxcars said he'd seen a dog running near the tracks. As my eyes scanned the strange place, I glimpsed something dark and quick moving in the shade between two train cars. Thinking it might be Violet, I pulled so hard on the leash that it came right out of the man's hands."

"I'd never run so fast in all my life as I did right then. I had my nose to the ground, then up in the air, sniffing. I caught Violet's unmistakable scent, mixed with the smell of oil and trains. It carried me forward, toward the dark shadow trying to hide itself by the wheels of a boxcar."

"'Violet!' I called out, knowing it was her. 'Violet, it's me!'"

"'Go away!' she snapped, angry and frightened. 'You've brought the man with you! I don't want to go back! I want to be free!'"

"'Please,' I pleaded with her. 'It's not safe here. If you're going to leave, at least let me go with you.'"

"'You're free, too, aren't you?' she asked, peering around the side of a large metal train wheel. Her dark eyes glistened, looking at the leash trailing on the ground behind me. 'We can run away together,' she agreed. 'But I won't let him catch me and take me back. I'm going to find my puppies. All of them.' With that, she turned and bounded down the tracks, glancing back as she ran."

"I ran after her, but was pulled short by the leash. I growled and whirled around, expecting to see the man behind me. It wasn't him, just the leash caught on a broken piece of track. I called to Violet, telling her to wait for me. She stopped and stared, watching as I struggled against the leash."

"Then the man caught up with me and saw Violet standing in the middle of the tracks. He called her several times, and when she didn't respond, he ran after her, leaving me behind." Magic sighed. "I fought, twisting and lunging against the leash. In a flash I was running beside the man, then passing him."

"Violet wouldn't stop for anything, not even for me. I watched in amazement as she ducked beneath moving train cars, narrowly escaping their crushing wheels."

"When she stopped to catch her breath, she was between tracks, with trains moving on either side of her. I caught glimpses of her from under the passing cars. Her head was hanging down, and she was breathing hard from running."

"'I won't go back,' she cried between gasps. 'I can't. I've got to find my puppies. All of them.'"

"The man was frantic, running back and forth, telling her not to move. The roaring and thundering of the moving trains filled the air and she couldn't hear what he was saying. Pacing back and forth, she looked for an opening, any opportunity to get away."

"I was terrified for her, afraid she'd be crushed beneath the wheels of the train." Magic lowered his head to his paws. "She was delirious from having run so hard, desperate to get away and afraid of getting caught."

"An opening finally came when the train directly in front of us passed. Seeing his opportunity, the man ran forward, calling her name." Magic shuddered. "I can still see her looking at him with wide, frightened eyes. She wasn't thinking of her own safety, just of getting away. I watched as she spun around and took a great leap, almost falling as she landed just inside the doorway of a moving boxcar."

"It all happened so quickly that I wasn't sure I'd actually witnessed it! One moment she was there, and the next, she was gone. It was almost as if she'd disappeared into thin air. I remember blinking hard, not believing my eyes, and for the briefest moment I saw her dark face peering out of the boxcar, which by then had moved further down the tracks. Just as quickly as I'd seen her, she ducked back inside."

"The man couldn't believe his eyes, either, but it was clear to me he thought she really did disappear. He wasn't quick enough to see her jump into the boxcar, and he didn't see her peeking out of it, either. Even after the train had passed, he stood for the longest time, staring at the place he'd last seen her, unable to comprehend how she could have vanished."

"In a strange way it was almost comical, seeing the man trying to understand what had happened. It was as if he were experiencing the confusion and panic that Violet herself had felt, each and every time a puppy had been taken away. As badly as I wanted to run after the train and join Violet, I didn't want the man to discover what had really happened. And so, as hard as it was for me to stay where I was, I did, because I loved her."

"I missed her terribly, and it wasn't until months later that she found her way into my dreams again. She was somewhere I'd never seen before, and it was a beautiful place with green grass, tall trees and bright sunlight. Most incredibly, she had newborn puppies with her, puppies that she fed and cleaned and played with. Proudly, she told me their names, and assured me they'd never be taken away from her. She was happy, and explained she wouldn't run away again, that she'd found exactly what she'd been looking for."

"I asked her about what happened at the trainyard that day, desperately wanting to understand where she'd been and where she was now. She wouldn't answer my questions about running away. She stared with those dark eyes of hers and told me it didn't matter, that her reasons weren't important anymore."

"She asked me not to be sad for her, and pleaded with me not to worry. She'd gone to the place where all dogs go when they die, and she couldn't have been happier. She promised to visit from time to time, and said she'd be watching over me and our children from the Happiness."

Magic lowered his voice to a whisper. "Sometimes, I know

she's with me. I can't explain how or why, but I feel her presence. It's the same way with Max. His presence here is very strong." He paused and shivered. "Suddenly, even in the sun it's cold."

Carolyn rested her hand on his coat, feeling the warmth of the sun and the sleekness of his short fur. As she stroked him, he trembled beneath her hand.

"To finish the story," he continued, "things, as you might imagine, weren't right with the man after Violet 'vanished.' I watched him bury her leash and collar in the backyard, and later on he planted a flowering tree over the place. I was ignored even more than before, and nothing I could do would get him to show me any affection."

"Then one morning he was gone, and I never saw him again. Lucky for me, the elderly lady next door set me free. She'd watched over me in the months after Violet had gone, bringing me water when my bowl was empty, and feeding me when the man was away at work. Sometimes she'd cook bacon and give it to me, as a treat."

"I had a chance to run away then, because she never kept me chained up. She was old and forgetful, always leaving doors and windows wide open. I stayed with her because she took good care of me and I knew she needed the company."

"Not long ago, I awoke to find that she'd died in her sleep. When the neighbors found her, I saw my chance and ran away. I didn't know where I was going, but I knew I had to get away. That night I fell asleep behind a restaurant and stayed there because they put lots of food into the garbage cans. After a couple of days, someone called the dog catcher, and when I was sleeping, they grabbed me and took me to the shelter." Magic closed his eyes. "And when I had lost all hope, there you were." He rested his head on folded paws, and sighed. "It's like remembering a lifetime," he murmured, feeling very tired. "I think I'll take a nap now."

"Sure," Carolyn said, not knowing what, if anything, she should say to him. His story was incredible, and it made her sad to learn how much had happened in such a short span of time. She wondered where his puppies were, and if they looked like him.

Watching the old dog's breathing slow as he began to fall asleep, she smiled and put her hand gently on his grizzled head. "I've got to stop off at my parent's house, and them I've got a few errands to run. Do you think you'll be okay here by yourself?"

"Sure," he replied sleepily. "I'll be okay."

She sat with him until he fell asleep in the sun. He dreamed that Violet slept beside him — a dream so real that when he awoke, he imagined he felt her body pressed tightly against him, her breath sweet and gentle in his face.

NINE

"YOU'VE BEEN PRETTY SCARCE lately," Carolyn's mother stood in front of the fireplace with her hands on her hips, and tapped her slippered foot impatiently. "Here, hold this end up high so I can see what it looks like." She stepped away from the fireplace to admire a strand of shiny garland. Carolyn balanced herself on the tall ladder, leaning forward to lower the decoration at her mother's direction.

From up high, her mother looked a bit smaller and a shade less intimidating, and

Carolyn smiled as she noticed some gray roots peeking past her mother's otherwise dark head. She'd always been vain about her hair, her home, and even her daughter, always pushing and pressuring for a better performance. Nothing was ever good enough, no grades were ever high enough, and no friends Carolyn had chosen were ever socially acceptable enough. Carolyn had to give her mother credit though, for in the years after she'd moved out, her mother had eased up on her daughter considerably, but she still was a formidable matron in her home and highly respected in social circles. In short, she had an image and was determined to maintain it.

"Well, I've been pretty busy," Carolyn replied, attaching the garland to the fireplace with a small hook. "That looks good, don't you think?"

"Mmmmm." Her mother had already moved on to the Christmas tree, and was adjusting some tinsel. "We can't just glob the tinsel on, dear," she said. "There, that's better. So, what have you been busy with?" She peered over her half-glasses at her daughter. "Careful now, don't fall!"

Carolyn sighed and steadied herself on the ladder, more for her mother's satisfaction than for her own safety. She couldn't help but feel sorry for her mother, and knew she was lonely now that her only child had moved out of the house. It wasn't that she didn't love her mother, on the contrary she cared very deeply for her and wanted more than anything to be close. But, her mother, being the perfectionist she was, had always seemed impossible to please and eventually Carolyn just quit trying.

"I don't know," Carolyn shrugged. "Just busy with things." She desperately wanted to share the news of adopting Magic, but knowing what the response would have been and not wanting to deal with disapproval on Christmas Eve made Carolyn decide not to say anything. It was easier to leave Magic out of the conversation than it was to deal with her mother's opinion of dogs.

"Anything you'd like to share?" her mother pressed, taking her daughter's silence for a secret. She studied her daughter carefully. "Did you get your hair cut, honey?"

"No Mom."

"Mmmmm." Her mother smiled. "Maybe you've met someone special?" The question came as no surprise to Carolyn. It was as much a part of every conversation they'd had lately, just as much as "hello" or "how are you" was. Her mother never failed to work the subject of men into their discussions. It was as if she, in fleeting moments of insight, caught a glimpse of her daughter's loneliness and wanted some reassurance that everything was alright.

Carolyn's green eyes widened at the question, and she thought of Magic and smiled, knowing full well what her mother meant, but unable to help herself. *Sure, I can tell her I met a talking dog yesterday,* she thought. *That would go over real well with her.*

"Carolyn?"

"Hmm? Oh, yes, Mom. I guess you could say I've met someone."

The smile that lit up her mother's face was like a ray of sunlight breaking through a dismal day, brightening the woman's features and making her look, for the briefest moment, quite pretty.

"That's wonderful, honey!"

"It's nothing, really Mom." Carolyn reached into a box and pulled out a string of lights. "Where do you think we should put these?" she asked, trying to change the subject.

"Wherever you like, dear." Her mother lit on the sofa like a little bird and perched on the edge of a cushion. "So why don't you tell me all about him," she pressed.

Backed into a corner with nowhere to go, Carolyn realized she was trapped in her ruse. "Oh, I really don't think you'd be interested in him," she said, burying her head in another box of decorations. "What happened to those snowmen we had last year?"

Carolyn's mother sighed. "You know, I do care about what goes on in your life, young lady. Even though you're out on your own, I still worry about you. Now, why don't you forget about the snowmen and sit down here. Tell me all about your new friend. I am interested. Have you seen a lot of him lately?"

Carolyn nodded. "Every day."

"Wonderful!" her mother beamed. "Then maybe you should invite him over to join us for dinner sometime. Why, how about tonight?" She tapped her fingers excitedly. "Maybe you should invite him over tonight. It would be fun."

"Oh, I don't know Mom," Carolyn hedged. "I don't think it's such a good idea . . ."

"Nonsense! Any friend of yours is more than welcome here, honey! Why don't you go ahead and invite him. Unless he's spending Christmas Eve with his family," she added. "He hasn't asked you to join him, has he?"

"He hasn't got any family," Carolyn replied. "But I just don't think . . ."

"No family! Well, then I must insist you bring him along this evening." Her mother stood and planted her feet firmly in the carpet. "No family! The poor dear!" She hurried off into the kitchen, leaving her daughter standing in the living room shaking her head.

Well, Carolyn thought, grinning to herself as she located the snowmen she had been searching for. *She did insist, didn't she?*

And so that night, in a move of uncharacteristic boldness, Carolyn brought Magic along to meet her mother and the rest of the family.

Every year, it was a tradition for her parents to invite family and friends over for Christmas Eve dinner. Guests from near and far flocked to the grand old Victorian house, eager to experience what her mother fondly called "an old-fashioned Christmas."

Carolyn's parents spared no expense, decorating their home lavishly with bows and garlands and poinsettias at every turn. An enormous tree towered in the two-story foyer, decorated in the same ornate fashion as its smaller balsam twin in the living room, nestled comfortably near a roaring fireplace. Christmas music played softly from cleverly hidden speakers, and the entire house was aglow from within with warm golden light that spilled out the tall windows onto brilliant white snow below. A multitude of multi-colored lights decorated the spires and towers of the house, flowed down the vast expanse of front porch and filled the shrubs and trees of the landscape like a child's Christmas dream.

Magic gasped when he saw the splendor of it all, his breath steaming up the windows of Carolyn's vehicle, blurring out the sight. Eagerly, he wagged his tail in anticipation of a Christmas feast.

"This is so beautiful!" he exclaimed, hopping out into the snow. "I've never seen anything like it before!"

Nervously, Carolyn smiled and hefted the strap of her guitar case over her shoulder. "Well, try not to be too disappointed," she said. "Remember, my mother doesn't like dogs, and I think she'll be a little upset when she sees you."

"Not to worry," Magic assured her. "I will conduct myself like the well-bred dog I am." He chuckled. "She'll have no choice but to like me!"

Carolyn took a deep breath. "You're so confident," she said, smiling down at him. "Okay then! Let's go!"

As if in a dream they moved up the paverstone walkway that was lined with brightly burning luminaries, made their way up the salted steps of the front porch, and stood beneath the mistletoe at the front door. Not knowing quite how to make her entrance with Magic, Carolyn reached out and pressed the doorbell. "I don't think it would be a good idea to walk right in," she explained.

They jumped as the door flew open, and Andie stuck her head out. "Hey! Merry Christmas, Kay O'Lyn!" she squealed, throwing the door open wide. Light and warmth spilled from within, encircling Carolyn and Magic with the wonderful smell of Christmas dinner. "Oh! And you've brought Magic!"

Andie's enthusiasm was catchy, and Carolyn broke into a grin as she hugged her cousin. "Merry Christmas to you, too!"

"Andie, who's here?" Carolyn heard her mother's voice calling from the foyer. "You're letting in all the cold air."

"Uh oh!" Carolyn backed away. "Maybe this isn't such a good idea."

"Carolyn honey!" her mother appeared in the doorway, fashionably dressed in a red dress trimmed with gold sequins. The brilliant smile on her face melted like snow in the summer sun when she noticed the Basenji at her daughter's feet. "Oh, Carolyn honey," she said, her eyes scanning the porch behind Carolyn. "Where's your date?"

"I think that would be me." Magic opened his mouth in a wide grin, and lifted a paw expectantly.

"Merry Christmas, Mom!" Carolyn began. "Hey look, mistletoe!" She leaned forward and planted a kiss on her mother's cheek. It softened the harsh look on her mother's face, and she took a deep breath.

"You've got a dog with you," her mother said flatly. "Whatever were you thinking? Dinner's almost ready. Maybe you can leave him in the car or something. Oh, good! I see you remembered your guitar!"

"Oh, NO Auntie!" Andie wailed, scooping the startled Basenji into her arms. "Oh, it's way too cold outside to leave him in the car! We can't do that! And, Carolyn hasn't got time to take him home, because like you said, dinner's almost ready! I'm sure he won't be any bother at all!" With that, she whisked Magic past her aunt and into the house, and was gone.

"I suppose that dog is your date for this evening?"

"I'm sorry, Mom." Carolyn replied sheepishly. "But you never gave me a chance to explain."

"Well, not much we can do about it now. I'm sure Andie has things well under control." Her mother shook her head. "But I expect you to watch that dog like a hawk, you understand? I don't want that dog to have an accident in here. You know how expensive these rugs are, young lady!"

"Yes, Mom," Carolyn replied sheepishly, wondering how she was going to survive what appeared to be the beginning of the longest Christmas eve she'd ever experienced.

"Well, come on in, honey. Don't just stand out there in the cold. Here, let me take your guitar for you." Her mother gave Carolyn a quick hug. "You can tune it up anywhere, dear. Just about everyone's here!"

Magic, as promised, was the perfect gentleman, although his curious nature did occasionally get the best of him, and he forgot himself many times in all the excitement.

Carolyn's mother was horrified when he climbed up on a sofa to sniff Carolyn's grandmother, and she had a fit when he lingered too long in front of the Christmas tree. Like a swarm of gnats on a hot summer day, she hovered over whoever happened to be petting him, reminding that person to be sure to wash their hands after touching *that dog*.

Not wanting to let her down, Magic boldly left a little surprise hidden behind a large green sofa when nobody was looking. He figured it would take her a few days to find it, but just to make sure, he found a box of tissues and shredded them to throw her off the trail.

As Carolyn had predicted, Andie immediately fell in love with Magic.

"Oh, Kay O'Lyn, he's so cute!" she exclaimed, rubbing the

top of Magic's wrinkled forehead. "You definitely made the right choice, adopting him. You've got quite a handsome mystery man here."

Magic eyed Andie carefully, taking note of her brilliant white teeth. "I bet she could really bite if she wanted to," he chuckled. "She went a little heavy on the perfume, but overall your cousin is a nice person." He leaned his neck forward so she could reach the itchy spot just under his collar. The scratching felt lovely and Magic's face wrinkled even more with pleasure.

"Such a sweet puppy!" Andie grabbed Magic's cheeks and rubbed her face on his. "Look at all those wrinkles! I could just kiss that face right up!"

"You've got quite a few wrinkles yourself, lady." Magic pulled away and hopped off her lap, scurrying to safety at Carolyn's side, pressing his body hard against her leg. He pawed at his face, for Andie's perfume still lingered in his nostrils. From a safe distance he eyed the auburn haired woman warily, wondering what would happen if he wasn't careful. Again she was reaching for him, clearly wanting to plant kisses all over his face.

"Make her stop, already," he pleaded, looking up at Carolyn for help. "I think she wants to eat me!"

"Magic doesn't like being fawned over, I guess." Carolyn couldn't hide her smile. "He's just like the books say. Aloof, reserved, dignified . . ." her voice trailed off as she caught a glimpse of Magic cleaning his "boy parts" as Andie had called them.

"Dignified?" her cousin laughed. "That's really dignified, isn't it?"

Magic looked up, and Carolyn saw the unmistakable glimmer of a smile in his eyes. "How about a kiss now?" he asked Andie, running his tongue over his gray muzzle. "How about a little kiss?"

"I can't believe you brought him here tonight," Andie whispered, leaning close to her cousin. "Your mother is simply having fits! She's made poor Jake wash his hands four times already!" She giggled, glancing around to see where her son had gone. "What ever got into you?"

"I don't know, exactly," Carolyn replied, putting a protective hand on Magic. "I suppose she would have been much happier if I would have found a real date." She sighed. "I guess I hedged a bit when I told her I would be bringing a friend tonight."

Andie laughed. "I'll agree with you there! She even set an extra place at the table! I don't imagine she'll be letting Magic eat his dinner up there, at any rate." Andie gave the old dog a pat on the head. "Maybe if he wore a shirt and tie she'd consider it. After what you've been through with your last date, I'd think your mother would rather have Magic at the table than see Ted again!"

"You had to remind me, didn't you?" Carolyn winced at the name, then frowned unhappily. "And on Christmas!"

"Honey, where he's spending Christmas is right where he deserves to be!" Andie said, putting her arm around Carolyn. "As far as I'm concerned, they can just lock him up and throw away the key forever!"

Magic glanced up at Carolyn, who shook her head. Clearly she'd had a bad experience with someone, and didn't intend to discuss the situation any further. He could see the distress in her face, and heard an edge of fear in her voice that hadn't been there before. He made a mental note to ask her about it later, when they were alone.

"I suppose bringing Magic with me tonight is a milestone," Carolyn said, eager to change the subject. "After all, it's taken me all these years to get up the courage to bring a dog into this house again." She snorted. "Christmases came and went, and birthdays too. More than anything I wanted a dog, because I knew I'd never have a brother or sister. Not that you weren't great to be with,

Andie," she added quickly. "But you know what I mean when I say it just wasn't the same. It wasn't fair that when I came home our house was big and quiet and there wasn't anyone for me to play with or tell secrets to, or share jokes or funny stories with. Even in my own home with my own parents, I was alone."

"I know it was rough," Andie agreed. "I used to try and convince Dad to let you come live with us. He would laugh at me and ask if I wanted to go live with you instead! Heck, he even would tell me that if we didn't live in separate houses, that we'd end up dressing alike!"

Carolyn laughed. "I remember him calling us the 'twins separated at birth.' Sometimes we would dress the same, remember?"

Andie nodded. "We had some great times. And now, you're embarking on a whole new adventure with Magic by your side. You've given him a second chance, and I have a feeling you won't regret it. He's a great dog, Kay O'Lyn."

"I hate to interrupt you girls," Carolyn's mother appeared in the doorway, blocking their view of the Christmas tree. "But dinner is on the table. You'll want to wash up, won't you?" She frowned at Magic, who stared back with wide brown eyes.

"Hi again!" he said, wagging his tail furiously. "Guess who I get to sit next to at dinner?"

"Oh, it's okay, Auntie," Andie replied, standing up and giving her aunt a quick hug. "My hands are spotless, see? Magic just finished cleaning them for me."

Carolyn's mother stiffened, and smiled icily at her niece. "Well, I don't worry about you so much, but little Jake doesn't need to eat dog germs with his Christmas meal. There's some antibacterial soap in the bathroom," she added. "Don't miss it." That said, she turned and left the room in a cloud of lavender perfume.

"Ten dollars says she puts on a different dress," Andie

quipped. "I'll bet those doggy germs are crawling all over her by now!"

"Andie, how could you! It's Christmas!" Carolyn wailed. "Now she's good and mad. I won't hear the end of it!" She hated the way her mother always seemed to be able to reduce her to feeling like an unruly child. But she was used to her mother's disapproval and sometimes it seemed worthless to try and fight it.

"Don't worry," Andie soothed. "You don't have to spend the night here, remember? You're all grown up and on your own." She giggled. "Well, lets go get some dinner, shall we?"

The evening ended earlier than Carolyn had anticipated, due to the sudden, severe headache her mother developed during dinner. Even the promise of hearing her daughter play Christmas carols on the guitar didn't seem to help ease her condition.

Magic knew he was the main contributor to her illness as he gurgled and smacked his lips, relishing the roasted turkey and mashed potatoes Carolyn served him on a small china plate. He assumed her mother would throw out the plate instead of washing it, for fear his Basenji germs would permeate all the fine china and render it unfit for human use.

I definitely do not like that woman, he thought, licking his plate with gusto. *I can't imagine Carolyn belonging to her!*

On the way home, Magic remarked to Carolyn that, in spite of her mother's obvious dislike for him, it felt good to be part of a family again. He complained that her mother hadn't given him a fair chance, and he couldn't understand why she didn't want to get to know him.

"She's always been that way," Carolyn explained. "Nothing, not a bird, a cat, a goldfish and certainly nothing as dirty as a dog has passed over her threshold in years." She became quiet, remembering how Max had only met her mother once, when he was very small. After he'd wet the rug he was never welcome again. She remembered her mother's words, harsh and unforgiving, and the frightened look on the puppy's face as the demon-lady flailed her arms and shrieked at his mistake.

Carolyn's arms could still feel the puppy-light weight of Max as she'd scooped him up and whisked him away from the terrible scene. She hated the unfairness of it, and hated the fact that no matter what she did or how well trained Max became, her mother's opinion of him had never changed.

Poor Max, she thought. *Poor, poor puppy.* Unwelcome tears choked her throat at the memory.

Laying in bed that night, she wondered what, if anything, would have been different that Christmas eve if her mother could have heard Magic speak. Would she have accepted him? In her heart Carolyn knew otherwise, of course. At the same time she wondered about herself, at the ease in which she had accepted Magic into her life. His voice had awakened something deep within her, making her wonder if there were other dogs who communicated the way he did. Magic was special — and Carolyn had to believe there was no one else quite like him in the entire world.

T E N

THAT YEAR, FOR THE FIRST TIME IN
ages, Carolyn declined Andie's New Year's Eve
party invitation. Instead, she elected to spend the
evening quietly at home with Magic.

"Why do you want to be alone on New
Year's Eve?" Andie whined into the phone.
"We'll have lots of company, and we'll have
champagne, too!"

"I won't be alone," Carolyn assured her.
"After all, I've got Magic to keep me company."

And, she thought, *I've got my own bottle of*

champagne! She didn't mention it to Andie, knowing her cousin would have lectured her about how terrible drinking alone on New Year's Eve would be.

"It won't be the same without you here," Andie insisted. "Besides, Kay O'Lyn, who's going to play *Auld Lang Syne* for us at midnight? No one can play the guitar over here except for you! And," she pressed. "Jake and Tyler were looking forward to seeing you and Magic again."

Carolyn giggled, thinking of her cousin's little boys. Jake, the two-year old, probably would enjoy hanging out with Magic. Tyler was just a baby and wouldn't know the difference if Magic was there or not. "Oh, Andie!" she laughed. "Leave it to you to bring the kids into this!"

"I'm just trying to keep you from being lonely," Andie replied. "I've never been alone on a New Year's Eve, and I can't even picture what that's like. It just seems so sad. You're not in college anymore, you know."

Carolyn was silent, thinking back to the time she had been in college and had refused to return home to spend the holidays with her family. Although she had desperately wanted to go home, she didn't because she knew her parents would do everything in their power to monopolize her time and keep her all to themselves. She understood their need to see their only child during the holidays, but it had become too stressful for Carolyn. While she wanted to make her parents happy, she wanted to feel free to enjoy the season with Andie's family even more. If she would have gone home, Andie would have strongly urged her to join their annual festivities, which they both knew her parents didn't attend anyway. Carolyn simply didn't like her loyalties being torn between the two. It was better to avoid the situation altogether than to face up to her parents and get her way.

Wanting to be with the people she loved but painfully used to being alone, Carolyn sometimes couldn't help feeling like an outsider at Andie's get-togethers. While she enjoyed the company of Andie's friends and never minded playing her guitar for an audience, she always felt an emptiness inside of her that she couldn't quite explain. Secretly, it frightened her to think she might find herself standing in a crowd at midnight, watching people as they hugged and wished each other a Happy New Year. Although it never happened, she always worried that she'd be forgotten, and that no one would turn to hug her. What if she was left standing all by herself, alone and embarrassed, at midnight?

I suppose it comes from growing up as an only child, she mused, thinking of the countless times her parents had left her with a babysitter while they attended dinners and social events. Not until she was older was she permitted to stay overnight with Andie's family. Their lively company made her wish she could stay with them forever, especially at New Years when they would have noisemakers and confetti and lots of what her mother would wrinkle her nose at and call "junk food." But to Carolyn, it was pure pleasure, a freedom from having to be the perfectly behaved, properly mannered daughter for her parents to parade in front of their distinguished friends. With Andie's family, she found the excitement of life awakened within herself. Only in her college years had the emptiness been felt, the longing to have that one special person in her life who would love her no matter what, who wouldn't be judgmental and who would always be by her side.

"So what do you say, Kay O'Lyn?" Andie's voice broke into her thoughts. "Please, please, please, please come over and spend the evening here. Please?"

Carolyn had almost given in to Andie and agreed, but when she glanced over at Magic sleeping near a heat register, her mind was made up. "I'd really love to, Andie," she said. "I've got Magic to think of, though, you know? I don't know how he'll react to all the noise and people at midnight. I think it would be best if I stayed here with him, just to be sure he's okay."

Andie sighed. "Well, like I said before, it won't be the same without you here, but I do understand. How about we get together tomorrow afternoon, okay? We'll have tons of food left over. We always do."

"I'd like that," Carolyn agreed. "I'll see you tomorrow afternoon then." Smiling, she hung up the phone. *Ah,* she thought, hugging herself happily. *If only Andie could know how different it really will be!*

Carolyn was usually a punctual person who planned things to perfection. She was never late for appointments, and she typically was the first person to arrive at family events and gatherings. This was due in large part to her habit of setting her clocks a few minutes fast, just to be safe. Andie claimed her cousin was living a few minutes into the future while the rest of the world spent its time trying to catch up.

And so it was that the clock on the bookshelf struck midnight a few minutes earlier that year, and the New Year came for Carolyn and Magic before it did for anyone else. As the last echoing chimes died away, Carolyn opened a small bottle of champagne and poured herself a glass. She dribbled a few drops into a bowl for Magic.

He lapped gingerly at the strange stuff, unsure about the taste, not liking the way bubbles tickled his nose. He sneezed, spraying champagne onto his coat. "What is this stuff?" he asked, pawing at his face. "Ugh!"

"Guess I should've known," Carolyn apologized. "Champagne is definitely not for dogs."

Magic sneezed again. "How can you drink that?" he asked, grimacing comically. "It's awful!"

Carolyn sipped her drink and found the bubbles made her sneeze, too. "I've got to agree with you, Magic," she said with a laugh. "This stuff is pretty awful. I don't remember it being this bad. It's the same stuff Andie always buys for her parties."

"Do you wish you'd gone?" the old dog asked. "You didn't have to give up your party and friends to stay with me. But," he added quickly, "I'm glad you did."

"It's no trouble at all," she replied, going into the kitchen to rinse out his bowl. She filled it with fresh water, and dropped in a few ice cubes as a special treat. "In fact, I'm enjoying being here with you more."

Magic lapped the water gratefully, washing the strange taste of champagne from his mouth. He watched as Carolyn moved across the room to where her guitar was propped up against a bookcase. With one fluid motion she picked it up and settled the strap across her shoulder, plucking the strings to make sure it was in tune.

"I started guitar lessons when I was seven," she told him, strumming a few chords. "I asked for a puppy for Christmas that year, and I got this plus lessons instead." She smiled and closed her eyes, feeling the soft notes ring clear in her head. "My parents never understood what little it would take to make me happy," she said. "All I wanted was a little love and attention."

"And that's why you wanted a puppy?" Magic asked. "You wanted one so you'd have someone to love and spend time with, right?"

"That's part of it," she replied. "More than that, I think, was that I wanted unconditional love. Someone who wouldn't care if my grades weren't perfect who would love me even though I had my own way of doing things. I wanted to have someone around who wouldn't judge me and make me feel like whatever I did wasn't good enough."

"But your parent's didn't give you that?" Magic asked, surprised. "I thought that's what being a parent was all about. I loved the puppies Violet and I had more than anything, and I always made sure they knew it. I can't imagine it any other way."

"My parents expected the world from me," Carolyn said,

putting the guitar aside. "And I can't blame them for wanting me to have the best, but," she added, sipping her drink, "they didn't give me enough room to be myself, and to simply be a kid. Even now I can't help but sometimes feel that they're disappointed in me. I'm a teacher, and I love what I do. I don't think they understand that it's not the money that makes my job worthwhile, but the fact that I'm doing what makes me happy."

Magic thought for a moment. "When I was young, I loved to chase rabbits. I loved the feel of the sun on my back as I raced across an open field. My muscles would stretch and grow warm, and my heart would pound in my chest. I never really wanted to hurt a rabbit; I just wanted to run with the wind and feel the world moving beneath me. I was doing what I loved to do, even though it wasn't my job. I was a show dog, and my people didn't like me running around like that too much. They were always afraid I'd get hurt." He sighed and stretched lazily. "Being happy isn't something that comes easy, and when you find your life's treasures and others don't or can't understand that you're content, it's not always easy to remember that your happiness is worth more than worrying about what other folks' opinions might be."

"To happiness," Carolyn said, raising her glass. "And to a happy New Year." She clinked her glass against his bowl, making the water move back and forth against the sides.

This he regarded with a wrinkled brow.

"A people custom," she explained. "It's for good luck, I guess."

"A new year," Magic said. "December never seemed like it was going to end, with all that went on." His eyes were dark, and glimmered in the light. "Every year, when you start out, December seems so far away. Strange how quickly it's here again, before we know it."

"Some years seem to move by quicker than others," Carolyn acknowledged. "Although I'm not sure why." She rubbed the old

Basenji's head gently. "This year will be different, don't you think? Maybe this year will be the best either of us has ever had." She set her glass down and scooped Magic into her arms, holding him close. He was warm and felt good in her embrace. She'd missed having a dog to hold, and now that he was there she felt a pleasant sense of completeness she'd almost forgotten. "After all, we've got each other now. What do you say?"

"This new year will be better," he agreed. Her face was close to his, and he smelled the sharp, sweet aroma of champagne on her breath. "At least, we can try."

Suddenly, a roar from the next apartment signaled that the rest of the world had finally caught up to them. Carolyn went to the doorwall, tugging on the handle until it opened. With Magic still in her arms, she stepped out onto the small porch.

The cold January air shocked them both, filling their lungs with the refreshing taste of winter. Diamonds glistened on the snow, catching the light from the half-moon and the nearby apartments. Everywhere people were cheering, clanging pots and pans and making noise with party favors, celebrating the arrival of another new year. Carolyn thought about the party that was in full swing at Andie's house, grateful for once that she wasn't there.

"Hear that?" she asked. "They're welcoming the new year." Impulsively, she shouted into the night "Happy New Year!"

Magic wriggled and she set him down into the fluffy snow. For the first time since she'd known him, he yodeled — a happy, thrilling yodel, loud and long. It carried far into the night, making all who heard it wonder what sort of creature it belonged to.

High above, a lone firework saved from some long-ago Fourth of July soared into the clear winter sky, bursting into a rainbow of brilliant colors.

Magic caught the acrid smell of the burning firework hanging in the air, and it reminded him of a time long since past. He remembered the man setting off fireworks, and thought of how Violet would press her body close, trembling with fear and excitement at the strange fire in the sky.

But it wasn't so long ago, he thought. *She was with me then.*

Carolyn stood with her eyes closed, and Magic imagined she was watching the firework's image left behind in her mind. A contented feeling came over him then, a feeling he was experiencing more and more the longer he was with her.

This will be a good year, he thought, closing his eyes and seeing fireworks. *It's got to be.*

"Oh!" Carolyn exclaimed. "I almost forgot! Wait right there, Magic! I'll be right back!" She disappeared into the apartment, leaving the old Basenji staring quizzically after her, wondering what she was up to.

A moment later she reappeared, holding her guitar in hand. Strumming it softly, she smiled. "Andie mentioned this earlier, and I'm glad I remembered. I always play *Auld Lang Syne* on New Years."

"I'd like to hear it," Magic offered, enchanted by the sounds that came from the instrument. He cocked his head from side to side as she plucked a few more notes, wrinkling his forehead in amazement. "I don't think I know the words, though."

"They're easy," came the reply. "Listen through once, then we'll do it together. Ready?"

"Ready!"

Carolyn strummed softly, her voice ringing out clear and strong in the night. As she played, Magic forgot about the cold and the night, and about the fact that another year had gone by. The music wrapped itself around him, touching his heart and making it feel happy and light. He closed his eyes, feeling the last echoes vibrate pleasantly in his ears.

"I've never heard anything quite like it," he exclaimed. "That was wonderful!"

Applause from the next apartment startled them both, and they turned to see several people standing on the balcony. "That was beautiful," one of the women called out, smiling and waving. Her companions echoed her sentiments. Then, from the balcony above, several men leaned over the railing and smiled.

"Would you mind playing that again?" one of the men asked. "We didn't hear all of it the first time. Please?"

"Yes, please?" Mr. Feldman, her next door neighbor, had pushed his wife's wheelchair to their open doorwall. She'd tucked an afghan around herself to keep out the cold. "We heard your music, and had to tell you how much we enjoyed it," he said.

Embarrassed, Carolyn felt herself blush happily, and she smiled at Magic. "Oh, I don't know," she said, watching him wag his tail appreciatively. "It's starting to feel pretty cold out here."

"Please?" Magic pressed. "They'd like to hear it again as much as I would. I'll even join you this time, okay?"

"Okay." Carolyn nodded, and her neighbors applauded. She nervously plucked a few strings, took a deep breath, and began to play, thrilled to hear her neighbor's voices join in, filling the night air with song. Her confidence soared and she played louder, feeling her guitar vibrate with each note.

Not to be left out, Magic yodeled right along, holding the last note as long as he possibly could, which drew even more applause.

"Take a bow, Magic," Carolyn said, bowing to her audience. "They're clapping for you too."

"No one's clapped for me in ages!" he replied happily, pleased to be included. He yodeled once more, drawing a final round of applause.

"That concludes our concert for this evening," Carolyn waved at her neighbors. "Happy New Year!"

Once inside, she felt her knees grow weak. Almost falling to the sofa, she sat breathless, her face flushed. "That's never happened to me before!" she exclaimed. "I didn't think I'd have it in me to play like that."

"You were great," Magic said, settling beside her. He leaned into her, and she put her arm around him, smelling the winter in his coat.

"Thanks for believing in me," she whispered, planting a kiss on his cheek.

"I should thank you for believing in me."

They stared at each other solemnly for a moment, then burst into laughter.

"We're starting the new year off just perfectly, I'd say," Carolyn giggled. "Maybe we should get a band together and go on the road."

"I like to travel," Magic said. "We should go somewhere, sometime."

"Maybe we will," Carolyn replied. "We've got a whole brand-new year to work with, don't we? Where would you like to go?"

"To the ocean," the old dog replied without hesitation.

"Really? Why?"

"I go there in my dreams a lot," he answered, curling up beside her. She gazed at him, trying to understand what he meant. She knew he had vivid dreams, for he'd talk in his sleep and often wake up terrified from nightmares he wouldn't discuss with her.

She stroked his wrinkled forehead gently, and decided not to press him for an explanation. They sat together until sleep overtook them both, sweeping them away into contented dreams.

ELEVEN

ONE SNOWY SATURDAY AFTERNOON
in February, Carolyn disappeared into the
bedroom. Magic heard her rummaging around in
the closet, his ears detecting the unmistakable
rustling of a plastic shopping bag. When she
finally returned her face was flushed and she
looked very pleased with herself. Holding her
breath, she placed a slender white box on the
sofa in front of him, impulsively planting a kiss
on his forehead.

"Today's a special day," she explained. "It's

Valentine's Day."

"Ah," Magic said, appreciating the tone in her voice, but not fully comprehending what the fuss was about. Christmas was easy, and Halloween had long since ceased to be much of a mystery. He had never known anyone who made a holiday of a cold February day. "For what it's worth, Valentine can have it! What's so special about a snowy winter day? Christmas is over; that much I do know."

"Valentine's Day is a holiday to celebrate the ones we love," Carolyn explained. "I've never had anyone special," she added. "At least, no one to share Valentine's Day with."

She'd never celebrated the holiday, not even with Max. Not having someone special like a boyfriend or husband to exchange valentines with was a painful part of life she didn't like to dwell on.

"There must have been someone special for you," Magic pressed, looking hard at Carolyn, realizing she wasn't telling him everything. "I've had two very special loves in my life," he added. "And, now that you already know about Violet, I'd like to hear about yours."

"Well," Carolyn admitted. "I was in love with someone once. At least, I thought I was." She settled on the sofa next to Magic. "I met him through work. He was a substitute the school had hired to take the place of a teacher who had retired."

"All of us single women were whispering about the new guy — silly stuff like how nice he looked in the sport coats he always wore, or how his haircut was trendy. His name was Ted, and I thought he was one of the nicest guys I'd ever met." She smiled at the memory.

"We hit it off right away, since we were both teaching third grade. We'd stand together at recess and watch the kids, discussing everything from the weather to sports, to our dogs. Ted was the kind of person I could talk to for hours and never run out of things to say."

She rubbed Magic's belly, watching his tail uncurl as he relaxed. "Like the way we are," she said. "I can listen to you all day long and never get tired of hearing your stories."

"Anyway," she continued. "We'd gotten quite friendly, and one Friday afternoon he asked me to dinner and a movie. I'd always been warned not to get involved with someone at work, and I believe that's still a good rule to live by. But, I really liked the guy and I didn't think it would matter if we had a relationship outside of work."

"He took me downtown to a fancy restaurant, and then to a special screening of *Gone With the Wind*. I had the time of my life, and I figured he must have, too."

"Everything moved fast — almost too fast, really." She chuckled to herself. "I was so stupid, not seeing what was going on. Oh, I knew Ted liked me, that was plain enough. But, he also liked other women, and he made no secret about it, either."

Carolyn's expression grew dark. "We'd be walking through the mall, for example, and he'd comment on how other women looked, how they dressed, or how pretty their hair was. He had a way of making me feel inferior to other women. I spent all sorts of money getting manicures, going to expensive salons, and on makeup! I spent a fortune trying to become someone I wasn't, and the harder I tried, the more he'd find wrong. I don't know why I let it go on, but I thought I loved him, and I wanted him to love me, too."

"One day, out of the blue, he asked me to marry him. I was shocked, to say the least, and what could I do but accept? It's something every woman dreams will happen to her — you know, gorgeous guy falls madly in love with you, asks you to marry him, and you live happily ever after, right?"

"So what happened, then?" Magic asked softly. "You didn't marry him, did you?"

Carolyn shook her head. "No, and I'm glad I didn't. He started seeing someone else. I found out from one of the other teachers — she'd seen him around with another woman and told me all about it. At first I didn't believe it was possible, since he was engaged to me, and usually an engagement closes the door on your dating life."

"I got tired of hearing people whispering behind my back, so I cornered him and demanded the truth. Without blinking an eye he admitted he'd been with someone else. Then he said he really loved me, and asked for a second chance. As hard as it was, I told him I never wanted to see him again, and ended our engagement right then and there."

"Ted got real angry, then, and said terrible things. He wouldn't leave, and the more I told him to go, the angrier he became. Finally, he hit me." Carolyn shuddered at the unpleasant feeling that ran through her. She placed her hand on her cheek, and Magic knew in that instant it was where she'd been hit. "I fought him and eventually he stormed out, slamming the door so hard the pictures on the walls rattled. And poor Max was so afraid! He was cowering under the bed, terrified, the entire time."

Magic sat up, the hair along his back bristling. "I'd give my tail to take a chunk out of him," he hissed. "Oh, he'd better not ever, ever cross my path." He narrowed his eyes until they were nothing more than dark slits, pinned back his ears, smoothing out the wrinkles, and curled his lips, exposing sharp teeth.

"You won't have to worry," Carolyn reassured him, stroking his back until the hairs lay smooth again. "Never in my life had I felt so stupid and so violated. When Andie heard what happened, she called the police. Believe me, he won't bother me again." Tears filled her eyes. "What a terrible mistake I'd made," she said softly. "And ever since then, I've had a hard time working up the courage to trust anyone enough to get to know them better. I just don't want to get hurt again."

"Not everyone in the world is like that," Magic said. "There are plenty of good people out there. You just have to look harder to find them, that's all."

"Oh, I know," Carolyn said quickly. "But it's like that old saying — once bitten, twice shy."

"Someday you'll find someone," he assured her, resting his head on her lap and feeling loneliness in her he couldn't possibly fill. "Until then, you've got me to protect you. I won't let anyone hurt you," he promised. "Besides," he added. "If you ever find someone who likes Basenjis, they can't be all bad, now can they?"

Carolyn grinned. "You do have a point there."

Magic chortled. "And, you can ask my opinion any time you want. After all," he added, "I can read body language like nobody's business. If someone's not honest, I can spot it in a second. Nothing gets past a Basenji," he said proudly.

"Well, then," Carolyn hugged him tightly. "I'll just have to trust your judgment, then, won't I?"

"You can, you know," he said, determination shining in his unblinking eyes. "I trust you, and you can trust me."

"Hey, I almost forgot!" Carolyn placed the white box in front of the old Basenji. "This is something special for you."

He sniffed the box carefully, wrinkling his forehead with intense concentration. With one white paw he flipped it over and sniffed some more.

When it became clear to Carolyn that he didn't know what to do with the box, she picked it up and held it out to him.

"Go on, then," she urged. "Take a look at what's inside."

He nosed the box and pawed it, loosening the lid slightly. "I'd hate to tear this," he said, although he wanted to very much.

"Okay, I'll help you out a bit." Carolyn lifted the lid on the box, pulling a piece of cotton batting from it.

Magic's eyes lit up, wondering if the cotton was his gift. He always loved sinking his teeth into fluffy things. Much to his surprise, she set the cotton aside.

"This," she said, "is for you." With a flourish she presented him with a brown leather collar. Attached to the collar was a heart-shaped identification tag and a blue bone-shaped dog license.

The old Basenji regarded the collar carefully. "I haven't had a collar like that in years," he admitted. "The shiny parts do glisten in the light, don't they?"

When Carolyn pointed out his name engraved on the gold heart, he became quiet and thoughtful, remembering part of a dream he had once before.

Find love again, believe in friendship and trust, and find your way back home.

"Is something wrong?" she asked, curious about his silence. "Are you okay?"

"Nothing's wrong," he replied. "Your gift made me remember something I thought I forgot." Graciously he thanked her for the gift, and wished he could have done something for her.

"It looks good," Carolyn said, placing the collar around Magic's neck. "Like it was meant for you."

He jumped off the sofa and paced back and forth in front of the floor-length mirror in her bedroom, admiring his new gift from every possible angle. The heart jingled merrily against the dog license when he shook himself. Delighted, he thanked her again for her thoughtfulness.

"I don't have anything for you," he said. "I'm sorry I can't give you something to show you how much I appreciate you."

"You already have," she replied. "You've given me your trust and friendship, and that means a lot to me. I've never had a friend like you before, and I don't imagine I ever will again." She smiled. "I guess what I'm trying to say is, thanks for being here."

Magic stared at his reflection in the mirror and didn't reply.

August Magic

Carolyn's words, so similar to the words from his dream, lingered in his mind, making him feel happy and confused all at once.

TWELVE

THAT NIGHT, WITH TROUBLING thoughts of Carolyn's gift on his mind, Magic had a hard time staying asleep. He awoke when the clock struck one, two and then three o'clock in the morning. Except for the ticking clock and Carolyn's steady breathing in the other room, the apartment was quiet.

He stretched and yawned in the darkness, and thought about walking to the kitchen for a drink. Deciding to skip the drink, he hopped off the sofa and settled into Carolyn's favorite chair, feeling the upholstery cool and smooth beneath him. After a few moments he left the chair and padded silently into the bedroom, jumping lightly onto the bed where Carolyn slept. Circling twice, he curled up against her and stuck his nose into the space between his front paws. His breath warmed the space quickly, and it wasn't long before he was fast asleep.

He dreamed he was young again, a curious pup exploring the world for the first time. Leaving the security of the house behind, he made his way down weathered cedar steps to a brick path that turned into gravel and ended at the dunes.

He followed a narrow, well-worn path through the tall grass that grew there, watching as the grass moved and swayed in the steady ocean wind.

He heard the roaring ocean, and the familiar sound of waves crashing and rumbling on the sandy beach filled his ears, sounding like music. Nearby, a tall brick lighthouse, painted with black and white stripes, soared into the blue summer sky.

The path ended abruptly at the top of a small hill. From there he looked down on a grassy valley, green and lush, sheltered from the sea and wind by tall dunes and scrub bushes surrounding it on all sides. He sat on the hill, feeling the hard-packed earth warm beneath his bottom. His dark eyes stared all around, watching the rolling sea in the distance. Not knowing why, he felt a tingle of expectation race down his spine, and waited for something wonderful to happen.

For a long time nothing happened. He watched seagulls with gray-tipped wings and sun-yellow eyes float high in the summer sky. A dark line of dirt-brown pelicans skimmed over the surface of the sea, occasionally diving into the waves for fish. A speckled ghost crab scuttled by, pausing just long enough to stare at him with beady, stalk-eyes.

Suddenly, a small, quick movement caught Magic's eye, drawing his attention back to the valley below. Then, from the other side of the valley, another quick movement made him turn the other way. Then still another, then another, then yet even another.

Magic's nose twitched, his whiskers vibrating in the humid, salty air. The wind wasn't quite right, and he couldn't pick out any definite scent. His mind questioned what his eyes were seeing, and he peered into the sunlight, wondering if he'd seen those shapes before, certain he recognized the shadows, but knowing shadows didn't move the way those did.

Shadows don't move at all unless they're attached to something, he remembered, suddenly alarmed. *What was it? Who was it?*

He realized with a start what he saw weren't shadows at all, but lean, brown rabbits making their way through the thick grass. He watched in amazement as at least twenty rabbits moved in and out of hidden burrows, their coats sleek and shiny in the afternoon sun. They didn't see him or smell him as their tiny noses cautiously sniffed the air. Their translucent pink ears turned this way and that, catching the sound of the wind and the ocean, the breeze tickling their quivering whiskers.

A seagull cried from high above.

At the sound the rabbits panicked and scattered. Slowly, they reappeared once they realized no harm had come to them. One by one, they moved into the sunlight again, standing around, blinking at each other with shiny black eyes. The largest rabbit sighed loudly and began to feed on the juicy grass, encouraging the other rabbits to follow his lead. Magic heard the sound of their teeth ripping and chewing the sweetness. He could smell the fragrant grass as they ate, the aroma warm and heavy in the air. The rabbits had relaxed and let their guard down.

Magic's body tensed and tightened, flexing as he crouched low to the ground, watching the rabbits eat. Then, in a sudden burst of energy, he bolted down the steep hill, his paws hardly touching the ground as he raced toward them, not knowing which to chase first, wanting to chase them all.

Once they'd seen Magic, the rabbits scattered in all directions. He ran in a zigzag pattern after them, determined to catch one but was unable to tell them apart. They ran in circles and taunted him, telling each other not to worry, that this was an old dog who couldn't catch a single rabbit. Their words angered him, for he knew he wasn't an old dog at all, but a young and strong one, and he was determined to catch each rabbit and teach it a lesson. Never tiring, he chased them until the sun was low in the sky and the tide had pulled away from the beach.

As he ran, he marveled at how wonderful it was to be young. His breath came easily and his heart pumped a steady rhythm in his chest. The rabbits couldn't run forever, he knew, and he felt as if he could.

The dream disappeared as the clock sounded four in the morning. Even though he had awakened suddenly, he felt as if he had slept an eternity, full of energy and ready for anything.

I was there, he thought. *That was my home.*

Surrounded by the afterglow of his dream, Magic made up his mind right then. Before another sun had set he would tell Carolyn about his dreams, because he knew what they were all about now. He'd tell her about the old cedar house, about the path that led through the dunes, about the lighthouse and the rabbits. He knew there had to be even more to it, but try as he might, he couldn't remember it all.

Maybe if I sleep some more it will come to me, he thought excitedly. *Maybe I can go there again.*

Not knowing how Carolyn would react when he told her bothered him terribly, but the feeling the dream left him with was so strong he couldn't keep it to himself any longer. He thought about waking her up, then decided he'd be better off waiting until morning. He fell into a dreamless sleep, still cloaked in the warm glow of his dream.

Tomorrow, he thought. *I'll tell her all about home. Carolyn, if she loves me, will understand.*

THIRTEEN

MAGIC TOOK THE OPPORTUNITY TO

tell Carolyn about his dream the next morning

after breakfast. Second thoughts crept into his

mind when she set her cereal bowl on the floor

for him, as she did every morning. He lapped at

the sweet milk, enjoying the delicious flavor

spreading over his tongue.

He found comfort in the routine, comfort in

the fact that every morning there was cereal, and

after the cereal was gone there would be milk

left in the bowl, just for him. He lingered over

the bowl, licking it several times even though there was nothing left inside. The bowl banged loudly on the floor, and Carolyn took it away.

"You're awfully quiet this morning," she said, pouring herself a cup of coffee, eyeing him with concern. "Are you feeling okay?"

"Sure," he replied. *I've got to tell her*, he thought anxiously. *How can I tell her?*

She peered at him over her cup. "Did you sleep okay?"

"Yes," he replied, trying to ignore the nervous feeling in his stomach. It soured the milk inside of him, and he swallowed as it threatened to come back up.

"Well then, you must have something on your mind." She sat on the floor next to him, stroking his face and neck. Her fingers were still warm from the cup. "Come on," she pressed. "Tell me what's bothering you."

Magic took a deep breath. "I had a dream last night," he said at last, looking into her wide green eyes, seeing himself reflected in them. "I dreamed of home."

"Home?" she asked. "You mean about us?"

"No, about someplace else. About where I came from, long ago when I was young."

She listened quietly with her eyes closed, as if by doing so she could see the picture he was painting in her mind.

With his voice he painted pictures of an ocean, a beach, and of warm summer breezes where brilliant white clouds drifted through deep blue skies. He took her to a lighthouse that stood tall and proud on the shore, and with her climbed every step of the spiral staircase to the top and stood beside her, looking out at the sand and waves far below. She smelled the cedar and sea on the air, heard cicadas buzzing in the heat of a summer afternoon, and walked a narrow path to the place where he told her the rabbits lived. Together they chased rabbits across the dunes through an open field, and when the day grew late they watched shorebirds as the tide came in and ate away at the beach, stroking it gently as the moon rose full in the east and the last rays of the sun disappeared behind the dunes into the still waters of the sound.

He finished telling the dream, then took a deeper breath. *I've got to do this*, he thought. *This is my one chance.* He led her out of the kitchen, to the sofa.

"I need your help," he said after a long silence. "That dream was very real to me. It made me realize I've been away from home too long." He paused, letting his words sink in. "I want to go home, and I need you to take me there."

Carolyn stared blankly at him, not comprehending his words. "I don't understand," she said, shaking her head. "You are home. This is your home! I've done everything to make this home!" She was afraid, and he heard it with every tremble of her voice. He hadn't meant to upset her, and he cursed himself for not being able to make her understand.

Deep in thought, Magic gazed out the window, seeing his reflection pale and ghostlike in the glass. He wasn't getting any younger, in fact, he was being forced every day now to admit that he was old. He hated the thought of getting old and wasting away. While he looked forward to seeing the Happiness some day, it irked his proud Basenji nature that being old and weak was all part of the plan.

Not knowing what to say or do, Carolyn paced around the room, straightening a crooked picture, then moving some magazines to the magazine rack by the window. It was something she always did when really angry or upset. From the time she was little, when she didn't get her way she would go into her bedroom, shut the door and methodically put things away. She would take everything off the bookshelves, clear away her dolls, and make her room as sparse as possible, even removing pictures from the walls and the curtains from the windows.

Without realizing it, she was making the room look as if she'd never been there, believing her parents would change their minds about whatever it was she wanted once they had an empty room and no sign of their daughter. It rarely worked, but she still found comfort in the old routine.

She'd cleaned out the apartment when Max died, shoving everything into closets and cabinets. The furniture had ended up in her bedroom, "Packed as tight as sardines," Andie had later remarked.

Andie had found her cousin sitting in the middle of the empty living room, her knees pulled tightly to her chest, her sock feet slipping maddeningly on the hardwood floor, and tears running down her cheeks. A lonely, well-worn tennis ball and a small tin that held Max's ashes were sole testament to her incredible loss. Andie had been there for her, and together they'd put the apartment together again, piece by piece.

Magic watched Carolyn's movements, reading them as easily as his nose read scents on the trunk of a well-visited tree. He realized she had grown to love him, even though most of his life was behind him. It hadn't mattered to her that he was old andhad been reduced to nothing more than a stray awaiting euthanasia in the shelter. She'd heard him, taken him in, and become his friend. In that instant he understood her distress.

"I didn't mean to upset you," he ventured. "I'm sorry if I did."

Carolyn had been careful to keep her back to him so he wouldn't see her tears, wondering if he could smell their saltiness in the air.

"I need to see the place where I was born one more time," Magic began, "I've lived a lifetime away from home, and now . . ." His voice trailed off. She wasn't paying attention.

He went to her and placed his paws on her blue-jeaned legs, feeling the well-worn fabric beneath them and realizing at that moment how much he loved her.

The shock of his touch stopped Carolyn where she stood, a vase in one hand and a basket of books in the other. She set the things down, and scooped the old Basenji into her arms. It was hard not to laugh as his tongue tickled her face, drying her tears.

"There's a place," he said between salty licks. "A place where the ocean rises to meet the sand, where islands stretch out to meet the waves. A lighthouse stands guard over it, watching over the sea and land and sky. My home was there, near the place where the rabbits live. I need to go back, to see it again, and I can't explain why but something inside of me is calling me to it. I need to be there again. Please try to understand! Can't you find a way to help me go home?"

She heard the longing in his voice and gazed into his eyes, expecting to see the place reflected in them. She could almost hear his memory of the roaring ocean and the cry of shorebirds.

Max never had a chance to grow old; he was forever young in her mind and memories. Magic, on the other hand, was in his autumn years, and she wanted to care for him and do the things she would have done for Max. This was her chance to thank him for helping her feel alive again, to give something back to the little Basenji who magically appeared at just the right moment, when she really needed a friend.

"I'll make you a deal," she said at long last. She ran her hand gently down Magic's back, and cupped his wrinkled face in her hands, staring into his eyes.

How could I have ever known another dog could mean so much to me? she thought. *I love him!*

"Stay with me until August. I get two weeks of vacation right before the new semester starts. That's when I'll take you home." She held out her hand, palm up, as if to seal the deal.

Magic regarded her carefully, taking his time to study her face. It occurred to him for the briefest second not to trust her, because she seemed to need him so much. A wave of guilt flowed over him, and he felt bad for thinking she wouldn't let him go. He knew she wouldn't let him down.

"Thank you," he said solemnly, placing a paw into her hand. A twinkle appeared in his eyes, and he yodeled happily. Carolyn smiled at the sound, and much to the old dog's surprise, tilted her head back and yodeled too!

PART TWO

JOURNEY

A lifetime of searching ultimately led me back to where I began. It was there that I finally found happiness. — Unknown

FOURTEEN

MICHIGAN IN LATE JULY WAS HOT AND humid. One could almost believe that the sun had slipped dangerously close to the earth, a blazing inferno bright in the steel blue sky. Ancient trees, their leaves faded to dusty olive, drooped lazily in the bright sunlight, barely perking up after brief afternoon thundershowers that left sidewalks steaming and warm puddles in the streets.

Fireworks and barbecues had been squelched by oppressive heat, forgotten in the days of air so thick it was like being in a perpetual sauna. Mosquitoes hovered in the welcome coolness of late afternoons, preferring to lurk in quiet shade, half-heartedly biting at anyone who passed. It was as if the whole world, wrapped in a steaming towel, had taken a deep breath and sighed tiredly, unable to change the weather but waiting patiently, secure in the knowledge that the weather would eventually change itself.

As she did every year, Carolyn volunteered her time and tutored at summer school, grateful that it was air-conditioned. Not having a husband or family to vacation with made her a prime candidate to take the summer position, and since she had nothing better to do anyway, it occupied her time and made the days go by.

Magic accompanied her to class every morning, since the rules were more lax during the summer months, and nobody seemed to mind when she'd suggested it. He had been eager to join her, for throughout the winter and spring she had entertained him with endless stories of the children. Clearly she loved her job, for her animated descriptions of the classroom and its occupants made him feel as if he knew each and every corner of the school.

Carolyn spent many hours wondering what it would be like to have Magic in class, and many more wondering if he would be a distraction. Her fears were laid to rest when she discovered how much more her students looked forward to their sessions with her, especially since they got to spend time with Magic.

Carolyn was amazed when some of the slower readers were motivated by Magic. It was a real treat to get out of the classroom and sit in cool shade under the towering maple trees, each child taking turns (and some even taking more than their fair share) reading out of school books to him. He took it all in stride, enjoying the singsong sound of their voices as they read him stories of kings and castles and far away places.

Often, she would watch from the window when the students

sat out in the grass reading to him. Her love for the old dog had grown more than she ever could have imagined. She saw herself reflected in him, understood their mutual love for the children, and shared the wonder of how much those children were capable of when given the chance.

She couldn't help but get a little teary-eyed when she saw how patient he was with kids, and hoped that he'd be welcome in her classroom that fall when school started up again. The end of summer school was fast approaching, and with it her two week break. Although Carolyn looked forward to spending her vacation with the old dog, she couldn't help but feel apprehensive about it at the same time. Magic wanted to find his home again, and the thought of him wanting to remain there frightened her.

What if he doesn't want to come home with me? she wondered, knowing in heart that if that's what it would take to make the old Basenji happy, then she'd have to steel herself and let it happen.

Losing Max had been difficult, and the thought of losing Magic now that they'd become so close weighed heavily on her mind. She'd grown to love him in a way she never thought possible, and as the weeks flowed into months he had become so much a part of her life that the thought of being without him was like not being able to live or breathe.

By virtue of his age alone she knew their time together was limited, and she feared the day when they'd go their separate ways. She often wondered what was wrong with her, why wasn't she able to find someone to fall in love with and marry. Magic had told her many times to wait, and eventually the right person would come along. He assured her she'd know it in a heartbeat, and she really wanted to believe him.

One warm spring afternoon he had described his North Carolina home to her. The doorwall had been open, and a warm spring breeze blew in from the west, causing the blinds to flutter in the wind. He had been dozing in a warm patch of sunlight, his tail unfurled and his eyes half-closed.

A fat, winter-fresh robin landed for a moment on the railing just out of reach, singing his springtime music. Magic's eyes popped open when he heard the melody, staring sleepily at the little bird as it sang a few more notes before flying off.

"Springtime," Magic sighed. "It's wonderful to feel spring again." He rolled onto his side, letting the sun warm it deliciously. "Winters here are too long."

Carolyn looked up from the papers she was grading. "It will be summer before you know it," she reminded him. "If we're going to plan our trip, then I've got some arrangements to make."

Magic lifted his head and looked at her for a moment, his brow deeply wrinkled. "I'm glad you agreed to go," he said at last, letting his head rest on the floor again. "I was afraid that maybe you might change your mind."

"I made you a promise," Carolyn replied. "And when I make promises, I always keep them." She shuffled some papers, dropping her pen to the floor. "I've been wondering about something. You never mentioned your birthday," she said, bending down to pick up the pen. "You must have a day you celebrate as your birthday, or at least know when you were born."

"I was born in the spring," Magic answered. "About this time of year, when it's just beginning to get warm."

"Isn't that unusual for Basenjis? They're usually they're born in the fall or winter, right?"

"Usually," he acknowledged. "But then again, my mother was an unusual Basenji."

He paused, stretching his neck and rubbing the side of his face on the carpet. "Most dogs will tell you their mothers are wonderful, smart, and beautiful, and I don't doubt it for a minute." He yawned, and gave himself a good shake. "My mother, she was all of those things, especially the last. She really and truly was beautiful."

Carolyn closed her eyes, trying to see the picture Magic was painting of his mother. What had she looked like?

He described a dark red Basenji, with markings similar to his own, with a face full of wrinkles and dark eyes. Her coat was like expensive velvet, soft and lush, wrapped around her short, muscular body like a cloak. Her ears were large and as expressive as her face, an extension of her fine head, creating an aura of independence and intelligence. As Magic spoke, Carolyn could see the mischief, with a little wildness mixed in, that gleamed in his mother's eyes, and her loosely curled tail, dipped in snow-white, wagging back and forth merrily.

Magic, his ears flushed from the heat, wandered a few steps until he was out of the sun. "My mother was an African-born dog," he said, closing his eyes, seeing her in his memory. "She was pure African, through and through. Her ancestors went as far back as time itself, and she would tell me stories that had been passed down through the generations. She knew wonderful stories, about how members of our family had hunted with great pharaohs and queens. When she was young she was taken away from her home in Africa, and sometimes she couldn't remember many of the details. What she did remember, she spoke of so fondly and with such feeling that I knew she missed it very much."

Carolyn nodded, thinking of Magic's desire to return home. "What it must feel like," she said, "to miss something that much." With a start she realized it was the same way with her and Max, although the feelings were starting to fade now that Magic was in her life.

Magic nodded in agreement. "She always wanted to go back, to return to the bush and to her tribe. She was such a proud dog; I don't think she ever would have admitted it was impossible for her to go back." He lowered his voice. "Once, she ran into the ocean and tried to swim home, and if her people hadn't saved her, she would have died. She never tried to go home again, but whenever things got to be too difficult for her, she would close her eyes and return there in her memories, as far as they'd take her."

"I guess I'm a lot like she was," he continued. "I remember being born, and I remember the first time I saw her face. I've been able to remember every corner of the old house where we lived, and I remember the sound and smell of the ocean."

"To the north of our house, far down the beach, was an abandoned lighthouse. I remember how big it looked to me back then, although I'd imagine time has made it smaller than I remember. Old red brick showed through in many places where the black and white paint had worn away from the weather and time. You may have heard of the place — Hatteras Island."

"To me," he said, "Cape Hatteras was a wonderful place to grow up. My mother showed me what to watch for when the pelicans flew low across the water, and she told me how to read the weather by looking at the clouds and sniffing the wind. She used to tell me fantastic stories she heard from the wild ponies that roamed there."

"What happened to her?" Carolyn asked, suddenly. "Your mother."

"I was sold and I never saw her again," Magic replied. "She's gone to the Happiness now." He became quiet, and Carolyn felt she had to say something.

"I'm sorry," she said, "I didn't mean to upset you."

"No, it's not that," he replied. "Being bought and sold, living and dying, it's all part of a dog's life. There's nothing sad about it, really, because we're all welcome in the Happiness. When you're a dog, it's just the way it is," he said. "Oh, I miss her sometimes, and often I feel she's with me, much the same way I feel Violet or Max."

Carolyn stiffened at the mention of Max's name. It was on the tip of her tongue to ask Magic how he knew Max was there, and she wanted to know what sort of feeling it was that gave his presence away. Knowing when the dog-spirits were near seemed to be second nature to the old Basenji, and it troubled her that her human senses were in some way dulled or not heightened enough to be able to know for herself. Deciding for the moment not to ask, she closed her eyes and sat very still, every part of her body listening and feeling for some change in the room, or some unusual air current – anything at all different that would let her know Max was there. As always, there was nothing, and she opened her eyes and smiled sadly at Magic, who was gazing at her with a puzzled look on his face.

"Are you okay?" he asked softly.

She nodded. "Oh, sure."

"Something wrong?"

She started to deny that there was, but changed her mind. "I was trying to see if Max's spirit was here," she admitted. "How will I know it? I guess I don't understand."

"Maybe you're trying too hard," came the cryptic reply. "Give it time; you'll figure it out. My mother used to tell me that when dog-spirits were about, she felt comfortable and at home. Even though Africa was so far away, the dog-spirits were always able to find her." He cleared his throat, moved by the memory. "Going home was something she could never do when she was alive. She used to tell me that when she died the Happiness would take her all the way back to Africa. Surely that's where she is, but whenever I dream of her, she's always on Hatteras Island, on the beach by the lighthouse."

"Could it be that she was happy there, too?" Carolyn ventured. "There must be a reason."

Magic rested his head on his paws. "It's almost as if she's helping me find my way back. I guess part of the reason I want to return to the island is because going home was something my mother always dreamed of, but never got to do in her lifetime." He stood and wandered back to the sunny spot, and lay down. "I've been to many places in my life," he continued, "and I've had many experiences along the way. I've been told that life is like a big circle, and I believe if I can find my way back to where I began, that somehow I'll be able to understand what happened to me there. It's like a piece of me is lost, and I need to find it again to be complete."

He closed his eyes and breathed the spring air. "I need to smell the ocean again, and to feel the sand warm beneath my paws. I want to look up at the sky and see all the right stars in their proper places. I want to see the lighthouse again, if it's still there." He laid his head on his paws and sighed. "And I need to find the place where the rabbits live. Don't ask me more about it," he said at last. "I'll tell you more some other time."

"I can respect that," Carolyn said. *Maybe sometime I'll tell you about Max*, she thought. *Sometime, when I can.*

In keeping with her promise to the old dog, she'd gone to the bookstore and to several travel agencies, gathering books and brochures. The pictures she saw in those books took her breath away, for the islands of North Carolina's Outer Banks were fantastically beautiful.

To her great delight, she discovered that pirates, pioneers, wild horses from shipwrecked Spanish galleons, and the Wright Brothers were all part of the history there. She learned that years ago German U-boats had prowled beneath the waters off of the Hatteras coastline, hoping to add to the hundreds of shipwrecks the Diamond Shoals, otherwise known as "the Graveyard of the Atlantic," had already claimed. Familiar with the landmark black-and-white spiraled Cape Hatteras lighthouse, she was amazed to discover that it wasn't the original one – that what little remained of its predecessor now slept beneath the waves, reclaimed by the

Atlantic Ocean. Further reading revealed that the ocean was threatening the current Cape Hatteras light, and plans were underway to somehow protect it or move it out of danger. The more Carolyn read, the more she was intrigued by the history and mystery of the Outer Banks, and how it was all tied into the mysterious history that Magic carried with him – the secret of who he was and why he needed to go back, and why his dreams haunted him.

"Missis Adams!" The children had finished their reading and returned to the coolness of the school room. She hadn't heard them come in at all.

"It's getting pretty hot outside," Magic told her, panting slightly. "And it's time for the kids to go home."

"Is it time for you guys to go home already?" she asked, looking at the six tanned and eager third-grade faces of her summer school class. They nodded in unison. "Have a nice afternoon, then, kids!" They scampered off, screaming with delight.

"I like them a lot," Magic said, sprawling belly-down on the cool tile floor. "They're good kids."

Carolyn nodded in agreement. "It's a shame their parents don't spend more time with them," she said. "If they did, then maybe they wouldn't have to be in summer school."

"Just like dogs," he offered, hoping she wouldn't take offense to the analogy. "If people paid more attention to their dogs, they wouldn't end up in shelters." He snorted. "But I assume people don't throw their kids away when they get tired of them."

"That's where you're wrong," Carolyn replied, much to his surprise. "Some people do. It happens to us, too. By the way," she added, "I have something to show you."

Carolyn fished around in her desk, opening drawers and pushing papers aside. "Where is it?" she asked. "Aha!" She pulled a yellow piece of paper from a drawer in her desk, and held it down at Magic's level, so he could get a good look at it.

"What's this?" he asked, reaching for it with his mouth.

"It's a receipt, for our trip." Carolyn grinned. "A surprise for you! In one week, we'll be headed for the Outer Banks of North Carolina, just like I promised. And you'll love the way we're going to travel. I've rented a motorhome!"

The old Basenji was stunned. Only one week! Time had, once again, moved incredibly fast.

"It's not a brand new motorhome or anything," Carolyn continued. "But it's really neat. It's not real big, but it's got a bunk over the cab, and air conditioning!"

Magic couldn't mistake the excitement in her voice as she chattered on about the wonderful motorhome she'd rented, about the things she had planned to pack, and about the places they would see along the way. He wagged his tail appreciatively at the news, hardly believing his dream might come true, but at the same time realizing it was going to do just that.

Unable to contain his excitement he yodeled several times, his voice echoing happily in the empty classroom.

F I F T E E N

Ever SINCE SUMMER ARRIVED, Carolyn
had been dropping hints to Andie about the trip
she was planning to take with Magic. The night
before they were ready to leave, she'd finally
broken the news to Andie over the phone, not
wanting to deal with her face-to-face.

"What?" Andie shouted, nearly dropping the
phone. "You rented a what and you're going
where? Alone! Are you nuts?"

"I need a vacation," Carolyn said, eager to
calm her raging cousin. "Cape Hatteras is

beautiful this time of year, and . . ."

Before she could finish, Andie cut her off. "A vacation! You need your head examined is more like it! Do you have any idea what driving a motorhome is like? And you want to do it alone?"

In frustration, Carolyn had put the phone on the counter and gone about her packing, picking up the phone at varying intervals, muttering a "yes" or "I understand," then putting the phone back down again. She'd learned long ago that when Andie had an outburst, the best thing to do was to let her ramble on and get her steam out.

"She'll still have plenty to say," she told Magic the next morning as she maneuvered the rig through the narrow streets of Andie's neighborhood. "Just you wait and see."

The street was quiet in the hot August morning, lined with neat rows of bungalows peering sleepily into the daylight. Here and there lawn sprinklers were set up, chattering from the cold water that flowed their spouts, freshening the manicured lawns.

"I don't have to wait," he replied, hanging his head out the window and yodeling, his yodel loud enough to wake anyone who was still sleeping. "She's waiting for us!"

Andie stood barefoot in the driveway, with her eyes wide as saucers. Her arms were crossed over her chest, and her mouth hung open. She tapped one bare foot on the cement, jumping back as Carolyn parked the motorhome at the end of the driveway — driving right over Andie's mailbox.

"Hey!" Andie bellowed. "My mailbox!"

Carolyn climbed out of the motorhome to inspect the damage. To her relief the motorhome was unscathed, but Andie's mailbox was in dire need of repair.

"Sorry," Carolyn stifled a giggle. "Gee, I don't remember it being so close to the road before. When did you move it?"

"It's always been there, Carolyn."

When Andie forgot to call her "Kay O'Lyn," Carolyn knew

she was in trouble, but she couldn't help bursting into fits of uncontrollable laughter when she saw what was left of the mailbox. Unable to keep her composure, Andie joined in.

"Don't worry, we'll fix it," she laughed. "So tell me now, what's going on here?"

"Well, I've rented this motorhome," Carolyn replied. "Magic and I are taking a two-week vacation to North Carolina."

"By yourself?" Andie asked, incredulous. "Alone?"

"As if we haven't had this conversation before." Carolyn rolled her eyes. "You must have said that a thousand times already."

"I don't think you were listening to me the first nine hundred times," her cousin pouted. She bent down to scratch a mosquito bite on her leg. "Really, going alone isn't such a good idea. At least let me come with you."

"I won't be alone because Magic will be with me," Carolyn replied. "I know what I'm doing. Besides, you've got plenty to do around here, and you can't just up and leave the kids, can you?"

"Okay, so you got me there. But Carolyn, that thing is a *motorhome!*"

"I hope so," Carolyn quipped. "It better not be an airplane. I *did* pay for a motorhome, after all." Seeing the distressed look that crossed her cousin's face, she relented. "Andie, think about it for a minute. I need a vacation, and I want to take Magic with me. I can't bring him into hotels, because dogs aren't allowed in the hotels there this time of year. That's why I rented the motorhome." She crossed her arms over her chest defiantly. "I know what I'm doing!"

"Well, at least you have the sense not to pick up a backpack and hitch your way to the coast. Honestly, I don't understand you lately."

"How about a little support here," Carolyn pressed. "After all, when was the last time I took a vacation?"

Andie shook her head slowly. "Look at this thing," she said, waving her arms like a magician. "This thing is like a bus! It's huge! It's a house on wheels!" She waved her arms again, as if by doing so she could shrink the motorhome into a smaller size, much more to her liking. "You drove it this far, but North Carolina isn't just across town you know!"

"I know, I know," Carolyn huffed, leaning against the motorhome. The sun had warmed its surface, and it felt wonderful against her back. "I'll be fine," she said. "Don't worry, okay? And don't try to stop me from going. The motorhome rent is paid for two weeks, it's got a full tank of gas, and that's that," she finished. "Besides, Magic loves the open road."

"What, did he tell you so?"

"As a matter of fact, he did."

Andie sighed. There wasn't any use in further discussion, because her beloved cousin had made it clear the issue was closed. "Well, at least promise to call," she said. "You've got your cell phone, right?"

Carolyn scowled.

"Right?"

Hearing no answer, Andie relented. "A postcard, then. Just let me know you two are safe."

"Fine, fine," Carolyn agreed. "And you remember what to tell my mother, if she asks, right?"

"You're going on a teacher's conference and training seminar and you won't be back for a couple of weeks." Andie recited in a monotone. "I've rehearsed that all night! I was beginning to hope it was true."

Carolyn could just hear her mother telling everyone how her daughter was going to be an easy target for villains and psychopaths who preyed on women who were, as her mother would say "stupid enough to travel alone." Not that thoughts of trouble didn't enter into Carolyn's mind — they had. She simply took the approach that as long as she was careful, nothing bad was going to happen.

"Well," Carolyn said at last, realizing Andie had finally run out of words. "I guess it's time to hit the road."

"I guess there's no talking you out of it, is there?" Andie bent down and rubbed Magic's head. "Watch over her, fella," she said. "That's the best cousin I've got!"

"Andie, I'm the only cousin you've got!"

"Whatever." Andie kissed Magic and pulled away abruptly when she discovered how wet his nose really was. "Ugh! Now, how do I explain what happened to the mailbox?"

The day was warm and the sun was high in the sky when the motorhome pulled away from Andie's driveway and headed east, toward the interstate. The embarrassment of hitting the mailbox behind her, Carolyn felt confident behind the wheel, and all she had to do was reach over and touch Magic to know that everything was going to be just fine. Already she was more excited about the trip than she had originally imagined she would be.

"This is great, isn't it?" she asked Magic.

"Wonderful," he grumbled, still bothered by the rules she had laid out for him regarding the trip. He thought he'd gotten pretty lucky when she allowed him to ride up front, but she had insisted on making him wear a red harness that buckled into the safety belt.

"I don't need you flying around if we hit something," she explained.

"Something like a mailbox, perhaps?" he retorted.

"Very funny. I just want you to stay safe, that's all."

"Well, then I hope there aren't any more mailboxes between here and the coast."

"Yeah," Carolyn said. "We'd take forever to get there if we stopped to hit them all!"

"Hmmmph."

"Is the harness too tight?" Carolyn asked. "Does it itch or anything?"

"Everything is fine," he mumbled, staring out the window at the fast moving scenery. After several minutes, he forgot about the harness entirely. "Look at that!" he exclaimed as they headed toward Detroit. The city skyline shimmered and sparkled in the heat of the day, making the skyscrapers look as if they could snag the white billowing clouds that drifted past. "It's been so long since I've been on the road that I'd forgotten how big the world really is!"

"We're going to see a lot of it in the next few days," she told him, rubbing his back with her free hand. "Sit back and enjoy the ride."

As the motorhome rolled across the miles of blacktop that stretched across the land as far as the eye could see, the industrial area of downriver Detroit melted into the rural landscape of southern Michigan and Ohio.

Farms dotted the open countryside, their fields green with soybeans and corn. Animals grazed in lush pastures, cooling themselves beneath vast expanses of shady trees. The motorhome passed cars and trucks going east and west, full of people and things heading to places that Magic could only dream about. He was mesmerized by the sights and smells of the world unfolding around him, an amazing rush of colors and sights that dazzled his mind with images he'd long since forgotten.

By the time they'd crossed the Ohio border into Pennsylvania, Magic was feeling pretty good about things. Excitement shone brightly in his eyes, quivered deliciously in his muscles, and he felt young again, like a pup seeing the world for the first time. He pawed at Carolyn, happy to see himself reflected in the dark lenses of her sunglasses, twin Magic's staring back at him with delight on their wrinkled faces.

"We're really going, aren't we?" he asked several times, wondering if it was all a dream from which he'd soon awaken. The feeling inside of him was like hovering on a cloud or flying like a bird through the air. It was a strange sensation, a heightened sense of awareness that left no doubt in his mind that he was really, truly alive.

"Oh yes," Carolyn replied each time. "Just like I promised. I'm taking you home."

"Home," Magic repeated, feeling an electric shiver of excitement run down his back, right down to his tail tip. It made the short, fine hairs along his back stand up deliciously. "I'm going home!"

SIXTEEN

THE MOTORHOME NOSED ITS WAY
into Breezewood, Pennsylvania shortly after six
that evening.

Breezewood was a busy, bustling tourist-
stopover town with plenty of restaurants, gas
stations, and souvenir stores all tucked securely
into the green Pennsylvania hills. The sight of
distant mountains had intrigued Carolyn long
before she'd actually driven into them, and she
wasn't disappointed with the town she'd chosen
as the stopping point for the night. Fresh from

sleep, Magic regarded the traffic and mass of people with amazement.

"This is a strange place," he said, sniffing the air. "There's so much going on all around us, but nothing here seems permanent." He snorted to clear the air from his nostrils. "It's as if everything in the world passes through here at some time or another, and brings with it the smells from all over."

"What I smell is dinner," Carolyn said, pulling the motorhome into a gas station. "I'm hungry, and you must be, too. Why don't you tell me what smells best to you, and we'll have something special to celebrate our first night on the road. There are quite a few places to choose from. What do you think?"

As Carolyn pumped gas, the old Basenji searched the evening breeze for food scents. He was rewarded by delicious aromas so overwhelming that they made him feel light-headed. Not knowing what all the wonderful smells were didn't help him decide on dinner. After several moments of intense concentration, he picked out the aroma of barbecued hamburgers, his nose searching for the direction from which the mouth-watering scent came.

"I think it's that way," he told Carolyn when she returned. "Go south, toward that low group of buildings."

At Magic's urging, Carolyn ordered dinner to go. The friendly cashier, who threw in an extra hamburger for Magic, further enhanced the festive atmosphere of their first day on the road. The smell of grilled hamburgers and salty French fries inside the white paper bag made both their stomachs rumble impatiently.

It had been a long time since Magic had dined on restaurant food, and he recalled how good it had been — the mixed-up, greasy delights he'd dug out of a dumpster the days before he'd been caught and taken to the shelter.

I'm not that dog anymore, he told himself proudly. *I'm not scared or alone anymore.* Belonging to someone again comforted him, and he wondered what would happen when he finally returned home.

He knew Carolyn cared a lot for him, and the thought of her love for an old dog warmed him through.

I love her, he thought, staring at her face as she studied a map, searching for a place to spend the night. *And she loves me.*

With a little bit of luck they found a small park nestled deep in the green hills overlooking Breezewood. A picturesque covered bridge crossed a cold stream just to the left of the parking lot where Carolyn found a spot for the motorhome. Her parking was a little crooked, and Magic pointed out to her how she'd narrowly missed hitting a yellow garbage can.

"You have better aim with mailboxes," he chuckled.

"Well, you can always drive," she retorted, feeling the smugness leave her. Except for the mailbox incident, she had been unbearably proud of how well she had handled the rig so far. "You do have a license, you know!"

Her reply amused the old Basenji, and it wasn't long before her laughter filled the air, mixing with his deep chuckle. "I suppose," he said at length. "You wouldn't care for my driving, at any rate."

Carolyn was amazed how human Magic seemed at times, and she wondered how different things would be if he were a person instead of a dog. What would he look like? What would he do for a living? Would they have ever met and become friends?

While the image of him sitting in the driver's seat was extremely comical, it saddened her to think that even though he was many things and had been many places, he was still just a dog. And she knew from experience that a dog's life was all too short.

Maybe Magic will find what he's looking for when we get there, she thought, staring into the blue summer sky. The air was fresh all around her, and she hugged herself happily. *Maybe things will work out for me someday, too!*

"Dinner is served," she called, looking around to see where Magic had wandered off to. He came trotting out of some low bushes, his tail curled tightly, his ears pricked forward as if they could literally catch the sound of her voice and scoop it into his mind.

"Smells wonderful," he said, licking his muzzle. "Where's my bowl?"

"Why don't you join me up here?" she asked, patting the empty space on the bench next to her. "That is, if you don't mind."

He regarded the invitation to join her at the table with surprise. "Unless you want to join me down here," he chuckled. "Although, I think it might look pretty strange to anyone who happened by."

The picnic table was old, carved with the names of many people who'd been there before. In between juicy bites of hamburger, Magic described the people who had been there before, whether or not they'd had dogs with them, and what those dogs were like.

As Carolyn listened, she secretly wished she could be a Basenji, too. Magic's world seemed so much more enhanced than her own. She couldn't help being just a little jealous to see how much information he could glean simply from sniffing the air around a park bench. She closed her eyes, wishing with all her might that for one brief moment she could see the world through the old Basenji's eyes, wondering if he ever longed to see how she viewed the world, curious as to what it was like to be up high on two legs.

Everyone has the ability to change the world in his or her own way, she mused. *Even by doing something as simple as passing through it. How strange this all must seem to a dog. All a dog asks for is a safe, loving home and companionship. Maybe a part*

of their purpose in life is to help us appreciate the simple things.
After all, what could be more important than love?

Delighting in the August summer evening, the two sat quietly listening to a symphony of crickets overtake the buzzing song of cicadas. Beneath a sky dotted with wispy pink clouds, they watched the brilliant orange sun sink low into the distant mountains. Once the sun had gone, shadows crept from beneath trees and buildings, bringing in the nighttime. Reluctantly, Carolyn and Magic were forced to abandon their picnic table, chased into the safety of the motorhome by hungry mosquitoes.

The night was fresh and warm, slightly humid but still comfortable in the gentle breeze that blew fresh from the mountains. Safe behind screened windows, they were able to look downhill at Breezewood as it glittered with neon and headlights.

The excitement of their journey, of what had taken place since she met Magic, and the anticipation of what was still to come took Carolyn's breath away, making her heart race with the unfamiliar beauty of the sight. Magic pointed out an airplane, visible only as a flashing red light in the sky, its fuselage dark against the stars.

"How little it seems, way up there," he said. "We must seem very small to them, too. I wonder what this place looks like from way up high?"

"Like a jewel," Carolyn decided. "I bet it looks just like a glittering jewel."

Magic agreed. "Or, maybe it looks like the stars, only they're below you instead of up above."

"Have you ever wished on a star?" Carolyn asked. "Andie's dad used to say that if you wished upon a star, your wish would come true."

"What would a star have to do with wishes?"

"I don't know," she answered. "But still, it's a nice thought, don't you think?"

After a moment of silence, Magic asked softly, "How does wishing on a star work?"

"Well," she replied, "you simply pick a star, and close your eyes, and make your wish. At least, that's how we always did it. Oh, and you can't tell anyone what you're wishing."

"Why not?"

"Because they say it won't come true if you do." Carolyn giggled. "Andie and I could never keep a secret. I guess that's why a lot of our crazy wishes never came true."

The old dog stared up at the sky, closed his eyes, and opened them again. "How do you decide what to wish for?" he asked.

"That's the tough part," Carolyn told him. "I guess you just wish for whatever you think will make you happy."

"Hmmm." Magic found his star again, closed his eyes, and thought to himself. *If it's true that wishes come from stars, and wishes are supposed to be what makes you happy, then my wish is for Carolyn. Nothing would make me happier than to see her with someone special. Someone who can make her laugh, someone who will love her for who she is, and someone who will take care of her when I'm gone.*

He opened his eyes and saw her smiling at him.

"Made a wish?" she asked.

"Yes."

"Was it a good one?"

"I'm not going say," he replied. "If there's a chance that this wishing on stars really works, I don't want to risk ruining it by telling."

"You'll let me know when it comes true, then?"

"Of course," Magic said, yawning. "Although, right now I'm wishing for a nice soft bed and a good night's sleep. It's been a long day."

They spent their first night on the road in the parking lot of a Breezewood truck stop; a bright red and blue neon sign flashing just brightly enough to make a pattern on the thin blanket Carolyn had thrown on the bed.

She watched the colors dance and glow on Magic as he lay on top of the blanket, and he in turn watched the colors dance and glow on her face until sleep overtook them both and the colors faded quietly into contented dreams.

SEVENTEEN

THE NEXT MORNING WAS RAINY AND

cool. The jewel that had been Breezewood the

night before was gray and dirty and didn't quite

glisten in the fog and dampness. Wisps of

ghostly white fog rolled off the mountains,

curled tightly around trees, and grasped at cars

on the road with feathery fingers.

Eyeing the dreariness, Carolyn became

apprehensive about continuing on. The thought

of maneuvering the motorhome over winding

roads and through a mountain tunnel seemed

like a daunting prospect, and she felt her conviction from the day before waver. To muster up her confidence, she studied the map she had highlighted with great interest.

Magic braved the rain, wandering off to do his business in a low cluster of bushes. He didn't like the way the wetness worked its way into his coat, making him damp and uncomfortable.

Sniffing around, he lingered in the bushes for a few minutes, disappointed that the rain had washed away most of the good smells, leaving behind only the strongest ones. Those he found he covered up carefully, letting the doggy world know who he was and that he'd been there. This done to his satisfaction, he shook the rain from his coat and hurried back across the puddle-strewn parking lot to the motorhome. When he returned, he found Carolyn sitting in the driver's seat staring at her map, shaking her head.

"Problem?" he asked, a concerned look darkening his wet, wrinkled face. He could tell something was troubling her, and if she was troubled, then so was he.

"Judging by the map, there's some tricky hills ahead," she said, absently reaching down to pet him. Feeling the wetness on her hand, she pulled it away and wiped the rainwater on her jeans. "Ugh, you're soaked! I'm not so sure I want to drive in this fog."

Magic turned east toward the mountains and the fog. Through the open window he inhaled the scent of cedars, pines and maple trees, and smelled auto exhaust and diesel fumes from the highway. His sensitive nose found the grassy-sweet aroma of milk cows hovering on the light breeze, and took in the musty odor of Breezewood encircled by fog.

The light rain became a steady summer rain, momentarily changing to a light mist, then resuming a harder tempo as dark storm clouds raced across the sky.

"I remember mornings like this," he said at last. "When the fog was so thick the only way you knew there was an ocean at the end of the beach was by the sound and the smell of it. Sometimes the wind would blow the fog away, but sometimes, when it was very still, a fine salty mist would fall. Those were the days for staying inside, in my opinion." He rubbed his face with a white paw.

"When I was very small and still lived with my mother, there was a man with dark hair and a gruff voice, a slight, red-haired woman who was his wife, and their son, a dark-haired dark-eyed boy." Magic began, moved by a memory that appeared out of the fog of his past.

"The boy — 'Nicholas' they called him when they were angry, and 'Nicky' when they weren't — never let the weather bother him. He was always out on the beach. It didn't matter if there was a storm looming on the horizon or if it was so hot that the sand burned your feet before you could make it to the water's edge. He loved the outdoors so much his parents used to tease him that he hadn't been born at all, but that they'd found him under a piece of driftwood, washed up on the beach after a summer storm."

"They called me 'Puppy' then, and it was the first summer of my life. Already my brothers and sisters had been sold, and my mother told me the day would soon come when I, too, would leave home and go out on my own. She said this happened to all puppies, and it was a part of growing up. Even after my brothers and sisters were gone, I found it hard to believe that I would ever live anywhere else or care about any other people."

"The place where we lived was full of things to keep even a busy puppy like myself constantly occupied. It was a wonderful time to be alive."

"Nicky was just twelve years old and as much a part of that beach as the ocean and the sand. He knew it well, so well that he could find his way back to the house in the dark of night when there was no moon — and I was certain we were lost." Magic chuckled at the memory. "My mother used to tell me I could learn a lot from him."

"One day we were out exploring the dunes, looking for tern nests, driftwood, shells — whatever interested a boy his age. Wonderful things always washed ashore before and after storms, and Nicky knew he was bound to find some sort of treasure in the sand when the tide pulled out."

"Several days before, I could feel the air pressure dropping. My mother explained to me that a storm was coming, a big storm. She warned me not to go far from the house, and she insisted I stay near Nicky so I could keep an eye on him." Magic closed his eyes, and saw his mother's face clearly in his mind, exactly as she looked when he was young.

"Nicky's mother had warned him to stay close to the house as well. She said the storm was going to be a bad one and they were going to the emergency shelter in town. Nicky's father said the police had already ordered an evacuation of the island. In their hurry to close up the house and leave, they were busy packing and didn't have time to keep an eye on Nicky. When he was sure no one was looking, he came and got me and together we slipped out of the house, unnoticed."

"I was just a young pup — what did I know of hurricanes? It seemed like my mother was getting all worked up over nothing but a summer thunderstorm, and I couldn't understand her trepidation."

"A hurricane?" Carolyn asked, her eyes wide. "You were in a hurricane?"

Magic stared out into the rain and fog, his ears turning towards the slow rumble of thunder growling in the distance. "I was," he affirmed. "And so was Nicky."

"What happened?" Carolyn pressed. "What was it like?"

Magic licked some rain from a paw. "We had wandered so far down the beach that our house was only a tiny dot in the distance.

Nicky was intent on discovering an intact conch shell or maybe even the remains of an old shipwreck, and he didn't notice how quickly the sky had darkened and how rough the ocean had become."

"Before we even knew what was happening, the wind picked up, gusting with incredible force. It blew fierce and hard, throwing sand into our faces, scratching our eyes and blowing into our ears. More than anything I wanted to go home and get out of the wind, to curl up against my mother's warmth and bury my head until the storm passed. But I had to stay with Nicky. It was my job, and I knew if I came home without him, my mother would have been terribly angry."

"The storm winds whipped up sea foam until it was a billowing froth, white against the darkness of the angry ocean. Nicky was smart enough to stay out of the water, because he knew the rip currents would be strong as the hurricane approached the island." Magic's eyes widened, and Carolyn could see their whites gleaming in the grayness.

"In the meantime, Nicky's parents had finished boarding up the windows on their house, and had packed up their pickup truck, ready to head to the emergency shelter in town. They searched the place from top to bottom, thinking he was hiding from them like he had many times before when they had to leave because of the weather. They knew he enjoyed storms, and they figured he was just trying to be difficult about going to the shelter."

"My mother told me later how she'd stood next to Nicky's father as he went out onto the porch in the wind and rain, calling to his son but getting no answer. There was terror in his eyes, and she could hear his voice tremble as he called Nicky over and over again. His wife joined him on the porch, and broke the news to him that I was missing as well. Hearing this, my mother immediately jumped off the porch and ran out into the storm, but she was brought back by a sharp command from Nicky's father. Before she could dash out of reach, he had her by the collar and had snapped a leash to it. He handed it to his wife and told her not to let go, no matter what. His face was grim as he explained he was going out into the storm to find us."

"His wife protested, urging him to get some men together from town instead of going out alone. But Nicky's father insisted that there wasn't enough time to get help.

"'Tie Savannah in the back of the truck,' he told his wife, "and get yourselves safely to the shelter. Whatever you do, don't let Savannah get loose or she'll be out there with me. I can't risk losing her, too. I'll find Nicky and the pup, and I'll meet you at the shelter before the storm worsens.' With that he gave my mother one last quick hug before closing the window of the truck cap.

My mother said she'd never forget how Nicky's parents had clung to each other in a long embrace, and she told me how frightened she was as she stared out the back window of the truck as it pulled away, pawing frantically on the glass, not wanting to leave her master behind. I can only imagine what went through his mind as he watched the truck disappear out of sight."

"And so he started out into the hurricane, determined to find us. He made his way over the dunes to the beach, and stood near where the dryline would have been, trying to decide which way to go. Any footprints he could have followed were blown smooth by the wind and pounded flat by the rain. I'm sure his heart jumped and raced when he saw someone moving slowly along the top of the dunes, and I can imagine how it sank when he realized it was my mother."

"Bleeding from a cut in her side and limping badly, she'd chewed through her leash and hurled herself against the truck window so hard she'd gone right through it. Bravely she fought against the wind and rain and her own injury so she could be with

Nicky's father."

'Savannah!' He called her name once, and she ran into his open arms. He held her close for a moment, and she told me how she trembled from fear and pain, afraid he would be angry with her for disobeying. He stroked her coat gently and took off his shirt, wrapping it around her cut to stop the bleeding, and secured it with his belt. He told her firmly that she couldn't go with him, that he had to find Nicky and promised to find me too. He told her to go home and pushed her away."

"She tried to follow him, and each time she did he would shout at her and push her away. Finally, he picked up a piece of driftwood and threatened her with it. She knew then he was serious, and the look on his face was enough to send her running back over the dunes to the house. She squeezed through an opening in the garage wall and cowered there, waiting for him to return. He never did."

"He didn't forget about her!" Carolyn gasped. "He didn't just leave her, did he?"

"No," Magic replied. "He simply disappeared. Many people believe he drowned in the storm surge."

"That's just awful!"

"My mother always felt that if Nicky had listened to his parents, that tragedy would never have happened. She used to explain it to me by saying that things always happen for a reason, and even though things may seem terrible at the time, there's always a life lesson buried in them somewhere. Unfortunately, sometimes you can live a lifetime and never understand the reasons why things happen, and it's difficult to forgive yourself when you know you could have done things differently."

"Did Savannah have any regrets?" Carolyn asked. "It must have been hard for her to leave Nicky's father alone out there."

"If she did, she never let on," the old dog replied. "She was devoted to him and was devastated to learn he was missing. She would spend afternoons sitting on the dunes watching for him, always hoping he would come back. It was hard for her to believe he had disappeared without a trace. His body was never found," he added sadly.

"So what happened to you and Nicky?"

"We were stuck in the middle of a hurricane with nowhere to go. We were too far from home to risk making it back safely. In fact," he added, "we couldn't even see where home was anymore."

"We took shelter in the abandoned lighthouse way down the beach. On sunny days we had played inside of it, and now it was our only protection as the winds grew stronger and the rain began to pound us."

"It was the Cape Hatteras lighthouse — a massive brick tower that soared into the sky. The lighthouse was old and it smelled like fuel oil and dampness. Large cracks spidered their way up to the topmost bricks, and many of the high, narrow windows at the top had been broken long before we made it our playground. The view from the top was dizzying, especially for a young pup." Magic's eyes grew bright with the memory.

"I'll never forget how the lighthouse shuddered and swayed in the storm. Nicky held me close as the storm raged. I remember feeling the warmth of his skin through his wet clothes and hearing the pounding of his heart."

"At one point water began to seep in from under the doors, and we knew it wouldn't be long before it soaked the floor we sat on. Nicky set me down and began to climb the rusted spiral staircase. He called for me to follow, and even though I was terribly afraid, I followed behind him. He didn't quite make it to the landing when a part of the staircase gave way." Magic flinched, remembering the sound of metal twisting and breaking.

"Nicky fell, hitting his head against the railing. It left a nasty gash that bled a lot. I was shocked to see it happen, and never having seen blood like that before, I was certain he'd been killed."

A drop of water that could have been rain or a tear ran down the old Basenji's cheek. "I hurried to him, frightened of what I might see. Blood covered his head, and it was on his face and in his hair. Luckily he was still breathing, and he moaned when I licked his wound. It was a deep cut, and it wouldn't stop bleeding."

"The lighthouse was dark, and I was distraught because Nicky had hurt himself. Fear settled in my heart — the dark sort of fear that comes from deep inside, when you suddenly realize you're helpless." He leaned against Carolyn's leg.

"I'll never forget the howling of the wind, and how it hurt my ears when it blew through the windows and whistled through the holes in the staircase. I get the same feeling when I hear a siren on a police car or an ambulance. The only way I can stop the hurt is to howl, and that's what I did."

Carolyn rubbed Magic's head gently, trying to imagine the fear he had faced while still a puppy. "What happened then?" she asked. "I don't know what I would've done!"

Magic continued. "I thought my howling would bring someone to help us. I hoped someone would hear me above the storm and know where we were. And, I desperately wanted to stop the sound in my ears and drown out the storm."

He pulled away from Carolyn's hand, and hung his head sadly. "I wish Nicky's father had heard me," he said, his voice heavy with regret. "I used to wonder if it would have made a difference if I had been just a little bit older or louder. Maybe then he would have found us instead of getting lost and dying the way he did. He didn't hear me, he couldn't hear me! But do you know that other creatures did?"

"Two small rabbits, soaked right through from the rain, squeezed their way under the rusted, old lighthouse doors. They stopped on the stairs just above the damp floor, twitching in fright when they saw us. I could tell they were thinking better of their decision to use the lighthouse to escape the storm. They were sniffing the air, smelling Nicky's blood."

"'We heard your voice,' the larger of the two rabbits said slowly, looking at me with unblinking eyes. 'Your voice carried far into the storm, and we thought it would be safe here.' His accent was strange to me, but his words were clear enough and I managed to understand them."

"I assured them they were safe, although it was against my very Basenji nature. Any other day I would have wanted to chase them, but the hurricane was raging all around us and we were in great danger. It was no time for playing."

"I remember the wind howling again, and when it did, so did I." Magic continued. "The lighthouse doors shook terribly, then flew open as a windblown pony pushed her way through them. A strong gust of wind caught the heavy doors, slamming them behind her with such a loud crash it made the lighthouse shudder."

"The pony regarded the rabbits, me, and Nicky with her ears pricked forward. 'If the rabbits feel safe here,' she said before I could speak, 'Then I think it's safe for me, too. You have quite a voice.' She shook the rain from her chestnut coat and moved to the wall opposite the door. From there she stared at Nicky, who was moaning and calling out for his mother. 'Poor thing,' she murmured, stretching her neck to get a better look. 'It looks bad for him.' She pawed at the ground, disturbed by the blood. 'Did you do this?' she asked me."

"'No,' I told her. 'He fell from up there.' I gestured at the staircase, and she craned her head up to sniff at the broken place."

"So many times through that terrible hurricane the wind howled and I howled with it. Other creatures heard my voice over the storm and followed it to the shelter of the lighthouse." Magic sighed. "By the time the eye of the storm passed over, it was getting crowded in there. Several shorebirds, a red fox, three house cats, and some other creatures I never learned the names of had joined our sanctuary."

"They all had voices, strange voices unlike any I'd ever heard before. Some of the shorebirds had such unusual speech that I never understood a word they said. The ones I was able to understand told me they'd heard my voice and said my howling had led them to safety in the lighthouse. They were grateful, and thanked me for saving their lives."

Magic paused, watching the storm clouds race across the rainy sky. "All those animals heard me," he said sadly. "They got to safety — but Nicky's father didn't. I've always felt partly to blame, because I should have known better than to go out with Nicky in a storm."

He rested his head on his paws. "Because Nicky couldn't hear me the way you do, he got hurt." He turned away from Carolyn, and trembled with the dampness in his coat.

"When the eye of the hurricane passed over, it got very quiet. I took advantage of the stillness and howled several more times. Some men who had gone out looking for us and Nicky's father heard me then, and they found us in the lighthouse."

"I'll never forget the looks of amazement and shock on their faces as they stared at the incredible sight of all those animals who were in there with us. The men took Nicky away, and I ran after them, not wanting to let him out of my sight. He recovered, but they said he'd always have a scar just above his eye from the fall. Everyone praised me and told me how brave I was for staying with Nicky during the storm, but I didn't feel like much of a hero when I learned that his father had been lost."

"I couldn't get over it," Magic continued. "And so I ran away, thinking that I could find him and bring him back, and then I'd be able to live with myself. I didn't get far before some people found me and brought me back. Eventually I was sold, and that was just fine by me." He stood and paced restlessly. "After I was sold, I never saw my mother alive again, or Nicky either. I thought no one wanted me around because I reminded them that Nicky's father was dead."

"But it wasn't your fault," Carolyn said. "He went out in the storm to find his son. It was a chance he took."

Magic stopped pacing and regarded her with tear-filled eyes. "Even so, I couldn't stand the guilt. Maybe they never even thought to blame me. If they blamed anyone, it was Nicky, because he'd wandered off when he was told not to. But I blamed myself because I didn't do what any good dog would have done. I should have gone out in that storm and found Nicky's father, and led him to the lighthouse. I guess I was too young and didn't know better."

"I think you found your answer right there." Carolyn scooped the old dog up into her arms and held him close, smelling dampness in his coat. He felt surprisingly light, reminding her of her grandfather when she was small and he was very old and frail, like a little bird. "Maybe you couldn't save him," she said, feeling the old dog tremble with a chill. "But you saved Nicky, and you did help those other animals. You've got nothing to feel bad about. You were too young to know any better, and it was out of your control."

"It's taken me many years to realize that," Magic said, leaning his head against her shoulder. "But there was no one to talk to, no one I could tell. Except you." He sneezed and raised a paw to his eye, rubbing it hard. "It still makes me sad sometimes. That's life, isn't it?"

Carolyn smiled. "That's life, alright. Now, let's dry you off and get you something to eat. This weather is nothing close to being a hurricane, but I think it might be a good idea to wait until the rain lets up before moving on."

EIGHTEEN

MAGIC SLEPT FOR SEVERAL HOURS before he awoke to a partly sunny afternoon. Telling his story of the hurricane had brought back troubling memories, but when he saw the sun shining it made him feel better about himself.

"There's always sun after the rain," his mother used to say. "Just wait and you'll see."

Carolyn heard him stir, and glanced up from her book to see him stretch and yawn.

"Hello, sleepy dog," she said, squinting

because the sun was behind him.

"I needed a good sleep," he said, moving away from the window and hopping to the floor. He lapped at some water she'd put down for him, then jumped into the driver's seat, hitting the horn with his paw. "Ready to go?" he asked.

"Sure," Carolyn replied, setting her book on the bed. "If you're ready."

With a yodel Magic jumped up on the bed, making Carolyn laugh as he pounced on her.

"Hey!" She giggled as he play-bowed and grabbed at the sheets with his mouth. Before she could stop him he was on top of the table in the eating area of the motorhome, giving the book he'd snatched from the bed a good swift shake.

"Bleah!" he spat out the book. "Tastes terrible!" His tongue moved quickly in and out of his mouth several times. "Not at all like the tissues at your parents' house!" There was a mischievous gleam in his eyes, and Carolyn laughed again.

"What would you know about tissues at my parents' house?" she asked.

He almost told her about the little present he'd left behind their sofa at Christmastime, but at the last minute he decided against it. He hopped off the table and into the passenger's seat of the motorhome. "Let's get rolling!" he yodeled.

"Crazy dog!" Carolyn said. "You are one silly, crazy dog!"

The mountains were green and freshly washed by rain, and their beauty was magnified by the brilliance of the sun that shone down between fluffy white clouds. In the distance, a rainbow appeared, vivid transparent colors arcing across the sky until the sun disappeared behind a small cloud. The rainbow reappeared moments later, then slowly faded into thin air as the fog dissipated.

A sporty red sedan with a blonde driver and an equally blonde Afghan sped past the motorhome as the road climbed higher into the mountains. The windows were down on the sedan, and the Afghan's hair was being tousled by the wind.

"Oh, he'll regret that!" Magic chuckled. "I've known Afghans, and when they get all tangled up, they're an awful mess!"

"Since when did you become the expert on Afghans?" Carolyn asked, raising an eyebrow.

"I've been to a few dog shows in my time," Magic said proudly. "Don't forget, I am a champion!"

The sedan disappeared over a hill, and with it the soon-to-be-if-not-already tangled Afghan. "I wouldn't mind seeing a dog show," Carolyn said. "I've never been to one."

"Really?" Magic's ears perked up, and his nose twitched. "Oh, you'd really enjoy a show," he said excitedly.

"When I was much younger," he began, "I heard my new people talk so often about how beautiful they thought I was, that I really began to believe it. Oh, you should have seen me strutting around the place, my tail curled tightly, my ears straight up and forward. I knew my coat glistened in the sunlight. All I had to do was strike a pose and the people would get all excited. I was beautiful then, and I was loving it."

"My first show was when I was only six months old. My people had hired a woman named Lydia to be my handler. She taught me how to walk in the show ring, and helped me become comfortable with the table." Magic chuckled. "What they sometimes call 'stand for examination.'"

"The table was the only thing I really didn't like — that's where the judge would put his hands all over me and look into my mouth to see my teeth, and then he'd reach around behind me and make sure I had all my parts. Really, that's what they do!" Magic snorted. "You'd think they could simply look, but no, they've got to go sticking their hands back there!"

"At any rate I simply adored Lydia. There wasn't a thing I

wouldn't do for her. She rewarded me often with the wonderful bits of boiled liver that she kept in her pockets." Magic licked his muzzle appreciatively at the memory. "Lydia always had liver in her pockets for me."

"I did very well at my first show. There were only two other dogs in my class, which at that time was the puppy class. I remember my people and several others I didn't even know making quite a fuss over my first blue ribbon. I got to live at Lydia's house after that, and she worked with me every day and took me to shows on the weekends. I collected more blue ribbons than I could even count, and everywhere I went people would admire me and tell me how wonderful I was." Magic puffed out his chest proudly.

"It wasn't long before things began to change. Where once the other handlers were kind and happy to see me, the more times I won, the angrier they all became. It really began to bother me. I didn't know why they all started to hate me — and believe me, it was hate I saw in their eyes and faces, and in the looks they would throw my way."

"If they were trying to shake my confidence, they certainly did. I missed the applause I used to get when I won a class or took a point. It saddened me to think that when I was on top of the world, people could be so mean and cruel, and make me wish I'd never been in the show ring at all. I easily finished my championship, but as time went on, strange things began to happen."

"At first it was nothing more than a terrible stomachache I had after a show one day. Lydia simply attributed it to a bad batch of liver, but I knew it wasn't her liver that had made me so sick." Magic sighed. "There were other things, little things, like handlers jostling me as I waited outside the ring. People would deliberately rush by me going very fast and bringing their dogs too close just to get me angry."

"If Lydia saw all this she did her best to ignore it, because I'm sure she chalked it up to the politics of the show ring. I remember her telling a friend — one of the few true friends she had — that she was incredibly pleased with me. She said I was beautiful and successful — everything she wasn't." Magic snorted.

"Imagine how that made me feel, to learn that even my handler envied me! Right then and there I vowed to put an end to the matter once and for all. Showing wasn't fun for me anymore."

"The solution came to me one evening when we were on the road. It was quite simple, really. I don't know why I didn't think of it before, but I had been happy in the show ring up until then. All I had to do was something I'd been wanting to do for quite some time."

"Anyway, at the next show the judge was going over me, and rather roughly I might add, I waited until he reached around toward my backside and that's when I made my move. Mind you, I didn't bite him, but I did growl and snap."

"That was enough to get me thrown out of the ring, disqualified. Since I was already a champion they couldn't take that away from me. However, my disqualification shocked and embarrassed Lydia terribly. Rather than take any more chances with me, she quietly retired me from the show ring and sent me back to the kennel. After that I didn't see Lydia again, and there was no more liver, but at last I was away from the people who didn't like me."

A worried look crossed Magic's face. "Don't get me wrong, though. Showing was pure pleasure for me. I was beautiful and I knew it. I liked nothing better than an outdoor show in early summer or late fall, when the morning air was still clean and fresh, and the sunlight would make my coat shimmer. It's just that people had to come along and spoil it, and there wasn't a thing I could do about it, except quit."

"Success can be tough," Carolyn said when he finished.

"Although, I can't help but wonder why someone isn't looking for you, or missing you? A champion Basenji must be pretty valuable to someone."

Magic turned and stared out the window. "Yes," he acknowledged. "Maybe someone would have wanted me back years ago, but now I'm too old to be much use anymore. Anyone who might have been looking for me would have given up a long time ago," he sighed.

"Being old doesn't make you any less of a dog," Carolyn said. "Why would you think no one would want you?" She paused, remembering that he'd been in the shelter, abandoned and unwanted. "I'm sorry," she said. "I guess I don't understand people sometimes."

"No one would want me now," Magic said sadly. "I've been away too long, and that part of my life is over. Besides," he added, "I like being with you."

"And I like being with you," Carolyn said, reaching over to rub his head. "I hope you'll never forget that I wanted you, and I always will. If we do find your home, and for some reason you don't want to stay, you can always come back home with me." There was hope in her voice that the old dog couldn't miss. "You'll always be welcome here."

"But I'm taking you home," Carolyn said. "That's what this trip is all about." There was hope in her voice that Magic couldn't miss. "I mean, if we get there and you don't want to stay, you can always come home with me."

"That's good to know," Magic replied. "I won't forget that."

For a while neither said a word. The miles rolled past and the sun moved across the sky, making the black ribbon of highway beneath them shimmer in the summer heat.

Carolyn played with the tuner on the radio, and found a station that promised a long stretch of fine summer weather and some good music. "What was your show name again?" she asked suddenly. "I'd like to hear you say it."

"Champion Windswept of Hatteras," came the proud reply. "But my people called me Blaze."

"It suits you," she said with a smile. "You were the blaze that burned up the show rings."

Magic didn't say any more, but she could tell he was pleased.

Nineteen

"**I** CAN'T BELIEVE HOW MUCH FUEL this vehicle takes!" Carolyn moaned. "I don't know how people who travel this way all the time can afford it."

They were at a gas station in Virginia, tanking up the endlessly hungry motorhome. The day had become unbearably humid and hot, the sun bright in a hazy white sky.

"Fifty-one dollars!" Her eyes widened at the numbers on the gas pump. Exasperated, she fished around in her purse and pulled out a credit card. "How do you like that!"

"I've never understood the thing with money," Magic admitted, reflecting on the times he'd been bought and sold. Hands had exchanged money then, but for some reason no money had been exchanged when Carolyn bailed him out of the shelter back in December.

"Well, to tell you the truth, sometimes I wonder about it myself." Carolyn held the credit card in her teeth. She pulled out a squeegee from a small bucket above the gas pump, and shook the water from it. "This should get the windshield clean," she said, scrubbing the windshield. Peering at the glass, she giggled. "Doesn't look much cleaner, does it? I'll pay for the gas and be right back." She headed towards the cashier, leaving Magic alone in the motorhome.

He hung his head out the window, resting his paws comfortably on the sill. All around him, the gas station was a flurry of noise and activity. He watched with some amusement as a large bald man with a cigar dangling from his mouth fueled an even larger Cadillac. The buttons on his too-small shirt screamed from the strain of holding the front closed, threatening to pop with each breath he took. From inside the car, his equally large wife squalled at him to get rid of the cigar, or at least, to put the darn thing out.

"You'll blow us all sky high!" she sputtered, shaking a fleshy finger at him through the window. "You'll blow this whole place to bits!"

"Yeah, yeah," her husband replied. He smiled broadly when he noticed Magic staring at him. The man rolled his eyes, clearly telling the old Basenji he thought his wife was nuts.

Across the way a family in a minivan waited for a gas pump to open up. A young Basset hound had its head hanging out from one of the open windows, slobbering down one side of the car from the heat. It saw Magic and woofed softly until a small boy pulled the dog's head inside and rolled up the window.

Magic's nose worked the air, catching the Basset's scent, discovering that it was a female as he'd guessed, although the strangeness of her scent told him she'd been spayed. He called out to her, curious to find out who she was and where she was going, but she couldn't hear him through the closed windows.

Magic sighed and laid his head on his paws, actively scanning the remainder of the vehicles for another dog to talk to. The acrid odor of gasoline hung heavy in the humid air, mixing with the smell of vehicle exhaust and the rubbery-hot smell of the highway. It was the highway scent that stirred a memory within him, carrying his thoughts back to a time long, long ago when he was a show dog.

He was young then, and lucky enough to have had the opportunity to travel. Letting the recollection overtake him, he closed his eyes, picturing a different gas station in a different town, one of the many he'd seen during his show career. Before long he was in a different vehicle, and there was Lydia, chattering happily to him as he waited for her, watching as she filled the car with gas . . .

"Hey, sleepyhead!" Carolyn's voice startled him, making him jump. His eyes flew open, half expecting to see Lydia standing there, but relieved to see Carolyn smiling at him. He wagged his tail sheepishly at her.

"I wasn't sleeping," he explained. "Only remembering."

"Hmmm." She turned the ignition key and the motorhome roared to life. Moments later they were back on the road again.

They drove in silence for a while, enjoying the view. Heat danced and shimmered on the road ahead of them, making mirage puddles appear in the distance. Late summer wildflowers bloomed brightly in roadside meadows, attracting fat bumblebees to their very centers. High in the sky a lone hawk soared on a breeze, searching for a wayward mouse or mole brave enough to venture above ground. The old Basenji took in all these sights, his eyes catching even the slightest movements and bringing them rapidly into focus. There was so much to see, and he wanted very much to see it all.

"Being on the road reminds me of Max," Carolyn said suddenly. She stared straight ahead, her green eyes hidden behind dark sunglasses. There was an edge to her voice, and Magic heard it clearly.

"I'd like you to tell me about him," he said quietly. "You've never told me his story." He held his breath and waited, afraid that she wouldn't continue. In all the months they'd been together, she'd only mentioned the dog in passing, for his memory seemed too painful for her to recall. Magic had refrained from asking too many questions, as it was the one subject that Carolyn had drawn an invisible line at and declared off limits.

"When I was a little girl, more than anything else in the world, I wanted a dog." Carolyn accelerated and moved the motorhome out to pass a slow-moving truck. "But, of course, my mother didn't want one around, and my father wasn't about to argue with her." She adjusted the rearview mirror, and reached over to pet Magic. Her hand was sweaty, and he licked it impulsively, tasting the saltiness.

"I can't imagine why," he snorted. "Your mother seemed to like me, alright!" He chuckled, remembering how the woman had made no effort to hide her disapproval. "What could make a person hate dogs, aside from a really bad experience? I've known a few bad dogs in my day, but for the most part, no dog is ever truly out to harm anyone!" Magic chuckled again. "I don't think your mother would stand still for it, at any rate."

"Well, I'm not exactly sure what happened," Carolyn admitted. "I think I remember my uncle — that's Andie's dad — telling me they'd had a dog when they were growing up. It was a little black and white dog, a Boston Terrier, I think, that my mother loved more than anything. Apparently the house caught fire and the dog was killed, and after that my mother wanted nothing to do with dogs again."

"That's a long time," Magic said, "to hang on to something like that."

"Sometimes, if you've been hurt badly enough, you avoid situations where you think you'll be hurt again," Carolyn explained.

Magic knew what she meant. The experience of being a young puppy caught in a hurricane had changed his life dramatically, in a way he never would have imagined. Losing Violet had been difficult, too, even though he knew she had gone to the Happiness.

"I can't promise you that the journey of life will be an easy one," his mother had told him on the day he was sold. "But if you believe in yourself, you will find strength you never thought you had. My thoughts will always be with you as they are with the rest of the pups. No matter where I'll be, I'll never forget you."

"At any rate," Carolyn continued, breaking into his thoughts, "getting a dog was simply out of the question." She flipped her hair back behind her shoulder, and glanced out the side window.

"Do you know that when Andie was ten she got a puppy for her birthday? Boy, let me tell you, was I ever jealous." She smiled ruefully at Magic. "When *my* tenth birthday rolled around later that year, I spent all my time hoping and praying that I'd be lucky enough to get a puppy too." Her voice grew quiet. "When that day came, there was no puppy. What I got was a new bike."

"I spent that entire day wondering if maybe my parents were keeping the puppy back as a surprise for me! I figured they were waiting for just the right moment and would bring it out when I wasn't expecting it." She paused, thinking. "I went to bed that night still expecting a puppy to show up at the last minute. Needless to say, none ever did."

Magic's brow furrowed, and he brought a paw to his cheek. He rubbed his face a couple of times and then sniffed his paw. In his mind he saw a sad little girl in a party dress with a new bike, looking eagerly around at her presents, hoping to see the one she wanted more than anything. Then he saw her crying, alone in the darkness of her bedroom, realizing that her one real birthday wish hadn't — and wouldn't — come true. The cruelness of the images saddened and confused him. Clearly Carolyn's parents didn't understand their daughter's special wish for happiness. And, Magic had to believe they'd been disappointed when she didn't seem to like her gifts.

Sadness all around, he thought. *Why do people do that to each other?*

"Andie and I were always close," Carolyn continued, "so it wasn't long before Andie and I made a simple arrangement. I let her ride the bike whenever she wanted, and she shared her puppy with me."

"He was an Irish Setter she named Lyric. Having Lyric around was like having another best friend. He never judged me, never told me I was wrong for being who I was. He simply accepted me and loved me, no matter what." She could still see his fiery auburn coat, and remembered the silky softness of his flowing ears.

"We had a lot of fun together. Andie would take my bike and ride up to the corner store, and I would take Lyric for walks or teach him tricks. It was almost like having a dog of my own, but I knew that when nighttime came, he'd be right at the foot of Andie's bed." Carolyn sighed. "All I had to keep me company was the stuffed toy cat my parents gave me one Christmas." She snorted. "Even when they gave me stuffed animals, they didn't give me dogs."

"Anyway," she continued, "the moment I moved out and got my own place, one of the first things I bought for my new apartment wasn't a microwave or a TV set, although I really needed both those things. No," she smiled. "The first thing I bought for myself was a puppy — a Golden Retriever."

"Max?" Magic asked, knowing it was, but wanting to hear her say the words.

"Max," came the reply. "His registered name was Starlite's Maximum Thunder, but to me, he was just plain Max."

Magic thought of his own registered name, and wondered if anyone besides himself would ever remember what it was. It occurred to him that Carolyn would always remember, and he hoped it would be with the same fondness as she remembered Max's.

"I was careful about choosing the right dog," Carolyn continued. "I went to several breeders, called around, scoured the newspapers and pet stores, and did all my homework. I bought leashes, collars, food bowls, a sweater and a bed — everything for the dog, but without having found him yet."

Carolyn laughed. "I was like Andie when she was expecting her first kid. Planning and preparing, obsessing over every detail. I wanted everything to be just perfect."

She reached over and rubbed Magic's neck where he'd told her his collar was beginning to pinch. "I found a breeder up in Baraga County, Michigan who had advertised Golden Retriever puppies in a magazine, and that's who I got Max from. I can't explain how I knew I was going to come home with a dog that weekend, but it just seemed right."

"So, I drove up to Baraga," she continued. "It was late in April, and spring was just beginning to take hold. I made a long weekend of it, all by myself. I wanted my first dog to be special, to be my best friend the moment he laid eyes on me. I didn't want Andie to tag along, because I was afraid he'd like her better or something. I know it sounds silly," she added, "but everyone — every dog — likes Andie! I just wanted it to be really special. I don't know, but in a way I had this little girl expectation of something magical happening between us. Like we'd both know when we saw each other that it was always meant to be."

"Love at first sight?" Magic asked.

"Exactly," Carolyn agreed. "I imagined it would be love at first sight."

"Was it?"

She smiled. "I believe it was," she said. "The funny part was, I needn't have worried at all. It was a blur, like a dream that happens so fast you can't remember all the details except the really important ones."

"Life is that way," Magic added. "It goes by so fast, and before you know it, you're old, looking back and wondering about the meaning of it all."

Carolyn removed her sunglasses and looked at him. "Being old isn't so bad," she said. "You've got a lot of wonderful stories to tell, and you've been so many places. It's when you're young that you don't take the time to 'smell the roses' as they say."

"So Max was young when you found him?" Magic asked. "What was he like, back then?"

A smile crept across Carolyn's face. "He was really neat. I saw him come toddling out of a pack of seven or eight puppies, and he made a beeline right for me, just like I'd always imagined he would." Her face took on a far away, dreamy look. "That little guy put his paws right up on my shirt, and covered my face with slobbery kisses."

"I'd never seen such dark eyes, nor felt such a soft coat. And he smelled so incredibly wonderful!" Carolyn breathed deeply, as if she could still smell the puppy-sweet smell. "He was perfect. Have you ever smelled how fresh puppies are when they've been playing outside on a spring day?"

"Yes," Magic answered, remembering how wonderful Violet's puppies had smelled. "You never forget that," he added.

Carolyn glanced over at Magic, who was smiling at his own long-forgotten memory of being in a new home with new people who showered him with love and dog cookies. Being new was a fine thing to be, he decided. Everyone always loved the new dog. But being old and being loved just the same, was something even more incredible. He realized Carolyn had started talking again, and he tried to concentrate on what she was saying.

"The ride home was long, but Max slept most of the way. We stopped a couple of times, because he was just a puppy, and it was such a pretty afternoon. I wish I had owned a camera then, because the day was as perfect a spring day as you could've ever asked for."

"Max was so silly with his puppy antics, running through the grass and tugging at dandelions. He would play for a while, then stop right in his tracks and smile at me, like I was his whole world." Carolyn smiled.

"That little puppy, who I had just taken from his brothers and sisters and mother, he didn't fret or complain or even act like he was missing them. For Max, life was an adventure that he really seemed to enjoy, and he was enjoying it with me."

She grew quiet a moment, brushing some stray hairs off her face, tucking the strands behind her ears.

"It was a dream come true," she said softly. "All my life I had waited for the day when I had a puppy in my life. And it really was like a dream, because everything worked out. No problems, nothing. Heck, I didn't even get lost on the ride up there!" She smiled sadly, taking a deep breath before continuing.

"And I raised him, helped him grow, took care of him, and did all those silly puppy things with him. We went to puppy preschool, to some basic obedience classes, and we always went to the park. Max loved the park. Especially the squirrels."

At the mention of the word "squirrels," Magic's ears perked up. Suddenly alert, his eyes stared out the windshield, looking around out the windows, and then back out the windshield. He relaxed momentarily, and Carolyn giggled. "Sorry," she said. "You weren't listening?"

"I *was* listening," he insisted. "I was imagining what you were telling me, and seeing it in my mind."

"Anyway," she continued, "Max and I were together for almost two years before he began to get sick. At first it was little things — things that, if they would have happened much later in his life, I would have attributed to his simply getting old." She lowered her voice. "I knew that it couldn't be that, though, because he was still so very young."

The hazy summer sky had grown dark with heavy thunderstorm clouds. A light drizzle coated the windshield, and Carolyn flipped a switch, turning on the windshield wipers. She and Magic followed them as they moved across the glass, mesmerized by the rhythm. The expression on Carolyn's face darkened as the sky above them darkened, and it wasn't long before the drizzle became a steadier rain.

"At first Max became picky with his food, and didn't want to run or go for walks as much. He began to mope around, and he slept a lot. It was easy to tell he wasn't feeling well." She wiped a tear from her eye.

"The vet checked him out and discovered that he had cancer, and it was slowly killing him." Her eyes began to tear up even more. Frantically, she searched the highway signs for a rest area to pull into.

"Max was dying, and there wasn't a whole lot I could do for him." She pulled the motorhome off the road onto the shoulder, and turned on the hazard flashers.

Pouring rain beat down on the motorhome. Angry streaks of white-hot lightning flashed across the sky, and in the distance, a sudden clap of thunder made them both jump, startled.

"The vet had me take Max up to the university — they've got

a really good veterinary college. She said they might be able to do much more for him than she could."

Carolyn was crying freely now, tears running down her cheeks. "The vets at the college explained that maybe they could save Max, but the treatment would be long and extremely expensive. They told me they couldn't guarantee anything." She leaned close to Magic when he put his paw gently on her arm.

"I was faced with a terrible decision," She continued, burying her face in the top of the old dog's head. He felt her warm tears wetting his fur.

"They told me I had to make the decision. I could either try to save Max's life or not. The vets, they weren't promising a cure! They told me the odds were so small, and Max was suffering. I couldn't look into his eyes without seeing pain staring back."

Carolyn cried, her breath coming in gasps. Magic leaned into her, comforting her as best he could.

"It's okay," he murmured, not knowing what else to say. "What did you do?"

"The only thing I could do. I had no choice."

Magic stared into her tear-filled eyes, frightened by the haunting sadness he saw there. He was reminded of the look he'd seen in Violet's eyes when her puppies were taken away — helpless, afraid, suddenly alone.

Carolyn found a tissue and blew her nose loudly. "Oh, I knew Max loved me and wanted to stay with me, but he couldn't keep fighting his pain." She blew her nose again, and sniffed.

"I couldn't afford to pay for the treatments, and of course there was no way I could ask my parents to help. Andie was just expecting her second son at the time, and couldn't spare any money either, although I know she would have given me everything if I had asked."

Rain pounded the motorhome, obscuring the outside world behind flowing sheets of water. Carolyn held Magic tightly as he leaned into her, supporting her, until she found her voice again.

"I had to end Max's suffering," Carolyn whispered. "It wasn't an easy decision, but it was the only thing I could do for Max that would set him free."

"All my life I dreamed of what it would be like, owning a dog. Max was the one bright star in my life, and I wanted to love and care for him and make his life as happy as he'd made mine. Sure, I knew that someday he would grow old and die, but never in my wildest dreams would I ever have imagined it would be so soon."

"When I knew there was no other choice, I held Max in my arms and told him what we had to do. I told him I wanted to ease his pain, but that it meant that he'd have to be put to sleep." Her voice trembled. "I think he understood, and I believe he was ready to go. Even knowing that, I wasn't ready to let him go. I put it off hoping for a miracle, but none ever came."

"I held him as he died," Carolyn continued in a whisper. "I held him as the vet gave him the injection, and I held him as his beautiful golden body went limp. I held him for the longest time after that, until he grew cold."

"The vet took him away and had his body cremated. A day later, she gave him back to me in a box, a box so incredibly small that I couldn't believe he was really in there! For a long time I didn't believe it, I didn't want to admit he was gone."

"Do you realize," she continued, "that I would get up at night to get a drink of water or to check the lock on the door, and I would move carefully and slowly so I wouldn't disturb Max as he was sleeping next to me — even though he wasn't there?"

"I'd go to bed, and it would be empty and cold, and I would cry because he was gone and it was my own decision that had made it so. I would tell myself that if I had the money, he'd have gotten better. I hated myself for not asking my parents for money and for not taking a second job to pay for his treatments. If I had, maybe he'd still be here with me."

"You made the right choice," Magic said quietly. "You gave Max what he needed and wanted. Nobody but you could have done that for him, and you did it because you loved him." He moved as close to Carolyn as his safety harness would allow. "There's something you need to know."

"You see," he said, burying his head in her embrace. "When dogs die, only their bodies stop living. Their dog-spirit lives on — always." He gazed intently into Carolyn's eyes. "When I was a pup, my mother explained to me that life and death are journeys we all take."

"All dogs who are loved by someone, sometime, become dog-spirits," he continued. "Wherever they were the happiest, wherever they were loved the most, they always go back and visit, and even stay awhile. It's what I was telling you quite some time ago," he said. "We never leave the ones we've loved."

"Sometimes, if you feel a gentle breeze on an otherwise still day, or when you feel a bit of warmth by your side late at night and think it was only a dream, know that Max is with you, watching over you, and loving you." Magic placed his paw on Carolyn's hand, watching as she took in his words.

"It's the truth," he told her. "Dog-spirits are all around us, everywhere. They come and go, and are always nearby when they're needed."

Tears of happiness formed in Magic's eyes. "Max is a dog-spirit; but he'd been held back because of your love for him," he explained. "Sometimes you can love someone so much, that you don't think you can ever let them go. Max, he's grateful for what you've given him, the freedom he has now." He pulled away from Carolyn's embrace, and placed his paws on her shoulders.

"You've done something wonderful by telling me about Max, by talking about him and by telling me his story, and you don't even realize how important doing so was! You've set him free, and that's the most wonderful gift you could ever have given him!" Excitement was in the old Basenji's voice, and he wagged his tail in appreciation. "You've set him free, Carolyn," he said. "You've given his dog-spirit true freedom!"

As Magic's words sunk in, the realization of what she'd done crept slowly over Carolyn, then washed over her like a wave. In her heart the loneliness and pain she'd felt for so long had lightened since the old dog had been in her life, and the feeling of relief that ran through her with his words helped ease her guilt over Max's death.

"Is he here now?" she asked. "If only I could've talked to him the way I talk to you, just one time . . ." her voice trailed off.

"He's not here, now," Magic replied. "He's free to come and go as he pleases. I imagine he'll be around often enough," he added, licking tears from Carolyn's face.

A rapid knocking at the window made them both jump. Carolyn turned to see a police officer, wet from the rain, peering at her through the glass, looking very concerned. When she glanced into the rearview mirror, she saw his patrol car pulled up on the shoulder behind her. Embarrassed, she looked out at the officer, and noticed that he was standing in a puddle.

"Is everything alright, ma'am?" The officer took off his glasses. "Are you having engine trouble?"

Carolyn lowered her window and smiled at him. "Everything is okay," she said. "Uh, my dog's safety belt snapped open, and I just pulled over to fasten it again."

The officer regarded her red, tear-stained face with mild curiosity. "A safety belt on a dog?"

"Sure," Carolyn said. "I figure, if they're good for people, then they must be good for dogs too. Don't you agree?"

"Sure, I guess so. Say, what kind of a dog is that?"

"Really, as if he'd never seen a Basenji before!" Magic retorted.

It was all Carolyn could do not to giggle. "He's a Basenji," she said. "It's an African breed of dog."

"One of those barkless dogs, eh?" The officer smiled and put his glasses back on. "Is it true what they say, that those dogs really don't bark?"

"It's true," Carolyn nodded.

"Really? Never at all?"

"Never."

On cue, Magic let out a short snarf that sounded very much like a bark.

"That sure sounded like a bark to me!" The officer winked. "Okay then, if you're sure you're alright, you might want to move along. With all this rain, the shoulder is sure to be soft, and we don't need you getting stuck out here. Drive safely, ma'am."

They both breathed a sigh of relief when he was finally gone.

"Shall we hit the road again?" Carolyn asked. "North Carolina is calling!"

Magic agreed that they should, but begged her to let him go back on the bed and nap for a while as she drove.

"After all," he said stretching as she unfastened the safety belt harness and removed it. "This seat wasn't exactly made for a dog's comfort, was it?"

They stared at each other for a moment.

"Magic?"

"Hmmm?"

"Thanks."

From the bed at the rear of the motorhome, Magic yodeled softly, and settled down for a nap.

TWENTY

"ARE YOU SURE WE'RE IN THE RIGHT
place?" Magic asked anxiously. "Maybe your
map was wrong."

"I'm sure," Carolyn replied, glancing down
at the map. "I don't think we made any turns we
shouldn't have."

"But I don't recognize this place! The road I
remember used to run right along the dunes, over
there!"

The old Basenji stared out the window in
bewilderment as the motorhome rolled into the

town of Kitty Hawk, North Carolina. The two lane highway he remembered as the beach road was just that — a side road that ran along the dunes near the ocean, jammed with tall beach houses built up high on wooden pilings. The five-lane road they were on was a new road, the main artery through a town that had grown considerably in the decade and a half since Magic had been born.

Where vacant dunes had once held scrub brush, sea oats, and shorebirds, now hotels, restaurants and sprawling shopping centers were firmly anchored in blacktop parking lots. The majority of the cars that passed the motorhome sported out-of-state license plates and contained families eager to vacation on the clean, sandy beaches. Four-wheel drive vehicles and convertibles crowded the streets, making it difficult for the few people on bicycles to get by. The only thing Magic recognized was the constant breeze from the ocean that made kites and flags dance in the bright summer sky. He couldn't believe that in the years he'd been gone so much had changed.

As the shock wore off, a gnawing fear started in his belly. Kitty Hawk was so different from what he remembered that it was like seeing it for the first time. What if things were the same all the way down the coast? Perhaps the place where the rabbits lived was long gone! He desperately hoped his home near the Cape Hatteras light was still standing.

"I don't know this place," he said again with a tremble in his voice. *What if I was wrong?* he thought. *What if nothing's the same?* He closed his eyes to shut out the view, settling his head forlornly on the seat.

Carolyn glanced over at him, and placed her hand on his back, feeling tenseness in his body. She'd expected to see excitement in his eyes, and had imagined him eagerly taking in the sights as they became familiar to him. But there he was, with his eyes closed, not wanting to see them at all.

"What's wrong, Magic?" she asked, stroking him gently.

"What's bothering you?"

"It's all so different," he said sadly. "I don't know this place, at all. It's not home!"

"We're just entering Kill Devil Hills," she reassured him. "Remember, we still need to pass through Nags Head, and then Hatteras is down the coast a ways, yet."

"But what if it's all like this?" Magic moaned, opening his eyes and wincing at the sight. "What if it's all built up with houses and stores and big wide roads, and what if there's lots of people? That's not how it used to be," he said. "It used to be different, quiet. You could hear the ocean," he added as they stopped for a traffic light. "All I hear is traffic." He turned a wrinkled, worried brow her way, tears welling up in his dark brown eyes.

"Oh Magic! It's not all like this!" Carolyn pulled out her map, and waved it at him. "Where we're going is National Seashore. When we get there, you'll see how different it is from here. Just have a little faith."

The old dog stared at her sadly, not convinced at all.

They drove for several more miles in silence. Carolyn racked her mind for some way to cheer up her companion. She got her opportunity when they passed through Nags Head.

"Look," she said, pointing to a billboard advertising the Cape Hatteras lighthouse. "That's where we're going. There's nothing but dunes and wildlife sanctuary for miles and miles, and then we come to some little towns. Trust me," she added. "A lot may have changed, but there's a lot they won't ever change."

Magic regarded her with half-closed eyes, wondering if maybe she was right. *After all*, he mused, pawing at his teary eyes. *She's done all the research and gotten all the maps. If something wasn't right, she would have told me. Wouldn't she?*

As Carolyn had promised, the hustle and bustle of Nags Head was soon behind them. The two-lane road they were on wound gently through the thin ribbon of land that stretched south from Nags Head out into the Atlantic Ocean. Its narrow lanes split the island in two, with high dunes on one side and lower marshy areas on the other. Low yaupon trees dotted the landscape, their waxy leaves deep green in the afternoon sun.

As the miles flew by, Magic perked up visibly, placing his paws on the windowsill so he could have a better view. A few times he leaned too far out the window for Carolyn's comfort, and she had to pull him in, afraid he'd tumble out

They stopped for lunch at the Bodie Island lighthouse, and sat enjoying the shade on the cool porch of the old lightkeeper's quarters. The humidity of the day disappeared in the coolness of the constant ocean breeze. Clouds drifted lazily past in the bright blue sky, making the black and white lighthouse appear to sway in the wind. Cicadas sang loudly in the low brush that surrounded the place, and high overhead seagulls called and swooped as they searched for any food the tourists were willing to offer them.

"It sounds rotten," Magic said, eyeing the black and white birds with thinly veiled disgust. "But don't give them anything. They're scavengers, and they won't think twice about dropping a surprise on you."

Carolyn looked up at the gulls, and smiled. "Okay," she said. "Then I suppose I'll just have to throw this bread crust away. I'm not going to eat it anyway!" She moved towards a trash container, and Magic jumped up, tugging at her shirt. "Hey!" she laughed. "What?"

"I'll eat it," he said, knowing full well that he always got the bread crusts from Carolyn's sandwiches. He eyed the tempting morsel in her hand, and licked his muzzle expectantly.

"Now who's a scavenger?" Carolyn chuckled and handed Magic the bread crust, watching in amusement as he wolfed it down greedily. "What makes it good for you but not for them?"

He grinned wickedly, his tongue hanging out in the heat. "I

won't drop a surprise on you!"

Back inside the motorhome, it took Carolyn several tries before the air conditioner was running properly. "There's no place to have it fixed if it breaks," she said. "What do you say we just keep the windows down, and see how it goes?"

"Fine by me," Magic said. "The summer air feels wonderful!"

They drove through the wide, flat expanse of saltwater marsh that was the Pea Island National Wildlife Refuge, past little towns of weathered cedar homes built high up on stilts — towns with names like Rodanthe, Waves, and Salvo. Carolyn had a hard time pronouncing the name of the lifesaving station they passed, and Magic proudly helped her out.

"Chicamacomico," he said slowly, letting the world roll off his tongue, loving the sound of it.

"Chicamacomico," Carolyn finally managed. "What a wonderful word!"

They passed several places where sand from the dunes had drifted onto the road.

"Reminds me of snow," Carolyn remarked. "Only, it's way too warm!"

Heat shimmered on the road and rose in steamy waves making the pavement ahead of them look as if it were wet.

"What we need to do," Magic said eagerly, "is cool off in the ocean."

"I'm up for that," Carolyn replied. "I think we're almost there, look!"

In the shimmering heat of midday, a lighthouse appeared on the horizon, slightly east of the road. At first it was tiny, resembling a birthday candle with black and white stripes spiraling up to the very top. As the miles disappeared beneath them the lighthouse grew larger and larger, prompting Magic to put his paws up on Carolyn's knee, leaning out her window for a better look.

The sight of Cape Hatteras light opened a floodgate of memories and stirred powerful emotions in the old dog. Excitement coursed through him, washing away what remained of his fears. Hardly able to contain his enthusiasm he yodeled loudly, thrilled to finally see the landmark of his island again.

"That's it!" Magic yodeled. "Oh, that's it!" He jumped off her lap and ran in circles inside the motorhome. He came bounding back into his seat, placing his paws on the instrument panel, his tail wagging furiously. "It's still there!" He yodeled again. "The lighthouse is still there!"

I can't believe it, he thought to himself. *I can't believe it! Home!*

"Settle down, already!" Carolyn told him, laughing. "We're here, it's there, and nothing is going to happen to either of us!" She'd never seen the old dog so animated before. Even their walks to the park hadn't held the excitement for him that the first view of the lighthouse did. Her heart swelled with happiness for the little dog who had led her here, bringing tears of joy to her eyes.

The thermometer read 87 degrees when they finally pulled into their oceanside campsite. From where the motorhome was parked they could see and hear the ocean, and much to Magic's delight, the tall spirals of the Cape Hatteras light were visible down the beach.

While Carolyn set up leveling stands beneath the motorhome, Magic trotted around busily, sniffing here and there, unable to get over the amazement of being on Hatteras Island again. Several times he ran down to the water's edge, spun around, and came tearing up the dune like a puppy, a wild look sparkling in his eyes. Out of breath, he rolled in the warm sand, grunting happily, his eyes closed in ecstasy.

"This is the island where I was born!" he told Carolyn, eager for her to follow him over the dunes to the beach. "It's been so long!" He paused for a moment, breathing deeply. She could see his snow-white chest rise and fall as he took in the ocean air, and smiled when she saw the sand in his red coat. "If this is a dream, I don't ever want to wake up."

"It's no dream," Carolyn replied, giving him a playful pinch. "See?" She gave Magic a wicked look. "The last one in the water is a rotten egg!"

After a quick dip in the warm ocean, they walked along the shore, chasing waves and searching for treasures. Carolyn squealed when she found a small conch shell.

"I think I'll keep this," she said happily. "Even though it's got a hole in it, it's the first shell I found on Cape Hatteras."

Tired from the long drive, but refreshed from the ocean and the breeze, they made their way back to a high spot on the beach to dry off.

"This really is a beautiful place," Carolyn said quietly to Magic. "I can see why you missed it so much."

"I can't find the words to tell you how wonderful it is to be here again," he replied, giving himself a good shake. "In some ways, I feel like I've always been here, that all the things that happened in my life were a strange dream and I've only just awakened."

For the longest time they sat together on the beach, at the high point just above the wet sand where the waves could reach their toes occasionally. The sand was warm beneath them, even warmer than the gentle ocean breeze that encircled them, carrying on its soft breath the sounds of shorebirds and children playing. In the distance, the unmistakable black-and-white tower of the Cape Hatteras light soared into the afternoon sky, reaching up to catch the fluffy white clouds as they drifted past.

They watched as sandpipers and surfboarders were replaced by surf fishermen who cast thin, spiderweb-like lines into the waves, hoping to catch something for dinner. Slowly, the sparsely populated beach emptied, until all that remained were Carolyn and Magic, the lighthouse in the distance, and a few brave sandpipers.

"I don't know about you," Carolyn said at last, breaking the spell. "But I'm getting hungry. I'd say it's past our dinnertime, for sure." She smiled at her companion, seeing happiness in his dark eyes and being happy she had helped put it there.

Magic stood and shook the sand from his coat, marveling at how the excursions he'd taken into the shallow, warm water had lifted years from his old body. "I'm ready for dinner," he said at last, pawing at a small ghost crab that scuttled past. "In fact, I'm starving!"

After dinner they sat in front of a small campfire and watched the sun go down over the still waters of Pamlico Sound, a fiery red ball in the western sky that looked as if it should sizzle when it touched the water. One by one, stars filled the night sky as the sun slipped beneath the stillness of the water. Behind them, the ever-present roaring of the ocean competed with the nighttime songs of cicadas and crickets.

"I think I'll leave my guitar in its case tonight," Carolyn said. "I'm enjoying the beach music. Maybe if I listen, I'll be able to figure out what makes it so special. Did you notice all the stars?" she asked. "I'll bet there's a million, trillion wishes up there."

Magic turned his wrinkled face upward, and gasped.

"What is it?" she asked.

"The stars are in their right places," Magic whispered. "I know where I am now. Maybe tomorrow we'll find the old house, and the place where the rabbits live."

"Welcome home, Magic," Carolyn whispered back, pulling the old dog close. She could smell the ocean on him, and when she kissed the top of his head she tasted saltiness in his coat. "Welcome home."

TWENTY-ONE

IT WAS GETTING ON TOWARD NOON, and the hot sun had baked the sand beneath their feet until it was almost impossible to walk on. Magic, proud as he was, decided it was best to let Carolyn carry him across the dune to the blanket she'd spread near the low-tide line. From this vantage point, it was only a small hop to the cool sand at the water's edge.

A few brave tourists lingered in the heat, their children having a grand time in the warm ocean water. From where he sat, Magic could hear their voices carrying on the wind, and they reminded him of Carolyn's summer school class. The ocean beckoned and sparkled in the sunlight, tempting him into the water to cool off.

Earlier, he'd explained to Carolyn that August was the perfect time to swim, for the jellyfish were few and the water was at its warmest. Although the park service newspaper she had picked up warned of hidden underwater currents and strong waves farther off shore, she'd been more worried about the creatures that lived beneath the briny waves. Magic, feeling full of mischief, made it a point to assure her that he'd keep a an eye out for sharks while she swam.

"Sharks?" Carolyn gulped fearfully. "You mean, there might be sharks?"

"Well, maybe," Magic replied. "But it's not likely. What you'll probably see out in the deeper water will be dolphins." He felt guilty for frightening her, and he hoped there would be dolphins for her to see.

Rising from the blanket, he waded into the salty water until it touched his chest, the sand swirling around his legs. When the waves moved away from shore he felt the current pulling him, and he splayed his toes, letting his paws sink deep into the sand. He closed his eyes blissfully, feeling the sun warm on his back.

It wasn't long before he decided he'd had enough of the water, retreating to his blanket to lick the salty water from his body, dearly loving the ocean taste. The breeze cooled his wet coat and made the small beach umbrella Carolyn had set up flutter and sway cheerfully against the cloudless blue sky.

He turned toward the north, where the Cape Hatteras lighthouse stood, tall and unyielding, proud and beautiful. He'd been delighted to discover that it wasn't abandoned anymore. Remembering Magic's descriptions of the tower, Carolyn had also been delighted that the lighthouse had been restored, and she happily read the details to Magic from a park service brochure.

He was amazed at how well this landmark of the Outer Banks had been restored by people who loved the place as much as he did. The red bricks beneath the paint didn't show through anymore, for it had recently received a fresh coat of paint, making its spiraling black and white stripes stand out crisp against the sky. The windows were all there and intact, and a new Fresnel lens had been placed in the tower. At night they had watched its phantom-like beacon reaching far out to sea.

An incredible thrill ran through him when he stood in front of the majestic lighthouse, making every hair along his spine stand up deliciously. In his excitement, he ran around the base several times, sniffing at the red brick and granite foundation like a long-lost friend.

The lighthouse still held a faint smell of fuel oil, intermingled with the musty smell that Carolyn told him was a part of all historic places. It was more impressive than Magic remembered, soaring into the August sky and looking as if it could stand forever. Even the old doors had been restored to a fine condition.

Although a sign outside the lighthouse clearly said dogs weren't welcome, Carolyn and Magic arrived early in the morning before many tourists had appeared. She'd even persuaded the park ranger to allow Magic in with her.

The old dog's face wrinkled in concentration, and he paused on the staircase, pointing out the place where it had given way so many years before, when he and the boy named Nicky had taken shelter from the hurricane. He stared hard at the place for a moment, letting the memory wash over him like a warm ocean wave. There'd been other times, fun times when he and Nicky had played in the tower, spending long afternoons looking for pirate ships and Spanish galleons on the horizon.

The world was so different back then, he thought, giving himself a good shake. *This place will always be a part of me.*

Together they climbed the spiraling red staircase, no longer rusty or dangerous, to the observation deck some 200 feet above the beach. The view from the top was dizzying and, Carolyn admitted, just a little frightening. She held on to the chest-high railing so tightly her knuckles turned white.

"You can see forever from up here," she breathed. "How tiny the houses and people are!"

"Time hasn't made the lighthouse seem one bit smaller," the old dog affirmed. "It's still as tall as it ever was!"

"I was thinking," Carolyn said slowly. "I've got the tin box with Max's ashes with me, in my purse. I know he's never been here, except maybe as a dog-spirit." She paused. "Do you think he'd mind if I set his ashes free from up here?" her voice trailed off. "It's just that it seems so right, and this place is so beautiful."

"I don't think he'd mind at all," Magic replied, "In fact, I think he would like it very much."

Reaching into her purse, Carolyn pulled out the small tin and held it in her hands reverently. "It's got a springtime design on it," she said, turning the tin around. "Because that's when we first met, in the springtime." Holding it close, she closed her eyes. "I've had this for so long," she said. "But I know this isn't him anymore. He's in the Happiness now."

"He is," Magic said softly. "You gave him the gift of your love when he was alive, and you've allowed him to move on now that he's gone. You don't need his ashes to know that he'll always be a part of you."

Carolyn held her breath and waited until she thought the wind was just right. Lifting the lid, she turned the tin upside down and watched the ashes disappear into the summer air. "You're free Max," she whispered with tears in her eyes. "You're free."

It wasn't until the park ranger began to let more people enter the lighthouse that Magic and Carolyn were forced to make their way back down again.

The climb had seemed easy for the old dog, for he had been

eager to do it. Much to his dismay he quickly tired on the way down, and Carolyn was alarmed to see him panting heavily from the heat and exertion. At her suggestion, and much to his relief, they rested at each landing, peering out the windows and enjoying the view.

"I know I must have said it a hundred times already, but I'll say it again. I can see why you love this place," Carolyn said, brushing her windblown hair back behind her ears. "It's beautiful." She stared out an open window, taking in the sight of the island far below.

"Yes," Magic agreed, placing his paws on the sill. "I wish we could stay up here forever." His voice was wistful, quietly sad. "I'd often wondered what it would be like to soar like the birds do, riding the warm breeze across the ocean."

"Tell me," she said, peering out the window. "Where was the house you told me about? Do you think we could see it from here?"

Magic turned toward the south, and studied the beach carefully. "I'm not sure, anymore," he said, scanning the horizon, his eyes moving down the beach. "It used to be visible from up here, it really stood out. The roof was a light color, not dark like some of those other homes."

"There aren't many houses right along the beach anymore," she observed. "I've read that sometimes hurricanes do a lot of damage down here. Gosh, do you think maybe the ocean got it?" Knowing how much finding his old home meant to Magic, she instantly regretted her words. To come all this way and discover it gone must be a terrible shock to him. "Maybe it's been painted," she said quickly, hopefully. "Or maybe they've moved it. They do that with houses, you know."

Magic was startled at how close the ocean had crept toward the base of the lighthouse. In fact, he scarcely recognized the beach at first, for much of it had disappeared. Where the lighthouse ended, the stretch of sand was very small, built up with large sandbags for support. Seawalls had been erected in the pounding surf to help fight erosion.

"It could have been taken in a hurricane," he said at last. "It's possible. There's definitely less beach here, and I remember some houses being over that way, but they aren't there anymore." He couldn't hide the disappointment in his voice.

"I can almost see you," Carolyn said when they stopped to rest at the next landing. "I can see you sitting there on the tile, with your nose turned toward the tower, howling." She smiled. "I don't suppose you'd be willing to howl for me, would you?"

"Of course," Magic replied, feeling the tile cool and hard against his bottom. He let out a short yodel, to warm up, then a longer one.

It was a frightening, exciting, mournful sound that echoed against the old bricks and carried way up into the tower. Carolyn closed her eyes, picturing a raging storm pummeling the lighthouse, seeing a small Basenji puppy protecting his boy, crying out for someone, anyone to hear. The powerful image sent chills through her.

"Wow," she breathed when he'd finished. "That was something!"

The howling had not gone unnoticed by some tourists, and it wasn't long before the park ranger found them and urged them to hurry along.

The sound of Carolyn's voice released Magic from his memories of the morning's events. Alarmed at her cries, he sat up, not seeing her right away. His eyes scanned the shoreline, looking for her familiar shape. She wasn't there.

He looked out into the ocean and was horrified to discover she was caught in a rip current that was pulling her out to sea.

He ran into the ocean and swam toward her, calling her name. Like a terrible nightmare he realized she wasn't able to hear him.

A large swell broke over her head, and for a heart-stopping moment she disappeared, lost beneath the waves.

The old dog swam as hard and as fast as he could toward his beloved, feeling every muscle in his legs protesting the exertion. His heart pounded painfully in his chest as strong waves kept pushing him back towards shore. The harder he fought the waves, the harder they seemed to push him back. Panicked, Magic knew he had to get to her, to save her! He couldn't lose her!

Suddenly, someone was swimming next to him, then passing him. He glanced over to see a young man with a surfboard racing through the water at a blinding speed.

The man called out to Carolyn in a calm voice, telling her he would help her, instructing her to keep her head above the water. He rode his surfboard over the waves easily, almost as if he'd been born in the ocean.

"Just another moment, and you'll be okay," he shouted above the wind. "I'm almost there!"

An overwhelming sense of relief washed over Magic when he realized the man was better able to help Carolyn than he could. Magic paddled in the water, only turning back towards the beach when he saw the man grab hold of Carolyn and help her get a grip on the surfboard. The three of them made it safely to shore at about the same time.

"Carolyn!" Magic was panting, dripping wet, and exhausted from the swim. "Are you okay?"

Carolyn's legs went weak. She sank down into the wet sand, trembling. Magic leaned against her, grateful for the steadying hand she put on his back. "I'm okay, fella," she said, pulling him close. He looked up to see that the man was still there, leaning over them both, looking very concerned.

"Are you sure you'll be okay?" the man asked, his eyes and teeth brilliant against his darkly tanned skin. "Those rip currents are something else!" He threw down his surfboard and joined

Carolyn in the sand. "That's some brave Basenji you have," he said, reaching out so Magic could sniff his hand. "He was swimming like a crazy fool toward you, like he wanted to help you. Good boy," he said to Magic, who allowed the man to rub his head, not minding the wet hand gentle between his ears.

"I thought I was going to die!" Carolyn gasped, and began to sob. "I was so scared! Thank you," she said, recovering her composure. It wouldn't do to cry in front of a stranger. "And thank you!" She gave Magic a big hug.

"Thank him," Magic grunted, laying down in the sand. "He saved you, not me."

Carolyn looked at Magic, then glanced back at the man, pleased to see he was smiling at her. "I'm not from around here," she said, extending her hand. "I guess I need to be more careful, huh?"

The man laughed and took hold of her hand. "To tell you the truth," he said, "you'd be surprised how many people I know who get into scrapes like that from time to time. It's a good idea to respect the ocean," he added. "It likes to play tricks on you, especially when it comes to rip currents. By the way, I'm Nick," he said, standing up and taking a bow. "Nicholas Dare, at your service, milady."

Carolyn blushed, and realized she must look like a drowned rat and not at all attractive. "I'm Carolyn Adams," she said, recovering her poise. "And this is Magic." She gestured toward Magic, who was staring at Nick as if he'd seen a ghost.

"Magic." Nick said, smiling. "He's up there in years for a Basenji, isn't he? I don't think I've ever seen one with that much gray around the muzzle." He brushed a lock of hair from his forehead, and Magic stared hard at the scar above Nick's left eye, the place slightly lighter than the tanned skin around it. "In fact, you don't see too many Basenjis around here. There aren't any on the island that I can think of, anymore." He smiled. "Looks like you're the only one," he said to Magic. "You're a good-looking fella, aren't you?"

It couldn't be, Magic thought incredulously. *It simply couldn't be.*

Carolyn was surprised to learn Nick knew that Magic was a Basenji "How'd you know?" she asked, "I mean, you know Basenjis?"

"Oh yes," Nick said. "When I was young my parents had an African Basenji bitch who had a litter of pups. I know Basenjis, alright."

"It can't be," Magic said, staring wide-eyed at Nick. "It can't be you, Nicky!"

"Nicky?" Carolyn asked, forgetting herself and turning towards Magic. "You don't mean . . ." Her voice trailed off when she realized it probably wasn't a good idea to be talking to Magic with Nick standing right there.

"What?" Nick looked at her strangely. *It must have been the water in my ears,* he thought. *She didn't just call me Nicky. No one's done that in years.* He gazed at Magic, wondering what had spooked the dog. Something about the old Basenji was familiar, but then, he'd seen many Basenjis in his lifetime.

And, something was intriguing about the girl, but he couldn't quite put his finger on it. *Must've been the scare she had in the ocean,* he decided. *I guess I don't blame her for being disoriented.*

"I think it's Nicky," Magic repeated. "He's got a scar over his eye!"

"Now's not the time," Carolyn hissed through gritted teeth. She glanced up at Nick and smiled. When he wasn't looking, she whispered in Magic's ear. "We'll talk about it later, okay?"

"What?" Nick asked, confused.

"Oh, nothing," Carolyn said, standing up and walking to the water's edge to wash the sand off her legs. "Say," she said, "I've got my motorhome parked up in the campground. Would you like to join me for a soda or an iced tea? That's the least I can do, after you saved my life." She looked at Magic, and she heard him sigh.

"I'd love to," Nick replied. "You'll have to tell me all about yourself, and your dog, too."

Together the trio made their way up the beach to the motorhome, stopping only to retrieve the beach blanket and umbrella, which had blown over when the wind picked up.

TWENTY-TWO

NICK STRUGGLED WITH THE motorhome awning, finally loosening a clasp that had shifted and stuck. The awning groaned loudly as he pulled it down, bringing shade and immediate relief from the hot North Carolina sun.

"Thanks," Carolyn said, removing two beach chairs from their storage compartment inside the motorhome. "I was wondering how I'd ever get that down."

"I guess it's a good thing I came along,

then." Nick smiled, opening the chairs and setting them into the soft sand.

They sat in the cool shade, sipping iced tea from plastic cups, letting the balmy ocean breeze dry their bathing suits. The roaring of the surf was muffled by the flapping sound of the awning as it danced in the wind. Cicadas buzzed loudly in the heat of the day, comfortably hidden in the tall grasses and sea oats of the dunes.

Nick sat with his feet propped up on the bench of a picnic table they'd dragged through the hot sand into the shade, leaning back easily in his chair.

"Have you toured the lighthouse yet?" he asked, pointing down the beach. "I'm always amazed when I go back there. Everyone's put a lot of time and effort into restoring the tower and the outbuildings. It's hard to believe the place was ever abandoned."

"Magic and I went up this morning," Carolyn replied. "It was fantastic! The view from the top was breathtaking!"

"So they let you take Magic up there?"

Carolyn grinned. "Well, it took a little persuading, but yes, he got to go too."

Nick regarded the old dog with admiration. "That's quite a hike," he said. "I remember when I was small, my Basenji used to tag along with me to the lighthouse. We'd spend all day up at the top, watching for pirates or storms." He smiled at the memory. "It was a great place. Still is."

"You don't have Basenjis anymore?" Carolyn asked.

Nick shook his head. "No, Savannah lived to a ripe old age, and along the way we'd lost track of her puppies. By now they would probably be pretty old. I always thought I'd like to have another one, but only if it was somehow related to Savannah. I've had friends who offered me puppies on occasion, but I'm convinced that a Basenji is the only dog for me. You're pretty lucky to have Magic," he added. "The shape of his head and the way his face wrinkles on the side reminds me a lot of Savannah."

"Magic's great company," Carolyn acknowledged. "I couldn't ask for a better traveling companion."

"You're traveling alone?" Nick asked, surprised. "It seems like such a big rig to be all alone with." He gestured at the motorhome in a way that reminded Carolyn of Andie.

"What's wrong with traveling alone?" Carolyn asked, reaching down under her beach chair to where Magic lay, belly-down in the cool sand. "Besides, that's what my cousin Andie said — about the motorhome being big. It's not, really." She smiled. "It handles the interstate pretty well, once you get the hang of it."

"Hmm. What brings you here, to the Outer Banks?" Nick asked. "It seems like most people stop before they get down to Buxton. They usually stay in Kitty Hawk or Nags Head."

"I'd heard it was all built up, up there," Carolyn replied. "And that's not what I was looking for. When I drove through it seemed too commercial for me," Carolyn said, afraid of sounding rehearsed. She planned on using the stock response in case anyone asked, but she hadn't thought she'd meet many people on this trip, let alone someone as attractive as Nick. "I was looking for something relaxing and quiet. I wanted to hear the ocean, not the traffic."

"I'd have to agree with you there," Nick acknowledged. "It's much quieter down here. So what do you think of the 'Banks so far?"

Carolyn giggled. "Well, the water can be a bit rough, but," she added, "I simply love it here. This is a part of the country I've always wanted to see. I wish I'd come out a lot sooner."

"I've never been to Michigan," Nick admitted. "As a matter of fact, I've lived here most of my life." He smiled again, and Carolyn noticed how little wrinkles appeared at the corner of his eyes. Fabulous! "I went away to Virginia, to college," he continued, keenly aware that she was staring at him. "But there's something about this place." He gestured towards the ocean. "Once you've been a part of it, you can't ever live without it. I know it sounds a little romantic and silly, but it's where I feel at home."

Carolyn glanced down at Magic, who was listening attentively to their conversation, although his eyes were closed. At the mention of the word "home," his ears perked up and turned forward, toward the sound of Nick's voice.

"Well," she ventured, "I don't think there's much work in hanging around beaches waiting for people to get washed out to sea, so you can't be in the lifesaving business."

"Oh, no." Nick chuckled. "Actually, I only save swimmers as a sideline. I'm a builder," he said. "You've seen the houses around here — the ones up on pilings? That's the kind I work on," he finished proudly. "Family business."

Carolyn nodded appreciatively, and ran her fingers through her hair. *I must look terrible*, she thought, her green eyes meeting his dark ones and stopping there. She tore her gaze away, and fussed with her beach towel for a moment. "I've been admiring those," she said. "The houses, I mean. I'll bet they cost a fortune!"

"Oh, they do," he agreed, nodding. "And believe me, the work we get after a hurricane costs a fortune, too. After all," he added, "after a storm everyone wants their house fixed right away. One thing's for sure — there's never a shortage of work. But, this time of year I usually take time off to enjoy the sun and the ocean."

Nick stretched and set his cup down on the picnic table. A sudden gust of wind tipped the cup over, tossing it into the sand. "Oops," he said, bending to pick it up.

His eyes caught Magic's eyes, and locked into their intent gaze. He had the inexplicable feeling that the dog was familiar to him, although why escaped him. It was almost as if Magic *expected* to be remembered and recognized. Nick was certain he'd never seen Carolyn or her dog before.

"Let me get you another cup," Carolyn said, reaching for the sandy one Nick was holding. "That is, if you'd like more iced tea." She didn't want him to leave, because if he did, she was afraid she'd never see him again.

Don't be silly, she chastised herself. *What do you think you're doing? You just met the guy, you hardly know him, and now he knows you're traveling alone with a dog in a motorhome.*

Nick squinted up at the bright sky, brushing a lock of hair from his temple. It was on the tip of his tongue to decline Carolyn's invitation, to tell her he had somewhere he had to be, but he was enjoying the cool shade and her company.

"Sure," he said at last. "Another glass of iced tea would be great."

He watched Carolyn disappear into the motorhome. Again the dark lock of hair fell forward on his temple, and he brushed it away, revealing a scar over his eye.

Could it be Nicky? Magic asked himself over and over again. *Is it possible?*

Nick felt Magic staring at him, and he turned his attentions back to the old dog, speaking quietly to him. Magic's eyes were wide and dark, and Nick could see himself reflected in their depths. It had been a long time since he'd been so close to a Basenji.

"Here, boy," Nick said, snapping his fingers and tapping his knee. "Come over here and let me see you for a minute."

Magic eyed the man before him, debating, as his Basenji nature dictated, whether or not to indulge Nick's request.

"I remember you," Magic said. "Don't you know who I am?"

Nick tapped his knee again, whistling through his teeth. "Come here, fella. I know all about Basenjis, you know. Years ago, when I was little, my best friend was a beautiful Basenji girl named Savannah. You remind me so much of her, so much that if I didn't know better, I'd think you two were related."

He can't hear me, Magic thought sadly. *He doesn't hear me at all. Maybe if I try hard enough, if I want it badly enough, I can make it happen. After all, Carolyn can hear me.*

Nick laughed at Magic's hesitation. "Typical Basenji, through and through, aren't you?" He leaned back in his chair, feigning disinterest. He turned his face towards the sky, seeing the sun faintly through the awning, and whistled. "On second thought, why don't you just stay right there, and we can stare at each other instead."

Magic chuckled and made his way over to Nick. Nick bent low and cupped the old dog's face in his hands, marveling at the resemblance to his long-gone Savannah. He put his face right up to Magic's and breathed, enjoying the warm grassy smell of his coat. The scent brought back a rush of memories to him, and he wondered who Magic really was, and where he'd come from.

Magic's mind was working busily too, recalling Nick's scent from his memories. He carefully pushed the top half of his body onto the chair and sniffed Nick for a moment before settling down again into the sand at his side. Wave after wave of memories washed over him as he took in Nick's scent, so overwhelming that it made him feel light-headed.

If Magic had doubts before, he didn't have them any longer. He knew beyond a shadow of a doubt that Nick was the same person, his Nicky, who'd been only a twelve-year-old boy when Magic was born. The realization sent a chill of excitement through the old dog, and although the day was hot, he shivered.

How can it be? he wondered. *After all these years I return home, to the place I was born, and who do I find?*

It occurred to him that maybe his mother, Violet, or perhaps even Max was looking out for him and helping him along. The more Magic thought about it, the more likely it seemed that someone was watching over him, making sure things worked out. He stared into the sky, squinting into the clouds and brightness where the dog-spirits played, and silently thanked whoever had led him home.

Carolyn returned with two fresh cups of iced tea, and she was balancing a water bowl for Magic.

"Here, let me help you." Nick took the water bowl from her and setting it in front of Magic. "There you go, old boy," he said, watching as Magic lapped at the cool water, noticing how he drank from the center of the bowl.

"Does he always do that?" Nick asked. "Drink from the middle like that?"

Carolyn giggled. "He knows what he likes, and he does what he does. That's Magic for you," she replied. "A Basenji, through and through."

"I don't like splashing water all over my chest," Magic explained. "Besides," he added between laps, "a few ice cubes sure would be nice."

"How long have you had him?" Nick asked.

"Since Christmas," Carolyn replied. "I adopted him from an animal shelter."

"Oh." Nick's face fell, clearly disappointed. "Don't mind me," he explained. "I think it's great that you adopted him. I was just hoping that maybe you knew who he was, and what his background is. It's just that he reminds me so much of Savannah, that I thought . . ." his voice trailed off. "Just being silly, I guess."

"I wish I knew more about him, too," Carolyn said, avoiding Nick's gaze. Her heart was pounding from his mention of Magic possibly being related to Savannah. "The shelter didn't have any records on him, though." She longed to tell Nick who Magic was, for it seemed as if all the forces in the universe had worked to bring them all together for this one moment. It was amazing and incredible, but Carolyn knew she couldn't just tell Nick that she could hear Magic's voice.

Flustered, she reached into her drink and fished out an ice cube. Holding it between two fingers, she watched it melt and slip in the heat. "Here you are," she said, handing the cube to Magic's eager mouth. "Is that better?"

Magic replied that it was, and thanked her for her trouble. He noticed Nick looking at them strangely, as if he knew he had missed something between the woman and her dog, but wasn't sure what.

"Better watch your guest," Magic said. "After all, he can't hear me so we must look strange to him."

Carolyn glanced at Nick, and blushed. "He likes ice cubes," she explained. "Even in the winter, he likes them."

"Hmmm." Nick sipped at the iced tea, feeling the coolness shock the back of his throat, following it all the way down. "You didn't say what you did for a living," he said.

"I'm a teacher," Carolyn replied. "I just finished working the third grade summer school session."

She was silent for a moment, watching a jagged line of pelicans skimming over the ocean, their bodies dark against the bright sky.

He doesn't need to think I'm crazy, she thought. *But, I guess in some ways, if I knew someone who drove all the way out to the ocean just to make an old dog happy, I'd think they were a little crazy, too!*

"Say," she said, suddenly. "I'd like to thank you for saving me from the ocean today. I don't even want to think of what might have happened if you hadn't come along. I'd like to invite you to stay for dinner, if you'd like." There. She'd said it.

If I am crazy, better just go ahead and be impulsive!

Nick looked at her strangely, watching how the wind made her hair dance, noticing how the sun had touched her skin, and even though she was still wet from the ocean, he found her beautiful.

"Well," he began. He glanced down at Magic, who was watching him with an intense look of concentration.

"I'd like that," he decided, realizing that he enjoyed Carolyn's company very much. "In fact, I'd like that a lot." He'd never done anything on impulse like this before either, and it gave him a strange and wonderful feeling. "In fact," he added, "how about I take you someplace around here, someplace that will really give you a taste of Outer Banks cooking."

"Say yes, say yes, say yes already!" Magic's excited voice urged. "Tell him you'll go!"

"Sounds good!" Carolyn grinned. "I'd like that." She cleared her throat, suddenly feeling self-conscious. "What time?"

"Around, shall we say, six, then?" Nick stood and handed her his empty cup. He picked up his surfboard, and held it lightly with one arm. "You'll be here?" he asked, thinking how he'd feel if he did show up to find the motorhome long gone.

"I'll be here," Carolyn promised.

"Great," Nick smiled. "See you then!"

He ducked under the low part of the awning, disappearing into the heat of the day, not minding the hot sand beneath his bare feet. He decided right then that he wanted to see more of Carolyn. A nagging familiarity about her dog bothered him, though. There was something about the Basenji he couldn't put his finger on.

Whatever it is, he told himself, *it will come to me.*

TWENTY-THREE

GETTING READY FOR DINNER WITH

Nick turned out to be more of an ordeal than

Carolyn could have ever imagined. She found

herself going through all of the clothes she'd

packed, looking at some things and discarding

others in an attempt to find the perfect outfit to

wear. She despaired often and loudly to Magic.

"Doesn't it just figure!" she wailed. "I've got

absolutely nothing to wear! Nothing at all!"

Her clothes were strewn haphazardly about

the motorhome, as if a hurricane had blown

through each and every drawer and cabinet. Magic sat quietly in a pile of clothes she had designated as "maybes," watching her with thinly veiled amusement, chuckling to himself.

Her fascination with appearance wasn't at all foreign to him, since he'd been a show dog and was keenly aware of the importance of making a good first impression. Watching her brought back fond memories of his days as a show dog. He remembered how carefully Lydia had groomed him for the show ring, making sure his coat was perfectly smooth and shiny.

He ducked as a pair of denim shorts went whizzing past his head, dangerously close to his ears. "Hey!" he growled, pawing at his ears to make sure they were still there. "I'm a Basenji, not a target!"

"Ugh!" Carolyn held up a green T-shirt and stared at it critically. The front of the shirt was printed with the word HAWAII, and beneath the word a teddy bear was dancing the hula in a grass skirt. "Why did I bring *this*?"

She flung the shirt away, sending it through the air, across the motorhome. It landed with a small *whump* in the sink. "Oh," she despaired. "Maybe I still have time to go out and buy something." She hunted for her watch, checked the time, and groaned. "No, I don't! Oh!"

"I like this," Magic said, pawing a sleeveless floral dress that lay in a crumpled heap on the floor. He nudged it with his nose, and sniffed the corner of it that was closest to him. It smelled of fabric softener, clean and nice.

Carolyn didn't hear him, for she had her head buried deep in the tiny closet. "I just don't know!" she mumbled, frustrated. "Why even bother, really? It's not like it's a real date!" She stood up too quickly and hit her head on the shelf above. "Ow!"

Magic picked up the sundress lightly in his teeth, careful not to damage the soft material that was cool and smooth against his tongue. "Here," he said, nudging her with it. "Wear this!"

Carolyn took the dress from him grudgingly. It was half on her mind to reject it simply out of frustration, because it was a bit damp from his mouth. She didn't remember exactly why she'd packed that dress.

Impulse, maybe, she mused. *How could I ever have known I would be going out to dinner with a guy on my vacation?*

"Will you wear it?" Magic pressed, raising a paw to touch her leg. "I've never seen you in it, but I'm sure it'll look nice."

How strange, Carolyn thought, holding the dress up to her chest, staring at her reflection in the floor-length mirror on the back of the bathroom door. *First, I almost drown in the ocean. Then, out of the blue a really nice guy that actually seems like he might be interested in me saves me. And, to top it all off we make a dinner date.*

Even stranger and more incredible was how Magic believed Nick was the same person he'd known so many years ago. Although Nick didn't appear to remember Magic, he did know about Basenjis, and he genuinely seemed to like the old dog.

This is like a dream, she thought. *These things don't happen in real life. It's like a dream or a movie.* She glanced down at Magic, who stared patiently back at her with dark, Egyptian eyes. *But I also used to believe dogs only talked in dreams or movies.*

"Okay," she said at last. "Thanks, Magic. I'll wear this."

Leaning comfortably against two pillows and a pile of clothes, Magic watched as Carolyn continued to ready herself for dinner. Although he'd seen her go through the motions of getting ready for work many times, this was the first time he really took a good long look at her. His dark eyes followed her movements as she washed her face, ran a brush through her hair, and stared at herself in the mirror. He wondered if she saw the same person reflected there as he did.

He'd never completely understood the fascination people had with mirrors. *They'd stare at them for hours if they could,* he reflected. *What do they see in there?*

He jumped off the sofa and stood in front of the floor-length mirror, staring at the old Basenji who stared right back. He peered at his graying muzzle, and tilted his head slightly to take in the rest of himself, surprised to see that the Basenji who stared back had his bristles up.

"Grrrr!" he growled, peeling his upper lip back to expose an ivory canine. "I am a formidable Basenji!" He raised his paw to bat playfully at the image, and watched his twin do the same. He'd been alarmed many times before whenever he'd caught his reflection in a window or in a mirror, sometimes forgetting the profuse growth of gray hair around his muzzle and face. *When did I get to be that old?* Leaving his twin, he returned to the sofa and laid down with a sigh.

Carolyn took another brush out of her bag and ran it though her shoulder-length hair, noticing the beginnings of sun-bleached highlights mixed with a little bit of red. She fished around in her bag and pulled out a shiny barrette, scooping her hair into it neatly. Humming softly to herself, she stepped back and admired her work.

Pretty, Magic thought, although he didn't say it. *She's really very pretty.*

Carolyn was brushing her teeth for the third time when a tapping sound at the door startled them both.

"It's Nicky!" Magic bolted to the door and stood on his hind legs, peering out the window. "He's here!"

"Oh nuts!" Carolyn wiped the toothpaste from her mouth and gasped in exasperation when she realized how messy the motorhome was. Frantically she began to pick up the clothes she'd so carelessly strewn about the place. "Help me, Magic!" she whispered, so Nick wouldn't hear.

"What can I do?" Magic asked, grasping at a blouse draped over a lamp. He pulled on the blouse and it fell down over his head, blocking his vision. "Hey! Help!"

The tapping sounded again, and they heard Nick's voice through the door. "Anybody home?"

"Coming!" Carolyn shouted, shoving clothes into the bathroom and pulling the door shut, nearly catching Magic's tail. She pulled the blouse off his head and stuffed it into a nearby drawer.

"Oh, there you are!" he chuckled. "I was wondering if you'd already left."

"Very funny! How do I look?"

"You look great!" Magic assured her. "Wonderful!"

Carolyn opened the door just as Nick was preparing to knock again. "Hi," she said, brushing some stray hairs from her flushed face. "I was just, um, cleaning a few things up."

Magic snorted. "Running around like a fool is more like it," he said, wagging his tail in greeting. "You should have been here to see the trouble she went through for you!"

Carolyn glared, but Nick didn't notice.

"Hey, Magic!" Nick bent down to greet the old dog. "Will he be alright here, all by himself?" he asked, rubbing Magic's neck. "We can do something else for dinner, instead, if you want." Impulsively he planted a kiss on Magic's forehead. "Some people don't like to leave their old dogs alone for very long."

"Go on ahead," Magic urged Carolyn, letting Nick's "old dog" comment slide. "Oooh, that feels good." He tilted his head for Nick to scratch some more.

"Oh, he'll be okay," Carolyn replied. "He's still pretty tired from his big swim in the ocean."

"Okay, then. Perhaps later he'd enjoy a walk on the beach?" Nick stood and held his hand out to her. "Shall we continue, my lady?"

Carolyn blushed. "You'll be okay?" she asked Magic again, feeling guilty about leaving him behind. He could see the happiness in her eyes and hear the unmistakable excitement in her voice. "You be a good dog, okay?" she said, for Nick's benefit.

"Sure," Magic yawned. "A nap sounds about right, anyway. Have a good time," he added wistfully. Peeking out of a window, he watched for a moment as Nick helped Carolyn into his Jeep.

I wish I could go along, he thought. It was one of those rare times in his life when he found himself wishing he could be a person. *People are lucky in some ways*, he mused. *Sometimes they really do get to have more fun.*

After a quick drink of water he fell asleep on the bed, wondering what his relationship with Carolyn would be like if he wasn't a dog. *Would she still love me?* he asked himself. *Would she?*

TWENTY-FOUR

NICK TURNED THE JEEP OFF THE MAIN road onto a narrow gravel driveway. The sign for the restaurant was made of the same weathered cedar as the building, and it had the words *The Sea Star* printed in dark blue. It was nearly obscured by the tall sea oats that flanked it on either side, and if Nick hadn't told her where to look before they turned, Carolyn was sure she would have missed it.

The restaurant was hidden from the road by more tall grass and short, tough-looking pines.

Like almost every other building Carolyn had seen, it was built of cedar up off the ground, although not as high as some of the houses she'd noticed. Weathered by the salt air and sea, its gray boards looked as if they'd been there for a long time.

As Nick pulled the Jeep into a parking space, the breeze died down, replaced with humid evening air. The evening songs of crickets and cicadas was almost deafening.

"They sing louder and faster, the hotter it gets," Nick said, unfastening his safety belt. He reached behind the seat for his wallet, which had fallen out of his pocket. "The cicadas," he explained. "My dad used to tell me that you could tell the temperature by counting their chirps. Heck," he laughed, helping Carolyn out of the Jeep, "I don't think anyone could count that fast!"

"It's sure hot," Carolyn acknowledged, wishing they could have driven longer. The breeze had been cool and refreshing on her hot skin. "Is it humid like this all summer long?"

"Pretty much," Nick replied. "Although you'd be surprised how easily you'd get used to it, especially living right on the ocean side. There's a steady breeze off the ocean most of the time, so it really doesn't feel as hot as the thermometer says."

They entered the coolness of the restaurant, and learned there would be a short wait.

"Look at this," Carolyn said, leading Nick to a painting that hung in the pine-paneled lobby.

The painting was a view from of the top of the Cape Hatteras lighthouse. A little boy stood with his arms hanging over the railing, looking out at the ocean. In one hand, he held a pair of small binoculars. Seagulls soared nearby, and the sky was a deep shade of blue. Below him, tiny houses dotted the coastline. "This is so neat!" she exclaimed, marveling at the artist's attention to detail.

Nick smiled. "There's more hanging inside the main part of

the restaurant, too. And," he added, a gleam in his eye, "they're all for sale."

He led her back outside onto the wrap-around porch. Deck chairs had been scattered on it, and a hammock hung in one corner. There were several rope-and-wood porch swings hanging from the ceiling.

"You'll like this," Nick said, settling into a swing. It creaked and groaned loudly under his weight. Although it looked comfortable, Carolyn regarded the swing apprehensively.

"I don't know," she said, uncertain. "It sure is making an awful racket." She seated herself gingerly next to Nick. "I hope we don't bring it down!"

Nick laughed and pointed to the enormous eyebolts that held the swing securely to the ceiling. "Those could hold an elephant," he joked. "Not that we weigh that much," he added quickly.

They sat for a while on the swing, listening to the sounds of the Atlantic summer evening moving and breathing all around them. When Carolyn commented on how comfortable the swing was, Nick told her that it was made right there in Buxton.

"Maybe you'll want one to take home," he said. "The shop isn't too far from the campground."

Carolyn shook her head. "I'd love one, but I don't know where I'd put it," she said. "I live in an apartment." She ran her hand along the smooth wood, and felt a little silly. "Maybe I should just hang it in the living room," she giggled, envisioning Magic lounging in the swing, bathed in afternoon sunlight.

Suddenly, she remembered that maybe he wouldn't be returning home with her. The thought of going home alone made the smile disappear from her eyes.

Nick looked at her curiously, wondering what had made her so sad. "Look," he said, waving to a man that had ridden up to the restaurant on a bicycle. "That's the guy who painted the picture you liked."

The man smiled and waved back, and disappeared into the restaurant. "He comes here a lot," Nick explained. "He did a painting of my parent's old house, the one that was destroyed in the hurricane. The old house was the color of this wood," he said, gesturing at the weathered cedar porch. "And it had bright white shutters. On really humid days, you could smell the cedar for miles." He grinned. "Well, at the time, it seemed like it."

"What happened to the painting?" Carolyn asked.

"Oh, someone bought it before I could get up enough money to do it myself. I was just starting with my uncle in the construction business, and I didn't have two dimes to rub together." Nick stretched out his legs until they touched the porch railing in front of him. "But that was a long time ago. Every so often, I think about asking him to do another painting, but I never seem to get around to it. It may sound a little funny, but it's the same way I feel about the house. You can build another one, but it's never quite the same. I guess in a way I'm afraid it will seem less special, not quite as magical as I remember it, if he duplicates it."

Poor Magic, Carolyn thought. *He was so looking forward to this trip, and to finding his home again, and it's not even there anymore. At least he saw the lighthouse,* she reflected, suddenly cheered by the thought that maybe he would return home with her.

She tried to imagine Nick as the little boy Magic had told her about. If she squinted her eyes just right, she could almost see a dark-haired, dark-eyed little boy wearing a faded blue T-shirt and blue jean shorts. Her mind's eye showed her his wind-tousled hair and a summertime tan. She closed her eyes and let the rhythmic rocking of the porch swing take her back to a different time, long ago, where a little boy named Nicky ran happily through tall grass and dunes, chased seagulls, and had a little red and white Basenji puppy tagging along.

"Hey," Nick said, bringing her back to the present. "That's us. Lets go get some of the best seafood you'll ever eat."

"Guaranteed?" Carolyn smiled as the little boy in her mind faded away, replaced by the handsome man next to her. He winked and stood, holding out his hand to help her up.

"Promise!"

They were led to a small table next to a window that had a view overlooking the sound. Carolyn watched a fishing boat silently move past, barely making a ripple in the still waters, and Nick was quick to point out a snowy white egret on tall stilt legs standing in the water, waiting for its dinner to swim by.

"There are so many decisions," Carolyn said, tearing her gaze from the window to study the menu. "What's the specialty here in the Outer Banks?"

"Well, let's see. Crabcakes are excellent," Nick replied, setting his menu down. "But the soft-shell crabs can't be beat. Right, Doreen?" He nodded at the waitress who had just returned with their drinks and some fresh bread. "Doreen is co-owner of *The Sea Star*. All the fish they serve is caught right from their own boat, which, appropriately enough, is also called *The Sea Star*."

The older woman with salt-and-pepper gray hair smiled at Nick. "It's all so true," she told Carolyn with a wink. "Every last word of it! Speaking of catches, you'd better net this fella before I do! He's darned cute, and one of the finest catches around here!"

Nick blushed. "Aww, don't pay any mind to Doreen," he said. "Between her and my mother, I'd be married up twenty times or more, by now!" He laughed.

"His daddy was a handsome man," Doreen said, putting her hand on Nick's shoulder. "And Nick has grown up to look just like him! If I was younger, I'd scoop him right up and keep him for my own." She leaned toward Carolyn, and whispered, "I always say, why settle for flounder when you can have the caviar!"

Carolyn laughed. "We've only just met," she explained.

"Well, missy, I wouldn't wait too long," Doreen pressed. She winked again. "Well, back to work. What will you two have?"

"I'd like to try the soft-shell crabs," Carolyn replied, handing her menu to Doreen.

"Me too," Nick added. "Oh, and let's have some of that wonderful seafood gumbo of yours."

"Excellent choices," Doreen said. "The boat just came in an hour ago, so the crabs are really fresh. We'll have those right up for you!"

"Wow," Carolyn said, watching Doreen disappear into the kitchen. "She's pretty neat."

"Our families have known each other ever since they settled on the 'Banks," Nick explained. "Years and years and years ago. It's quite an exciting history. We've even got pirates in our blood," he laughed.

Carolyn's eyes grew wide. "Really?"

"Sure," he replied with a twinkle in his eyes. "Blackbeard was well known in these parts, and some folks will claim to be descended from him."

"And you?" Carolyn asked. "What about your family?"

"Well, my mother is from Ocracoke, and my father was born right here on the island. He's got a memorial site up in Buxton Woods cemetery."

"I'm sorry," Carolyn said quickly. "I didn't mean to bring up sad memories."

"That's okay," Nick replied. "He died in a hurricane when I was twelve, but I had some really great years with him. Buxton Woods is beautiful, and the cemetery is on a small hill that overlooks the ocean. He loved that ocean, and in the end it was the ocean that took him away from us. I always thought it was appropriate that we put his memorial there. So," he smiled, "what about your family?"

Carolyn laughed. "I'm afraid they're not terribly interesting. My father is a senior partner in a law firm back in Detroit. My mother is a professional housewife who didn't think her only daughter should become a third-grade teacher. I guess she was really disappointed when I didn't follow in my father's footsteps."

"But the main thing is that you followed your own star," Nick said. "As long as you're doing what makes you happy, they should be happy for you."

"That's what my cousin Andie says, but sometimes my parents — especially my mother — can make me feel like I'm six years old! Maybe they didn't want their little girl to grow up, you know? They hate the fact that I've got Magic."

"Really? I think he's great."

Carolyn giggled. "I don't know what got into me, but on Christmas Eve I brought him over to meet the family. You should have seen the look on my mother's face when she opened the door and saw me standing there with Magic!"

"You didn't by any chance lead her to believe that you were bringing a date, did you?"

Carolyn nodded, and Nick burst out laughing. "Good for you!"

"That's what Andie said."

"So who's this 'Andy' I'm hearing so much about? He must be pretty special."

"*She* is," Carolyn replied. "Andie's dad is my mother's brother, although you'd hardly know it because they're as different as night and day. Andie and I grew up together. Our houses were just a block away."

Doreen appeared with their gumbo, and set the steaming cups gently on the table. "So, did you ask her yet?" she asked, nudging Nick with her elbow.

"Ask her what?"

"To marry you, silly!" Doreen laughed as Nick blushed. Some people at the next table turned at the sound of Doreen's voice and smiled expectantly.

"Oh, don't worry," she told Carolyn. "He'll get around to it. You're a real pretty girl. You two would make a great couple." She scooted away before Nick or Carolyn could reply.

"Wow," Carolyn said.

"I'm sorry about Doreen," Nick began. "She just likes to gossip, and believe me, just by being here we've given her plenty to talk about."

"She's just having fun, Nicky," Carolyn said. "I don't mind, really."

He gazed at her with his dark eyes, and gave her hand a squeeze. "No one's called me Nicky in years," he said softly. "And here you've gone and done it twice in one day."

It was Carolyn's turn to blush. "I guess it just slipped out," she stammered. "I don't know why I did it."

"It's okay," he said. "My dad used to call me that all the time, and I've really missed hearing it. I don't mind at all."

Carolyn didn't know what to say, so she smiled and fiddled with her napkin. His hand was still on hers, and she felt the warmth of his touch flow through her like electricity.

"Tell me more about yourself," he said. "I'd like to know what you do when you're not teaching school or driving to Cape Hatteras in a motorhome with your Basenji."

"Actually, not much else," she admitted. "I guess life was kind of boring before Magic came along." She felt silly for saying it, even though it was true. *Andie would have been making up an exotic life story if she were here,* she thought. *I'd love to tell him about Magic, but what would he think of me then?* Deciding to change the subject, she asked, "What do you do when you're not building houses?"

"Well," Nick sipped his iced tea. "The construction business keeps me pretty busy, but when I can I like to spend time in the ocean. I like to kayak, and surfing is fun. I also like to go windsurfing on the sound side. But other than that, not much else," he laughed. "See how much we have in common, after all!"

Carolyn laughed along with him, enjoying the sound of his voice. "Don't let Doreen find out! Between her and Magic, there would definitely be some matchmaking going on if we let them get away with it."

"Speaking of Magic," Nick said. "Were you ever able to find out anything more about him? What's his story? You don't often see Basenjis his age, and I can't imagine the shelters in Michigan are full up with them."

"He was the only one," she replied. "He was sitting all by himself, and he was scheduled to be put to sleep. When he asked me to take him home, I couldn't find a reason why not." She felt tears welling up in her eyes, and brushed one away before it escaped. "Just last August I'd lost my dog Max to cancer. I didn't think I'd ever be ready to open my heart again, but there he was, and I just couldn't leave him there to die." She smiled. "His owner had moved away and abandoned him, and he was rescued by the next door neighbor. She was a lonely old lady who took care of him up until she died. Magic ran away after that, and they found him wandering the streets and that's how he ended up in the shelter. Beyond that, I don't know too much about him."

"That's quite a story," Nick said. "I'm surprised you know that much. You say they found him wandering the streets?"

Carolyn was horrified, realizing quickly that she had told Nick more than she could have possibly known. "I'm a teacher," she said quickly. "If I can get answers out of third graders, then I guess I know how to ask the right questions. The man at the shelter was very helpful."

"Hmmm." Nick scratched his head.

"I just couldn't leave him," Carolyn said.

"Got a soft heart?" he asked quietly. "That's really admirable, you know. Not many people would open their heart to an old dog they found in the shelter, especially one that's as old as Magic."

"It's more than that," she replied. "Magic is really special to me. I never thought I'd be able to love another dog after I lost Max. His death left an awful emptiness in my life, but it's not like Magic just took his place. It's hard to explain, but Magic has filled an emptiness I didn't even know I had."

"From the way your eyes light up when you talk about him, that's easy to see. I can't get over how much he reminds me of our first Basenji girl, Savannah."

"What was she like?"

"To understand Savannah, you have to understand her life. Savannah was a dream my father had." Nick's face took on a far away look. "He always loved dogs, and he'd read a story about a Basenji years ago. Maybe you've heard of it? It's called *Good-Bye, My Lady* by James Street. At any rate, he had a friend who was going to Africa on an expedition to find some of these Basenji dogs in their native Zaire. The plan was to find a few and bring them back here, and blend them into the American breeding programs. They wanted to expand the genetic pool, I guess." Nick smiled. "And so when his friend returned, my father acquired one of the puppies. She was a little red and white female, with a dark red coat and the most expressive, far-seeing eyes I had ever seen on a dog. My father called her Savannah, after the grasslands in Africa. As a matter of fact, she was one of only a handful of pure African Basenjis that the American Kennel Club allowed to be added to their registry."

"Do you have any pictures of her?" Carolyn asked eagerly. "I'd sure love to see what she looked like."

Nick shook his head. "Unfortunately, when my mom lost the house to Annabelle, she lost everything."

"Annabelle?"

"That was the name of a hurricane that came through and wiped out a lot of the beach homes, my childhood home included. Mom lives in town now, near Buxton Woods." Loud laughter a few tables over interrupted his thoughts. He turned to see what was going on, and frowned when he recognized the people who were making all the noise.

A woman at the noisy table glanced up to see Nick staring at her. She tossed her long blonde hair over her shoulders, grinned and waved. Nick made a face and looked away, but he couldn't help but glance over again. When he did, the woman leaned over and kissed the man sitting next to her. The large diamond ring she wore caught the late afternoon sunlight, making it glint and glimmer.

Although Nick did his best to keep up a friendly stream of conversation with Carolyn, before long it became obvious to her that the loud party at the table behind her distracted him. She watched him throw furtive glances over her shoulder every now and then, and felt slightly annoyed each time he did so.

When their dinner arrived, Carolyn looked at the soft-shell crabs on her plate with apprehension. "Uh, Nick," she said. "These still have their legs on!"

Nick laughed and explained to her that with soft-shell crabs, one ate the entire crab, legs and all. He watched as she took a tentative first bite, grinning as a delighted smile crept across her face.

"These look strange," she said at last, "but they sure are good!"

Eating took the place of conversation for a while, and it gave Carolyn time to study Nick more closely. She could see streaks of red in his dark hair, probably from the time he spent in the sun and sea, and noticed the scar Magic said he'd gotten so many years ago when they were trapped in the lighthouse. As much as she wanted to ask him about it, she didn't dare, for fear of what he might think.

The key lime pie Doreen had said was on the house had just disappeared from her plate when the couple from the table behind her got up to leave. They passed by Nick and Carolyn's table on the way out, and the woman smiled broadly at Nick, then at Carolyn.

"Hey, Nicholas Dare," she said, throwing her long hair over her tanned shoulders. "Long time no see."

"Hey Nick." The blonde's partner smiled at Nick, who glared back.

"Hi," he growled. "Enjoy your dinner?"

"Who's your friend?" The blonde leaned forward, and Carolyn could see where her skin was sunburned beneath her tan.

"This is Carolyn," Nick replied, forcing a smile. "A friend of mine from Michigan, here on vacation. Carolyn, this is Angela and her fiance Tony." He spat out the words as if they left a terrible taste in his mouth.

Angela's eyes widened. "Nicholas, I didn't know you had friends from Michigan!" she exclaimed, her voice sticky-sweet. "Staying in one of Mr. Nick's vacation homes?" she purred. "He does build some beautiful ones, doesn't he? Honestly, I don't know what would have become of me if Tony's folks hadn't bought one years and years ago."

Nick looked extremely uncomfortable under the couple's watchful stares. Carolyn quickly realized that this act was some sort of game for Angela, and she didn't like it one bit.

"Actually," Carolyn said, putting her fork down on the table with a bang. "I'm from Romeo, Michigan. I'm sure you must have heard of it?" She paused, letting that bit of information sink in, reveling in the puzzlement that appeared on the couple's faces. "I'm staying at the campground in my motorhome. Your friend Nick was just telling me about two of the houses he's working on.

I can't decide which one I like more, and he's just about convinced me to buy them both."

There, she thought wickedly, watching Angela's eyes grow wide with amazement. *That ought to shut her up. Andie would be proud!*

"Uh, Carolyn's just a good friend," Nick said, looking as surprised as Angela. "She's only down here for a couple of weeks."

"Pity," Angela said, not sure who to believe. She forced a smile Carolyn's way. "I'm sure Nicholas could show you such a good time." She winked at Nick, as if they shared some personal secret. Laughing, the couple left the restaurant, none too soon for Carolyn's satisfaction. She glared after them as they left, glad to see them gone.

"Hey," Nick said. "Buying *two* houses, are you?"

"What was that all about?" Carolyn fumed, feeling angry and hurt, not understanding what had just taken place. "Those people were *friends* of yours?"

"Not exactly," Nick said sourly. "Believe me, they were the last two people I needed to see."

He looked embarrassed and uncomfortable as he sipped his iced tea nervously. Water droplets that had condensed on the side of the glass dribbled down his light blue shirt, leaving dark blue stains where they fell. "Damn," he said, blotting at them with a napkin. "I guess this wasn't such a good idea, was it?"

They were silent for a moment, listening to the clinking of silverware against dishes and murmured conversations all around them. Carolyn wished with all her might that she hadn't accepted Nick's offer of dinner at the same time he was wishing they'd gone somewhere else. He had wanted it to be a nice evening, and now after seeing Angela and Tony, he felt that the evening had become a disaster.

"Hey, I'm really sorry," he said, feeling embarrassed and sad all at once. "I don't know what to say."

"It's okay," Carolyn replied, feeling uncomfortable as well. What had she been thinking? Things seemed to be going so well, but for some reason everything had gone wrong. She wracked her mind for something she might have said or done, and came up empty-handed.

"Hey, don't look so sad. I really did want us to have a nice evening." Nick reached out and touched her hand. Instinctively, she jerked it away, causing a glass of water to crash to the floor. "Kind of like a bad dream, isn't it?" Nick was quiet for a moment, staring at the water and ice. "Wow," he added. "Couldn't get much worse now, could it?" He began to laugh.

Carolyn suddenly found herself laughing, too.

"Awkward, that's what that was!" she giggled. "I can't imagine what's going on here!"

"I can explain, if you'll let me." Nick's eyes twinkled. "Why don't we just get out of here and go somewhere else? How about a ride on the beach?"

They left the coolness of the restaurant, and stepped out into the humid evening. Across the small parking lot was a pond, and on the other side of the pond a deer, antlers still in velvet, stepped out of the brush to drink. Nick and Carolyn watched it silently, not wanting to move and scare it off.

The stillness was finally broken when a dark blue car with Massachusetts plates pulled into the lot. Its occupants got out, talking loudly and slamming doors. Smoke from their cigarettes curled in the humid air, carrying the rank odor across the pond. The deer, which had looked up curiously when the car approached, bolted and disappeared into the brush when it saw the people.

"Oh," Carolyn said, disappointed. "Too bad they had to come along and spoil it."

"Tell me about it," Nick said angrily. "Summer people can

really wreck things around here sometimes." He turned towards Carolyn, who realized that she was what Nick would have considered to be 'summer people.' He was doing a good job of making her feel like she didn't belong. Tears welled up in her eyes, and she desperately wanted to be somewhere, anywhere else.

"Oh, hey," Nick broke into her thoughts. He placed an arm around her shoulder, and she immediately stiffened and pulled away. "Come on," he said. "You must think I'm a complete idiot."

Carolyn nodded, not trusting her voice.

"I can explain," Nick began.

"Don't bother." Carolyn found her voice, angry and sad at the same time. "You've been a jerk, alright. All through dinner you were somewhere else, watching someone else. I don't know why I let myself be talked into going out with you. I don't know what I was thinking. Maybe you think that people who don't live around here are just ruining it for the rest of you, and that maybe we don't belong here, but to go out of your way to make me, a visitor to this place, feel like I don't belong, well, that's just horrible!" She stormed off, leaving him standing next to his Jeep.

"Where are you going?" Nick followed her to the end of the parking lot. "You just can't walk all that way back to the campground!"

"Oh yeah?" Carolyn replied. "Watch me!"

Nick grabbed her arm and spun her around to face him. "Listen," he said. "I'm sorry. Really, believe me, I am sorry."

Carolyn glared.

"It's a long story, and I can explain, if only you'll let me! Please," he begged her. "Don't leave. I really want to get to know you." His eyes were dark, pleading. "I know I was a jerk, and I don't blame you for wanting nothing more to do with me. But please, give me a chance to explain my behavior."

Carolyn stared at him, her anger turning to confusion. "Listen, Ted — I mean, Nick," she said, pulling her arm free. "I came here because I needed a vacation, because I needed to get away and enjoy myself, and because I made a promise to Magic. I didn't come here to be treated like this, and I certainly don't intend to spend the rest of my vacation thinking that I should have never come!"

Carolyn realized that she'd slipped and called him Ted, and she'd also mentioned Magic. She knew Nick would take her for a lunatic if she told him the real reason behind her trip. Ignoring the strange look he gave her, she continued. "Anyway, why should I give you another chance? I'll be leaving in a week, and you'll never have to see me again. What more fun can you possibly have with me?"

Nick threw his hands up in the air. "I guess I really blew it." He turned towards his Jeep. "At least," he said, turning back around to face her. "At least let me give you a ride back to your campsite."

Carolyn considered her options and realized that it would be a long walk back to the campground. The sandals she was wearing wouldn't be much protection against the little cactus plants that dotted the roadside. And anyway, it probably wasn't very safe to just go traipsing across the island all alone, especially since the sun would be setting soon. She drew a deep breath, squared her shoulders, and sighed. "Fine, then," she said. "You can take me home."

TWENTY-FIVE

THEY WERE SILENT ON THE RIDE back, each lost in thought, wondering what the other was thinking. The humid evening air rushed past them as the Jeep sped down the two-lane road, making conversation impossible. Out of the corner of her eye Carolyn caught a glimpse of a snowy white egret standing in a marshy area they passed, and she turned to watch it disappear into the tall grass. Losing sight of the magnificent bird, she leaned back in her seat and closed her eyes, thinking of Magic.

Nick noticed the egret too, and glanced over at Carolyn, watching as she stared wistfully after it. He felt terrible about how the evening had ended, and it bothered him that Carolyn was angry with him. He put himself in her position and realized he couldn't blame her for feeling the way she did. Suddenly inspired, he turned the Jeep around and headed back towards town.

"What now?" Carolyn asked, suddenly fearful. "You're going the wrong way!"

"I know a shortcut," Nick explained. "We can drive on the beach and find our way back. At least let me make it up to you by showing you the beach."

"Looks like I don't have a choice," Carolyn murmured. *Oh Magic*, she thought. *You're sure going to hear about this!*

They drove to where the road ended abruptly near a small parking lot. The pavement became a sandy path, and Nick expertly guided the Jeep over a dune on what he called an "access ramp."

"They put these ramps in," he explained when Carolyn asked, "to keep people from driving on the dunes. These dunes are very fragile, especially when you consider that this whole island is nothing but a big ol' sandbar!"

As they crossed the dune on the access ramp, Nick pointed out the tall grass on either side.

"Those are sea oats," he said. "They help keep the sand from moving around too much and eroding during storms, or in the wind."

Carolyn drew in a breath of amazement when they reached the top of the access ramp. Down the beach there were perhaps thirty or so four-wheel drive vehicles, some with fishing poles, deck chairs, and beach umbrellas strapped to their front bumpers. The sun was sinking low into the sound, making the dunes and water sparkle with gold and red.

"Beautiful," she breathed. "This place is incredible!"

They drove down the beach, past the vehicles that were lined up along the water's edge by the dryline, and right to the end of the beach that Nick called "the Point."

"This is where Hatteras Island ends," Nick told her, his eyes skimming the horizon. "That's Ocracoke Island, there." He pointed toward the small island on the horizon. "The only way you can get there is by ferry boat," he explained. "This time of year the ferry pretty much runs constantly. It's a nice ride, and the island is pretty neat, too. They've even got some wild ponies there."

"Is that the ferry?" Carolyn pointed to a blue and white boat that was approaching the Point.

The boat had a strange shape, and was loaded with cars. The flag high atop the ferry fluttered in the steady ocean wind. As the ferry passed, several of the passengers waved, and Nick and Carolyn waved back.

Nick stopped near some other vehicles, and they got out to walk around. Carolyn found a large conch shell half-buried in the sand. When she held it to her ear, she knew the music in it was the ocean roaring all around her. She decided to keep it, for Magic.

"Need to make a call?" Nick was beside her, close enough that his shirt touched her bare arm as the wind blew around them. He took the shell and held it up to his ear. "Sounds like long distance," he said, handing it back. Their fingers brushed against each other, and they were both startled by the electricity between them.

"What happened back there?" Carolyn asked, settling on the bumper of the Jeep, looking out to sea. "At the restaurant, I mean."

Nick followed her gaze out to sea, where he spotted the lights from the Diamond Shoals light tower some twelve miles out across the water. He took a deep breath, and tasted the ocean in the air.

"I've been asking myself that question for quite some time," Nick began, dropping his gaze to avoid Carolyn's. "You see, Angela and I grew up here, on the island." Unwelcome memories came flooding back to him in a rush of colors and emotions that made him feel light-headed.

Angela had always had that effect on Nick, ever since they'd first met as children. There was something almost unreachable about her, something that, in later years, drew Nick and a host of other admirers to her side.

Nick stared out to sea, watching the waves break on the shoals offshore. "As a kid I had a crush on her, but then, so did most of the guys. I always felt like I had the edge over the other guys because her family lived just across the road from mine. Unfortunately for me, Angela was an only child and I became more like the brother she never had than the boyfriend I wanted to be."

"Being an only child isn't as great as it's made out to be," Carolyn offered, following Nick's gaze to the horizon.

"You sound like you're speaking from experience," he said, turning as she nodded. "You were an only child too?"

"Me too," she replied. "It was really lonely sometimes." She thought of Andie, and of all the fun they'd had together. Andie was more than just a cousin, even more than a sister could have been. She was like an extension of Carolyn, the person Carolyn had always wished she could be — daring, fun, free and unafraid of being herself. "But, I had Andie," she added. "And we always had fun together. I don't know what I would've done without her. I bet Angela thought the world of you, too."

Nick thought for a moment, then nodded. "Living out from town the way we did, there weren't many kids around. My brothers were too old to be bothered with me or my friends. Angela and I are the same age. We always attended the same schools, so we had a lot in common. If I wasn't at her place, then she was over at mine," he chuckled, remembering.

"What changed your relationship?" Carolyn asked softly. "It sounds like everything was just great with you two."

"Summer people." Nick spat out the word as if it left a terrible taste in his mouth. "My uncle got this brainstorm one year to start building homes on some land he'd purchased near the ocean. The land was adjacent to ours, and as the homes went up, my uncle would sell them to folks who wanted a vacation cottage away from the hustle and bustle of the mainland. Just like a lot of his friends, he wanted to cash in on the tourist dollars. And so, as the houses were finished, the summer people moved in."

"That's where Tony comes in, right?"

Nick nodded. "Tony's parents bought the cottage that was about a quarter of a mile down the beach from where we lived. They moved in the summer I was ten, and stayed until the end of August. Tony and Angela met that year, and even though I was reluctant to share her with him, I didn't have much of a choice. My brothers were all out working with Dad on the boat, and there wasn't anyone else around to hang out with. Dad didn't think I was old enough to be on the boat with him, so I was stuck at home." His mind raced back in time, remembering what it was like meeting Tony for the first time. He recalled how painful it was shortly after, realizing that he was no longer number one in Angela's life. She'd found a new friend, an exciting friend with wealthy parents who came from New York City on their own private airplane.

"Angela was starstruck with Tony and the life he led," Nick continued. "Being from New York City gave him a worldliness that I just couldn't compete with. And so, as the summer wore on, Angela and I drifted apart as she and Tony solidified their friendship. At least I had Savannah to keep me company," he added. "I don't know what I would have done without that Basenji to talk to."

Carolyn smiled, thinking of the conversations she'd had with Magic along the way. It was easy for her to understand how a person could turn to a dog for comfort. He had needed a friend, someone who would love him no matter what, and he found that someone in Savannah. "She was special," she said. "Savannah."

"She sure was," Nick agreed. "When Tony's family left at the end of August, I was ecstatic, because Angela began to seek out my company again. As the fall and winter moved on, I was sure she'd forgotten all about the summer she spent with Tony. But," he added, "Tony's family arrived in June that next year, and once again she forgot I even existed."

"And the next year?"

"That was the year an early season hurricane destroyed Tony's summer house," he said. "I was glad to see the house gone, glad that he wasn't coming back. We didn't see Tony again until seven summers later. I had Angela all to myself, and it wasn't long before I had fallen in love with her. I really believed she'd fallen in love with me, because we began dating seriously, and everyone assumed we'd end up married after high school."

Carolyn smiled at the thought, reminded of how Andie had married her husband right out of high school. They were a great couple, and had a strong relationship that Carolyn someday hoped she'd find for herself. She recalled how often she'd dreamed of finding a man as wonderful as Andie's husband, but as time passed, she wondered if she ever would. She thought of how it would feel to have Nick hold her in his arms, to have a relationship with him. The thought sent a tremor of excitement through her, and she shook her head to clear it. "But you didn't get married," she said. "What happened?"

"Tony came back." The words hung heavy in the air, like the sound of distant thunder. "He drove down from New York in his new convertible, fresh from his first year at Yale. He was taking the summer off to see how construction was going on his family's new summer place, and wasted no time sweeping Angela off her feet. That was four years ago, and they're getting married next week." Nick shrugged and smiled sadly at Carolyn. "And that was the end of me and Angela. I'm really sorry she treated you poorly back there, really I am." His voice was soft, his eyes watching her earnestly.

Carolyn studied his face, trying to read his thoughts. "Do you still love her?" she asked, feeling her heart race as what seemed like an eternity passed between her question and his answer.

"No," he replied. "No, I can't love her, and I don't. She seems to be happy with her decision, and I'm happy for her."

"Losing someone you've loved is never easy," Carolyn ventured. "Letting go is one of the hardest things a person can do."

Nick turned toward her, and the wind caught a lock of his hair, dropping it down over his eyes. He pushed it back without thinking, in an easy, fluid motion that told Carolyn he'd done it many times before, perhaps even his whole life. "It sounds like you're speaking from experience again," he said. "I don't know why it was so easy to tell you all of this, or why I feel like it all doesn't matter anymore," he added, leaning against the Jeep, very close to her. "It's so strange, but wonderful at the same time. I feel as if I've known you for a long time. You're easy to talk to, you know?"

A rush of emotions flowed through Carolyn, and she didn't know what to say, so she said nothing. Nick's closeness was as exciting as it was unnerving, and she fought back the urge to fall against him, desperately wanting to feel his arms around her, afraid of what he might think. Memories of Ted drifted into her mind, and she angrily pushed them away. Nick was nothing like Ted had been — in fact, he seemed to be the complete opposite. Being with Ted had always made her feel like there was something dark looming on the horizon, and he had always moved in a manner that made one feel as if there might be something dangerous about the man. That unrelenting promise of danger had manifested itself in the end, and Carolyn couldn't bring herself to believe it would be that way with Nick. Being with Nick made her feel protected and free, and there was a familiar, comfortableness about him. In that comfort and familiarity, she had begun to believe there could be more to their relationship — if only she could let herself go and give him a chance.

But what if I get hurt again? She couldn't help but ask the question, and more than anything wanted reassurance that it wouldn't be anything like the last time. *Maybe it will be different, especially since we've both been hurt in our own ways. I'm not the same person I was back when I met Ted. A lot has changed.*

Removing her sandals, she moved away from the Jeep and made her way across the short strip of dry sand to the water's edge. The sea swirled around her bare toes, and she felt the sand melting away beneath her feet as the ocean pulled away from the shore. Looking back, she realized Nick was watching her, gazing at her as if he were really seeing her for the first time.

Ted never looked at me like that, she thought, turning to watch the waves offshore. *I wanted him to, but he always seemed to be looking at someone else. Nicky isn't Ted,* she chastised herself. *In so many ways, he's just like me.* She closed her eyes, enjoying the feel of the warm water lapping against her legs. *We're both looking for something we're afraid we might not ever find. I wonder if he's thinking of kissing me?* She entertained the girlish thought, smiling in spite of herself.

In a flash, like a vision from a dream, Nick appeared by her side, startling her. He placed his hand on her elbow to steady her, and she leaned into him timidly, letting the hem of her dress fall into the water.

"You're not mad at me, are you?" he asked. "I'm really sorry about the way this evening turned out. I guess I'm a little out of practice when it comes to taking someone out for dinner." He stood in the water, not knowing what to do with his hands, wanting to place them around her shoulders, afraid of what she might think if he did.

The sun was setting low in the sky, just touching the still water of the sound behind them. Colors from the sky danced on the clouds and as they turned to watch the sunset the colors danced on their faces, warming them with the last golden rays of the day.

"I enjoyed your company at dinner tonight," Nick whispered, not wanting to break the spell. "And I'm enjoying this sunset more than I've enjoyed any in quite some time. Sunsets here are always spectacular, but I can't remember when I actually took the time to sit back and watch one." He paused, not wanting to scare her off. "I'd like to make the evening up to you," he ventured, gazing at her intently, trying to read her thoughts. A hint of a smile blossomed into a grin that spread across her face, and he found her beautiful.

"I've enjoyed this," Carolyn replied, "and I wouldn't mind seeing you again." She rocked back and forth, feeling the water on her legs, loving the smell of the ocean.

The breeze played with her hair, tossing it back behind her shoulders to caress Nick's face. He could smell the cleanness of it mingled with the scent of the summer evening and the ocean.

"I've never thought anything could be so beautiful," she whispered before he could say anything. "This place was here the whole time, and I never knew it. How could I have missed it?"

"Maybe you never had a reason to know it," Nick replied. "Something made you come here," he added. "Whatever it was, I'm glad it brought you here."

It was Magic, she thought. *Magic brought me here.* Instead of saying the words, she closed her eyes and listened to the music of the surf. "I was thinking of making a day trip to Ocracoke Island," she said at last. "And I was planning on taking Magic along with me. Maybe you could come with us and show us around a bit." She giggled, breaking the tension that had built up between them. "That is, if it's alright with Magic, of course."

Nick grinned happily. "Of course," he confirmed. "Let me know what his answer is," he said, taking her hand in his. "I hope his answer will be 'yes.' "

TWENTY-SIX

AFTER SAYING GOODNIGHT AND dropping Carolyn off at her campsite, Nick felt wide awake and restless, so he drove back out to the beach. He parked his Jeep on the soft sand just beyond the access ramp, turning off the motor and the lights.

The Outer Banks night was alive with the sound of the ocean and wind. All around him, nighttime creatures moved in the sand. Tiny ghost crabs with dark eyes scuttled in and out of their holes. Nearby a nest of sea turtle eggs had hatched, the babies making their way from their sandy home toward the beckoning waves.

The night was warm, the ocean breeze comforting, and the sound of the waves on the beach wrapped around him like the arms of an old, beloved friend. It had been a long day, an amazing day, and a wonderful day. Nick breathed deeply, filling his lungs with the familiar perfume of the ocean and the island.

Not surprisingly, his mind raced with images of the day, and he found that Carolyn and Magic were all he could think of. He stared out at the moonlight that danced on the waves, wondering what would have become of Carolyn had he not seen her struggling in the surf. He thought of her Basenji, Magic, and how the brave old dog had been willing to risk his life for her. In his mind he saw the image of Magic paddling against the waves, heading toward his mistress who was in trouble.

From his own experience he knew that Basenjis were loyal to those they loved and would protect their people no matter what the danger. Nick was certain the old dog knew he was no match for the ocean and the powerful rip current, but it didn't stop him from trying to save Carolyn just the same.

Nick had built houses for many summer people, people from all walks of life who fell in love with the Outer Banks and had to have a piece of it for their very own. He found it strange that Carolyn had traveled all the way to the island from Michigan — doing it in a motorhome, alone. Granted, she'd made it clear that she didn't consider herself to be alone at all — in fact, she seemed content with only Magic for a companion.

There was something mysterious about their relationship, Nick decided. What it was, he couldn't put his finger on. He realized that it was probably her devotion to the old dog that he looked upon with a little bit of envy. Anyone who loved an old dog as much as she did and received that love back had to be someone very special indeed.

Leaning back in his seat, Nick stared into the midnight sky, the multitude of stars above taking his breath away. High in the sky toward the northwest, he could make out the shape of a comet, brighter than the surrounding stars, its long tail glowing milky against the darkness. He made a mental note to tell Carolyn about it, and he hoped she would come to the beach with him again after sunset to take a look. Selecting a star, he closed his eyes for a moment and wished she would.

He imagined he could smell the oncoming storm, the one that had recently been upgraded to a hurricane. Gazing out to sea, he wondered about the swirling mass of clouds and wind that was heading toward the peaceful, unsuspecting coastline. He'd weathered hurricanes before, and he wasn't going to let this one scare him off.

Nick knew the rumor of a storm somewhere out in the Atlantic was enough to send many tourists packing, scurrying back toward the safety of the mainland. It wasn't often that an actual evacuation took place during the summer season, although storms had been known to cut vacations short. Nick was surprised when the possibility of evacuating saddened him. He knew Carolyn wasn't the type to stick around if an evacuation was ordered.

Maybe the storm will turn away, he thought hopefully. *After all, that happens more times than not. Besides, it's such a long way off at this point. Who can predict where it will go?* He stared out at the Atlantic, wondering.

His thoughts drifted to their conversation in the restaurant, and subsequent drive out on the beach. He'd been so close to kissing her, he realized with a shock. He hardly knew her and already he'd thought about kissing her. He ran his fingers through his hair, and turned his face into the wind.

Angela and Tony's presence at the restaurant had been unsettling for him, like a bad dream where he was unable to change the outcome. All his life he'd wanted Angela to like him as more than just a friend, and once he'd come so close it was painful to recall. Only now was he realizing that, at best, a friend was all he'd ever be to her, and he wasn't sure he even wanted that anymore. Stranger still was the fact that in the short time he had known Carolyn, thoughts of Angela that had plagued him ever since the announcement of her engagement seemed unimportant, almost a distant memory.

Yawning, he settled back into his seat and watched the tide roll in. He recalled the many summer nights he'd spent camping out on the beach with Savannah, and the memories brought a smile to his face. There had been fewer people then, and life had seemed so much simpler. Slowly, without even knowing it, he drifted off to sleep, the sound of the ocean lulling him into dreams.

He dreamed of Carolyn in the ocean, wading far offshore. He became alarmed, for somehow he knew the ocean floor dropped off sharply beyond the sandbar she was standing on. He called out to her, telling her not to go any further. She turned at the sound of his voice, and waved happily. He called out to her again, and still she didn't seem to hear his words over the roaring of the ocean. He felt panic rising inside of him, twisting his stomach painfully, for he knew that if she stepped off the sandbar, she'd be pulled under by the strong ocean current. She was in danger, and although he tried to move, he couldn't. He felt paralyzed, and could do nothing to help her.

Magic appeared on the beach next to him, his dark red coat wet from the surf. His long pink tongue hung out of his mouth, and he was panting heavily.

"Why don't you save her?" Magic gasped, falling to the sand, clearly exhausted. "I've been trying and trying, but I just can't do it. You know you swim better than I can."

"She can't hear me," Nick replied. "How can I make her

understand?"

The old dog regarded him with dark brown eyes. "She doesn't hear you?" he asked, blinking in surprise. "I don't understand. She can hear me just fine."

Nick stared at the Basenji, and the dog seemed very familiar to him. Magic's face changed until it became Savannah's, then changed back again until the two seemed to be the same dog and he couldn't tell who he was looking at. He wanted to ask Magic who he was, and why he was on the beach instead of out in the surf, but he found that the dog had turned his attentions back to Carolyn.

"It's the ocean," Magic said, finally. "She's got the ocean in her ears, can't you tell? That's why she can't hear you." He stood and shook the water from his coat, the droplets spraying Nick, releasing him from his paralysis. "The hurricane will swallow her for sure if we don't help her!"

"But I've got to warn her!" Nick cried, racing to the water. "Why can't she hear me?" He stared out at the water, but Carolyn was no longer there. He heard her voice calling him, and he saw that she'd gone up into the lighthouse, and was waving at him from the top of the tower.

"Maybe she never could," Magic said simply, turning away. "Sometimes a person can be right in front of you and you don't even see or hear him until it's too late. You know, she can hear me just fine. I know the right words."

Nick watched the old dog trot up the beach toward the lighthouse. "Do I know you?" he called. "Magic? Savannah? Who are you?"

In a crazy rush of wind and clouds, the sky was suddenly dark and the ocean was angry, and Carolyn was gone. Nick was a little boy again, lost in a terrible storm. He fought his way up the beach toward the lighthouse, the wind threatening to push him over into the dark water that swirled around his ankles. The sand gave way under his feet, and he was falling, falling. He felt a sharp pain in his head, and he cried out.

He lay on the cool tile floor of the lighthouse, listening to the storm roaring outside. He felt safe in the old lighthouse, and didn't want to move for fear he'd broken something when he fell. His head was fuzzy and it hurt him terribly. All around he could hear strange voices, murmuring above the sound of the storm. The howling he'd heard earlier had quieted, and he felt something warm on his face, licking away the pain. He tried to look up, but his eyelids were too heavy to open.

Again he heard the murmuring of strange voices, and the nicker of a pony. He could feel the pony's warm breath on his face as she sniffed him, gentle puffs that smelled like fresh grass and sunshine. He called out for his Basenji puppy, and the puppy was there, curled up by his side, keeping him warm with his little body. He could hear the puppy talking to him, in a voice that was the same as Magic's. The puppy was telling him not to be afraid, that he was safe from the storm.

"You'll be alright," the puppy said, and Nick could feel his tiny wet nose close to his ear. "I'm so sorry for not being able to do more. I'm so afraid!"

Nick wanted to tell the puppy not to worry, that he would protect him. He felt the puppy curl up and rest his tiny head next to his own, and when he opened his eyes he saw Magic staring back at him. Unable to stay awake, he drifted into unconsciousness, and when he heard a pony nicker again, he opened his eyes.

The ocean was smooth, with barely a ripple as it lapped quietly at the beach. Fiery red, the sun had just begun to rise over the water, the sky brightening slowly as the day began. High overhead, a lone pelican soared dark against the sky. Sandpipers on impossibly thin legs picked their way through the wet sand at the waters edge, looking for breakfast. Farther down the beach, several vehicles were already parked, their owners fishing in the stillness of the early morning surf.

Nick yawned and stretched, realizing with a start that he'd spent the entire night on the beach. Remains of his strange dream lingered in his mind, making him wonder what it all meant.

He rubbed the sleep from his eyes as his mind traveled a million miles a second, remembering the events of the past day. He thought of watching the sunset with Carolyn, and he smiled when he remembered how beautiful she'd looked in the last light of day and how her smile had lit up her whole face.

I wonder if she's watching the sunrise, he thought suddenly, feeling a bit lonely and wishing she were there beside him. The thought that she might be watching the day begin from her campsite cheered him, and he pictured her sitting on the beach with Magic by her side.

The wind would be blowing her hair back right now, he reflected. *And when the sun touches it, it will shine even more. Ah, what I wouldn't give to be close to her like Magic must be.* He wondered what she'd told the old dog about their date, and he hoped she hadn't changed her mind about seeing him again. *I used to tell Savannah everything,* he remembered. *I wouldn't be surprised if it's the same between her and Magic.*

Leaving the Jeep, he waded into the warm ocean and splashed water on his face. Moving into deeper water, he floated on his back, letting the gentle rolling of the waves carry him for a few moments before he swam back to shore. *She said she wanted to see Ocracoke today,* he remembered, hopping into the Jeep so he could head home and shower. *I hope she hasn't changed her mind. I can't wait to see her again!*

PART THREE

BELIEVE

Where is he now, my beloved dog? Does he
play amongst the stars, chasing comets
across the vast, unending heavens?
— Unknown

TWENTY-SEVEN

THE MORNING DAWNED HAZY AND hot, with only a few wispy clouds high and bright in the brilliant blue August sky. The ocean was still, almost glasslike, lapping gently at the beach. After a quick splash in the warm, shallow water left behind by a little rivulet when the tide pulled out, Magic settled onto one of the two beach towels Carolyn had laid out in the soft sand. He dug around until the sand beneath the towel was to his liking before stretching out to soak up some sun.

Turning his wrinkled, time-grizzled face to catch the breeze, he sighed and closed his eyes, breathing in the wonderful ocean smells that were familiar and comforting to him. He smelled the fresh cleanness of the cotton towel, and through it the sand beneath him, pleasantly warmed by the sun. As he licked his paws dry, he tasted the salty ocean on his coat. He could smell the sweet fruitiness of suntan lotion lingering in the warm air all around him, and he opened his eyes to see a line of brown pelicans skimming over the surface of the water in search of fish.

I've really missed this place, he thought to himself, watching Carolyn as she collected shells from the beach.

When she had returned from her dinner with Nicky, fresh-faced and windblown, he had eagerly clung to her every word as she recounted her adventures of the evening, including the sunset drive she had taken with Nicky on the beach. He couldn't help but notice the way her green eyes lit up when she spoke of Nick, and he could tell she liked him very much.

"Hey." Carolyn, her body wet and glistening in the sun, sat down next to Magic, getting water and sand on the empty beach towel. Magic noticed that her dark red swimsuit gave away the fact that she had a little bit of a tummy, and that endeared her to him more. "Enjoying the beautiful day?" She shook the water from her hair, sending a spray of salty droplets flying.

"It's great," Magic replied, leaning over to lick water from her arm. "Do you really like it here?" he asked, knowing the answer but wanting to hear it anyway.

"I do," she answered, wondering if Nick would come by to see her today. "Nick builds houses," she said, looking down the beach. Over the dunes the tops of some houses he had pointed out to her as ones he'd worked on were clearly visible. "Wouldn't it be great if he could build us a house? Then we could stay here all the time." The moment the words were out of her mouth, she instantly regretted them. "But, I can't afford that," she added quickly.

Magic's heart leapt and raced when he heard her words, but he knew that she didn't mean it, that she couldn't possibly mean it. "Not many people can afford to live like that," he told her, letting her know it was alright and he wasn't offended. "Lots of people here are summer people," he said. "They only stay a few weeks out of the year, and rent their houses out to other tourists." Magic shifted, then sat up to scratch his ear. "It's the way it's always been, as far as I can remember."

"Nick doesn't seem to like summer people much, and I can't say that I blame him." She played with a corner of her towel, flipping some sand off with her index finger. "Angela and Tony gave him a pretty good reason not to like summer people. But, I'm summer people, too." She smiled. "And I guess we get along okay."

"I remember Angela," Magic said. "Long ago, he had a thing for her. But she just wasn't ever serious about him. Even as a puppy, I knew that much." He directed his attentions to Carolyn's leg, where water droplets were abundant. "Do you like him?" he asked between licks. "Nicky?"

"Nicky? Sure I like him." She removed her sunglasses, setting them carefully on the towel so they wouldn't get covered with sand. Reaching into her beach bag, she pulled out a bottle of suntan lotion. "He's nice, good looking, and he's fun to be with." She rubbed a bit of lotion on Magic's nose where it was beginning to look a little too pink. "I really do like him," she finished not knowing what to say and certainly not wanting to sound too hopeful. "Don't lick it off."

The warning didn't come quickly enough, for Magic's tongue was even quicker. "Bleah!" Magic wrinkled up his nose and pulled his lips away from his teeth. "That's awful stuff!" He shook his head, trying to rid the terrible taste from his mouth.

"Tell you what," Carolyn said, standing up and shaking out

the beach towel. "Let's head back to the motorhome and I'll give you something to get rid of the bad taste. How about some cookies and fresh water? I'll even throw in some ice cubes."

Together they headed up the beach and over the dunes. Refusing to be carried, Magic hopped and pranced as the hot sand burned his paw pads, alternating feet so they all didn't touch the ground at once.

Once back in the coolness of the motorhome, Magic ate a few cookies and felt better.

"I had a girlfriend once," he began, "before Violet." He licked his muzzle, searching for crumbs that might have gotten past him.

"Well, now." Carolyn handed him another cookie, which he crunched slowly. "What was she like?" She sniffed one of the dog cookies, and nibbled on a corner curiously. "Hmmmm. Interesting." She handed the remainder to Magic.

"Her name was Diva," he replied, "and she was the most beautiful creature I had ever seen in my life."

"Her full name was Mystrybrook's Miss Devious, but they called her Diva because of her voice. When she yodeled, it was the prettiest sound you could ever imagine, high and sweet, and very feminine. I was crazy about her," he said, wrinkling his brow. "But then again, so were all the boys." He closed his eyes, savoring the memory.

"Diva was beautiful and she knew it, and she made sure everyone around her knew it, too. She caught my eye the very first time I saw her in the show ring. She had a stunning tricolor coat, with the black so dark and shiny it gleamed when the sun hit it. Her white was dazzling, and she had dainty, perfect little paws. She used to wrinkle her forehead so much that you'd think the red pips above her eyes would touch." Magic sighed. "She had a tail that triple-curled. And," he added, "was she ever a flirt!"

"I was well established in the show ring when Diva first started, so it wasn't long before she noticed me. She used to do silly things to get my attention." He rolled his eyes. "As thrilled as I was that she was interested in me, I played hard to get with her, and it drove her up a tree! She was a silly, young thing."

"When I'd pass her by she would pull right to the end of her show lead until it was tight on her neck, and she would rise up on her hind legs to paw the air behind me." He chuckled to himself, the picture of Diva's white paws batting the air with a charming kittenness that was unique to Basenjis and was absolutely irresistible when she did it. "We were both so young," he added. "Sometimes I forget what that used to be like."

Magic stood and stretched, flexing his toes and unfurling his tail, then wandered off to get a drink of water. Discovering an empty bowl, he pawed at it until it banged loudly on the floor. Carolyn hurriedly apologized and filled the bowl with fresh, cool water.

Magic lapped greedily, drinking directly from the center of the bowl and being careful not to get any water on himself or the floor. When he finished, he ran a tongue over his muzzle, and rubbed it thoroughly on the carpeting where the sofa met the floor.

"No wonder dogs drink out of toilets," he muttered under his breath. "It's the only water that's always there!"

"I said I was sorry." There was a hurt tone in Carolyn's voice, and it irritated Magic.

"It's a fine thing to depend on someone for your food and water! After all, if the tables were turned, do you think *I* would forget?" Magic's voice had an uncharacteristic edge to it. "No," he concluded. "*I* wouldn't forget."

He hopped on the sofa, and curled up into a tight ball. "I need a nap," he muttered, not liking the way he felt at all. All of a sudden his heart was beating rapidly, and his breath came in short, difficult gasps. His head was pounding, and he felt terribly hot.

It's the heat, he told himself. *The heat's gotten to me. And, I just need to rest. Being out in the hot sun today wasn't such a good idea, after all.*

Alarmed by his uncharacteristic outburst, Carolyn studied the old dog carefully, trying to judge his temper and wondering if there was something more that was bothering him than just the heat and an empty water dish. She almost asked him straight out, but decided to trust his judgement that maybe all he really needed was a good nap.

"Poor fella," she murmured, opening up the freezer compartment and getting a few ice cubes out of a tray. She dropped them into his water bowl, and they clanged against the stainless steel, splashing water over the sides. She took one of the cubes to where he lay, and he accepted it from her, crunching the coolness into smaller bits that he could swallow.

"Thanks for the ice," he said, feeling bad that he'd gotten angry.

"You'll be okay?" she asked softly, placing a gentle hand on his back and feeling the rhythm of his breathing as it slowed. She often forgot that he was an old dog, for his stories and words made him seem younger than his years. She could see him in her mind, young and strong and beautiful. He was beautiful still, but in a different way, in the way that old people are beautiful. The thought brought tears to her eyes, and she wiped them away before he could see them.

"Yes," Magic whispered, drifting off into a troubled slumber. "Don't worry, I'm sorry I was short with you." He sighed and closed his eyes, his graying muzzle tucked into his paws, his breath warming them comfortingly. "It's the heat and humidity," he murmured. "Forgive me. I'll feel better after a nap, I think."

He slept for nearly two hours, lulled by the steady hum of the air conditioning unit above him. Several times he awoke with a start from bad dreams, but he wasn't able to remember them clearly. He thought of Diva and the story he'd started to tell

Carolyn, and he felt bad for not finishing it. He didn't understand why the heat suddenly seemed to bother him. The day was bright and sunny, but the air pressure and humidity made his head ache terribly. He made himself as comfortable as he could, and drifted off to sleep once more.

Carolyn sat outside the motorhome, her feet propped on a picnic table. Half-heartedly she strummed her guitar, the soft notes hanging in the thick summer air. The humidity was getting to her, too, and it didn't help that the cheap lawn chair she sat in was making her back itch. She'd left the motorhome door open just a bit so she would know when Magic awoke. Several times she heard the old dog talking in his sleep, and although she couldn't make out the words, she knew his dreams were troubling him again. She continued to play, knowing that he enjoyed the music and hoping it would help soothe his troubled dreams.

"Oh, Magic," she said aloud. "I would give anything to help you be happy!"

"Hello!" Nick appeared around the corner of the motorhome. "Hey, you play guitar? That sounded great."

Carolyn hadn't heard him arrive, and she jumped in surprise when she saw him. "Nicky!" she exclaimed.

He was carrying a large watermelon in his arms. A big grin spread across his face when she called him Nicky. "Brought you a little something to help you cool off on this hot day." He glanced around, looking for Magic. "Where's Magic?" he asked. "I know he'll enjoy some of this watermelon. Our Basenjis always did."

"He wasn't feeling good, and I think the heat's gotten to him today. He's inside taking a nap," Carolyn answered, watching as Nick placed the large melon gently on the picnic table. She could see that the melon had been chilled, for there were large droplets of water condensing on it. She reached out as it started to roll, diving forward to catch it at the same time he did, grasping his hand instead of the melon.

"Oh," she said, pulling her hand back, suddenly shy. "Sorry. It was going to fall."

Nick smiled. "If you've got a knife, we can cut this open and have some," he said, feeling his face redden a bit. "It's nice and cool, and I guarantee it will be wonderful." He studied the watermelon the way a painter might a fine work of art. "And, if I'm not mistaken, we'll need plenty of napkins or paper towels."

He followed Carolyn into the motorhome, and their voices woke Magic from his nap. The old dog yawned loudly and stretched, nearly falling off the sofa.

"Good afternoon, sleepy," Carolyn said, reaching down to pat the old dog. "Are you feeling any better?"

"This will work," Nick said, turning around. He had found a long knife in a drawer near the little motorhome sink, and held it in his hand triumphantly.

Still dazed from sleep, Magic took one look at the knife and panicked. "Look out! Look out!" he screamed. "He's got a knife!" He jumped up, peeling his upper lip back menacingly, exposing sharp Basenji teeth.

"What?" Carolyn turned back towards Nick. "Don't be silly," she whispered. "He's just brought us a watermelon and we needed the knife to cut it, that's all." She glanced at Nick. "Uh, we just startled him," she explained. "He's not quite awake yet."

Nick eyed the Basenji warily. "He looks like he could eat me right now." he said. "I guess I don't blame him!" He put the knife down and crouched to Magic's level. "Hey, old boy," he said, letting Magic sniff his fingers. "Hey, I didn't mean to frighten you." His voice was kind and low. Slowly, the hairs on Magic's neck smoothed out, and he wagged his tail meekly.

"Good old boy," Nick said, scratching him under the chin. "Good old Magic."

Magic looked up at Carolyn, and rolled his eyes. "Old boy indeed," he said, standing up and giving himself a good shake, right down to the tip of his tail. "Sorry for the scare," he said sheepishly. "Tell him I'm sorry, won't you?" he asked. "I would tell him myself but he can't hear me."

Carolyn scooped the Basenji into her arms and planted a kiss on his nose. "Magic's sorry he got angry," she told Nick. "He does want to be friends."

"That's good to know," Nick said. "I hope he likes watermelon, because we've got a lot of it."

At the word "watermelon" Magic's ears pricked forward. "He brought *watermelon*!" he asked, incredulously. "Wonderful!" He licked his muzzle in anticipation.

The watermelon was as cool and refreshing as Nick had promised. Magic ate his fill, careful not to get the sweet juice all over his fine coat. He couldn't help getting a few drops on himself, but these he carefully cleaned from his coat.

It wasn't long before tiny bees made their appearance on the scene. Magic snapped playfully at the little bees that were drawn to the watermelon's sweetness, until Carolyn teased him, telling him that he'd better knock it off unless he wanted to get stung.

"You sound just like a parent," Magic joked back. "It wouldn't take a genius to figure out that you're a teacher!"

Carolyn smiled at his remark, and made a mental note to ask him to finish the story about Diva later. She knew there had to be a lot more to the story than he'd initially let on. And anyway, it wasn't like Magic to leave a story unfinished.

TWENTY-EIGHT

WHEN THEY HAD THEIR FILL OF THE
watermelon, the trio piled into Nick's Jeep and
headed towards Hatteras Village for an afternoon
on Ocracoke Island.

"I suppose I get the back seat," Magic
grumbled, eyeing the open Jeep critically.

"Unless you want to stay here." Carolyn
gave him a look that clearly told him to knock it
off.

For half a second Magic thought about
staying behind, but the day was so beautiful he

decided to go along. Certainly, he hadn't come all this way to sit inside a motorhome on such a perfect summer day.

"The back is fine," he decided, stretching out across the rear seat Nick had covered with a soft blanket. "Let's go!" He yodeled loudly, making them laugh.

Black-capped seagulls hovered eagerly in the warm summer air, their cries carried on the gentle breeze. Houses and stores rushed by, and the wide, knobby tires of the Jeep hummed happily on the hot pavement. As they approached town, traffic increased. They arrived at the ferry docks in time to see one ferry pulling away, loaded with cars. Another ferry, empty except for a couple of vehicles, waited to unload.

"Looks like good timing," Carolyn remarked. "That one just got here!"

"This is only one of several ways to get there," Nick explained. "You can get to Ocracoke by ferry from Hatteras Island, here, or from the mainland at Swan Quarter."

"I've noticed those blue signs that say 'Evacuation Route,'" Carolyn said. "Will people actually stay on the island in a hurricane? It's a bit frightening to think that there are only a couple of routes on or off the island."

"The evacuation routes are there mainly to get folks out of here if a hurricane threatens." Nick ran his fingers through his hair. "Remember last night when we were on top of the access ramp by the dunes? If you looked east then west, it's easy to see how narrow Hatteras Island really is. Ocracoke isn't much different. When a hurricane warning is posted and the islands are asked to evacuate, they usually start by getting all the tourists off of Ocracoke. Then the evacuation moves up the islands." He steered the Jeep into a short line of cars, stopping just short of a car with Michigan plates. "Hey, they're from Michigan, too." He grinned. "Do you know them?"

Carolyn giggled. "No, I don't know who they are. It's such a beautiful day," she added. "It's hard to imagine that a hurricane could blow in at any time."

"Well, it's not that dramatic," Nick said. "They don't just appear on the horizon one afternoon like a thunderstorm does. We get plenty of warning, and there's enough time to evacuate if we have to. In fact," he added, "there's a hurricane out there right now." He ran his fingers through his hair again. "August is a good month for hurricanes, actually." Seeing the concerned look on her face, he added "But don't worry. This storm is far enough away, and moving slowly. Don't let it ruin this beautiful day."

"I feel a little silly admitting it, but since I've been here I haven't even turned on the television or listened to the radio." Carolyn said. She glanced back at Magic, who was dozing happily in the sun. "I usually pay attention to weather reports."

"You don't think Magic is too hot back there, do you?" Nick asked. "We could put the top up, if you want."

"Don't bother," Magic said, yawning. "The sun feels good, and the breeze has picked up enough that I'm not all that hot. I feel just fine now."

"He's fine," Carolyn said. "He'll let us know if he gets too hot."

"Well, then we'll just have to listen for him." Nick turned on the radio, and tuned it to a news station. "Just to set our minds at ease," he said. "Let's see what the weather report says."

"Looks like it's our turn," Carolyn said, noticing the car from Michigan had moved forward in line. "I've never been on a ferry like this."

Nick drove the Jeep forward until the wheels contacted the metal gangplank. One guide directed the Jeep to the forward-most position on the ferry, where all that was between them and the ocean was a chained-off area and a small railing.

"Yikes," Carolyn exclaimed. "They sure do pack them on here, don't they?"

"We can get out and walk around when the boat gets underway," Nick said. "It's about a forty minute ride to the island."

Carolyn watched in amazement as the ferry operators and guides quickly loaded the remainder of the vehicles onto the boat. The ferry was a flat, barge-like vessel that could easily hold thirty vehicles. The vehicles were loaded around the perimeter of the boat, and in the middle was a two-story passenger area and the captain sat high inside the topmost tower.

"These ferries are operated by the state as part of our highway system," Nick explained. "There's no cost to go from here to Ocracoke, but if you want to get from Ocracoke to the mainland, there's a fee."

Magic watched all the commotion with great interest, his ears swiveling this way and that, picking up different sounds. "Would you believe I've never been on a boat before?" he asked. "Born and raised here, and you'd think I would've spent some time on a boat!"

A horn sounded from the tower above, and the ferry began to pull away from the dock. It moved slowly at first, then faster as it headed towards the island in the distance.

Magic stuck his head out the front of the ferry, letting the warm wind blow over him, caressing his body. It felt like the gentle touch of his mother's tongue, rolling down his back, wrapping itself around his legs, finding its way into his ears and eyes. He closed his eyes and relaxed his tail, feeling free and peaceful.

He'd heard about the island of Ocracoke, and of the wild ponies that lived on it. Thinking of the island made him remember the wild pony that had followed the sound of his voice to the safety of the lighthouse in the hurricane so many years ago. What had happened to her, Magic could only guess. Buried deep in his memories was the hugeness of her, the damp horse smell that was touched with saltwater and sunlight, a smell that was so very much like the ocean wind.

The ferry moved and vibrated beneath him, and when he turned away from the wind, he could smell diesel fuel, metal, and automobiles. His ears caught the rhythmic flap-flap-flap of the flags high atop the pilot house. All around him people were milling about, some staying with their vehicles and others, like Carolyn and Nick, were walking around, leaning over one edge of the ferry or another, taking pictures and enjoying the ride.

One little girl, not more than three years old, stared at him shyly for a moment before walking over and reaching out a chubby hand for him to sniff. Instinctively, the bristles on his back stood up, but he felt them relax under her caress. She smelled delightful, like suntan lotion, baby powder, and apple juice.

"Doggy," she said. "You pretty, good doggy!"

"Yes," he replied, watching her eyes grow wide with excitement. "I'm a nice doggy."

In that instant he realized that she had heard him, as clearly as if a person had spoken to her. He took a few steps back from her, visibly shaken. He'd never had anyone else except Carolyn hear him, and he wondered if maybe everyone on the ferry could hear him as well.

It can't be, he thought. *How can it be?*

He followed the little girl as she wandered back to her parents, wanting to know more.

"Doggy talked to me, mommy," she said breathlessly, pointing at Magic. "He's a good doggy."

Her mother gazed down at the old Basenji and smiled. "I'm sure he did, honey," she said. "He seems like a nice doggy."

Magic stared hard at the woman, desperately wanting to know if she could hear him too. "Hello," he said. "Nice day, isn't it?"

The woman glanced down at him in annoyance. "Go on back

to where you belong, now," she said. "Go on, shoo!"

Magic regarded her for a moment. "Hello," he said again, louder this time.

"Doggy says hello, Mommy," the little girl chimed in, throwing her arms around his neck. "He likes me."

"Never mind," Magic said, disappointed that only the child seemed to hear him. "Well, good-bye, then." He worked his way out of her grasp and hurried back towards Carolyn and Nick, who were watching a parasail that was hovering high in the sky with a rainbow-colored chute.

"Hey," Magic said, pawing at Carolyn's leg. "Can you believe that I just talked to that little girl and she understood me?"

"You did what?" she asked. "You talked to who?"

"What?" Nick turned and saw Magic. "Oh, hey, where've you been, boy?"

"I did!" Magic insisted. "That little girl over there! I talked to her and she heard me!"

Carolyn didn't know what to say. She crouched down and pulled Magic close. "We'll talk about it later, okay?" she whispered, wishing she could share her secret with Nick.

I can't do that, she thought. *He'd think I was crazy.*

The air cooled considerably as they met open water, and Carolyn felt a little chill. *Somewhere out there's a hurricane,* she thought, imagining its swirling clouds and powerful winds.

"Did you hear that? We've officially got a hurricane watch," Nick said, turning off the radio. "But there's no need to worry about it just yet. This storm is pretty far off, and the forecasters say it's moving slowly and might fizzle out in the Atlantic."

"Isn't a hurricane watch like a tornado watch?" Carolyn asked. "It sounds pretty serious to me."

"It's okay," Nick assured her. "It just means the weather service has indicated that the storm is heading in this general direction. There's no guarantee it will hit here, and it's too far off yet to really be certain." A glimmer of something in the water caught his eye. "Look at that!" he exclaimed, pointing to the waves. "Dolphins!"

"Look," Magic shouted, at about the same time. "Dolphins!"

A school of dolphins had appeared off the port side of the ferry. There were about six or seven, and they were swimming right alongside the boat, taking turns playing in its wake. When they broke through the surface of the water, their skin glistened silver-grey in the sunlight.

"I'm glad I remembered my camera." Carolyn said. "I've got to get a photo of this!" She snapped a few shots of the dolphins, and turned toward where Nick was standing next to the Jeep, patting Magic on the head. He'd taken his shirt off, and he was darkly tanned.

"Nicky, smile," Carolyn said, feeling a bit silly. "You guys are quite a couple," she added. *I want to remember this day*, she told herself. *I don't ever want to forget this beautiful place, and my new friend.*

"Here, let me take one of you," Nick said, reaching for the camera. His fingers brushed against Carolyn's as she handed it to him. "Then maybe we can get someone to take one with all of us in it."

He stepped back a few feet, and peered through the lens. "I have an idea," he said, putting the camera down. "Why don't you put Magic up here." He patted the hood of the Jeep, pulling his hand back when he felt how hot the surface was. "Nope! Bad idea. Here." He opened the driver's door and placed his shirt on the seat. "Hop inside, Magic," he said, patting the cushion. He closed the door and Magic put his paws on the window ledge, leaning against Carolyn as she stood next to him.

"Say cheese!" He snapped a second picture, loving the way Carolyn's smile lit up her face. Enlisting the help of another passenger, Nick stood beside Carolyn, gently placing his arm around her shoulders.

"I hope you don't mind," he whispered in her ear.

"Not at all," she smiled, enjoying the feel of him next to her.

Magic yodeled as the passenger snapped their picture, thrilled to see the seeds of romance blossoming between his two friends. Excitedly, his mind raced ahead, wondering how far the relationship would grow.

Could this mean she won't go back to Michigan? he wondered, feeling his heart race at the thought of remaining in the Outer Banks with her. It was too early to tell for certain, but Magic had a feeling the day's adventure would draw the couple even closer together. *And that,* he thought anxiously, *would be wonderful for all of us!*

TWENTY-NINE

ALL TOO SOON THE FERRY RIDE WAS

over. Nick guided the Jeep carefully down the

gangplank, and before long the hot sun was

cooled by the rush of air as they sped down the

two-lane road to the village of Ocracoke.

"Would you believe this island was once a

hideout for pirates?" Nick asked. "This place is

full of history as well as mystery. Many a

famous pirate strode across these sandy shores

and anchored his vessel out yonder." He pointed

out to sea. "When I was little, we'd visit my

grandparents here, and I would spend hours digging up the beaches looking for buried treasure."

"And did you ever find any, pirate Nicky?" Carolyn laughed.

"I did," he joked back. "Only, I wanted to be sure the other pirates wouldn't find it, and so I buried it. I drew a map so I could remember exactly where it is. Unfortunately, I buried it too. Say, did I mention that I once pulled a mermaid from the briny waves?"

"But she wasn't big enough so you threw her back?"

"No, I kept her because she was so beautiful." He paused and gave her hand a squeeze. "Do you like horses?"

"Horses? Sure, why?" Carolyn gazed at the small barns and fenced-in area just off the road. "Are we going riding?"

Nick laughed. "I don't think you'd want to ride these horses," he said. "This is the pony sanctuary that was built to keep the wild ones in. It's huge, so the ponies still think they've got the run of the place, but it's safer for them. There were too many wandering onto the road and getting hit by cars, and they'd developed a fondness for people's gardens that was pretty unpopular."

They got out of the Jeep and leaned up against the fence. Several dark bay and pinto ponies were grazing in the lush green paddock, their tails swishing rhythmically.

"These are true mustangs," Nick explained, putting his arm around Carolyn. "They're believed to be descended from the horses brought by the Spanish to this area. As the story goes, the Spanish galleons ran aground and were shipwrecked on the shoals just off the coast. The ponies swam their way to the island and made it their home. Another popular theory is that these ponies came from an English ship called *Tiger*. It was the flagship of the vessels that carried some of the first colonists to Roanoke, north of here." He whistled softly and several horses turned their heads, their fine ears moving toward the sound.

"They're beautiful," Carolyn breathed. "And at the same time mysterious. So no one really knows what their true background is?"

"That's right," Nick replied. "In a way, they're kind of like Magic. Maybe you'll never really know who he is or where he's been, but it really doesn't matter because he's with you here and now, and you love him just for being him."

Carolyn gazed into Nick's eyes, wishing with all her heart she could tell him that she did know all about Magic, including where he came from. "Wouldn't it be something," she ventured, "if we could find out?"

"I don't know how you'd begin," Nick replied. "He's not tattooed, so you can't trace him that way. You'd at least need registration papers on him, or find someone who knew him long ago." He stared at the old dog, who seemed to be listening to their conversation with great interest. "Magic's about twelve or thirteen, isn't he?"

"The vet guessed fifteen," Carolyn said, and thought *Actually, Magic told me he was fifteen.*

"Well, he'd be about the right age if he were one of Savannah's puppies," Nick said, and Carolyn's heart raced, knowing he was unaware of how close to the truth he really was. "But," he added, "we didn't sell to anyone from Michigan. I think I'd remember it if we had."

"People move," Carolyn insisted. "And dogs are bought and sold all the time. Especially show dogs. You have to admit, it is possible."

A troubled look crossed Nick's face, and he stared at Carolyn with wide eyes. "We did sell two pups as show dogs," he said slowly. "One male and one female." *But there's no way it could be the same dog,* he thought, shaking his head. *That puppy, the male, was the last one sold, right after dad died, I think. I don't remember ever knowing what happened to him after that.*

"No," he said finally. "No, I don't think it's possible. As much as I would like it to be, and as much as he reminds me of Savannah, it's just not possible."

The look of shock on Magic's face mirrored the one on Carolyn's. A gust of wind blew through the trees, shaking the leaves and startling the horses. Still troubled, Nick stared up at the sky, watching the clouds in silence. "The wind is changing," he said quietly. "I'd be willing to bet that if the hurricane doesn't make it up this far, some rain from it will."

Anxious to talk more about Magic, but suddenly fearful of the hurricane, Carolyn let the topic of Magic's past drop. "Where will the horses go when there's a hurricane?" she asked, watching a small foal kicking up its heels with another. "I can't imagine them just hopping on the ferry and riding off to safety.'"

"Oh, they stay on the island," Nick said. "They're tough survivors. They've been here for hundreds of years, and I'm sure they've got their tricks and hiding places. They know how to ride out a storm."

He told her about how, in times past, the residents of the island would capture the wild ponies, tame them, and use them in their daily lives. "It wasn't until quite recently in their history that they even had reliable telephones or cable television out here."

Magic watched the horses intently, trying to hear what they were saying. Their language was entirely different from his own, for they mostly communicated with pictures in their minds, something he wasn't used to. They didn't use as many words as he did, for their wildness and freedom from domestication had made words almost unnecessary.

He could sense an uneasiness in the animals, and he wasn't sure if it was because they'd caught wind of his scent or if it was because they could feel the subtle dropping of the air pressure all around them, signaling the approaching storm. As the horses milled around, their unshod hooves kicked up small puffs of dust that swirled and danced in the hot air. Magic had to believe these horses knew the weather signs better than he, for it was born into them, a part of their genetic makeup.

Leaving the ponies behind, they drove some more on the two-lane road that wound its way through a saltwater marsh, where the grass was tall and brown, and hid strange birds in its thickness. Canals were cut through the marsh in various places, and Carolyn saw several people in ocean-going kayaks drifting silently by. Cicadas screamed in the heat, their constant buzzing something that she and Magic both were learning to ignore.

The town of Ocracoke was made up of old buildings set low to the ground and several newer structures that were built up high on pilings. Nick explained that the settlement was very old, and they toured the area and saw several historical buildings, including the short white lighthouse.

A man with a backpack approached them, and asked if they'd mind taking his picture for him, explaining that he was taking the summer to walk his way down the coast, from Maine to Florida. He handed Nick his camera, posing proudly with his backpack in front of the long walkway, the lighthouse in the background. On impulse, Carolyn told the man that it wasn't right that he be alone in the picture, and she persuaded Magic to join her in the next one Nick took.

"That was nice," Nick said after the man had left. "I think you made his day."

Carolyn smiled. "It just seemed kind of sad, being all alone in a picture on your vacation," she said. "Now he's got something fun to remember."

"Speaking of remembering," Nick said. "Look how they've remembered their storms." He pointed out the places where the residents had painted "high water marks" on the sides of their buildings, and had written the dates and the names of the hurricanes that had caused them.

"My grandparent's house is now the island museum," Nick

explained. "A couple of days a week my mother acts as curator and gives tours. I'd love to show it to you, if you're interested."

"I'd like to see it. Is it nearby?"

"Actually, it's not far from here, just down the road a ways. We can walk to it from here."

Hand in hand they strolled along a quiet gravel road that was shaded by a canopy of ancient trees so wide that their branches arched over the roadway, making a tunnel of leaves. Bits of blue sky were visible through the thick greenery.

"We've got trees like this back in Romeo," Carolyn said, gazing up into the sky, watching the sunlight dance in the leaves. "In the summer it looks a lot like this does, and in the fall the leaves are vividly bright with yellows, oranges and reds. I used to pretend I was an elf who put the colors on the leaves when I was little."

Nick laughed. "We make a great team – a pirate and an elf. Well, here we are." He stopped before a freshly painted white clapboard house. The scent of cedar from the porch wood and shingles hung heavy and pleasant in the humid air. "I used to love coming here when I was a kid. Still do."

A tiny set of wind chimes jingled as Nick opened the screen door and held it for Carolyn and Magic. At the sound, a woman appeared in the front room of the old house. She was tiny and dark, her skin deeply tanned by the sun and weathered by the seasons. Her hair was colored a soft shade of red, and her dark eyes glistened in the dim coolness. She wore a white button-down blouse and a pair of khaki shorts.

"I'm sorry, miss," she said, not noticing Nick right away. "But I'm afraid you'll have to leave your dog outside."

"It's okay mom," Nick said. "She's with me."

The woman's eyes lit up and she smiled broadly. "Nick!" she exclaimed, throwing her arms around her son. "I didn't see you there! Who's this you've got with you?"

"This is Carolyn Adams," Nick replied, placing his arm around her shoulders. "I'm showing her around the island. Carolyn, this is my mother, Emily Dare. And this," he added with a flourish, "is Magic."

"A Basenji! Oh, he's an old one, isn't he?" Emily crouched low and extended her hand. "Here, puppy puppy puppy," she crooned. "And how are you doing today?"

"I remember you!" Magic cried, bounding forward and placing his paws on her knees. He sniffed her excitedly, his tail wagging so fast it was a blur. "It's been a long, long time, but I remember you! Do you remember me?"

"He likes you," Carolyn said happily. She wondered if Nick's mother would recognize Magic, hoping she would.

"We had Basenjis years and years ago," Emily said, cupping Magic's face in her hands. "He does remind one of Savannah, doesn't he Nick?" She studied the old dog's face carefully, and as she did her expression changed. Clearly troubled, she stood and took a few steps back from Magic. "He looks so familiar," she said quietly. "But maybe it's because he looks so much like Savannah. Every Basenji I see reminds me of her," she explained. "So," she changed the subject, "my son is showing you around the island. Must be serious!"

Carolyn blushed, and Nick shook his finger at his mother playfully. "Now, don't you start with me," he teased back. "We already got the third degree from Doreen last night at dinner."

"I know!" Emily clapped her hands together happily. "She called me right after you two left. But now let's get to know you a little better," she said, taking Carolyn's arm. "And you can get to know us, too. Let me show you around the museum."

Emily led Carolyn and Nick through the small house, chattering happily. She pointed out photographs of Nick's grandparents, Nick's father, and even one of Nick when he was a little boy. And, much to their surprise, she let them into a room where a small framed newspaper clipping hung on the wall next to an old leather dog leash and collar. Yellowed and slightly water damaged, the clipping was in a dark oak frame behind glass. Carolyn gasped when she saw it, and together she and Nick leaned close to read the caption.

"It's Savannah and the puppies!" Nick exclaimed. "I didn't think you had any pictures of her or them!" Almost reverently he removed the picture from the wall, and held it up to where sunlight streamed in through a window. "That was my Savannah-girl," he said, touching the image with his finger. "And there are all her pups."

"Your father was so proud of his African dogs," Emily said with a smile. "He bragged so much about them that the paper had to do a story on them. Savannah was the first Basenji on the Outer Banks, and her pups were the first Basenjis born here."

Carolyn stared at the photograph, easily picking out Magic from the lineup of puppies. He was standing by his mother, with one paw up on her shoulder. "She was beautiful," she whispered, picking up Magic so he could see the picture.

He stared at the picture in wonder, taking in the image from his dreams and memories of long ago, amazed to see it before him. "There we all are," he breathed, feeling a tremor of emotion run through his old body. "We were all so young!"

"My husband was so fond of those dogs," Emily said softly. "And so was my son." She reached up and tousled Nick's hair. "Remember how Savannah used to sit on the dunes after your father died? I liked to think she was waiting for him, hoping like we all did that someday he'd come back and things would be like they were. I miss having them around," she added.

"Me too," Nick replied, his voice a whisper.

The tension in the room was thick, and no one quite knew what to say. Uncomfortable with the silence, Carolyn said "Magic looks a lot like that puppy," and pointed to the image Nick still held in his hands. "He looks a lot like that one right there, on the end."

"So he does!" Emily exclaimed. "Well, what do you know?" She leaned forward and patted Magic's head. "So have you come home to visit us, then?" she asked with a grin. "Wouldn't it be grand if it were you in that picture?"

"Could it be?" Nick asked quietly. "Do you think it's possible?"

"Anything is possible," Emily replied. "But there are a lot of Basenjis in this world, and the odds of this old boy being the one in the picture aren't real good. As far as I know, all those pups are gone now," she added sadly. "I wish I could tell you otherwise. It's been so long, I wouldn't even remember who we sold them to."

Carolyn bit her lip, watching Magic's reaction to Emily's words. She felt the old dog tense up in her arms, and felt his heartbeat quicken. They were looking at his picture – she was sure of it! *But what can I do, insist?* she thought sadly. *They'd think I was crazy, for sure! I can't just up and tell them Magic has told me all about his life, and that he was once their dog. Maybe it's better this way. Even if only he and I know it, he's found his way back home, back to the people he loved. We both know who he is, and that's what's most important.*

They stayed a while longer, and Carolyn found she enjoyed Emily's company immensely. As they prepared to leave, Emily gave Carolyn a quick hug, and planted a kiss on her cheek.

"It was so good to meet you, Carolyn," she said. "You enjoy your stay on the island, and take good care of my boy now, won't you? And, take special care of that Basenji of yours, too!"

"I will," Carolyn replied. "It was great meeting you, too."

"He's a great fella," Emily whispered with a gleam in her eyes. She pulled Carolyn close, and whispered, "You don't let him out of your sight, okay?"

Carolyn blushed, and watched as Emily stood on tiptoes to whisper something to her son that made him blush as well.

"Well, now," Emily said. "We can't forget about you." She knelt next to Magic, gently stroking his grizzled head. "Old dogs are the most beautiful dogs of all," she murmured. "You really do remind me of our Savannah." She kissed Magic's forehead and gave him a quick hug. "I'd like to think you are one of her pups come home again. If you don't mind, that's what I'm going to believe. I always wondered if life is all about going full circle to find our way back to the place where we began." She cleared her throat, her voice trembling with emotion. "Those two make a great couple," she added, loud enough for Carolyn and Nick to hear. "Keep them together for me, won't you Magic?"

"Certainly," the old dog replied with a twinkle in his eye. "I'd be glad to!"

After a light lunch of crabcake sandwiches, iced tea, and chips, they drove out on the beach. Nick maneuvered the Jeep across an access ramp, and found a spot along the ocean side of the island. They set up a beach blanket and a couple of chairs, and Nick firmly planted an umbrella in the sand for shade.

The ocean was no longer calm. Large waves crashed against the shore, throwing glittering spray into the bright summer sun. Carolyn stared out at the horizon, wondering about the hurricane that was out there, half-wishing in a silly way that she'd get to evacuate. Although evacuating sounded frightening, the thought stirred something deep inside of her, making the wild, untamed beauty and vulnerability of the Outer Banks seem even more mysterious and exhilarating. It was exciting to know that a hurricane was lurking out in the Atlantic, swirling and churning the waters and the clouds.

"It's really out there, isn't it?" she asked, facing into the wind. "I wonder what the hurricane looks like?"

"It's out there, alright," Nick replied. "When we get back into

Buxton, I'll show it to you on the radar. I know the guys at the surf shop. They've got a computer tied to the weather service, and they get constant updates and satellite images. It's pretty impressive."

"So they can see how far away it is, and how fast it's moving?"

"Sure. But you don't need radar to see how the ocean's changed, and how the waves are building. You can bet the currents are getting pretty strong out there, and most folks won't go into the water when it's that rough. Only the die-hard surfers are crazy enough. They love this kind of weather." Nick smiled. "Maybe you'd like to watch them sometime?"

"That would be great," Carolyn replied. "But I suppose this weather isn't too good for the beach, is it? The shore really seems to be taking a pounding."

"That's one of the worst things about storms, whether they're hurricanes or nor'easters. We lose a lot of beach with some storms. Hopefully, this one will pass us by." Nick gave Magic a pat on the neck. "I think I'm up to cooling off in the waves," he said, offering Carolyn his hand. "We won't go out far, and it's pretty shallow here. What do you say?"

"Great," she replied, taking his hand. "Want to come?" she asked Magic. "The water will be wonderful."

"No, I'm fine here," he replied. "Go on, have some fun." He watched as she followed Nick toward the shoreline, looking very happy.

He lay belly-down in the sand frog-dog style, his legs stretched out behind him. The sand was pleasantly warm beneath him, and when he became too warm he got up and moved some of it away, exposing the cool dampness beneath. He settled back into the sand, feeling it cool his belly. He unfurled his tail, shifted to a more comfortable position, and turned his attentions to a quarter-sized hole in the sand directly in front of him. He breathed slowly and waited patiently, and was rewarded by a subtle movement from below.

A ghost crab, no bigger than the pads on Magic's feet, slowly and carefully began to emerge from the hole, its dark eye stalks twitching at the slightest movement. Its beige coloring made it almost impossible to see unless it moved, and its tiny pincer claws opened and closed gently. Magic knew that bigger crabs could deliver quite a pinch, but this little crab was harmless to him, and he watched with growing interest as it ventured out into the sun.

The little crab, tentative and wary, came part way out of the hole. Magic inched forward slightly, dragging his legs behind him in the sand, silent, swift — but not swift enough. The crab darted back into the hole, and it was several minutes more before it found the courage to make an appearance again.

Magic played with the crab for a little while longer before growing bored with it. He started down the beach, but instinct got the better of him, and he turned back towards the crab hole, sniffing it to make sure the little sea creature was still inside. Convinced that it was, he began to dig, throwing sand behind him in a brown arc.

"Whatcha got there, boy?" Nick and Carolyn came walking up the beach, stopping in front of Magic and his hole.

"A crab," Magic said. "I know he's in there, but darned if I can get to him!"

Carolyn laughed. "Keep on digging," she said. "Maybe you'll catch it."

"What's he got there, a crab?" Nick bent down to inspect the hole. "Looks like he got away from you," he said at last. "These guys are pretty smart. They've always got a back door somewhere else, so they don't get trapped inside." He rubbed Magic's back gently. "Look over there, see?" He pointed a few feet away, where a little crab had emerged safely from its hole and was scuttling down the beach towards the water. "Better luck next time!"

"No wonder," Magic said, thinking it through. "I've never been able to catch one of those things, and now I know why." He gazed at Nick with thinly veiled admiration. "Live and learn," he said, shaking the sand from his coat. He knew Nick couldn't hear him, but it made him feel important to have Nick talk to him, and he wished with all his heart that Nick could hear him, just once.

THIRTY

THE FERRY DOCKS WERE JAMMED
with cars — so many cars, in fact, that Carolyn
found it hard to believe the island was actually
able to hold them all. People grew impatient in
the humid air of the summer evening, their
happy vacation smiles disappearing into
murmurs of discontent as the lines to board the
ferry lengthened. For some reason everyone was
in a hurry to get off the island.

Nick leaned against the rail on the starboard
side of the ferry, staring at the sea and the sky,

trying to read the winds. As he looked toward the southeast, a concerned look darkened the fine features of his face, causing little worry-lines to appear on his forehead. He hadn't mentioned to Carolyn that, back in town at the Coast Guard station, they'd just put up hurricane warning flags. Although the portable hurricane evacuation road signs hadn't been put into place yet, the radio he'd heard playing inside the gas station was advising tourists to evacuate Ocracoke Island.

I should have told her as soon as I found out, he chastised himself. *Any moment now she'll figure out why all these people are leaving.*

The sun, dimmed by high clouds, still burned brightly, but there was an unsettling thickness to the humid air. Nick gazed at Carolyn, loving the way her dark hair billowed silky in the strong breeze. She had her sunglasses on, and Magic was in her arms, one of his dainty white paws just touching the railing for balance.

It was no secret to Magic that something was bothering Nick. The old dog could see the worry in his friend's eyes, and he'd noticed back at the gas station how he seemed to have paled beneath his dark tan. He'd been quiet on the ride back to the docks, every so often reaching back to rub Magic's head gently. Magic had mentioned the strange behavior to Carolyn, who had only shrugged at the old Basenji's questions.

"There's something he's not telling us," Magic ventured. "Why don't you ask him what's going on?"

Carolyn turned toward Nick, staring at his profile. She noticed the worry-lines on his face, and saw the darkness in his eyes. She watched as he stared into the sky, following the clouds as they passed overhead. She wondered what he was thinking, and she was about to ask him why people around them were chattering about the hurricane, when it was still so far out to sea, when he turned toward her and smiled sadly.

Her cat-green eyes met his dark ones and stayed there for

what seemed like an eternity. *What's with him?* she asked herself. *Why is he looking at me that way?*

Feeling uncomfortable under his intense gaze, she turned her head and pretended to be terribly interested in a ferry boat that was approaching from the other direction. As it drew closer, she noticed that it was empty. Alarmed, she asked him about it.

"That one's empty," he replied, feeling an unfamiliar uneasiness growing in his stomach, "because they're not allowing anyone to go to Ocracoke Island." He took a deep breath, and tasted the ocean in the air. "I heard about it at the gas station when we tanked up a little while ago. They need to evacuate the tourists from the island, because a hurricane warning was issued a little while ago."

Carolyn felt her mouth drop open, and her arms grew weak. Gently, she set Magic on the deck, unable to hold his weight any longer. She leaned against the railing and removed her sunglasses, pushing the hair from her face, and stared hard for a moment at the sunset, wishing she could stop it from sinking low in the sky.

The sun was a deep red inferno, burning slowly into the horizon, threatening to turn the entire soundside molten red as it settled in the west. Waves churned against the sides of the ferry, and seagulls cried above the rumbling of the diesel motor. Angrily she brushed away a salty tear with the back of her hand.

"I'm sorry I didn't say something sooner." Nick apologized. "It's just that we were having such a good time. I didn't want to scare you." He looked at her, saw the fear on her face, and felt terrible.

Having lived his entire life on the Outer Banks, Nick had long since accepted hurricanes as a fact of life and over time had learned to respect, not fear, them. Even so, it wasn't difficult for him to understand how disappointed and uncertain Carolyn had become at learning the news. She'd never seen an angry ocean beating mercilessly on the beach, or felt the apprehension of huddling inside a hurricane shelter surrounded by people who said little as they stared into the darkness and listened to unbelievably powerful wind and rain. Only in news reports had she seen the devastation that a hurricane could leave in its wake, and she had no idea what it was like to stand on the beach afterward and know the ocean had claimed the only home you'd ever known. Everything about a hurricane was an unknown to Carolyn, and the fear that came from not knowing what to expect was something Nick had learned to live with long ago.

"I don't understand," Carolyn whispered, her knuckles white from the choke hold she had on the railing. "How can there be a hurricane warning when the sunset is so beautiful? And look at the gulls! They don't seem to be in any hurry, do they?"

"The warning was issued because the islands are in the path that the storm will most likely track," Nick replied, placing his hands over hers. "You can see a few clouds building in the southeast, over there. That's the direction the storm will come from."

Magic paced restlessly back and forth, watching the waves break against the side of the ferry. He remembered well the fury of a hurricane, and knew in his heart that evacuating was the safest thing to do. As desperate as he was to go back to the lighthouse and try and find the place where the rabbits were, as much as he wanted to understand his dreams, the last thing he wanted was to have anything bad happen to Carolyn. "The ponies back on the island knew the storm was coming," he said softly. "I'm sure of it."

Carolyn was silent, not daring to look at Magic or Nick, although she wanted to very much. Emotions were all jumbled up inside of her, making her want to laugh and cry at the same time. Leaning over the railing, she wondered how things could be going so wonderfully one minute, then so awful the next.

"Carolyn?" Nick asked tentatively. "I know you're

disappointed, but don't worry. Things will work out. Look, it's only Ocracoke that's being evacuated right now. You've got a day or so before they'll evacuate Hatteras, if they do it at all. Hurricanes have a funny way of turning away sometimes."

"But you can't say for sure, can you?" she retorted. "I'm sure evacuations aren't decisions the authorities make lightly. There's got to be a darned good reason why they're making these people cut their vacations short and leave!"

Nick sighed. "Look, maybe you're overreacting, just a bit?"

"We are talking about a hurricane, aren't we?"

"Yes, but —"

"And they're evacuating the island because of the danger, right?"

"Well, yes —"

"Then I can't stay much longer, can I? People die in hurricanes, Nicky. You of all people should know that! I'm sure you'll understand if I don't want to stick around and see one firsthand." Carolyn's voice trembled, and she crouched down to hug Magic for comfort. Scooping the old dog into her arms, she buried her face in his neck, letting her tears dampen his coat. "I don't want to leave, really I don't," she whispered to Magic. "But you know how dangerous it could be if we stayed."

"I understand," Magic replied, disappointment clearly in his voice. "I don't like it at all, but we can't take chances when it comes to storms like this."

"Carolyn?" Nick put his hands on her shoulders, and felt her body tighten, then relax. "I do know that people die in hurricanes all too well. But you've got to understand that we all make choices, and we have to live by the consequences. My father thought he was doing the right thing when he went out looking for me in the storm."

"I'm sorry," Carolyn said. "I didn't mean —"

"It's alright," Nick answered. "The reason my father died was

271

because I didn't listen to him when he wanted us to evacuate. I took my Basenji puppy and went out on the beach when he warned me not to. We got lost in the storm and hid in the Cape Hatteras lighthouse. We were safe, but my father had no way of knowing it. I don't remember much about that day, but I do know that he took a chance that many people wouldn't have taken, and he ended up losing his life. There's not a storm that goes by that I don't think of him being out there looking for me, and not a day that I don't regret my decision to go exploring." Nick sighed and looked out to sea. "Believe me, I'd never risk mine or anyone else's life when it comes to these storms. The weather service, the Coast Guard, the local authorities — they all have ways of tracking hurricanes and determining where and when they will strike."

He kissed her cheek softly, pulling her to him, not minding the wet nose Magic stuck between them. "Listen for a moment. The evacuation is only for Ocracoke Island right now. I've seen lots of evacuations, so believe me when I say it'll be at least a day or two before they evacuate Hatteras, if they ever even have to. Even then, there will be plenty of time to get to the mainland before the storm hits."

"But what if the storm gets stronger?" she asked, meeting his gaze with wide green eyes. "What if it moves faster, and what if it heads toward Hatteras?"

"We'll have plenty of warning," Nick assured her. "Let's try not to worry until we have to, okay?"

Carolyn turned toward the sunset, realizing with a start that if Hatteras Island was going to be evacuated, there was little time for Magic to find what he was looking for. She wondered if he'd insist on staying behind, and she resolved not to let that happen. There was no way she would leave him behind. She felt him take a deep breath and rest his head on her shoulder, taking in the evening with his entire self.

"A hurricane," he murmured, feeling the bristles on his back stand up. "What if I don't find the place where the rabbits are? What if it was only an old dog's wishful dream?" His voice was shrill, clearly upset by the sudden turn of events. Panic washed over him in chilling waves, making his heart race painfully in his chest. "Oh, we can't leave! Not until I've found the place!"

Holding the old dog close to calm him, Carolyn crooned softly, fresh tears wetting his warm coat. "I'm so sorry Magic," she sniffed. "But if we have to evacuate, we will, and I won't leave you behind!"

"Carolyn, everything will be okay," Nick told her, turning her to face him. His strong arms closed around her, pulling her close. "I'll take care of you. Don't worry."

At his touch Carolyn burst into tears. Nick let her cry, stroking her brown hair gently, squashing Magic uncomfortably between them. "Shhh, it's okay. C'mon, honey, don't cry."

"I can't breathe!" Magic gasped, wriggling between them. "Squeeze me any tighter and I'll break!"

The old dog's outburst and wriggling broke the tension and made Carolyn begin to giggle. Magic jumped from Carolyn's arms and gave himself a good shake, right down to his white tailtip, muttering to himself about being squashed.

"Poor old guy," Nick reached down and gave the Basenji a gentle pat. "I hope you're not angry, too."

"No," Magic replied. "I'm a little flatter now, though!"

"Look at us!" Carolyn said sheepishly. "I don't know what came over me." Her eyes met Nick's, and she gladly took the hand he offered her. He pulled her close again, and gave her a quick kiss.

"Things will work out," he said quietly. "They always do."

Carolyn nodded, not wanting to trust her voice. Nick kissed her again, and she welcomed him, her fingers finding their way to the back of his neck, where the hairs curled up just a bit.

Magic cleared his throat, and jumped up, placing his paws on Nick's leg. "Don't forget about the dog," he muttered.

Carolyn laughed and pulled away from Nick. "We won't forget about you," she told Magic. "I don't think you'd let us!"

"The sunset is pretty," the Basenji offered. "Let's enjoy it together, okay?"

Carolyn nodded, and Nick looked at her strangely, feeling as if he'd missed something between her and Magic.

If I didn't know better, I'd think he was talking to her, and she was answering him! he mused, shaking his head to clear it of the thought. *I guess I've got the hurricane on my mind.*

He watched as she extended her hand and smiled, her windblown hair beautiful in the fading light. "Watch the sunset with us, Nicky."

Taking the hand she offered, he moved close and placed his arm around her shoulders. He felt her sigh and lean into him, and together they watched the sun dip below the clouds, disappearing into towering thunderheads.

THIRTY-ONE

TWO NIGHTS LATER, THE NIGHTTIME
was loud with the sound of an angry ocean
churning sand and sea foam as it broke against
the shore. As the ocean pounded the beach, it
began to roar, and the sound found its way into
Magic's dreams, pulling him from the comfort of
sleep.

He lay next to Carolyn in the darkness of the
motorhome, staring into the blackness and
listening to the world outside with a heightened
sense of alertness. His nose worked the air

feverishly, smelling ozone and impending rain in the humid summer night. How Carolyn was able to sleep through it all was a mystery to him; she hadn't even stirred when the wind changed direction, amplifying the sound of the surf.

Confirming the worst fears of everyone on the Outer Banks, the weather service had reported earlier in the day that the hurricane had strengthened out in the Atlantic. Increasing in power and speed at an alarming rate, it was moving in a direct track across the water, preparing to sweep across the barrier islands as many storms had before.

Storms had a way of changing what they encountered in a dramatic way. They thought nothing of moving the fragile coastline seemingly overnight, sweeping through and wiping the beaches clean of homes and landmarks, or removing the blanket of sand from the skeletons of old shipwrecks while making others disappear again. Wild and unpredictable, they were like thieves, stealing property and lives, changing things forever.

As Magic reflected on the hurricane of his youth, he wondered how his life would have been different if that storm had never occurred. Maybe he would have stayed with Nicky and his mother, and maybe Nicky's father would still be alive. He could have lived his entire life and never left the Outer Banks, yet when he thought of all that he'd been through, he found it hard to imagine his life being anything other than what it was.

Time had a way of changing things as well, only in a slower, gentler fashion. Time brought friends into lives and somehow showed them the way out, gave freely of joys and sorrows, and never asked for anything more than to be allowed the privilege of gracefully draping the mantle of old age upon a body. Magic knew he'd had his fair share of time, and he'd lived longer than any dog he'd ever known. Even so, he had so many questions that still needed answers, and he hated to be so close to knowing those answers but unable to reach them.

Knowing their stay on the island was limited, Carolyn had spent as much time as she could with the old Basenji, asking him questions and taking him where he thought he might find the place he'd dreamed about. Even with Carolyn's help, they were unsuccessful, and Magic became discouraged.

Frustrated at being unable to locate the place where the rabbits lived, Magic had found them running in his dreams again. Strangely, each time he dreamed about the place, something was added. As time went on his memories moved in mysterious ways, filling in all the openings, enhancing details, adding colors and scents and sensations so real he would sometimes awaken confused, wondering which was reality and which was only the dream. It had always seemed so real to him, and he believed he'd actually seen the place before.

At the sound of a large wave crashing, Magic awoke, having dozed off briefly again. The dream was part of his memories now, a welcome escape from an old body that tired easily on short walks and couldn't run very well anymore. He'd often wondered if dying was like falling into a beautiful dream, where the lines between sleep and awareness were blurred into a sea of colors and sounds, wrapped up in an incredible warmth of an ever-blazing summer sun. He hoped that when his time came, that's exactly the way it would be.

How could I come this far and not find it? he asked himself, resting his head on Carolyn's arm as she slept. *I need to see the lighthouse again, just one more time,* he thought suddenly, feeling an urgency growing within him. He couldn't shake the feeling that he'd forgotten something there so many years ago, and he had hoped the trip to the Outer Banks would make the feeling go away, but it hadn't. Surprisingly, it had grown stronger, and it had something to do with the one piece of his dream he hadn't been able to fill in.

I have to know what it is.

He felt terribly guilty, knowing that in order to go out into the night he would have to deceive Carolyn. She always kept the motorhome door locked when they slept, and there was no way he could open it without her help.

His confidence wavered as he stood over her, watching her chest rise and fall gently as she slept. She had a smile on her face, and her breathing revealed to him that she was having a happy dream.

I'm sorry, he thought, gazing at her. He studied her face for a moment, her pretty features tanned from the sun, framed by her silky brown hair. *I don't want to leave you now, but I must. I promise I'll be back as soon as I can.*

Pawing at the covers, he gently pushed against her until she awoke.

"What is it?" she asked sleepily. "Magic? What's wrong?"

"Nothing," he whispered, "I need to go out, that's all." He hated lying to her, and he knew if she'd been more awake she would have questioned him more closely, and possibly seen through his ruse.

Sleepily, she threw back the light sheet from her body and shuffled the few steps to the door. Unlocking it, she murmured, "Let me know when you come back in. You can wake me up, and I'll lock the door again." She yawned and stretched, still half asleep. Magic wondered if she really knew what she was doing, and it eased his mind to think that she might not even remember letting him out. He could slip back in before she awoke the next morning.

This must be like a strange dream to her, he thought. *At least she won't worry, and I'll be back before she misses me.*

He stepped out into the humid night, the familiar sound of crickets and cicadas overtaken by the roar of the sea. The door closed behind him with a barely audible click. The sound was frighteningly final, echoing in his ears like a rifle shot.

Now is the time, he told himself. *Follow your instincts and see where they lead.*

He crossed the dune, stopping to paw at a silken spiderweb that stuck to his face. It was damp and unpleasant, and he rubbed his face furiously to get rid of it. He hadn't seen the web stretched across the path, for the night was dark. There was no moon, only starlight faintly glowing behind high, thin clouds. He could see the comet Nick had pointed out to them one evening, its long tail faint in the sky. The ocean rumbled and crashed at the shore, and the wind was strong at his back.

Magic continued on, his gaze focused on the lighthouse in the distance, its beacon flashing, reaching out a tendril of brightness into the night. *That's the place to start*, he thought. *That's where I have to go.*

He climbed back on the top of the dune, catching a glimpse of the steady line of cars that were heading towards the mainland. The evacuation of Ocracoke had started two days ago, and Hatteras the day before. Yet still there were cars leaving, even at this late hour. Magic thought of Carolyn alone in the motorhome, and he resolved to make it back before she awoke.

Everyone is leaving, he thought sadly. *And in the morning, so will we. If I don't find the rabbits tonight, then maybe I never will.*

Nick had grimly advised them that the weather reports weren't favorable, and that Hatteras was in the direct path of the hurricane. He had promised to accompany Carolyn and Magic to the mainland. He had been hard at work boarding up several houses late yesterday afternoon, and he planned on meeting Carolyn in the morning to help her break camp and leave.

Magic left the dune and walked on the hard sand near the water, jumping from time to time as ghost crabs scuttled across his paws. A frothy finger of ocean reached out from a wave that broke on shore, seeming to grasp at him. He jogged his path further away from the ocean, suddenly fearful that it would capture him and swallow him up in its angry swells.

The lighthouse, he thought, repeating the words over and over, trying to calm his racing heart. *To the lighthouse.*

Stumbling briefly on a piece of driftwood he hadn't seen, he stopped for a moment to catch his breath.

"Animal."

A voice whispered in his ear, and was carried off into the wind. Magic turned toward the sound, not seeing anything unusual in the night. He turned the other way, and in the darkness made out the shape of a large sea turtle.

"Animal go away."

It was a large female who had found her way out of the ocean to lay her eggs. He could see that he frightened her, but he also knew she wouldn't leave until she was finished. Her head was raised, making her appear large and fearsome, like something out of the prehistoric past.

"I won't hurt you," Magic said, stepping towards her.

She opened her mouth as wide as she could, and hissed at him. "Go away now. Leave babies be." She moved her rear legs, digging herself deeper into the sand. He sniffed the air around her, smelling seaweed, saltiness, and something that made him think of the deepest part of the ocean.

"Must finish, go away." Her voice pleaded with him. "No time. Big storm. Now go."

"How much longer?" he asked. "When will the storm be here?"

The turtle eyed him cautiously, moving her heard from side to side like a snake, sniffing the air around him, taking in his unusual odor. Although she'd never encountered a dog before, there was something about Magic that made her realize she had nothing to fear from him.

"You are old," she observed, relaxing a bit. Her voice was husky, raspy in her throat. "You will find what you look for, but not tonight, animal." She shook one of her front flippers at him, and he was reminded of Carolyn chastising her students. "I must finish. You go now."

"I'm looking for the place where the rabbits are. Have you seen it?" Magic asked, stepping closer to the turtle, who hissed and lunged at him.

"I have little time!" she shouted. "Leave me be."

"I'm sorry," he said, taken aback by her anger. He stared at her for a moment longer before moving away and continuing up the beach.

She watched him go, following his shape until it disappeared up the beach. "Wait," she called after him, raising her body slightly. "Animal," she whispered into the wind. "Old animal, go to the lighthouse. It will protect you."

As he walked, Magic sniffed at the sand, discovering the tracks of a wild pony who had been there not long before. He jumped in surprise when a large crab scuttled by right under his nose. *I've got to be more careful,* he thought as a wave reached far up onto the shore, carrying the crab away in swirling water and foam. *If I get caught in the water, I'm done for.*

He found himself at the base of the lighthouse, gazing up at the beacon some two hundred feet into the sky. Low clouds had moved in, and the light from the old lighthouse raked across them, splitting the sky into two as it moved in a wide arc. It occurred to Magic that if he were to climb to the top of the lighthouse, he'd be able to touch them. *I could slide right down the light, all the way to the water,* he mused, chuckling to himself at his little joke.

When the wind shifted, he heard cars approaching, and it wasn't long before their headlamps appeared, blinding him. He'd heard their loud radios long before he'd actually heard the tires on gravel. Suddenly fearful, he was certain they'd seen his eyes glowing in the brightness from their headlamps. He ducked into the tall grass and lay low, breathing heavily. What was going on?

Several teenagers, dressed in shorts and T-shirts, climbed out of the cars, talking loudly even after their radios had been silenced. Magic could smell the beer on their breath, hanging low and heavy in the humid night. Smoke from cigarettes drifted like ghostly fog in the air, filling his nostrils with the strong odor. He pawed at his face and rubbed his eyes, not liking the way the smoke made them water, almost sneezing once, but catching himself just in time.

"All the way to the top!" One of the teenagers yelled, weaving back and forth, falling for a moment against one of the cars.

"Yeah, race you there!" another replied. "If you can make it that far!"

Loud laughter followed. Magic heard the muffled scuffling of their shoes on the wooden boardwalk. Someone coughed and spit into the sand.

The first one to make it to the lighthouse laughed crazily. "Looks like I am the winner!" He drew long on his cigarette, making the end glow in the darkness. "Watch this!" he called to his friends, managing to climb the granite steps and pull himself to the top of the red brick base with a beer still in hand.

"I am the lighthouse king!" he cried into the night. "And this is my castle!" He jumped down and tried the lighthouse doors again, rattling the padlock in frustration. "Awww man! It's locked up tight!"

"Naw, Chris!" Another teenager, tall and red-faced from the sun, fumbled in his pockets. "You won't believe this!" He fumbled some more, then pulled out a set of keys. "We can get in!" he laughed, and gulped some more beer. He threw the empty can on the ground and made his way up the stairs to the massive lighthouse doors.

"The keys to the castle," someone said, lighting up another cigarette.

"What luck!" The other teenagers crowded around the one with the keys. Out of a pocket came a small flashlight. It flickered for a brief second, threatening not to come on at all. Its owner banged it on the bricks and it came to life, shining brightly on the padlocked doors, throwing shadows high onto the lighthouse tower.

"Put that out!" the one with the keys hissed. "You want to be seen?"

The one called Chris let his legs dangle from the short wall. "What're you worried about?" he asked. "Ain't nobody around to see us here! They're all too busy evacuating!" he laughed. "Got a big scary storm and all the tourists are running home! Ain't no one around here! Didn't you see the sign when we pulled in? CLOSED!" he laughed again. "How 'bout another beer?"

Someone tossed him a beer. "Thanks," he said, discarding his partially empty can in the tall grass. It hit Magic on his back, and he yelped in spite of himself. Cowering lower into the weeds, he held his breath and felt his heart pounding in his chest, so loud that he was sure they would hear it over the wind and waves.

"What was that?" The one with the flashlight spun around, shining the light in Magic's direction. "Who's there?"

"Probably just the wind," the one with the keys said, "There!" The key he was trying clicked in the lock, and he pushed the doors open. "Got to remember to thank my sister, little miss park ranger, for leaving these laying around," he laughed. "All the way to the top!" he cried. "Last one there buys the beer!"

As they entered the lighthouse the light from their flashlight faded and Magic once again found himself surrounded in darkness. He could hear the teenagers as they ascended the stairs, their shoes and voices echoing inside the tower.

They don't belong in there! he thought angrily. *What are they doing?*

Fear was replaced with determination as he crept from his

hiding place and silently climbed the stairs. *I have to stop them!* He stuck his head inside, taking a few moments to let his eyes grow accustomed to the blackness. A faint light from high above glowed from their flashlight.

Magic could still hear their voices, way up high and out of sight. *What to do?* He racked his mind for something, anything. He thought of how the lighthouse used to look, with broken windows and graffiti on the walls, and it made him sad to think these intruders could do that sort of damage again. The lighthouse was his sanctuary, and they had no right to be there, sneaking around in the darkness! Then, an idea came to him.

I wonder if I could scare them off?

He sat down just beneath the last flight of stairs and cleared his throat. Swallowing several times, he closed his eyes, willing the pounding of his heart to settle. *I can do this!* he told himself bravely. *The lighthouse will protect me!*

And so it was that in the darkness, the old Basenji took a deep breath, pointed his nose to the heavens, and began to howl.

It took only a moment for the sound to carry up into the tower. When the first echoing notes sounded in their ears, the teenagers were immediately silenced. Magic paused, listening to their terrified whispering. A grin spread slowly across his face.

I may not be big or tough or young, he thought. *But I can make them leave!*

He howled again, louder, longer, more terrifying than before. The sound bounced off the bricks and mortar, twisted its way up the metal spiraling staircases, and lingered in the darkness like an unseen specter. The sound was further amplified by the massive tower, making it seem as if a hundred starving wolves were crying out to a full moon on a starry night.

"What's happening?" Magic heard a trembling voice from above whisper.

"Who's there?" another voice asked.

Someone else gasped. "It's ghosts!"

"Let's get out of here!" A scrambling of footsteps from above indicated that the teenagers were on their way back down. Magic grinned to himself, and howled again, loud and long.

Basenji music! he chuckled happily. *Love that Basenji music!*

"What's going on in here!" A deep voice stopped Magic and the teenagers cold. "Who's up there?" A North Carolina state trooper stood in the doorway, silhouetted by the headlights of his patrol car. He shone a light towards the spiral staircase, stopping on the second landing where the beam caught the pale, terrified faces of the teenagers midway down the stairs. One of the teenagers had frozen in mid flight with a beer can still in hand. Seeing the officer, he let it drop to the floor. The sound of the can rolling on the tile echoed loudly in the tower.

"This place is haunted!" one of the teenagers cried, sounding like a frightened child. "Didn't you hear them?"

"It was ghosts!" another chimed in, his voice a husky whisper.

"Oh, no!" another voice moaned. "Cops!"

"You boys have a lot of explaining to do," the trooper said grimly. "Get down from there — NOW!"

"But didn't you hear them wailing? This place is really haunted!"

"That's enough, already." The trooper threw the beam of his flashlight on the staircase. "I want you all down from there, and I don't want to hear anymore babble about ghosts."

He escorted the frightened teenagers out of the lighthouse, holding them at bay until two other patrol cars arrived. The troopers shook their heads sadly as the teenagers told them about the sounds they'd heard inside the lighthouse.

"Haunted, indeed," one trooper snorted. "More like a little too much beer and the howling of the wind, if you ask me!"

Much to Magic's surprise, the troopers who searched the lighthouse didn't even notice him hiding in the shadows, peering out of the little well at the bottom of the staircase. He waited quietly, almost expecting a flashlight to blind him. Any moment he expected to feel their strong hands reaching down to whisk him out of the darkness and take him away to a shelter. Terrified, the old dog held his breath and waited.

The flashlight never blinded him, and no hands appeared from above. Apparently, no one knew or even suspected he was hiding there. Magic wondered if he should run and make a break for it, but he could clearly see that it would take some extra effort to climb out of the hole he was in, and he certainly didn't want to risk getting caught. And so, he waited.

Unfortunately, he waited too long, for once the teenagers were handcuffed and searched, the trooper who had first entered the lighthouse climbed to the top for one last look. It took some time before he was satisfied that there wasn't anyone else hiding inside. Whistling, he made his way down the stairs, pausing for a moment to look out one of the tall windows at the angry ocean.

"Damn hurricane," Magic heard him mutter. "Damn kids!"

An empty beer can was kicked from the second landing, banging its way down the stairs. It landed near the well where Magic was hiding.

Suddenly the trooper was there, so close that Magic could smell the clean starchiness of his uniform. As his hand reached for the beer can, Magic made himself as small as possible in the shadows. He closed his eyes, waiting to feel the hand on the back of his neck, lifting him up and out of the hole.

"I hope that's the last one." the trooper said, almost in Magic's ear. "I'm sick of these kids leaving beer cans everywhere." The can disappeared, and the trooper with it. Magic let his breath out with a long *whoosh* of relief.

Here's my chance, he thought, standing on his hind legs, stretching toward the top of the hole. *Now if I can only jump just a little higher.* His thoughts trailed off as his ears caught the unmistakable sound of a padlock snapping closed.

"No!" he cried, scrambling out of the hole. He ran to the doors, scratching frantically on them. "Don't leave! I'm still in here!"

Darkness closed in on him as he heard the patrol cars pull away, their tires crunching gravel beneath them on the road. In one terrible moment he realized he was trapped inside the lighthouse. His hopes of finding the hill with the rabbits, and of returning to Carolyn, vanished like waves on the shore.

What am I going to do now? he asked himself over and over. *I can't get out, back to Carolyn! She doesn't know where I am!* Tears welled up in his eyes as he sat mournfully in the dark, empty lighthouse. *This wasn't supposed to happen!*

He howled once, long and mournful. This time, there was no one around to hear him.

THIRTY-TWO

"MAGIC'S GONE!" CAROLYN WAS frantic when Nick arrived at the campsite. "I can't find him anywhere!"

"What do you mean, he's gone?" Nick asked. He stared blankly at her, not fully comprehending. "Where would he go?"

"I don't know!" she said, clearly frightened. "He got me up late last night, and told me he had to go out." She began to cry. "I figured he just needed to go to the bathroom, and I let him go outside. I fell back asleep, and didn't realize until I woke up this morning that he was gone," she sobbed. "I feel terrible! It's all my fault!"

Nick placed his arms around her, pulling her close to comfort her. He could feel the sadness in her, and an inexplicable fear. "There, there," he murmured. "Let's go out and try to find him. Where have you looked?"

Carolyn told him she'd searched every inch of the campground, and that she'd only found a few of Magic's footprints in the soft sand. "I can't begin to guess which way he went!" she said. "The wind has blown the sand all around. I don't know if I'm looking at old footprints or new ones!"

Nick sighed and gazed out the window, towards the dunes and the sea. Dark angry waves crashed away at the fragile shoreline, claiming precious sand with each pounding of the surf.

From where he stood he could see several beach homes that faced the angry sea and sky, their windows hurriedly boarded up with fresh plywood, making them look as if they'd closed their eyes on the world and on the storm. Nick had boarded up those windows himself just yesterday, hoping to shut out the danger that loomed over the water that was, with each passing moment, growing closer and more frightening.

If the beach the houses could have looked down upon the beach, they would have seen it was barren and empty, the summer tourists long since evacuated to the safety of the mainland. No campers lingered in the campground; in fact, except for Carolyn's motorhome, they were all long gone. Even the little ghost crabs had buried themselves deep in the sand and waited silently, wondering what was happening to their world.

"Let's go out again and try to find out what happened to him," Nick offered. "But we'll have to work fast. The storm is moving in, and we haven't much time left to evacuate. If we don't leave soon, our only chance will be to go to the shelter in town."

For several long hours they searched. Hour by hour, the

weather worsened, and a spitting rain began to fall, pushed into their faces by the ever-strengthening wind. The ocean, which had been angry before, became a furious beast, tearing and clawing at the beach with dangerous, pounding waves. The sound of it was a constant roar that was unrelenting and nearly deafening. As the hours passed and there was no sign of Magic, Carolyn grew more and more fearful of not finding him.

"We've waited long enough," Nick said reluctantly after a time. He felt fear growing inside of him, and he was unable to stop the pounding in his heart and the roar of the wind and crashing waves that echoed in his head. He hated the thought of the old Basenji lost out in the storm, but he knew they didn't have much time left to get to safety.

"I've got to wait longer," Carolyn pressed. "Something's happened to Magic, and I've got to know what." Thoughts of his death drifted in and out of her mind, and she pushed them away angrily. There wasn't time to think of him being dead; she wouldn't allow herself to do it. "I won't leave without him."

"We've got to leave, and leave now." Nick insisted. "As it is, we won't make it across the causeway before the full force of the hurricane hits, no matter how fast we drive. We've got to get to the shelter in town, now!"

They were sitting in the motorhome, damp from the rain, tired and depressed from their fruitless search. The motorhome, which everyone had claimed was once so large and unmanageable, looked like a child's toy in the abandoned campground, small and fragile against the threatening sky. High winds were buffeting it from all sides, and it seemed as if the storm would scoop it up at any moment, toss it high into the air, and send it hurling back towards the earth.

The thin aluminum walls shuddered as strong wind gusts hit the sides. Over the roar of the sea and the pounding of the rain, Carolyn heard a pinging sound from part of the awning that had broken loose, torn out of its bracket by the wind. Already the power was out, and it wouldn't be long before the surf covered the only road off the island.

Carolyn stared out the rain-streaked windows, looking out into the grayness that worsened with each passing moment. Magic was out there, somewhere, and it was all her fault. She wasn't going to leave without him; she couldn't.

"We've got to go out again and find him," she said at last, turning a frightened, determined face towards Nick. "I can't leave without him. I won't."

"Carolyn, listen to the wind and the sea! Don't you understand?" Nick shouted, throwing his arms into the air. "If Magic is out there, he's going to be dead before we can even get to him. There's no guarantee that we'll be able to find him now! This is a hurricane we're in, not some little summer storm! We've got to get out of here, and we've got to do it now! We've waited too long as it is . . ." his voice trailed off. He was choking back tears, and he saw tears in Carolyn's eyes, too. His heart went out to her, and he regretted his outburst immediately. He knew how important the old dog was to her, and it broke his heart to be unable to find him.

Their eyes met, and traveled down to the key ring that Carolyn had left on the table. Nick moved toward the keys, and in that same instant she grabbed them and sent them flying across the motorhome. She winced as they hit a window, causing it to crack from top to bottom. She hadn't wanted to lose Magic this way. How could she simply give up looking for him when he might be hurt or lost? Breaking down in to uncontrollable sobs, she leaned her head down to the table, resting it in her folded arms.

"I'm sorry," Nick whispered, putting his hands on her shoulders. "I know what Magic meant — I mean, means to you," he said, pulling her close. "But we can't risk our lives, too. I don't think he'd want us to do that, do you? The situation we're in is really getting serious," he added. "Carolyn, please listen to me."

Through his wet clothes, he could feel her body tense and relax in his strong hold and he smelled the sweetness of her hair, and felt it soft against his cheek. Everything about her felt so right, like he'd known her his whole life, like they were always meant to be together.

It's the storm, he told himself. *You're frightened, that's all. Besides, how could she possibly love you when she only met you less than a week ago?* But in his mind he knew that he did love her, and more than anything he wished he could wave his arms and stop the storm, even bring Magic back to her — anything just to see a smile on her face again. He gazed into her eyes and kissed her gently, surprised when she kissed him back.

"Please, Carolyn. We need to get to safety," he whispered. "Let's go now, okay?"

"No," she replied. "Not without Magic."

"He was an old dog. Maybe it was just his time."

"What do you know about him?" Carolyn shouted. "You, of all people! You didn't even remember who he was!"

She pulled away from him, and it pained him that she was pushing him away. She studied his face intently, the way he'd seen Magic stare at him from time to time. It was as if she was committing his face to memory, taking everything in for one last time so she'd never forget.

"I am going out there, and I am going to find him, Nicky." Her voice trembled. "Maybe you don't understand, and maybe you don't know him the way I do. He's counting on me, and I won't leave him behind!" She jumped up, knocking Nick to the floor. Before he could stop her, she was out the door and into the hurricane.

"Carolyn!" He scrambled to his feet, grabbing the small flashlight from the table. "Carolyn, come back!"

The force of the wind took Carolyn's breath away. As she ran to the beach, wind-driven rain and sand pelted her body. Sea oats, bending crazily in the storm, whipped her arms and legs painfully. It was only moments before she was drenched from the rain, her clothes and hair plastered to her body.

"Wait!" She heard a muffled cry, and in another instant Nick was by her side with a flashlight. He held her arm, steadying her in the wind. "You can't go alone!" he shouted in her ear. "I'm coming with you!"

They fought their way down the beach slowly at first, then faster as the wind changed direction and pushed them along. "We've got to stay away from the water," Nick shouted. "If we get caught in those waves, we're done for!"

Carolyn eyed the angry surf, terrified of the enormous waves that sent foam and spray into her face. It wouldn't be long before the waves overtook the dunes, she could see that plainly enough.

Magic, she thought, *where are you?*

THIRTY-THREE

ALL AROUND HIM, LIKE THE MOST
terrifying nightmare, the hurricane swirled, an
angry, soulless thing with a black heart and evil
intent. It was as if all the terrors and nightmares
of a thousand lifetimes had been set loose upon
the lighthouse, ready to swallow it up whole in
less than a heartbeat.

Lightning flashed at varying intervals;
sometimes as sheets of brightness against the
windows, filling the entire sky with an eerie
glow that illuminated the churning hurricane

clouds. At other times the lightning became jagged, broken streaks that screamed and tore across the sky, ripping open the clouds, violent and deadly. Magic heard the scrabbling sound of sand being pelted against the old painted bricks and thick glass windows of the lighthouse, sounding like thousands of tiny crab claws grasping and tearing at it from all sides.

As the storm tried to get inside, the lighthouse groaned and swayed in the wind, arrogant and strong, doing battle with it, daring it to unleash its most violent fury. As he had been so many years before, Magic found himself cowering on the first landing of the lighthouse — not young and frightened, but old and terrified. And, worst of all, he was alone.

Why is this happening again? He asked himself this question over and over, racking his brain for an answer that wasn't there. It took all his Basenji resolve not to simply give up and submit to the terror that gripped him. It was as if all his most feared nightmares had joined forces and created this storm, this hurricane that was the culmination of all he feared.

I'm all alone, he thought sadly. *I followed the dream, and it's led me to this.* He shuddered at the thought of what might happen if the lighthouse flooded, or if it began to break up in the storm.

This time I have to face it all on my own, he thought, remembering his mother's words. *The lighthouse is built of a circle, and it will protect you.*

Magic's mind turned to thoughts of Carolyn and Nick. He wished with all his might that he could be with them and that he'd never gone out into the night. He had followed his dream because it seemed to have promised him the answer to a question he'd been asking himself all his life. Instead, it led him here, to what he presumed could only be his death. But even if that was the case, he couldn't understand why he was all alone. Why wasn't Violet, or his mother, or even Max there to comfort him at these final moments of his life? Had all the dog-spirits deserted him?

His stomach was empty and it pained him. Suddenly feeling weak and small, he leaned against the cold brick wall like a frightened puppy. His heart pumped and raced in his chest, as if it wanted to leap right from his throat.

Where is everyone? Where is Carolyn? What am I going to do now?

Impulsively, he began to howl as the wind howled, long and lonely. It was a haunting, plaintive sound that carried to the very heights of the lighthouse, winding its way around the spiraling staircase to the flashing beacon at the top. He howled and howled, certain that death was imminent, terrified to be meeting it alone.

Carolyn, Nicky! Help me! Help me! he cried between howls. *Please Carolyn, Nicky, find me!*

He wondered what had happened to them. It made him feel sick inside to think that they could be out in the storm looking for him. Carolyn loved him too much just to leave him to the hurricane, he knew. But Nick knew the awesome power of such storms, and Magic suspected they'd quit looking when the full force of the storm hit. They would be foolish to continue their search. Clinging to the one last hope that they might be out there, he cried out again on the desperate chance they would be near enough to hear his voice.

Out of the storm a strange sound filled his ears, and he heard a rustling that came from somewhere up above. Was someone trapped in the tower with him? Magic jumped as something warm and furry brushed against him in the darkness.

"Who's there?" he whispered hoarsely, barely able to make out a dark shape when the lightning flashed. "Who are you?"

"A friend," a gentle voice answered. "You helped me when I needed it, and now I can repay my debt to you."

THIRTY-FOUR

NICK AND CAROLYN STRUGGLED

down the dunes, towards the lighthouse.

"That's the only safe place now! We've got

to take shelter there." Nick had to shout over the

roar of the wind. "If we wait any longer, it will

be too late!"

A loud banging sound filled the air, and

something hard and sharp caught Carolyn in her

shoulder, knocking her to the ground. There was

a throbbing pain in her arm now, and she could

see blood seeping from a cut just above her

elbow.

"Nicky!" Carolyn choked on sand that found its way into her mouth when she fell. She felt the salty grittiness on her teeth, and had to spit several times before it was gone. Wind whipped around her, disorienting her and taking her breath away. "Nicky!"

"Here!" he called, appearing in a swirl of rain and wind. "Are you okay, Carolyn?" He helped her to her feet. The pain in her arm and shoulder made her head swim with dizziness. She swayed, fighting back the urge to close her eyes and drift off into the peaceful darkness of unconsciousness.

"We've got to give up," Nick said in her ear. "It's no use!" He moved his hand to where the object had struck her. "You're hurt! Oh, you're bleeding! We're going back."

"No!" Carolyn stepped forward, stumbled and fell to the sand, grabbing at it with hands that became fists, ignoring the pain. "I won't leave without Magic! I won't!" Torrential rain pelted her, and somehow the wind seemed to help her to her feet again. "He's out here somewhere!" she shouted. "I won't leave him!"

Nick shook his head. Was she crazy? Was her fear of the storm making her take leave of her senses? "We can't stay here!" he told her, his face close to hers. Debris from a roof flew over their heads, spinning and turning in the wind. He pulled her close, and held her tightly in his arms. "It's too dangerous!"

Lightning split the sky into several pieces, and Carolyn saw the angry ocean, full of foam and froth, pounding furiously at what was left of the beach. She realized they were in great danger, and she knew they should get to safety. But the thought of Magic lost somewhere out in the hurricane terrified her, and strengthened her determination to find him.

"Come on!" Nick shouted, starting back up the beach. "If we can get to the lighthouse, we'll be safe until the storm passes!"

Wind and rain swirled in the air around them, beating down on them without mercy. Already they were soaked to the skin, and Carolyn could taste the salty water in her mouth, and sand stung and burned in her eyes. A roaring that wasn't from the waves filled her ears, and when the lightning flashed again she could see a waterspout that had formed in the ocean, very near to land. The sight of it terrified her all the more, and she stumbled as the wet sand gave way beneath her feet. The wind and waves were eroding the beach at an alarming rate. Already the ocean had claimed a good portion of it.

"This way!" Nick jerked her arm so hard that it felt as if he'd wrenched it from its socket.

New pain shot through her, awakening her and spurring her to move faster. Through the driving sheets of rain Carolyn could see the steady beacon of the lighthouse, warm and reassuring in the darkness.

"We'll wait out the storm in there," Nick shouted. "Hurry!"

It was painfully slow going. As they drew closer to the lighthouse, a strange wailing sound filled the air. The sound was quiet at first, so quiet that Carolyn almost thought it was the wind or her imagination. But as they moved closer to the lighthouse, the wailing was transformed into a distinct howling sound.

"Magic!" Carolyn screamed. "He's in there, Nicky! The lighthouse! Can you hear it?" She was frantic now, moving as fast as she could toward the sound. "I can hear him! I can hear Magic!"

Nick turned toward her, his face wet with rain and his hair dripping with water. He grabbed her with both arms, and shook her hard. "It's just the wind," he shouted, certain she was delirious and imagining things. "It's just the wind!" He pulled her forward again, and she jerked her arm out of his grasp. She ran against the wind and rain, toward the sound of Magic's voice, losing Nick in the swirling grayness.

"Carolyn! Help me!" Magic's voice was loud and strong above the wind and roar of the ocean. Carolyn heard it as clearly as if he'd been right next to her.

"Where are you?" she screamed into the storm. "Magic, where are you!"

Lightning flashed, a brilliant sheet that illuminated the entire sky, reflecting ghostly silver on the beach. Something moving on the dune caught Carolyn's eye, a dark object she glimpsed briefly several times as the lightning continued to flash. As the object grew closer, she realized it was actually two figures that appeared out of the wind and rain. Both were soaked from the storm, bending low as the winds gusted.

"Hey!" Carolyn cried into the darkness. "Hey! Over here!"

At the sound of her voice the figures turned, and she saw a man dressed in jeans and a white T-shirt. He appeared to be in his late forties, with short dark hair and a wiry, tanned body. By his side was a large golden dog, his honey-colored coat darkened by the rain and matted down by the wind.

"You shouldn't be out here!" The man was by her side in a flash, shouting into her ear. "It's not safe! You've got to get to shelter!"

The golden dog pushed his way between them, and Carolyn reached out to touch his coat. He wore no collar that she could make out under his thick fur. Why were they out in the storm?

"Are you from the campground?" the man asked. "You don't live around here, do you?"

"No," Carolyn replied, stumbling forward as the wind pushed her. She almost fell, but the golden dog caught her with his back and side, steadying her and helping her find safe footing again. His body was powerfully strong against the brutal winds, and his wide feet held firm in the wet sand. He sniffed her hands as she cupped them around his muzzle, and the warmth of his breath traveled through her, warming her right through.

"Who are you?" she asked, wondering if the man could hear her over the wind. "Where did you come from? Are you lost too?"

The man shook his head slowly, and turned, motioning her to follow. "This way!" he shouted.

"Who are you?" she asked again, her voice a whisper.

Through the wind and the rain, over the sounds of the storm, a deep voice spoke to her clear and calm in her mind, blocking out the roar of the sea and storm. Gentle and reassuring, it was strangely familiar to her. "Follow us and we'll take you to safety," the golden dog said. "We know where he is. Trust us, and we'll take you to him."

Carolyn tightened her grip on his strong back, feeling the broadness and warmth of it on her wet skin. Her fingers wrapped around the long wet hairs, feeling their silkiness. "Nicky!" she cried out. "Nicky! Over here!"

He was by her side in a heartbeat, and took her injured arm in his firm grasp. Immediately he noticed she was hunched over, standing as if she were hanging on to something he couldn't quite see. "We're almost to the lighthouse!" he shouted into the wind. Lightning flashed, and he caught a glimpse of the dog by her side.

Not believing his eyes, Nick fumbled with the flashlight and saw the dog's dark eyes glowing, reflecting the dim light. It gazed at him calmly, and Nick could see its long tail wagging slowly from side to side in a friendly greeting. Clearly the dog appeared to be leading Carolyn, and it seemed to be oblivious and unafraid of the storm.

"Where'd he come from?" Nick asked. "That dog?"

"He's with that man," Carolyn replied, spitting as the wind tossed some wet hair into her mouth. "We've got to follow him! He knows where to go!"

Nick and Carolyn followed the man and his dog across the beach to the lighthouse. Warmth and energy flowed from the dog into Carolyn without her even realizing it, and through Carolyn it flowed into Nick. He felt the amazing force strengthening them both, and marveled at the calmness and certainty in which the man and dog led them to the lighthouse. As much as he wanted to catch up with the man, Nick stayed by Carolyn's side. There would be plenty of time to talk once they were out of the storm.

"We're almost there." The golden dog was illuminated briefly by a burst of lightning from above. "Careful now, don't fall."

The lighthouse loomed before them, and they were led up the rain-slicked granite steps to the doors. "Help me give those doors a push," the man said to Nick. "They're not locked."

Letting go of Carolyn, Nick pushed his full weight against the doors. They flew open with a loud groan and crashed against the inside of the structure. Stumbling into the darkness, Nick could hear the muffled sounds of the storm raging outside, and the howling sound Carolyn had described echoing inside. It stopped abruptly as the dog led Carolyn into the sanctuary of the tower. Together, Nick and the man pushed the massive doors closed, shutting out the storm.

Feeling dazed and terribly weak, Carolyn sank to the floor, her back against the coolness of the brick, and began to cry.

"It's alright, we're safe now," Nick whispered, taking her into his arms. "Shhhh," he breathed. "It's okay. You're alright now."

Thunder crashed outside, and the sound of it made them both jump. "Magic!" Carolyn called out into the darkness. "Magic!" She fumbled for the flashlight, shining its dim beam around the room.

His familiar voice came to her, soft and gentle and not afraid anymore. "I'm here," he said, stepping out of the darkness into her open arms. "I was afraid you'd forgotten me."

"Oh, no, Magic, never!" She held him tightly, crying tears of happiness into his sweet-smelling coat. Nick put his arms around them both, and breathed a long sigh of relief.

"I'm so glad to see you! I thought I'd never see you again!" the old Basenji's body trembled. "I was trapped in here, and there was no way out! I was so afraid!"

Carolyn buried her face in his neck, then turned to look up at Nick. He pulled back suddenly, as if he'd been shocked. Leaning back, he took the flashlight from Carolyn and pointed it at her, then at Magic, staring at them both. He had heard another voice in the room.

"Magic?" he asked softly, suddenly afraid. "Magic?"

Carolyn stared at Nick, visibly shaken. "What?" she stammered. "Nicky, you heard him? Did you? Could you — you heard Magic's voice?"

"Nicky," Magic whispered. "Do you remember me? Do you know who I am now?"

Nick's face was pale, and his eyes were wide with wonder. "You!" he gasped, hardly believing his ears. "I can — you're talking — I can hear you!" He rubbed his face with his hands. "I can't believe I'm hearing you!" He turned to Carolyn. "You could hear him the whole time, couldn't you?"

"Do you remember me?" the old Basenji pressed, moving forward into Nick's outstretched arms. "Do you remember the hurricane so long ago, when you fell from up there?" he turned toward the metal staircase. "That's how you got the scar over your eye," he added, feeling tears well up in his eyes. "I was just a puppy then, but I was there."

"Little puppy," Nick whispered, his mind racing back to the storm of his childhood, remembering the strange dreams that had haunted him on countless nights afterward. He held the old dog close, feeling Magic's heartbeat strong in his chest. "You really are Savannah's son," he said quietly.

"I wanted to tell you the other day," Carolyn said. "But I didn't know how. I didn't think you'd understand."

"Magic is the perfect name for you," Nick smiled at the Basenji in his arms. Suddenly self-conscious, remembering the man who'd led them to the lighthouse, Nick turned and looked around the room. Not seeing him, he shone his flashlight all around, trying to make out his shape in the darkness. "Hello?" he called. "Hello?"

"What is it?" Magic asked. "There's nobody here but us."

"I want to thank that man for leading us here," Nick said, turning to Carolyn. "What happened to him, and what happened to the dog he was with? Did you see where they went?"

Carolyn stared back at Nick, the sudden realization of who the man and dog were flowing over her like the storm surge itself. "That dog was Max," she said quietly, "And I think you can tell me who that man was, Nicky." She was silent for a moment, trembling with fear and astonishment. "They've done what they needed to do, and now they've gone back home."

THIRTY - FIVE

THEY SPENT THE REST OF THAT DAY
and night in the lighthouse, sheltered inside its
thick walls as the hurricane raged all around
them. Safe in each other's arms, they talked long
into the night, sharing memories of times past.
Magic and Nick recounted the events that had
taken place since they'd been apart, filling in the
spaces where time had taken them down
different paths. Carolyn told of finding Magic in
the shelter, and shared with Nick the wonder of
having heard the old Basenji's voice. She

told

Nick how beautiful her relationship had been with Max, and how her difficult, failed romance with Ted had made her fearful of commitment. Through it all, Magic had been the thread that wove their lives together, bringing two lonely people together, and making his wish to return home come true.

"I think I understand what you meant about happiness," Carolyn whispered to Magic as they drifted off to sleep. "We've found it here, haven't we?"

"We have," the old Basenji replied softly. "This barrier island may be where I was born, and I've called it home and traveled here many times in my dreams. But up until now I hadn't realized that a place isn't home unless you've got someone who loves you there." He sighed, and rested his head between his paws.

"Magic's right," Nick said sleepily. "Being loved lets you know you're in the right place. And," he added, giving Carolyn a quick kiss, "I think we're all in the right place."

As they slept, the hurricane howled its last, miraculously turning as it passed, just brushing against the North Carolina coastline before heading back out into the Atlantic. As suddenly as they had appeared, the powerful winds died down. Storm clouds rode away with the winds, and one by one the stars came out and filled the night sky with millions of brilliant white lights.

That night, curled up snugly between Carolyn and Nick, Magic dreamed of starlight in the wide-open sky above him. He found himself standing on the hill where the rabbits lived, for he knew exactly where to find them now. The final part of his dream was in place, and the urgent feeling that had driven him to keep searching for the answers had quieted in his heart, stilling his mind and warming him with a deep-running feeling of contentment.

Starlight danced on the waters, gentling the rolling ocean. It sparkled and glimmered in the soft sand beneath his paws, and settled easily on his body like a cloak, feeling like snowflakes or raindrops, only warm and caressing.

Magic awoke from his dream feeling strange and light. He moved away from Carolyn and Nick, and when Carolyn stirred in her sleep he stopped, watching her for a few peaceful moments as she dreamed. She had a sweet smile on her face, and he knew that her dreams were happy ones, and he hoped Max was running through them, for she'd told him how much she loved it when he met her there. Slowly, reluctantly, he moved away from her.

Out of her dream, she stirred again and whispered, "Need to go out?"

Half asleep, half awake, still dreaming her dream, she heard Magic's familiar old voice say "Yes."

Sleepily, she moved through the lighthouse, down the spiral staircase from the second landing where Nick still slept, and somehow opened a door for him. She smiled at the old dog dreamily, telling him she'd wait for him to come back in. Impulsively, instead of closing the door she left it open just a bit, and felt the ocean breeze cool on her skin. Leaning back against the brick wall, she slid down it, settling comfortably on the cool tile floor.

She was asleep before she could see Magic slip off into the darkness.

When she saw him again he was in her dream. He appeared on a high hill, his body dark against the starry sky. The white markings on his coat reflected the starlight from above, making him glow in their ghostly blue light. There were trillions of stars in the sky, and there was no moon. In her dream she could hear him calling out to her, telling her to hurry, hurry because soon it would be time to leave.

"You don't want to leave here," Carolyn implored. "This is your home."

"If you want, it can be yours, too," Magic replied. "It's all so simple. The secret was that you had to find love again, believe in friendship and trust, and find your way back home. Thank you for being my friend, and for bringing me home." He disappeared behind the rise of the dune into the tall grass. "I'll be waiting for you here," he called back. "Don't forget, this is where I'll be if you need me."

When Carolyn awoke she was in Nick's arms. She heard birds singing outside, and saw bright sunlight streaming in through the tall lighthouse windows. She allowed herself to fall back asleep for a just a moment, then awoke with a start when she realized Magic was missing.

"Nicky!" She shook him hard. "Nicky, wake up! Magic's gone!"

"What?" Nick yawned and stretched, and was suddenly wide awake. He sat up quickly, looking around for the old Basenji. "What's wrong?"

"It's Magic!" Carolyn stood and ran to the lighthouse doors, pushing one of the heavy doors open. She stepped out into the sunshine, shielding her eyes from its brightness. "He's gone!" She ran down the granite steps, and circled the base of the lighthouse, calling the old dog's name. "Nicky! We've got to find him!"

"Magic!" Nick's voice carried over the dunes and into the wind. He turned toward the ocean, surveying the hurricane damage that littered the beach. "Magic!" he called again. "Magic! Where are you?" *Oh, please!* he thought frantically. *Oh please let him be okay! I can't lose him again!*

Together they ran along the top of the dunes, calling out to the old Basenji, but getting no answer. In despair, Carolyn sat down in the sand, put her head in her hands, and began to cry.

"We've got to keep looking!" Nick said, putting his arms around her. "We can't give up now!"

"Last night," she told him between sobs. "Last night, he needed to go out, and so I opened one of the doors and let him go. I must have fallen asleep," she sobbed. "I don't remember seeing where he went. Oh why didn't I stay awake?"

Nick held her and let her cry, feeling tears in his eyes as well. "Don't worry, we'll find him," he promised. "We found him once, and we'll find him again. We just need to keep looking."

Like a flash from a camera, the memory of her dream from the night before appeared in her mind, making her sit up quickly.

Don't forget, this is where I'll be if you need me.

"I know where Magic went! I saw the place!" Carolyn grabbed Nick's hand, pulling him to his feet. "Remember he was talking about the rabbits, and how much he loved to run with them? Come on!" she cried, running down the dune toward the shore. "I know where he is!"

Together they ran with all their might, the roar of the wind and the ocean drowning out the sound of their racing hearts.

EPILOGUE

.

THEY FOUND HIS BODY WHERE HE'D

left it, at the crest of a small hill overlooking the

place where the rabbits lived.

Carolyn let out a little cry when she saw him

and placed her hand gently on his coat as she had

a thousand times before, and realized with a start

that there was still a small bit of warmth left in it.

He hadn't been gone long, and she wondered for

a moment if he'd waited for her, and she wished

she'd been there so she could've said good-bye.

The wind blowing off the ocean seemed to

tease her, tossing her hair back into her face. Angrily, she wiped her tears away and for a moment thought she saw him running along the dune, chasing a rabbit.

The morning sun had burnished his red coat into dark auburn, and she could see that the years had left his body, that it was sleek and strong and hard and without gray. He chased the rabbit over a small rise in the dune and disappeared behind it into the tall grass, just as she'd imagined he would. She wanted to call out to him but was afraid if she did the spell would be broken. He reappeared once more, and for the briefest of seconds tore his gaze off the rabbit and looked directly at her. She knew then that he was finally home and had found the Happiness.

It was the startling warmth of Nick's hand on top of hers that finally broke the spell. She turned into him, and buried her face in his shirt, apologizing for wetting it with her tears. He kissed her gently, and murmured to her his condolences. He knew she'd loved the old dog, and he knew before that fateful night in the hurricane he'd only scratched the surface as to how much. He understood her pain, and felt his own cutting deep inside him. He held her close, and swore that he would take care of her, the way Magic would have wanted him to.

She had the old Basenji's body cremated, for she knew he wouldn't be needing it anymore. She brought the small box of ashes to the top of the lighthouse, and when the wind was right she lifted the lid and let them enter its embrace. Nick stood beside her, his arm across her shoulders. The shock of what life might be like without her flowed through him, just as when he first realized he loved her, and in that instant it seemed he understood everything about life, death, and the mystery that surrounded it all. He realized what Magic had meant to them both, and as he watched the ashes disappear on the wind, he knew he never wanted to be without Carolyn by his side.

"Carolyn," Nick began, pulling her into his strong embrace. "I know you've got to leave here, that there's nothing more to keep you here, but you don't have to go back to Michigan if you don't want to. I'd really like for you to stay."

Carolyn's heart jumped at the thought, and her spirit soared with the possibility. She leaned into him, feeling the quiet contentment of the island settle into her. Turning toward Nick, her cat-green eyes met his dark ones, and she was immediately overwhelmed by the love she saw gazing back.

"We've got a great school here," he went on, kissing her lightly on the forehead. "And they're always looking for dedicated teachers. I know it's probably not quite the same as what you're used to." He paused, studying her face. "What I'm trying to say is that I love you, Carolyn. Please say you'll stay."

As she began to answer, she thought of what her parents would have to say about that little bit of news. Then, she saw Andie urging her forward, telling her she deserved all the love and happiness the world had to offer.

Find love again, believe in trust and friendship, and find your way back home.

Magic's words echoed in her mind, and she knew she'd made the right decision. *Let my parents think what they will. In time, they'll understand that their daughter has found her own happiness, and is following her own star. By finding Nicky I've found love again, and Magic has shown me trust in a friendship that will always stay with me. This island, this place both he and Nicky have called home, feels more like home to me than any place ever has before. This is my home, too. I belong here, with Nicky.*

"Nicky," she smiled, happy and secure in her decision. "I don't want to go back. I want to stay here with you!" She turned into the wind, and opened her arms to it. "Thank you, Magic!" she shouted. "Thank you for everything! We've both come home, and now we're both free!"

Nick followed her lead, and shouted his thanks to the little Basenji who'd miraculously returned home, and brought Carolyn with him. Carolyn, his love.

They embraced each other again and held on tightly.

And although they didn't notice, in the tall grass far below, a large golden dog and a small red and white Basenji watched, their dark eyes bright with happiness. After a moment the two turned and disappeared over the dunes, leaving Carolyn and Nick alone for the moment, giving them privacy as they kissed.

"This is like a dream come true," Nick whispered. They turned and faced the wind again, looking out at the narrow strip of land beneath them.

"What's that?" Carolyn leaned over the railing, pointing to the tall grass far below. "Look, down there."

At first, Nick saw nothing but the wind bending the green and gold stalks of grass, making them sway back and forth playfully. Then, out of nowhere, a movement that wasn't part of the grass at all caught his eye and made his heart race.

They flew down the narrow, spiraling staircase, sometimes taking the steps two at a time. Breathlessly the reached the entrance and stopped on the granite steps of the lighthouse.

"There!" Carolyn cried. "Over by those pines."

Hand in hand they made their way to the place, startled to see a multitude of small pawprints left behind in the sand.

"Must have been a cat," Nick said, disappointed and embarrassed to have gotten his hopes up.

The wind gusted, and Carolyn turned to face it, letting it flow through her hair and dry the tears that had formed in her eyes. Nick came up behind her and placed his arms around her shoulders, letting her lean into him. He could see her tears and he knew she thought she had seen Magic, just as he had.

"I don't know what I was thinking," she said quietly. "It couldn't have been him, I know that. He's gone! We saw his body, we set his ashes free." She turned to Nick. "Maybe I'm going crazy imagining things."

He gazed into her eyes and shook his head slowly. "No, you're not. I thought the same thing, too." He sighed and pulled her close. "Come on, let's go walk on the beach a bit and talk."

She nodded and took the hand he offered, unable to resist turning once more to look back at the pawprints in the sand. They were still there, she hadn't imagined them at all.

Probably was just a cat, she thought, following Nick toward the beach. *And anyway, they're too small to have belonged to Magic.*

As they reached the top of the dunes the wind gusted, howling through the trees, sounding very much like a Basenji yodeling. As the wind died down, the yodel continued, loud and long, calling to them. They stopped, and Carolyn felt Nick's grasp on her hand tighten.

"There you are!"

They stared in wonder as a young Basenji, not more than five months of age, stepped out of the tall grass and stopped a few feet away from where they stood. His velvety coat was a deep burnished red, and the white markings on his face, chest and legs were brilliant in the sunlight. His eyes were dark and exotic, lined with smoky black.

"Magic!" Carolyn and Nick called his name in unison as the little dog bounded into their open arms, wiggling with excitement.

"How?" Carolyn breathed the word, unable to believe what was happening. Magic was back, alive and young, and in her arms!

"We've got all the time in the world," the young dog replied. "If you'll walk with me along the beach, I'll tell you all about it."

"But will you – can you stay?" Nick asked, afraid to break the spell. He held his breath and knew Carolyn did the same, waiting for what seemed like an eternity for the answer.

"I'm here to stay," came the reply, accompanied by a yodel. "I'm not going to leave either of you for a long time. It's such a beautiful day. How about that walk on the beach?"

Together they crossed the dune and walked along the water's edge, not minding the waves that reached from the ocean toward their feet, smoothing out the footprints they left behind.

THE END

Also Available from Windigo . . .

The Secondhand Basenji Handbook: The Guide to Adopting and Living With a "Rescued" Basenji by M.W. and P.J. Cotter.
ISBN 0-9658488-0-9.

An excellent resource for folks interested in adopting a Basenji, *The Secondhand Basenji Handbook* takes the mystery out of Basenji rescue and adoption. It's the only guide of its kind — dedicated to the experience of adopting and living with a "rescued" Basenji.

The Secondhand Basenji Handbook has over 200 pages packed with information and photographs covering topics like:
• How to choose a rescue group
• How the adoption process works
• Questions you should ask, and questions you'll be asked
• Training tips even a Basenji will enjoy
• "Tail Tips" — Down-to-earth advice on living with our curly-tailed friends

Even "firsthand" Basenjis and the people that love them will benefit from the tips, advice, and guidance in *The Secondhand Basenji Handbook*, and it's only $12.00 (U.S. funds), plus shipping.

Check your local bookstore or use the order form on the next page to order directly from Windigo!

Attention Basenji Rescue Groups!!!

You can't tell them everything firsthand . . . So why not do the next best thing? Send them home with a copy of *The Secondhand Basenji Handbook*.

Our "Rescue Pack" gives you ten copies of *The Secondhand Basenji Handbook* for only $62.00 (plus shipping). Rescue Packs are available to all rescue groups and clubs that support Basenji rescue.

Want additional copies of *August Magic* or *The Secondhand Basenji Handbook?*

Check your local bookstore or order directly from Windigo!

ISBN	Quantity	Description	Price Each (U.S. Funds)	Total
0-9658488-2-5		*August Magic: A Novel*	$12.95	
0-9658488-0-9		*The Secondhand Basenji Handbook: The Guide to Adopting and Living with a "Rescued" Basenji*	$12.00	
		Shipping Charge (See information below.)		
		For deliveries in Michigan, add 6% sales tax		
		TOTAL (Checks payable in U.S. funds only, please.)		

All prices are subject to change. Contact Windigo for latest pricing, quantity discounts, and availability.

Mail To:
Windigo
P.O. Box 183176
Shelby Township, MI 48318-3176

E-mail: info@windigo.net

Web Site: http://www.windigo.net

Shipping Charges:
•For orders up to $20.00, add $3.00.
•For orders from $20.01 to $60.00, add $5.00.
•For orders over $60.00, add $7.00.
If shipping outside of North America, please add $5.00 to the above shipping charge.